Death in Londinium

Death in Londinium

JOHN DRAKE

LUME BOOKS

LUME BOOKS

This edition published in 2022 by Lume Books

Copyright © John Drake 2016

The right of John Drake to be identified as the author of this work has been asserted by them in accordance with the Copyright, Design and Patents Act, 1988.

All rights reserved. No part of this publication may be reproduced, stored in a retrieval system, or transmitted in photocopying, recording or otherwise, without the prior permission of the copyright owner.

ISBN 978-1-83901-514-4

Typeset using Atomik ePublisher from Easypress Technologies

www.lumebooks.co.uk

For Len Morgan
Dedicated Re-enactor of Roman Glories,
Artillery Engineer without equal,
Craftsman and Scholar,
Patient answerer of questions,
And Inspiration for the First Javelin of this book.

Salve Leonius Morganus Fortis Victrix!

Chapter 1

"They'll kill us," he said, "all of us." The huge, fat man grabbed my arm, but looked over his shoulder at the hysterical mass of slaves cramming into the great atrium and he wished he had kept his mouth shut, because there was a wild moan of terror. He was Agidox the major domos, an expert from Gaul, who ran the biggest staff in the city with effortless ease. Normally he went upon his way with stately tread and serene authority. But not now. Now he was barely in control of his bladder.

"Come here," he said, and dragged me into a corner between a pair of big marble statues, and he shook me, trying to spring me into action. "You're clever," he said, "you must know what to do." I searched for words, but, before I could speak, a woman came shrieking through the mob followed by five children.

"Agidox!" cried the woman, "Don't let them take us!" and she howled in fear. Her and her little ones, and the slaves, gaped as Agidox's family threw themselves on him. "Husband!" she said, because slaves pretend marriage even if the law denies them it, and she clung to Agidox while the girls screamed and hung to his robes, and the boy, the youngest and smallest, climbed into his father's arms and bawled in terror.

"Hush, hush," said Agidox to his favourite. He patted the boy with infinite tenderness as a sudden, higher pitch in the crowd's noise showed it was not just Agidox's woman that had heard the news, and run to her man with her young behind her. The whole building echoed with cries and running feet, then a sudden shout of surprise as the atrium gates crashed inwards and a centurion staggered in with a dozen square-shield regulars behind him, with more filling the vestibule that led to the streets. They were identical in their uniform gear: inhuman and infinitely menacing.

"Oh no!" said Agidox, "They've come to kill us!" The rest heard and there was unhinged panic and scrabbling for escape, blocked only by the press of slaves coming into the atrium from the rest of the house.

So I did what I could to calm them.

"Look!" I yelled. "We're safe. They haven't drawn steel."

The slaves heard, and they paid heed because my reputation was strong, and so they looked and saw that every sword was still in its scabbard. The troops were simply pushing their way in with their shields, heaving and shoving, with their boot nails skidding on the marble. So there was a sigh of relief from the packed mass, and I shouted again.

"They're here as the law," I cried, "nothing more." It was in my mind to add '*not yet*'. But I had the sense not to say that.

"Ahhhhh!" they said, in a deep, soft sigh; ever credulous, as house boys always are, for they are mostly illiterate, mostly superstitious and are ruled by the most primitive fancies and desires. Thus the mood swung in an instant, and they were content for the moment that this was not a death squad come to strike them down on the spot.

They were like children, but who can blame them? How else can slaves behave? They bear no arms, they cannot fight, and they are bred up to servility. A slave may not even defend his family: the most sacred duty of a man. Thus slaves are not men at all, but cattle, and yet they have all the feelings of men: joy and despair, greed and fear, and they love their children as dearly as any citizen.

"Right!" said the centurion to his men. "Fall back and secure the house." They backed out through the vestibule and into the street, leaving the atrium doors wide open. "So!" said the centurion and straightened his cloak and glared at all present. He was young for a centurion, but absolutely confident of himself, with his men behind him and only slaves in front. He frowned because these slaves were pressing close in great numbers, and that was improper. So, he struck out, sharp and precise with his vine staff, and those who were beaten, cringed and made way without a sound, because that was the duty of slaves.

He nodded in satisfaction and looked round.

"Who's in charge here?" he said. "Where's this smart-arse Greek?" But he had already spotted me, because Romans know a Greek when they see one. They have a special sensitivity for a Greek's nose, a Greek's chin, and a Greek's brow.

"You!" said the centurion, pointing his vine staff at me. "Over here. Now!"

So I bowed and moved through the crowd, with the slaves staring at me while their children trembled beside them. Then I stood before the officer and gave another bow, very low, and there was silence.

"Now then *boy*!" said the centurion, for all slaves were boys, including me. I had long since grown to a man's strength, and grown above average size and build, such that I was both bigger and older than him. So, after his contemptuous greeting, he came close and looked at me and gave a tiny, polite nod that was almost a bow. "Where can we talk," he said, "in private?" I saw what was in his mind. I had seen it before in young Romans, because respect for their elders is drilled into them as children. So when one of them looks up at a creature like me, with grey hair and obvious education, it is in his Roman bones to give respect. Added to that, although I had been ten years a slave and ground into that servile condition by the mill of the Roman state, I had not been born a slave and was not ground quite so small as those who were. Thus a little of my own self had survived and I did not look at a Roman with the limitless humility of the true-bred, well-flogged slave, and, for an instant, this young Roman looked to me as if he were a pupil looking to his teacher. But I was very careful not to presume upon this, because experience had also shown that the Roman could, and would, flip from respect to anger with the speed of a tumbling athlete and never even know he was doing it. So I was polite.

"If the honoured officer would follow me," I said, and led him to a side room, a small library painted with hunting scenes and fitted with bright windows for illumination. I stood back as he entered.

"Shut the door, boy," he said, which I did, and his manner duly shifted as he turned on me. "This is all your fault," he said, "I'm blaming you!" I felt a spear thrust of fright that I might myself be held accountable for the crime. But, by the grace of the gods, that was not what he meant. He was not really accusing me at all. He was worried, even frightened.

"It was you that summoned us, wasn't it?" he said.

"Yes, honoured sir."

"So why didn't you cover it up? Heave him in the river? Bury him in the garden, or just burn the blasted house down?" I breathed deep.

"Too many already knew the truth, honoured sir," I said, "too many tongues."

"Too many to kill?"

"Who would do the killing, honoured sir? There were only slaves in the house." He nodded reluctantly.

"Well, what about selling them off?" he said, "to anyone, anywhere!"

"Impossible, except in a longer time, honoured sir, and they would still have tongues and we are dealing with great numbers."

"Jupiter, Juno, Minerva!" he said, cursing in the Name of the Capitoline Triad: the greatest oath the Romans had. He found a chair, slammed his vine staff on a nearby table, pulled off his helmet and rubbed his curly hair with his free hand. He was barely in his twenties, smooth faced, unscarred and with olive-hued Italian skin. He groaned, and put his helmet on the table with the vine staff, and looked at me again, appealing to me, "So, come on, boy," he said, "I've heard about you. You're the Greek wonder brain. So how do we get out of this?"

"I don't know." I said, "Not yet."

"Gods help us," he said. "The wonder brain doesn't know!" He spread his hands in question. "So what do we do? Because if we do what we *should* do, there'll be big trouble. You've only got to blink at this province and it goes mad." He sighed. "That's why it's me that's here," he said. "The rest pulled rank. Nobody wants this." He shook his head. "It's all mine." He shoved his legs forward and slumped back. Then, he picked up his helmet, fiddled with the straps, looked at his boots, looked very young and spoke more to himself than to me.

"There's even a drill for it," he said. "Like there is for everything."

He marked off points. "Once the Lord Justice says *do it*, we dig a mass grave outside the city, then we block side streets to clear a way for the wagons." He paused. "For the bodies. Then we separate males from females, find a place where the rest can't see or hear." He paused again. "And to do the actual job, the book says *chose those in the ranks whose blood is hot*." He looked at me. "That means the nasty bastards," he said. "The maniacs. The ones we normally stamp on. We have to let them off the leash, and that's not good for discipline."

"You don't have to kill everyone," I said. "Only those of sexual maturity. The children are exempt."

"Oh gods be praised!" he said. "All stand and give thanks!" He glared at me. "And who makes that decision, boy? Not you!" he said, and shook his head and stood up. "I've got to do that, boy. *Me*!" He sighed and put his mind to it. "The little 'uns are easy," he said. "They go free. But what about those half grown?" He looked away in shame, probably imagining hysterical mothers pleading for the lives of their children, and he shook his head in disgust. "*Ugh*!" he said. "For them, I've got to lift their skirts and look!"

He put on his helmet, bucked his chin strap, led the way to the door and opened it.

"Go on then, Greek," he said, "You're s'posed to be the cleverest boy in the province, let's see you find a way round this!" He stood back and waited to see what I would do. So, I stepped through the doorway and I looked at the packed mass of slaves … and I myself wondered what I was going to do.

Chapter 2

And it all began so well, indeed it began in triumph. It began at a *salutatio*. The most important daily event in Roman life; the spring that feeds the Roman river, the cement that binds the Roman wall, the team that pulls the Roman wagon. It is the occasion when hundreds of citizens, the *clients*, gather at dawn outside the house of some great and powerful man, the *patron*, seeking favours, jobs, protection, money, whatever, and in return they vote as he tells them, they become his men in all things, and they march behind him in public processions.

Thus I stood in my hooded cloak in the damp Britannic pre-dawn, that most hideous of times in that most hideous of climates, in the piercing cold among a huge, murmuring crowd made up of masters and boys, torches and lanterns, stamping feet, clouding breath and red, running noses. It was a heaving mass that filled the wide street from pavement to pavement. Sounds echoing from the tall buildings, whilst all eyes looked towards the biggest house in the street, the home of my master Scorteus, Fabius Gentilius Scorteus, the richest man in Londinium.

He was my master and my owner, because I, Ikaros of Apollonis, who had once been a soldier, a nobleman and an engineer, was no longer a human being at all. I was a possession. But if so, at least I was an expensive one. I was an *exotic*, like the beautiful boys and girls who sell for millions, except that I was not bought for my body but for my mind.

Meanwhile the crowd chattered in the horrible Britannic dawn: red light showing over the eastern housetops, and looked at the gates of the enormous house which occupied an entire city block.

There were three sets of gates behind a fine stand of pillars under an elaborate pediment, carved and painted in bright colours. There was a big pair of citizen gates in the middle, a small pair of trade gates to the right, and an even smaller slave gate to the left. The citizen gates were shut, but the others were open to admit the vast quantity of supplies needed to feed an enormous household. Slaves and traders were streaming in and out with clattering feet, squealing wheelbarrows and much shouting and talk.

I moved round taking care not to jostle citizens, because that is a flogging offence for a slave. I looked and learned, because people are endlessly fascinating, and the slaves nodded warily at me, as slaves always do, while the citizens ignored me. They had no time for a slave when they were bellowing at each other, hitching their robes, and being important. So they ignored me even though they all knew me, and some even knew that, in my own city, I had been a senator. I had moved through such a crowd as this with men bowing and seeking to catch my eye. But that was in the past, and now I was better known for the mind-reading tricks I had to perform to entertain Scorteus's dinner guests.

Then I was stirred from my miserable thoughts by a roar of laughter, a jarring screeching. I looked round and saw that outside the trades-gate, the procession of incoming supplies had stopped, and slaves were grinning and resting their loads. They were looking at four old women in trailing shreds of dirty black rag. The greasy, dirty, remains of unidentifiable old garments, all tattered and bound together with clumsy ragged stitches. The women were vile, unwashed, unclean, with straggling hair, jet-black fingernails, faces like leather. They yelled at the gate-keeper in furious anger, while wise men kept clear for fear of what might be hopping and crawling about their persons.

"Sod off the lot of you!" cried the gate-keeper, losing his temper and raising his cudgel at the old women. "This house don't want nothing off you today!"

"Don't you threaten me, boy!" screamed one of the hags. "We're freeborn women, we are not fart catchers like you!" This brought roars of laughter from the audience, followed by a pure filth of language from the old women as they shrieked out curses and stabbed their gnarled fingers. The onlookers joined in with jeers and wit, vainly attempting to match the appalling profanity. Finally, to cheers and more laughter, the old women despaired of mere words, turned their backs, bent over, and threw up their skirts to show their bare behinds to the gate keeper.

They were the Corvidic sisters, a shared joke for the whole city. They were fish wives who had once been plump and fresh. But now they were shrivelled and stank and had lost their minds: often turning up at the wrong house, or with the wrong order, and never admitting fault but swearing that those who accused them were wicked liars.

Then a gong sounded within the house as the water clocks pronounced dawn, and there was a cheer as the citizen gates opened, masters and slaves surged forward, pushing the old sisters aside, light beamed forth. Twenty slaves marched out in the livery of the House of Scorteus, led by Agidox, the major domos, with the gong bearer going before, clashing and clanging in tremendous importance.

Agidox wore layers of fine robe. He advanced bearing a wand of office as stout as a spear shaft, and bowed to left and right acknowledging favoured citizens. Then he stopped in the middle of the crowd and four slaves placed a dais before him. He climbed three short steps, and raised his wand, bringing instant silence because only Agidox's word could get a man past the house guard of eight huge black Africans who blocked the citizen gates, magnificently naked but for white loin cloths. They stood with grim brows, arms folded, and conscious of their tremendous beauty even as their most precious parts began to freeze.

Thus began the ceremony of the salutatio, just as it was beginning all over Londinium outside other houses. Scorteus's salutatio was bigger than most, but was otherwise identical except for one thing. Elsewhere the citizens wore formal dress. They wore the toga, the massive, fearfully expensive length of white woollen cloth that a Roman citizen draped round his body to proclaim his rank. But there were no togas outside the House of Scorteus, because his event was not a salutatio; it was only *morning calls*, even if it was exactly the same thing.

It could not be a salutatio because only a Roman citizen could hold one of them, and Scorteus was a Britannic Celt who, despite his vast wealth, public works, and steady years of bribing the great and powerful, was not a Roman citizen. But it was his uttermost ambition to become one for the huge advantages it would bring him in public life. These including the cherished privilege of putting his son on the *cursus honorum*: the noble pathway of increasingly senior, civic and military offices that could take a young Roman all the way to the senate in Rome. Thus denial of citizenship was a maggot in his soul, as was the poisonous irony that many of the clients who bowed before him were themselves citizens, such that when he led them to vote in the Forum, they voted as he told them, but he himself could not vote!

Meanwhile, a slave handed Agidox a great book tablet, bound in glossy red sandalwood, hinged in gold and displaying two wax sheets a foot wide by two feet long. He opened the book, put it down on a lectern at the front of his dais, while slaves raised torches, and he made a great business of consulting the pages while the crowd waited patiently until he looked up.

"Citizens of Londinium," he cried. "My honoured master, Fabius Gentilius Scorteus." He paused expectantly.

"Blessings be upon his house!" roared the crowd. Agidox nodded and continued.

"My master admits, as first and dearest friends, the following citizens ..." Groans and cheers greeted the names, as a privileged few were summoned before the rest, and the Africans let them pass.

I did not stay long. I was only there to see who was in favour, and I went into the house by the slave door, and straight to my suite of rooms: bedroom, bath chamber, study and workshop, of which the workshop was my favourite. Lit by glazed windows, a luxury few citizens could afford, it was full of benches and instruments, and the biggest bench was covered with an eight-by-ten-foot scale model. My two boys stood and bowed as I entered, for slaves have slaves under Rome. I gave them my cloak and looked at them and I wondered what to do next.

I wondered because it was time to start the day's work, but I had no work, and I saw the depression coming like a black cloud to cover my sunshine. In those days I was wounded in spirit and burdened with guilt, because I, who had been born so high, was living in shame, being unable to take the advice of the Roman philosopher Seneca, who said that *no man can be a slave who knows how to die*. Worse still I did not know why I was unable to follow his advice. Not when Socrates, greatest of all philosophers, taught the stoic doctrine that while a man cannot control the insults of fortune, he should be in complete control of his reaction to them.

Thus I was still alive because there was something within me that would not let me die. This was because my mind, or to be precise my personality, was standing still. It was in *stasis* as we say in Greek. It had stopped as a cart does when its wheels sink into the mud and no force of man or beast can move it. So, I was not the man that I had been, because he would never have behaved as I did. I had accepted slavery, I had become self-centred and irritable, I was prone to say foolish things, and parts of my memory were closed, especially those concerning the last days of my city. So I was a mystery and an oddity: both to myself and to others, and there was much about myself that I did not know. What I did know was that I was being punished for being alive: most probably by myself, because there is no justice if the guilty are not punished. One of my punishments was chronic insomnia, which affliction I soothed with the wine flask, even though the only real cure was hard work. But now the two projects that had filled my days were completed, and I was afraid of idleness.

I looked at the model: project number one, my machinery to raise water for the Imperial Baths, using the power of the river Thames to turn waterwheels to drive force pumps. It was another attempt to persuade the Romans to make Scorteus a citizen, because Londinium had no aqueduct and the Imperial Baths were having to shut twice weekly to allow inefficient, slave-driven pumps to fill the huge cisterns that fed the baths.

The plan was that once the model was complete, it would be carried in state by the Africans, followed by Scorteus and his clients, into City Hall: the Basilica. The councillors would be awestruck, Scorteus would offer to pay for the real thing, at a blinding cost, there would be thundering cheers and Scorteus would gain citizenship. Or, so we hoped. I sighed. The model had taken months to design and build, and now it worked. But the job was undoubtedly finished. I saw my boys looking at me and frowned.

"This room is filthy," I said, "Clean it before the dominus gets here."

"Yes, your honour," they said, and found brooms and mops.

The *dominus* was Scorteus, the master, who loved the workshop and came here most days after morning calls. But the room was not filthy. I was just annoyed that the boys were looking at me, knowing that I had nothing to do. Then, when I saw them pointlessly cleaning the clean floor, I felt foolish and told them to stop and tried to smile at them, and, of course, they smiled back with the practised deference of slaves, which meant absolutely nothing.

So I sat by the window at my reading bench, doing nothing, because there was nothing to do. The bench was purpose built, with rows of shelves and pigeon holes, and brass lamps fixed to the sides. It was covered with the clutter of a scholar's desk and was my favourite place in the world when I was busy. But now I stared at a stack of books that had occupied me even more than the pumps.

They were the second big project: the holy books of a notorious Jewish sect which was the morbid fascination of the entire province. The sect had been banned and its priests imprisoned, because while Romans are astonishingly tolerant of alien religions, there are some things they will not permit, and ritual cannibalism is one of them. The rumour was that the sect ate the flesh and drank the blood of virgins, having first ravished them. Indeed, the sect priests never even denied the charge of cannibalism and had raved of it as the Lord Chief Justice's men arrested them. But his Lordship wanted evidence, and Scorteus set me to translating the books to gain favour with the second highest man in the province; another bid for citizenship.

I opened one of the books and looked at the curvilinear script that ran right to left across the page. The language was Aramaic, kindred to Hebrew which I knew and had used as a bridge to understanding. I sighed. The pumps were enjoyable engineering, but the cannibal project was the more fascinating, because it illuminated some private research that I was doing on the nature of gods, and their triumph over death. It was my vanity that I might write a book on the subject, assuming anyone would want to read it. That is what I believed in those days, but now I realise that it was more than vanity. It was myself seeking proof of survival after death and re-union with those we have lost. I sought proof of that cherished fantasy of the bereaved, which every rational observation denies. That is why I tried so hard and read so deep, and knew so many languages.

But then my door banged and Scorteus charged in with a huge smile on his face. He was a short, heavy man in his forties, with thick arms and legs, a round face with a round nose, long hair scented and oiled, and thick black eyebrows. He was smooth shaven, dressed in layers of expensive tunics and wore a fortune in jewellery: neck chains, brooches and rings.

He was new money and delighted in it. But everything he owned had been won by hard work and great talent. Thus he was tremendous in commerce, being especially ingenious in spotting opportunity and taking risks which others feared. And, people liked him as a man because he was honest, made jokes, seized hands, slapped backs, and ate with his mouth open, spraying crumbs, while speaking coarse dog Latin. It was his charisma, but it was also the reason why Romans thought him irredeemably vulgar.

I stood and bowed, as did my boys.

"Dominus!" we said.

"Yes, yes," said Scorteus, and got straight to business. He went to the big model and peered at its wheels and levers. "So it'll do the job, will it?" He already knew because I had already told him. But, of course, I was polite.

"Yes, dominus," I said, and stood beside him and pointed to a brass crank," If you would care to turn this handle?"

Standing behind Scorteus, and scowling viciously, was his Syrian secretary who was also his junior business partner. He was a shrivel-faced man with a chicken's neck, a thin beard, intensely black eyes, an ever-worried expression and nervous habit of plucking at the hairs of his neck when agitated, which hairs he then brushed, unconsciously, off his garments. If he stood in any one place too long, he left a little scattering of short hairs and skin flakes upon the floor. He was a freedman, who had once been Scorteus's slave. Thus he should have been happy, but he was not, because once he had also been Scorteus's personal confidante, acknowledged as the cleverest man in his service. But now that was me, and the Syrian hated me for it.

"This handle here," said Scorteus.

"Yes, dominus," I said, and he turned it and the model clanked and sighed, and water gushed. He nodded, but with less enthusiasm than I had expected.

"What about the cannibal thing?" he said, "Have you cracked it?"

"Yes," I said. "Just yesterday."

"And?"

"I'm afraid there's nothing there. Nothing interesting."

"No?" he said.

"No," I said. "It's not real cannibalism. It's a sacrament."

"What's that?"

"A ceremony with religious meaning. They eat bread and drink wine and believe it gets turned into the flesh and blood of their founder."

"And who's he?" said Scorteus. "Anyone I should know?"

"He is, or rather was, a rabbi."

Scorteus frowned.

"What's that? A rabbi?"

"A Jewish teacher. A scholar. A religious leader."

"Is it though?" he said, entirely without interest. "Go on."

"He was a rabbi called Jesus Bar-Joseph who was crucified in Judea, under the Prefecture of Pontius-the-straight in the year of Sulpius and Sulla." I thought of what I had read of the case. "There was a bit of scandal at the time," I said. "It was controversial."

"Never heard of it," said Scorteus. "And what's Sulpius and Sulla?" He asked because Romans have the odd habit of referring to years by the names of the two Consuls who lead the Senate at the beginning of each year. They do also number the years, counting from the foundation of their city; but they regard the numbers as crude shorthand.

"That's sixty-seven years ago," I said, and could not help adding, "It's quite interesting actually. The sect believes their founder was a god incarnate who was resurrected after death, like Osiris the Egyptian god of the afterlife, or Tamuz the Babylonian god of vegetation. Resurrection is common in these eastern religions …" I would have continued, but I saw the look on his face. Nobody is interested when I discourse on such matters. It is a small tragedy that I have to bear.

"So," he said, "no butchered virgins? Not even one?"

"No," I said. "And no thanks from the Lord Chief Justice, because we've destroyed his case, not proved it," He nodded and I looked at the Jewish books on my desk, "Would you like the books back, dominus?"

"No, you have them," he said, and I bowed in thanks. For, although he had no personal interest in books, he was being hugely generous. Slaves supposedly had no wages or possession. But it was customary to let good slaves keep a little of the money they earned; a *peculium* as the Romans say. But the ritual books were worth the price of a good farm.

Then he looked at me and put his head on one side. "Never mind that," he said, "just be my clever Greek and tell me what's going on." I looked back at him and he laughed. "Bugger that!" he said, "Don't give me your solemn little smile with the eyebrows raised. Just tell me!"

He was referring to my principal mind trick: my unfortunate ability to guess what people are thinking. It is something everyone does to some degree, taking clues from context and facial expression. Thus, if a man picks up broken glass we know he fears cut fingers, and we can all tell a smile from a sneer. But I did it better than most, just as some people have better eyesight than most, or shoot better with the bow. I was especially good at reading faces: the flick of the eyes, the droop of the mouth, the turn of the head. The skill sounds desirable, but was not, because it led to my being seen as strange. It led to others whispering about me as I passed, and it led to my seeing untruth in those that I liked, or even loved. I saw their deceit, their guilt and their shameful deeds. Not that these were great or wicked faults, because we are all imperfect, but it was poison knowledge. So I looked at Scorteus and drew conclusions from the evidence before me. Thus he had paid little attention to my success with the pumps, or my failure with the translation. Also, I knew that there was only one subject that would so totally capture his imagination, and finally I could see delight in his eyes.

"You've found a better way," I said.

"See?" he said, and nudged the Syrian who forced a smile.

"You've heard something new."

"Yes!"

"About *someone*." That was easy. Nothing moves in the Roman world without influence. "Someone very important," I added. That was obvious, but Scorteus was so delighted that he blurted the rest without my having to work for it. People often do that, and afterwards believe that I see into their minds. Then they run round telling others that I work magic, to the greater glory of my reputation. It is ludicrous, but what can I do? Anyway, who complains when the court makes a false judgement in his favour?

"It's the Governor himself!" said Scorteus. "One of the clients whispered in my ear."

"Ah," I said, and I understood, because the salutatio was about news as well as power. The patron was one of the small circle of great men who ran the city, so he was first to learn news of great matters which he passed down to his clients. News such as when the new theatre would be built; whose faction was failing in the senate; would there be war with the northern tribes. In return the clients passed up all the local, street-level affairs; for example who was giving short measure; whose sons were breaking windows at night; whose wife was a whore behind his back. Since clients competed for the patron's favour, anything really tasty would be whispered in strict privacy after the client had taken extremely good care to check the truth of what he was saying.

"So what did he say?" I asked, and Scorteus, darted forward, grabbed my head and whispered in *my* ear, to the fury of the Syrian. Scorteus stood back when he was done, and took a breath.

"Well?" he said.

"Subtle," I said, "different."

"So," said Scorteus, "what do you know about drugs?"

"To bring sleep while the surgeon cuts?"

He nodded.

"Yes, dominus," I said, "there is such a drug. It's described in volume four of …"

"Doesn't matter where," he said. "Is it any good? Does it work?"

"Oh yes. I have seen it used." I had indeed. As a young man I considered a career in medicine. I even studied it for a while. But the lure of engineering shone brighter in the end.

"Good!" he said. "So why don't the Romans use it?"

"Because it is addictive, dangerous, hard to prepare, it tastes vile unless skilfully formulated, and it is extremely expensive."

"Bugger the expense! Come on my clever Greek. Are you saying you can't make it work?" He looked again at the scale model. "You know about more than this stuff, don't you?"

"Yes," I said.

"That's my boy!" he said, and reached out to pinch my cheek. Then he thought again, and did not. Slaves have no dignity, but some masters are kind enough to pretend that they do. "So can you do it?"

"Can the girl be weighed?"

"What for?"

"The dose depends on body mass."

"Ah!" he said. "So you can do it."

Next evening, very late, I was given the patient's weight, and I made my calculations and set to work. It was intense, careful, systematic work which entirely banished my depression. The drug was poppy resin dissolved in spirits of wine, and, while the resin cost a fortune, at least it could be bought, but the solvent was unknown to Roman science so I had to make it myself by distillation. Thus all was peace and contentment through the long night, alone with the hot smell of the still, the clink of glass vessels and finally the steady crunch of poppy resin ground in the mortar. The scent of spirits of wine, added slowly, and stirred with the pestle, and mixed with honey masked the bitter taste.

The steady discipline brought profound contentment and memories of days when work was fulfilment in itself, not service to a master however kind. So I was sad when the task was done. But eventually it was and I measured the liquid into a bottle, inserted the ground-glass stopper, sealed it with molten wax, then sent it to the surgeons with written instructions. I sighed as I gave up the bottle and wished it farewell. I would very much have liked to have seen it in use, and to observe the surgical procedure, which sounded fascinating. But I knew that, in this case, any such request would have been denied absolutely. So one of my boys took the bottle, and went off with the Africans, armed with clubs to protect him, and with torches to light them through the dark streets.

A month after that, Scorteus received a summons from His Grace the Governor.

Chapter 3

The summons was delivered by an imperial slave: highly educated, excellently dressed and escorted by lesser slaves. This was a serious problem for Agidox, because imperial slaves were owned by the Empire: in theory by the Emperor himself, and they ran the Empire's bureaucracy, wielding great power. Yet still they were slaves.

So by which door should one be admitted to the House of Scorteus? What bad example might be set to the household slaves? What would the neighbours think? What would the clients think? But the messenger gave warning before his arrival, and Agidox was a master of protocol, who knew that the bearer of summons from His Grace, passed as if he were the Governor himself.

So the imperial slave marched in through the citizen gates, and was taken with his followers to the great atrium, with its richly-glittering furniture, its painted walls, its mosaic floor, and its square opening to the sky. The so-called *compluvium*, fringed with bronze spouts in the form of dolphins to direct water into the ornate marble pool below, the *impluvium*, when rainwater ran off the roof, which in Britannia it usually did.

Scorteus was informed, and came in due dignity, having left the summons bearer waiting for a proper time, while the senior staff were turned out to give honour and the best wines in the house were offered in hospitality. So I was there with the rest, lined up in rows, and watched Scorteus break the seals and unroll the document, while the imperial slave stared at the collection of gaudy portrait busts in gold, silver and bronze, that looked down from marble niches in the walls. In a Roman house these would be portraits of noble ancestors, carved in honest stone or modelled in wax. But this was not a Roman house, there were no noble ancestors, and the visitor sneered.

"Ah!" said Scorteus, and among all those present he beckoned to me. I went to him, and he showed me the document. It was written in purple ink, on real Egyptian paper. It was signed by the Governor, and was a command for Scorteus to attend a personal audience of His Grace, the next day at the third hour at Government House. It was a colossal honour.

"This is all down to you," said Scorteus. "You and your magic."

"It's not magic," I said. "I've told you many times." But, he laughed aloud and, in the joy of his gratitude, he made me a great promise.

Next day Scorteus set out in his litter, a carved and painted monster with opulent cushions, dangling tassels and velvet curtains. It was some load, even for the eight Africans who were the litter bearers. While two dozen hefty farm slaves went before and behind, with staves to beat back the common herd, I followed behind with the fancy boys. There were four of them, body slaves responsible for the master's dress and appearance. They were slim creatures who minced and pranced, spoke in high voices, and slapped each other's hands in mock chastisement. I had to walk with them because I could not ride in the litter. Protocol forbade that to a slave, but the Syrian got a ride, and took opportunity to leer in triumph, whilst I reflected that his disdain no longer mattered, not now. So I thought.

It was a long walk through the busy streets of the biggest city in the Western Empire. For Londinium was a prodigy and a marvel; a vast, modern city planted in a land beyond the known world and in the face of ferocious native opposition. It was a typical, ruthlessly planned, grid-pattern Roman city, with plazas and avenues, blocks and apartments, plumbing and drains. Where there had been swamp and rushes, there were baths, theatres, law courts and shops. The raucous noise of a huge population here for the tremendous trade focused on the capital of the Imperial Province of Britannia.

I looked at the grinning faces peering at Scorteus in his litter, as they chattered and pointed, and packed the broad pavements. There were men and women, citizens and slaves, robes and rags, manners and insolence, with little girls cherishing dolls, while little boys piddled in the gutters. I heard every language in the Empire and saw every colour of skin, for as well as imported slaves and citizen colonists, there were many immigrants from backward lands here to seek work and a better life. Among the din I kept hearing the loud, shouted discussion of the latest news: rumours of a Caledonian revolt in the far north. This was a very ugly thought indeed, because only forty years ago Londinium itself had been massacred and burned in a native rebellion, Boudicca's rebellion. Britannia was as violent as that: never entirely stable, never completely safe.

But, at last the Africans could lower the litter at the steps of Government House, where a squad of the Governor's Guard stood to attention in elaborate parade armour: bronze cuirasses, broad-blade spears, and the antique helmets and oval shields of the old republic, for soldiers love the obsolete when it comes to dressing up.

Here Scorteus was extracted by the fancies, stood up, brushed down, wiped over, then towelled and perfumed, and made in all respects presentable, whilst I waited, dressed for the occasion in a Greek chiton that left the right arm and shoulder bare. That was Scorteus'ss idea, to impress the Romans, with their mawkish admiration of classical Greece. Which probably it did, because I was not the only Greek on show in a chiton.

"Fabius Gentilius Scorteus!" cried a polished and elegant figure, who stepped out from Government House. I recognised Petros of Athens, the most senior of imperial slaves, and personal secretary to His Grace the Governor. Petros had a clever face with a neat beard and moustache, and intensely black hair heavily receding at the temples, with a thin peak over the brow. He was the Governor's man, having come to Britannia in his service. Petros was famously efficient, and constantly attended by six shaven-skull, stone-face slaves, hand picked for intellect. Each one bore a sheaf of notes and an abacus. They were a library, record office and calculating engine, all in one and all on legs.

But, today, Petros bowed low to Scorteus, who stood erect, beckoned me to follow and walked up the steps into Government House, whilst an officer bawled a command and guardsmen stamped a crashing salute. Thus Petros escorted Scorteus, while the Syrian and I walked beside the six bald heads. We nodded to each other, formal and unsmiling, and followed our masters through bronze gates, massively cast in scenes of mythical antiquity.

Once inside the dull building, everything changed. The outside was plain by Imperial Decree, to remind the Governor that his residence was not a palace, nor was he a prince. But the inside was his to decorate as he pleased, so there was an enormous entrance hall, floored in a checkerboard of black and white slabs, and lined with dozens of alabaster columns with life-like, painted statues between. Glazed silver lamps hung on silver chains, suspended from rings held in the mouths of silver lions, and a fountain sprayed water from the lips of a bronze nymph in a central pool.

Then a band of legionary trumpeters blasted out a bone-shivering fanfare, and five military tribunes stepped forward to greet us.

This was the greatest honour yet, for tribunes were the most senior of army officers, representing not just military strength but political power. They were young aristocrats on the cursus honorum: destined for government and serving their time in the army before moving on to higher things. Each was a Knight of the Equestrian Order: the second highest rank in the Empire. They stood in gleaming steel, with helmets under their arms, and raised voices in formal chant.

"We give you good day and good blessing, O Fabius Gentilius Scorteus!" they cried. We bowed in return. Petros of Athens beckoned, and we set off into the interior of the great building, slow paces, grim faces, to an enormous marble staircase, and so the floor above, and to the throne room where yet more guardsmen threw open the doors and a marching tribune sang out in ponderous Latin.

"All hail to His Grace! Marcus Ostorious Cerealis Teutonius! Governor of the Imperial Province of Britannia! Chief Priest! Conqueror of the Teutonic Hordes! Three times Consul of ..."

"Enough," said a thin Roman, a mature man in the prime of life, who sat on the Governor's throne. Of all those name and titles, Teutonius was the one he used, and he wore the simplest clothes of anyone present, a tunic and cloak of unbleached wool. He smiled. "We are informal here today. This is all *in the family*." The Governor laughed and we laughed with him. Even the tribunes laughed, but then they bowed their heads in salute. They might be knights, but he was a nobleman of senatorial rank: the *highest* in the Empire. He smiled at Scorteus, and incredibly he smiled at me. I bowed, then studied his face, but very carefully and without staring.

He had the manner and bearing of a Roman aristocrat, born to rule and taking it for granted. All Romans affected that look, but Teutonius, by reputation, was the real thing. The eldest son of a powerful family, he was a career soldier and a gifted administrator who could bear the strain of high office. This was not surprising, because only the Empire's foremost men were sent to govern Britannia with its permanent garrison of three legions plus auxiliaries, the biggest army in the Empire. It was a huge force, needed to counter the constant threat of rebellion. Thus, while Britannia was not an especially rich province, it offered the chance of military glory which Romans valued above everything.

Against this was the fact that the Governor's huge army made him dangerous unless Rome could trust him completely. Since Rome trusted nobody completely, the Governor of Britannia was watched very closely indeed, and must be able to bear that too. But, Petros was speaking,

"Your Grace," he said, "There stands before you that friend of Rome, that man of public affairs ..." He was introducing Scorteus. He did so at length, and I looked round. I suppose things *were* informal by their standards. The turnout was just five tribunes, a dozen officials, twenty guardsman, plus Petros and his six, and various domestics.

But next to the Governor stood his wife, a Roman matriarch of exquisite refinement, tall, upright and splendid, in an immaculate, white, figure-hugging stola, the formal dress of a citizen's wife. Her hair was swept up and caught in a swirl within a plain golden crown. The effect drew attention to her gleaming neck, while five teenage daughters stood behind, dressed like her, but as nothing compared with the glory of the mother, and bizarrely outranked in place by a slave woman who stood right behind the matriarch. The slave was an odd creature, not old but wizened, and pure Greek, with the darkest skin I have ever seen in our race. I struggled to guess her age because she had the remains of great beauty, prematurely ravaged by hard experience. She was richly dressed with fine ornaments, and yet she was a slave who whispered in the ear of her mistress and stood between her and her kin. I wondered who she was.

But, I did not wonder for long. No man would ponder on the slave when he could worship the mistress. She was like a marble statue of Athena, only colder. She could have walked on water by freezing it with a glance. She could have killed men dead with a frown. She was formidably stern, and she was everything that Roman gentlemen seek in marriage, an institution perceived by them as a property contract made exclusively for reasons of financial and dynastic politics.

This was Her Grace the Lady Tertia, leader of fashion, patroness of philosophers, and champion of the arts. She was all that and more, because she came of the same clan, the Ulpii, as Emperor Trajan, and was related to His Imperial Majesty by blood. In terms of strict precedence, she therefore outranked even her own husband. The fact had the most powerful effect on me because, in those days, there were some events that my memory kept hidden and even what I could recall was fading.

Thus, after ten years, with neither pictures nor sculptures to prompt me, it was becoming hard to recall the appearances of those I had known in the days of my freedom. Worst of all, and to my great sorrow, the faces of my children were already gone, soft and unformed as the faces of children are. I had wept over this until I had no more tears. Now even my wife's face could not be fixed in the mind's eye, not in sharp precision. But in looking at Tertia and thinking of her exalted rank, the locked door of memory was burst open, and the image of my beloved lady suddenly came to me, prompted by the fact that *she* had outranked *me* as the daughter of a nobler house than mine.

I strained to see her, to fix the moment, to hold it fast, but it was like grasping smoke and the image was gone in a heartbeat. Then, since I was present on the most strict of formal duty, and since the image had indeed and definitely gone, I forced myself to pay attention to what His Grace the Governor was saying. It was my burden to do so. It was another punishment for being alive.

"Madame-my-wife," said Teutonius. "I present, Fabius Gentilius Scorteus, one of the province's leading men, and who is soon to become a Roman citizen." His words were life changing and momentous, and Scorteus bit his lip, hung his head in emotion and fought the tears, for he had been born of an mother squatting on the earth floor of a Celtic roundhouse and had pursued Roman citizenship for most of his life.

"Fabius Gentilius Scorteus," said the Lady Tertia, "I greet you and welcome you." Then she held out her hand for Scorteus to kiss, another tremendous gesture. Because, while her husband could grant citizenship, it was exclusively within *her* gift to accept a citizen as worthy to enter the salons, dinner parties and ceremonies of Roman high society, and the offering of her hand was that acceptance. This time, Scorteus could not hold back the emotion. He sobbed and the tears flowed. He was a Celt after all.

The Governor smiled kindly, small talk was made, then Petros leaned forward and murmured to His Grace, who suggested that Her Grace might show Scorteus the exotic plants of her private garden. It was another great honour, and Tertia left the chamber with Scorteus and her girls in line astern, and a diplomat's smile on her face.

Then doors closed and Teutonius stood up. He dismissed everyone except Petros, and beckoned me through a side door. At first I froze, because there are secrets that are dangerous to know, and I feared what lay behind the door. Petros saw my hesitation and spoke to me in classical Athenian Greek.

"Ikaros of Apollonis," he said, "be not afraid, for the benison of His Grace's favour lies upon you." But still I hesitated because I had just stood in the presence of the Governor's legally wedded wife. Then the Governor spoke.

"Boy!" he said, "Here!" So I stepped through the door and Petros shut it behind me. It was a small room, an office with bookcases, desks and papers. But a girl was there. She was obviously German, because she had the fabulous golden hair that is unique to that savage race, and she was wonderfully lovely. Her skin glowed, her eyes shone and her beauty touched the souls of all who saw her. She was richly dressed, but not in the stola of a Roman wife because she was a slave. She was Teutonius' slave and his darling.

"Ikaros of Apollonis," he said, seeking to calm my anxiety, "let not your mind be troubled." He too spoke Athenian Greek. Then the girl spoke guttural German and stepped forward and offered me her hand. I looked at Teutonius who nodded. I touched the hand, not presuming to grasp it, then bowed in deep respect, and the girl stepped back and took her place beside her master.

"My lady thanks you," he said, in flawless Greek, and he paused as she spoke again and he translated. "My lady blesses you in the name of Freya the mother, Nerva the wise, and Ilka the lovely." She nodded. She was done, but Teutonius was not. "And I bless you," he said, "by the Olympian gods of your heroic and noble homeland, that realm of poets, philosophers, and engineers."

"Gods bless Your Grace," I said, and looked at the girl. "For I see that the surgeons have achieved a cure." Teutonius smiled.

"Yes," he said, "it was a vaginal fistula. A debilitating and dolorous affliction, but well within surgery's art to cure, if only the patient may tolerate the pain. The surgeons had failed twice and it was you, with your drug, who enabled the cure." He paused to look at me, "You were summoned because I was curious to study you, Ikaros the Apollonite," he said, "since you are renowned for your penetration of intellect." He nodded thoughtfully and, in my innocence, I imagined that he was praising me as a man. But, he added, "It is a fortunate master who owns such an asset." Thus I was classified somewhere between intelligent apes and dogs that do tricks.

But the girl tugged at his arm and spoke to him again, and he smiled, as a man does at some small or easy matter, and he turned to me. "My lady would bestow the gift of favour," he said. "So should misfortune place you in need of my benevolence, then you may approach me in her name."

Later, Scorteus and I rode in the litter, with protocol trudging behind, beside the Syrian. Scorteus was intoxicated with joy.

"You did it boy," he said, and instantly corrected himself. "No!" he said, "I won't ever call you boy again. And no other bugger won't neither!" He reached under his seat and pulled out a big flask of wine. "There's another one under yours," he said. "Go on. You deserve it. Help yourself." I did. I like wine, and by the time we reached the house the flasks were empty, and I entered unsteadily, arm-in-arm with Scorteus, and the household bowing before us.

"So," he said, and jabbed a thumb at the Syrian, "he can draw up the document tomorrow, first thing. And he can get the lawyers round to witness it."

"Dominus," I said, "how can I thank you?" He laughed and swayed on his feet, grasping my shoulder for support.

"Crap!" he said merrily, "If I'm going to be a citizen, which I am, and it's all due to you, which it is, then you're going to be free. Ain't that what I promised?"

"Thank you," I said. "Thank you."

"So, first thing after morning calls tomorrow."

That night I slept badly because the huge disturbance of regaining my freedom, wonderful though it was, broke open my memory again, and showed me things that were not wonderful, but dreadful; teaching me that when memory hides its secrets, sometimes it does so through kindness.

I was in the past as the Romans came over the walls. I smelt fear, felt the weight of my armour, gripped sword and shield, and staggered under the shock of their charge as they broke us on the battlements and ran yelling down the stairways to open the gates for their main force. Then we who still lived were bound in honour to deliver our kin from the debasement of slavery. So I ran through a city under bombardment, with stone shot smashing roofs, and incendiaries starting fires. Flames roared as I entered my house and faced my wife and children. The children screamed at me, bloodstained as I was, so I threw off my helmet to show my face. But they screamed still louder as I drew my sword.

And so to the present, and the hour before dawn, and the simple matter of soap. The Romans thought it was good for nothing but cleaning floors, and they went to the baths to be clean because the baths were their club and their daily entertainment. But I preferred soap because it worked quicker and better, and the soap that I made smelt of roses. So, I stood in my bath chamber, naked on a wooden grating, and covered in lather. Lamps twinkled. Steam swirled. Cisterns ran with hot and cold water. The chamber was luxurious, a privilege of exotic status.

"Water," I said. My boys dipped pans into warm water and poured them over my head, washing away the lather, which ran into the drain below. "Again," I said, and the water gushed. All was peaceful, and I thought of the document that Scorteus was going to sign. I closed my eyes and tried to look forward. What would I do? How would I live? And in that moment there came the knock of doom, a polite tap at the bath chamber door.

"See who it is," I said, and the elder boy opened the door and looked out.

"It's one of the mice," he said. *Mice* was what superior boys called the lowest grade of unskilled menials. "What is it?" said my boy sharply. "His worship is taking his bath." There was a murmur of speech, then my boy looked at me. "He says he can only speak to you, worshipful sir."

"Bring him in," I said, "and get me some towels." I stepped off the grid, my boys wrapped me in linen, and the houseboy came in, bowing constantly. He was old and shrivelled and, like all the lower slaves, he looked towards me but not at me, because he thought I had the evil eye "What is it boy?" I said, as gently as I could and he rattled off a prepared speech.

"His Worship Agidox begs that His Worship Ikaros should join him with utmost despatch, as led by the willing hand of this boy here present."

"What for?" I asked, but the house boy merely bowed, and repeated his speech. I looked at the lined, old face and asked no more questions, because he was already afraid and it would have been cruel to press him. So I dressed and followed him through the house, which was at its busiest as the house folk prepared for morning calls.

Everything was bright with lamps, and noisy with chatter and laughter, as hordes of slaves ran to their tasks; males and females, young and old of every age and status. There were even more of them upstairs in a warren of dormitories, whole families of them. They were a community, a clan, a village; hundreds of them as is common in the house of a millionaire, since the usual way to display wealth is in the number of slaves.

So the elderly house boy led me through the vast complexity of the mansion: three atriums, stairways to upper floors, guest rooms, dining rooms, music rooms: all of them huge and all of them floored with mosaics, lined with paintings, and crammed with furniture. They dazzled the eye and besieged the senses. They were opulent beyond belief, and went on and on, with the house boy gasping and wheezing, and finally stopping in an ornately-decorated, bright-lit corridor, lined with exquisite bronze statues of dryads and fauns.

Here the house boy fell to his knees before Agidox the major domos, waiting with four senior boys outside the cedar-wood door that led into the master bath chamber. They all looked at me and said nothing, because they were shaken with horror. It was an uncanny moment and I did not know what to think. But I spoke the proper words.

"I give you good day, and may gods bless you, honoured Agidox," I said, and I bowed. But Agidox amazed me by ignoring all formalities as he stepped forward and gasped into my ear.

"I sent for you before anyone," he said. "Come and see." He pushed open the big door and led me in to the bath chamber, which was fifty feet square with a deep plunge bath in the centre, filled with steaming water sprinkled with flowers on cork dishes. There was a hot room, a cold room, shelves for cosmetics and perfumes, marble tritons in niches in the walls, and a vaulted ceiling lined with tiles beautified with coloured images of fish, while golden lamps shone from a ring of eight tall, black granite pedestals that surrounded the plunge bath.

The lamps gave bright and beautiful illumination, which showed pools of red all over the white marble floor. It was blood, as much blood as if a pig had been slit. But, it was not a pig. It was Fabius Gentilius Scorteus.

"What happened here?" I said to Agidox, but he looked away. He was afraid to speak and, in that instant, I knew. I read his mind and knew why he was afraid. Scorteus had been killed by one of his own slaves, and every other slave knew what that meant. They knew that, under Roman law, if any slave killed the master then every slave in the house would be put to death.

Chapter 4

Scorteus lay on his back with his mouth and eyes wide open. He lay grotesque and exposed in a thin tunic which had ridden up to show white flesh, pubic hair, and genitals nestling in the fat of the thighs.

I stared in disbelief. I stared and stared, and finally knelt beside him. I touched his foot, his leg, his face, and felt the warmth still in him. Then I closed his eyes and looked at the wound in his throat. A single cut from a sharp blade, delivered with great force. It was a death stroke that would have killed in the blink of an eye. It was common knowledge that he usually dozed in a chair in the bath chamber each morning, after a hot plunge, waiting for the barber. If he had been caught like that he would never even have woken up.

Then I had to stand, because I had been among the Romans so long that, instinctively, I wanted to raise hands in the Roman way: elbows bent, forearms vertical, palms turned outwards. It was their universal sign of respect, and of honour to the gods. So I made the sign, offered my respect, and gave prayer to Apollo in the name of Scorteus. But then I fell to my knees again and pressed my hands to his cheeks and called on Scorteus by name and shook his head, still refusing to accept what I saw.

Nonetheless he was dead and nothing could wake him, for resurrection thrives only in nonsensical eastern cults. In the real world it does not exist, and yet still we torture ourselves with self-inflicted pain. We torture ourselves with hopes, and with dreams and with memories: which hopes are never realised, which dreams are nightmares, and which memories are monsters of dread.

* * *

In that moment, the memories came staccato, like faces seen by a horseman as he gallops through a crowd, each face bright and clear but instantly gone. My wife and children lay with blood spurting from their wounds. I howled and screamed. I cursed the gods. I fell to my knees and beat the ground. Then the Romans came and I was chained. I was taken outside the burning city and looked back and saw the smoke. It was black and the fires roared. We were burning our libraries, burning five hundred years of science rather than give it to the Romans.

We were in a stockade for days. Hundreds of us. All men. The women were elsewhere. There was enough food and water to keep us alive. Everyone was chained. No shade, no peace, no help. The wounded died. They were dragged away. Days later the slavers came, those who followed the army and bought in bulk. A slaver approached me, fine robes and guards behind him. They killed the man next to me. Daniros, son of Cleon, captain of infantry. The slaver tried to examine Daniros, who snarled and struck him. A guard ran a sword through Daniros. The slaver looked at Daniros, laid bleeding and dying in the dirt.

"The least valuable of slaves," he said to me, "is a man who shows fight. I want skilled men who do as they're told. So show me your hands, boy." I showed him my hands. "Good," he said. "A skilled man. And are you literate?" I nodded. He asked many other questions. I answered and he smiled. I remembered only his last question. "How did Eratosthenes of Syrene calculate the circumference of the earth, having seen his own reflection down a well?" I told him and he laughed in delight. And so I was enslaved. I did not fight. I did not take my own life. Thus Daniros died a man and I did not.

So I wept in the past and I wept in the present, kneeling beside Scorteus. I wept for myself, because who would give me freedom now? But I wept for him too. The only man who did not treat me as a freak, and who looked me in the eyes and smiled. He was my owner, but he was the nearest thing I had to a friend. This thought goaded me into acting as a man and thinking of someone other than myself. So I put aside my weeping and looked outwards rather than inwards. It was a seminal moment in my life because I could just have easily have sunk into despair. It was a great struggle too, but strength was granted unto me by Apollo, and I stood up and faced the world, ugly and unjust as it was.

"Who did this?" I said to Agidox. But he was silent and staring at the floor. "Agidox!" I said, again.

"It was Mettorus," he said, "Mettorus the barber."

"Never," I said, "He's a nice little man. Everyone knows him."

"There was only him and the dominus in here," said Agidox. "There's only one door, and nobody else went in or out."

"Where is he?" I said. "Mettorus?"

"The Africans have got him," said Agidox, and moved close and whispered, "Ikaros. Can we hide this? Say it was suicide?"

"Suicide?" I said, and almost laughed. "When he'd just got citizenship?" But then my thoughts ran dark and deep. Could we hide the body? Say Scorteus had run off? Gone mad? Been killed by burglars? "No," I said. "Too many people know. Your boys and the Africans make a dozen, and they'd all be questioned under torture, and us too."

And so he groaned, and looked to me, he looked to the clever Greek, and my spirit trembled, such that I nearly fell back into tears. In my city, in my days of glory, I had been a senator and a military officer, making decisions and taking command. But that was years ago. Now, all I did was build machines, read books and perform at dinner parties. I feared that I had lost the strength to be decisive in crisis. But I did my best. I did not give up. I gathered facts.

"Where's the Syrian?" I asked. "And the family?" Agidox frowned as if I were asking the obvious.

"They're at the master's villa," he said, "for the countryside festival."

"Oh," I said, because I had a weakness with festivals. I could never remember them all, and still cannot. This one, sacred to the Celtic goddess Druantia, was a favourite with the women of the family. Although Scorteus never kept it, the Syrian did, believing that Druantia was a local incarnation of one of his Eastern gods. So I nodded and looked again at the corpse of our master, lying in his bath chamber, and I took a breath and spoke.

"I shall write letters to the family, and to the dominus' brother, who is his most important relative." I paused and took the final step. "I shall write to the Governor, the Lord Chief Justice, City Hall, and everyone else I can think of."

"What will you tell them," said Agidox, wide eyed with fear. Looking at him I wondered again if some life-saving tale might be contrived, even now.

"Leave that to me," I said. "Get a dozen of the young slaves. We will need runners to carry the letters." Then I gasped. "The clients! They must be outside."

"For morning calls," he said, which he too had forgotten until now.

"Get out there, Agidox," I said. "Tell them the dominus is indisposed. Tell them it's the Britannic phlegm." I looked at him. He was pale and trembling. "Can you do that Agidox?" He nodded, because he too was doing his best. So we got rid of the clients. I wrote the letters and we sent out our runners. Within two hours the young centurion arrived with his men, by which time the dreadful news was known to everyone in the house.

The centurion, Decimus Paulinius Marianus, did little. He just stood at my shoulder, superior to a mere Greek, but relying on him to solve the problem, which was typical Roman behaviour and which explains why he opened the door, stood back and waited to see what I would do. So I stepped through the doorway, I looked at the packed mass of slaves and I myself wondered what I was going to do.

They were not just working slaves, they were families, dozens of them. Males, females and children, and more cramming the corridors. Nearly four hundred adults were doomed to die, while the children would be left as orphans, to be sold if they were pretty and cast out to starve if they were not.

And now they looked to me in hope, because they had heard the centurion's words. More than that, they knew me and they believed that I could save them. They believed that, because they believed I had magic powers which was a comfort to them but a burden to me because

I knew that I did not. Meanwhile I had to get rid of them because they could not stand forever dithering in a milling mob, and because I needed time to think.

"Go about your duties," I said, "that is what the dominus would have wanted." But, they looked to Agidox.

"Go to your duties," he said, "and trust in the Greek. He will save us." And they sighed and smiled at me.

"Gods almighty," I thought. "Gods preserve and save us."

"Go on," said Agidox, clapping his hands, and they filed out and I turned to Marianus.

"Honoured sir," I said, "will you view the alleged culprit, and the body of my master?"

"Is that necessary?" he said.

"Yes, honoured sir. To see that the facts are as I have said in my letters."

"I suppose that's in order," he said.

"Where's Mettorus?" I said to Agidox.

Mettorus was downstairs in one of the cellars, where the Africans had thrown him. So we took lamps and went down into the dust and the dark, and found him unconscious on the stone flags beside a great stack of barrels.

"Who told them to beat him?" I said, and Agidox gulped in guilt.

"Nobody," he said. "They just did it." Marianus stepped forward and looked at the barber in the flickering lamplight.

"Huh," he said. "That's nothing. He's got far worse than that coming!"

"Only if he's guilty," I said.

"Can you prove he isn't?" said Marianus.

"Will you see the body of my master, honoured sir?" I said, ducking the question, and we went to the bath chamber, where Marianus removed his helmet in respect, and poked the body with his vine staff to check that he was dead. Then he glanced round, in superficial haste, as if he could somehow keep distant from this disaster.

"Yes," he said, "everything is as you said," He frowned at the corpse. "Get him covered up," he said. "He's not decent like that." And that was all he did, apart from placing guards on the gates, who were changed at intervals with the old guard marching back to barracks and Marianus with them once it got late, still trying to keep at arms' length from his loathsome duty.

Next day the family returned. They came with slaves running ahead, such that Marianus, Agidox, and I were waiting, with the soldiers stood to respectful attention, as a procession of litters and slaves approached, chanting a funeral dirge, and the neighbours turning out with their own slaves, to line the streets in hundreds. They raised hands and bowed as the litters passed and I expected some dignified ceremony at the gates, but Celts are Celts and there were howls and cries from the women, and one boy, in the litters, who jumped out and rushed weeping into the house. The Syrian was with them in his own litter, and he too was weeping, and between them they set the slaves off again. Half the city must have heard; it was chaos.

In the bath chamber, Scorteus's wife, his son and his three daughters were transported with grief, embracing his cold body, kissing his cheeks, chafing his limbs, and making the same futile attempts to rouse him as I had done. They even pulled him up into a sitting position, supporting the limp head, and the boy cried out, "Pappa! Pappa!"

Marianus frowned in contempt, because Romans show no emotion in public. He, Agidox and I were stood to one side and we watched as a richly-dressed old woman entered with her body slaves, and everyone bowed. She came leaning on a stick, while her slaves bore pots, jars, and white mourning sheets.

"Who's she?" said Marianus, over the crying and wailing.

"The lady Caradigma," I said. "My master's mother. She is the domina, honoured sir. The mistress of the house." Indeed she was, because Scorteus's wife was a pretty, plump, gentle creature, chosen for childbearing, while Caradigma was fierce and strong minded, even though her understanding was clouding with age, such that she rejected all opinions than her own, believing that she already knew everything worth knowing. She was a tiny woman, white haired, and much afflicted with arthritis. But she barked orders in the Britannic language, and made family and slaves stand behind Scorteus's son: Fabius Gentilius Fortunus, eleven years old, snivelling and crying and now supposedly head of the household.

Helped by her slaves, Caradigma draped the family in white sheets, tore each sheet to display grief, then spread ashes on every head, got the mourners into a ring around the body and beckoned to slaves who brought forward pots of earth, water and salt. Having knelt with utmost difficulty, she smeared these sacred materials on Scorteus's brow, one at a time, uttering ritual words to express the family's grief to the family's gods, which was very proper. It was all very well my seeking intercession from Apollo, but when a man dies he needs his own gods, those who know him and know where he lives.

Then she rose, aided by her slaves, and there was silence as she looked round, and beckoned to the Syrian who was waiting with his boys behind him. He came forward, bare chested, lamenting, and shedding tears which were entirely genuine because he owed everything to Scorteus. But he approached Caradigma and bowed low, speaking fluent Britannic, which I could follow only if it were spoken very slowly.

This was because my daily work was conducted either in the written languages of other civilisations or the everyday Latin and Greek that are ancestral kin to each other but are uttermost strangers to the Britannic tongues. Thus, even such basic words as *man*, *house* or *bread* are wildly exotic in Britannic and convey no hint of meaning to the Mediterranean ear. Likewise, the syntax, gender, inflection and what passes for case in Britannic are beyond reason or calculation and must be learned by rote. But I had given no time for such effort because Britannic was the speech of a conquered race and its prestige was lower than the sole of a Roman's boot. So I had ignored Britannic, and knew only what little I had picked up by absorption, diffusion or casual chance. Thus my understanding was like that of a child; it was slow, clumsy and weak. Such was my ignorance, such was my failure.

So the Syrian spoke and Caradigma listened, and I strained to read their thoughts if not their words. She was agonised with grief, tired with pain, and was balking at the burden of this apocalypse. Seeing this, the Syrian was offering himself as her champion. With Scorteus dead, a huge wealth of enterprise lacked a leader, and he would be that leader, he would take over. He would, in effect, become the new dominus.

It was a terrifying moment, because even though the centurion Marianus had told me to *find a way round this*, I was a slave under the orders of the domina. I could do nothing without her word. If the Syrian gained control of the house I would do nothing at all because I would be got rid of, not even with the grace of a swift dagger. In his malice the Syrian would sell me down the mines where slaves were worked to death by hideous labour and sadistic punishment. The trembling moment came when the Syrian fell silent, adopted a humble stance and raised his eyebrows whilst asking a question, begging a grace, seeking an outcome. Caradigma looked at him, and then at Agidox, and then at her grandson Fortunus, now wiping his nose on the tail of his mourning sheet.

"Bah!" she said, and turned from the Syrian, and lurched forward and bore down like a ram ship, then stopped nose to nose, glaring up at me. It is strange what a man notices in such moments. She had a tattoo on her left cheek: the tiny outline of a horse in graceful, Celtic strokes. I had never seen it before because I had never been close enough. Then she spoke slowly and carefully, making allowances for my deficiencies, but even so I stress that I did understand her fully in the instant that she spoke. It was only with effort that I resolved her speech into the sentences that I record here.

"My son always named you as the clever one," she said, and in that moment I blessed the name of Scorteus who would have freed me had he lived, and who even now stretched his hand across the River Styx to save me. "So you will protect this house," said Caradigma, "and all within its walls." She pointed to the slaves and I nodded, wondering whether it was their humanity that she valued or their market value. As I wondered, she gave swift orders to the slaves, who bore away Scorteus's body for washing and binding, before ritual cremation at sunset.

They cleaned the bath chamber too. They cleaned it of every sign of the murder, even as I realised that I should have given close attention to the scene of the crime. But now it was too late. Then Caradigma spoke to me again, slowly and deliberately.

"Come," she said, "I will see the slave who murdered my son." She chattered rapidly at Agidox, who bowed and led the way, with herself, myself, Marianus and the rest following, and the Syrian sticking to me like a lamb to its mother.

Agidox had got Mettorus out of the cellar into a small guest room, where we found him sat swaying on a stool, just about conscious. He was a small, middle-aged man, with battered, half-closed eyes, broken teeth and split lips. He tried to stand on sight of the domina, but she screeched and swung her stick. He jerked with each impact and she stopped only when she was tired. Then she shouted at me, miming throat cutting with her free hand. The Syrian began to translate.

"The domina says ..."

"I know," I said. "But, if he dies, we learn nothing. What if there were a plot?"

"A plot?" said the Syrian. "You mean there may be others?"

"I don't know, and if we kill him we'll never know." He told Caradigma and she spoke slowly to me.

"I thank you for your wisdom," she said, and looked at the barber. "He shall go to the torturers. They will find out what he knows."

"Oh no," said the barber, and the domina growled like a dog and raised her stick. But, I took her arm and did my best in Britannic Celtic, straining to draw words from my limited vocabulary.

"Domina. Man must live. For questions."

"Ah, yes," she said.

"I do questions?" I said, and she smiled, grateful even in her grief.

"I thank you," she said and patted my hand. "But you are too fine to do torture." I closed my eyes. That wasn't what I meant. But she nodded at the barber, "He goes to those who know the craft," the smile vanished. "He goes *at once*!" I could have groaned. Torture works if you can check the answers. It is useful for *where have you hidden the money?* But it is hopeless for *who else is in the plot?* The victim will say anything to stop the pain. He will give every name he knows then make up more and, in this case, it was worse than useless because I could have found out what Mettorus knew by patient questioning..

"Mettorus?" I said, switching to Latin, "you know me, don't you?" The little man stirred.

"Yes, sir," he mumbled. "You're Ikaros, sir. And I never done nothing, sir. Not to the dominus, gods bless him." He could barely see, he could barely speak, and I could not read his face, not in that condition. But I believed him because he was a decent man with a family who had everything to lose. He could not have quarrelled with Scorteus, for who would allow a razor at his throat if he had quarrelled with the barber? Certainly not Scorteus!

So I knew then that Mettorus was innocent. But, if he did not kill Scorteus, then who did? And why?

Chapter 5

In the moments that followed, I thought I had the answer, because the Syrian's behaviour was so odd. He attempted a private conversation in a room packed with ears, while several things happened all at once.

Thus the Africans came and seized Mettorus to take him for torture; the domina left with her slaves to prepare her son's body, and Marianus the centurion insisted that we move to the great atrium, where the business of a Roman house should be transacted. So there was much bowing and shifting and falling back according to precedence, even as the Syrian fastened on to me, and hissed words into my ear, while Marianus looked on in amazement. But the Syrian persisted, with his black eyes glittering with hatred, and something else besides. It was fear.

"Who did you write to?" he said, "I know you sent letters."

"Everyone," I said, "Every authority from the Governor, to the Street Wardens."

"What did you tell them?" he said.

"The truth," I said, and he frowned as if *the truth* were something bizarre. "Any deceit can be broken," I said, "and show us as liars."

"Us?" he said.

"Yes! You too. D'you think you're not part of this?"

"Not so much as you," he said. "I'm a freedman, so I'm not under sentence of death." He relished the thought with a nasty smile, and I looked at him. Perhaps I should have thanked him, because he had just concentrated my mind. What was I trying to do? What did Caradigma expect me to do? What did I *want* to do? Save four hundred slaves and myself from execution? Keep the household together and functioning? Find the killer, who I didn't think was Mettorus, but maybe it was? Or did I simply want vengeance for Scorteus?

The answer was 'yes' to everything. But above all and as a matter of the most profound principle, I wanted some redress and reparation in this capricious world, which may smite the innocent and cherish the guilty in rank injustice, and where newborn infants may by ignorant chance inherit freedom, riches and health, or slavery, poverty and a cleft palate, because the gods give no justice, only men, and we must fight for it. We are like the mythical Sisyphus rolling his immense boulder up a hill, but we must work harder than him because he failed every time to reach the top.

Thus everything depended on gathering evidence that Mettorus was not the killer, but somebody else was, and that the somebody was not a slave of the House of Scorteus; then proving it in a court of law, and all this I would have to do myself. I would have to do it because Romans regarded crime as a private matter, which seemed strange to me because in my city we had officers of police to catch criminals, who were prosecuted by the state. But Romans have none of this, believing that the state should remain impartial when citizens fall out, merely appointing magistrates to whom citizens could bring evidence for judgement. And as for a police force, Romans saw that as an outrageous interference in the liberties of free men.

But first I had to survive more pressing hazards, such as calming four hundred house slaves, who would need some better response to the master's death than being told to go about their duties. They could not be left suffering in their terror, or still worse to attempt escape and face certain death from the soldiers guarding the house. Finally, having thought carefully, I did not thank the Syrian, because he was hiding something. So I tried to find out what it was.

"What would you have said," I asked, "had you written those letters?" But he glanced at Marianus, Agidox and the rest, and his face showed nothing. So I ignored him and spoke to Marianus. "Honoured sir," I said, "with your permission I would like to call a meeting of the senior slaves."

He shifted his feet and looked away as if it were nothing to do with him. So I bowed and spoke to Agidox, who sent boys to summon the leaders among his staff, and soon I was facing several dozen frightened men and women in the great atrium, with the portrait busts looking down, and a grey, square of Britannic sky glowering over the pool. Marianus stood as far to one side as he could, while Agidox and the Syrian stood beside me.

I looked at the elite slaves: females as well as males, all leaders of departments within the house. I had to speak to them because the lower ranks spoke only Britannic, and it was vital that I spoke persuasively, which I could not possibly do in that language. So I made my speech, striving to bring calm upon the house. I told no knowing lies, but I gave an optimistic interpretation of the facts. What else could I do?

"The law which threatens us," I said, "is the *Senatus Consultum Silanianum*, which means a Senate decree in the year of the Consul Silanus." Agidox and the Syrian understood, but not the rest, "It means the law was passed ninety years ago," I said, "and it's bogeyman law. It's there to frighten you. They never use it!" I hoped that might be true. Decent Romans were ashamed of the Silanianum. It had not been used in decades, and perhaps they would not use it now.

"They used it for Pedanius Secundus!" said the Syrian, "in Rome itself." Everyone groaned. The case was famous. Every slave knew it because masters made sure that they did.

"That was sixty years ago," I said. "It was the only time they ever used it in Rome, and it was a disaster. They never tell you that. The mob turned out, the Senate was besieged, there was rioting for days, they sent in the army and there was blood in the gutters." Then I stopped, hearing voices outside the atrium doors, one of which opened slightly to admit a soldier who saluted Marianus and spoke quietly to him.

"Let 'em in," said Marianus, and the doors opened fully. There was a great genuflection from the slaves as two men entered with their own trail of slaves. The first man was Scorteus's younger brother, named in the city census as Lucius Gentilius Caractacus, but who always used his Celtic name, Badrogid. He came in response to my letter, and came in deep mourning, with ashes in his hair and a torn white sheet over shoulders.

Badrogid was like Scorteus, yet unlike him. The same complexion and features, but a younger and broader man, with enormous hands and great physical strength. He wore a rich man's caricature of Celtic dress: checked trousers, layers of tunics, plaited hair held back with a leather band, and a massive, golden neck ring, a torc, of classic Britannic style. He was proud and arrogant, taking no interest in the tanneries that supposedly he managed for his brother, and which were run by freedmen. He lived on Scorteus's generosity, he had a foul temper, and his slaves went in fear of him.

The other man was a Roman citizen in his toga, with his head covered within a fold of the white wool to show respect. He was Tullius Quintillius Dolbius, Scorteus's lawyer, a skinny, sharp-faced man, poised and sophisticated, and his toga displaying the narrow, purple band that proclaimed equestrian status. Thus he outranked everyone in the house. But he most carefully deferred to the non citizen, Celt, Badrogid, who might soon replace Scorteus as his best customer. So Badrogid advanced, with slaves bowing before him. He stared at all present and, with only the briefest nod to the centurion, he fixed on Agidox.

"Where's my brother?" he said.

"With the women, honoured sir," said Agidox, "being prepared for cremation." Badrogid sighed while Agidox stepped forward, knelt before him, and gave blessing upon the dead in the name of Jupiter Maximus. We all did, including the centurion. It was the decent thing to do and the room sighed with voices as we chanted the well-known prayer, which was rudely interrupted as the boy Fortunus rushed into the atrium, from the depths of the house, threw his arms around his uncle and buried his face in his robes. But we finished the prayer and stood, as Badrogid pushed his nephew to arms' length.

"Stand straight boy," he said, "for your father and your clan." I think that was what he said, for he spoke Britannic, which seemed odd to a boy that looked Roman from shoes to haircut. He even had a bulla round his neck, the amulet on a leather thong that Roman boys wear against evil. But Fortunus nodded, and did as he was told, although clinging to his uncle's hand while the lawyer whispered to Badrogid and pointed at me.

"Him?" said Badrogid, "The Greek?"

"Honoured sir," said Agidox. "The lady-your-mother has placed her entire confidence in Ikaros of Apollonis."

"I see," said Badrogid, but I doubt that he did. He shared none of Scorteus'ss interests and knew little of me. But I needed his help.

"Honoured sir," I said, "Brother-of-my-master, I beg in his name that I be allowed to speak a few words to these slaves of the house. It is most seriously urgent and important." Badrogid looked at me, and at the slaves, and perhaps he did understand, because he nodded.

"Yes. Go on. Get on with it," he said, and I bowed, and looked at Dolbius.

"Honoured and learned sir," I said. He looked at me without expression. "We need to reassure the slaves of the house. They are in fear of the Silanianum."

"The Senatus Consultum Silanianum?" he said.

"Which is dead law," I said.

"Ah," said the lawyer: a single, totally non-committal sound.

"It is pretend law," I said.

"Ah," he said.

"It is a law which has never been used in Britannia." This time he nodded.

"That is true," he said, and the slaves sighed with relief. So far so good. Now I had to rely on my reputation within the household.

"Therefore," I said, looking at them all, "I give my word as an Apollonite Greek, that the law will take vengeance *only* upon the killer of our master."

"Ah!" said Dolbius, stepping smartly aside from responsibility. "The Greek gives his word."

"The word of the cleverest man in Britannia!" said Agidox, and the Syrian turned on me.

"You give your word?" he said, "Before us all?"

"I do!" I said, and there was a glad murmuring and smiling from the slaves, while I whispered to Agidox, who took permission from Marianus and Badrogid and dismissed the slaves. They filed out, content for the moment, and Badrogid's slaves were sent out after them, while the centurion Marianus took swift opportunity to get away.

"I will not intrude on family matters," he said, and clicked his heels and went, which left Badrogid, Dolbius the lawyer, Agidox, the Syrian, and me, all stood by the compluvium pool, looking at each in the chilly downdraft from the open roof above. We could hear the traffic in the street through it.

"So," said Badrogid, "who killed my brother?"

"The barber!" said the Syrian.

"I'm not so sure," I said, and to my surprise Badrogid agreed.

"No," he said "I can't see him doing it. Not Mettorus."

"But who else could have done it?" said Dolbius.

"Can Mettorus be spared the torture?" I said, "and given to me?" Badrogid did not even consider the question.

"No," he said, "All slaves are liars, and cunning with it. Torture is the only way to get the truth out of them." I sighed because that is what everyone believed, and perhaps they were right. Dolbius the lawyer was already nodding.

"Indeed," he said, "it must be torture." I gave up and moved on.

"Honoured sirs," I said, "there are other matters."

"Such as what?" said Badrogid.

"If I am to make investigations," I said.

"About the murder?" said Badrogid.

"Yes, honoured sir. If I am to do that, I would wish to start by speaking to everyone who knows Scorteus, to ask many questions." Badrogid nodded. "And a slave cannot do that without the authority of his dominus, which means the *new* dominus."

"Yes," said Badrogid, and turned to the lawyer.

"Has the will been opened? My brother's will?"

"Not yet honoured sir," said Dolbius.

"Then open it," said Badrogid. "Now!" The lawyer smiled politely.

"I regret that it cannot be done, honoured sir. Not here. The opening of a will is a serious matter. It must be done at City Hall before witnesses."

"Then just say who inherits," said Badrogid. "Say who's the next dominus." Dolbius smiled again, the expression telling nothing.

"With regret, honoured sir, that is forbidden by professional confidentiality." But then he looked at me, and his eyes flicked to Fortunus: tear stained, childlike, undersized, and trying to be a man.

"Oh," I said.

"Ah," said the lawyer.

"What?" said Badrogid, who had managed to see nothing.

"And," said Dolbius, "even if we had the authority of the new dominus of this great house," he waved a hand at his magnificent surroundings, "there would still be problems." He looked at me. "In such investigations as you propose." So I bowed and looked at him. It was obvious that he was protecting himself. But at least he was neutral and I did not want to provoke him. So I found humble words.

"Purely for my guidance and correction, most honoured and learned sir, might I ask what are these problems?" He frowned and thought for a while. Then he spoke.

"How much do you know of your late master's business?"

"Less than he thinks!" said the Syrian, and an eye blink, flash of expression passed between Dolbius and him

"Shut *up*!" said Dolbius's eyes.

"*Sorry*," said the Syrian's in a tongue-biting apology.

So we all stood silently looking at one another, the Syrian and Dolbius sharing some dangerous secret, and myself wondering what it might be.

"What's going on?" said Badrogid, and Dolbius smiled and smiled.

"It really is not for me to say, honoured sir. But," and he looked at me, "if this so very, *very*, clever Greek proposes to question those close to Scorteus," I nodded, "he will soon need quite exceptional authority."

I looked at his careful face. I already knew that I would need the new dominus' permission to question Scorteus's household and professional associates. Likewise, the dominus could grant me power to speak in his name to Scorteus's clients, customers and friends, but beyond that I was unsure. What if I needed to question Roman citizens? Officials?

Councillors? I bowed still lower and asked another question. "Might I ask, learned sir, how great an authority would be needed?"

"How great can you imagine?" he said, and laughed. It was an odd laugh, with prim little lips and no humour. Had we been playing dice, it would have been a challenge that I could not throw double six, which was interesting because, just possibly, I could do exactly that. Thus I thought of yesterday's meeting with the Governor, and the moment when he had made a promise: *should misfortune place you in need of my benevolence, then you may approach me*. Those were his words; great words from a great man, and very splendid, except that great men have a wonderful skill at finding reasons to break promises. But what could I lose? If I could turn to Teutonius it was not just double six, it was *double*, double six. So I threw the dice.

"Learned sir," I said, "how about the authority of His Grace the Governor? Would that be sufficient?"

I thought that at worst Dolbius would sneer, or everyone would laugh at an uppity slave with delusions. Or perhaps Dolbius might be impressed, but the Governor would later renege on his promise. I thought that I had covered everything, but I had not because Dolbius did not sneer, did not smile and did not say anything at all. He just looked away with an expression so faint that I could barely read it. But I did read it.

"By all the gods," I thought, "*he doesn't know!*" I shook my head in amazement. The Governor's power was supreme within the province, but Dolbius did not know if that was enough.

What sort of task was I attempting?

Chapter 6

Dolbius recovered his composure.

"The authority of His Grace the Governor?" he said. "Do you claim some influence with Marcus Ostorious Cerealis Teutonius?"

"Yes," I said, and Dolbius surprised me by looking to the Syrian for his opinion who of course had not been present when Teutonius made me his promise. But the Syrian did know me. So he gave a small, non-committal shrug that signalled, *'Possibly. Maybe. I don't know.'*

"Hmm," said Dolbius, wondering. But Badrogid was in no doubt.

"You?" he said, "Influence with the Governor? A shitty-arsed house boy?"

"With respect," said Dolbius, "perhaps we might ask the Greek to explain?"

So I told them about the Governor's promise and they reacted according to their different personalities. Agidox nearly fainted with relief, Fortunus gaped, Badrogid ground his teeth at the thought of a slave rising above his station, while Dolbius, the careful, opportunist lawyer, gave a tiny bow and offered help.

"Let me make the first approach to His Grace, O Ikaros of Apollonis," he said, "Lest He should think your move inappropriate." He smiled greasily. What he meant was that Teutonius might be insulted by a direct approach from a slave, as indeed he might. But I did not trust Dolbius, with his glances to the Syrian. Also I could detect a nervousness, even fear, that was lurking behind his polite words.

"Gods bless your honour," I said, "but it is my belief that His Grace would give consideration to a letter, even from a slave, which was sent in the name of His Grace's lady." I bowed low. "Thus, while conscious of your gracious condescension, I could not, in all respect, trouble your honoured self with such a demand upon your professional services." This was laying it on thick, but Dolbius liked it, and even responded by doing me a small favour as further investment against the danger of my becoming powerful. Thus he got rid of Badrogid.

"Honoured brother of my late and lamented client," he said, "perhaps we might leave the Greek to make his appeal to His Grace?"

"What?" said Badrogid, and Dolbius bowed and spoke on.

"He will wish to write a letter, honoured sir," said Dolbius, "and, if investigation is to be made into the death of your honoured brother, as indeed it should, then who better an inquisitor than so cunning a Greek as he?" Badrogid pondered on these matters.

"Yes," he said, frowning at me, "He looks into men's heads, does this one. Or so my brother says ... *said*." He corrected himself. Dolbius nodded and continued.

"And now, honoured sir," he said, "like you, I wish to give respect to the dead."

"Yes," said Badrogid, and looked at Agidox. "Take us to him. My brother."

"Permit me, honoured sirs," said Agidox. The Syrian and I were left bowing as the two men went into the house, led by the major domos, now moving with his normal, ponderous dignity, while the Syrian blinked at me, and said nothing. He was subdued and quiet, keeping his thoughts deep hidden.

"Let's go to your office," I said. "Your boys are skilled at formal documents and mine are not."

"To write to the Governor?" he said.

"Yes," I said, and he nodded. He was as quick as Dolbius to guard against my gaining powerful support and so he was helpful.

"You'll need a funereal tablet" he said, "and a casket. We've got a stock of them for when important people die." Then he suddenly clutched at his mouth, and heaved in a sob of real sorrow, remembering who it was that had died, for he really did care for Scorteus. So I sent

Teutonius a letter in a black-edged, golden casket worth a year's wages for a skilled man. It had a wax tablet on top, which one of the Syrian's boys, inscribed with the words:

'To Marcus Ostorious Cerealis Teutonius in the mourned
and beloved memory of the late Fabius Gentilius Scorteus by the
hand of his tearful and reverential slave,
  Ikaros the Apollonite'

"Is this really what Romans expect?" I said to the Syrian.

"Oh yes," he said, and he was right. Although, I had to wait three days for a reply. In that time, the centurion Marianus contrived to dump his responsibilities on to a century of Numidian auxiliaries: mere natives compared with his own men who were Roman citizens, and we saw no more of him. Also I questioned many of the household slaves, confirming that nobody had entered or left the bath chamber between the time Mettorus the barber went in, and the time when he came running out covered in Scorteus's blood. I would have questioned the Syrian too, him before anyone, except that he locked himself inside his suite of rooms. But I did speak to someone else of great importance. I spoke to Allicanda the fish cook.

In a house so big as this, there were many specialist cooks, each with a dedicated kitchen at the back of the house. The fish kitchen was large and cool with great marble slabs, live fish flapping in lead-lined tanks, a store of crushed ice from the ice well, pumps for running water to wash the pots, and great bundles of herbs hanging from the ceiling. These and long racks of amphorae containing the endless varies of fish sauce, *garum* the Romans call it, which constitute a firmament of stars in their cuisine, and which all taste the same to me.

Normally the fish kitchen would be clattering with noisy life, but on that day the slaves were standing round, grey faced and muttering to each other. Although they fell silent and looked away I entered. But that was normal, house boys never looked me in the eye. Then Allicanda saw me and smiled.

She was a small, voluptuous woman, pale skinned, red haired, green eyed and much admired by men. She was a Hibernian, who held high rank through her exquisite palate. But she was far more than a cook. She was the hub of slave gossip, that heaving, swirling undercurrent of Roman life, because slaves are everywhere and see everything. They see it and hear it, and then they talk. They talk in the house, in the streets, in the wine shops, in the baths and at the games. They talk everywhere and, in this house, above all they talked to Allicanda because she was kind and sympathetic. Women liked her as much as men, and I liked her too. I liked her a lot.

"Good day Ikaros of Apollonis," she said.

"Good day Allicanda," I said, and looked at the smooth round arms that were uncovered as practicality, but which were so appealing, even in a woman in a long apron, with a boning knife and steel hanging at her side.

"Have you a moment to speak?" I said.

"For you, always," she said, which she said to everyone. "Would you like to come through?" she added. That was her familiar invitation into the little side room she had as an office, with two chairs, a small table and an excellent selection of wines. So we sat down and sipped wine. But as I paused to get my questions in order, she stretched out a hand and laid it on mine. I looked at the small, white hand on my own large fist, all weather beaten and marked with little scars, and one fingernail black where a hammer had hit the wrong target. I had engineer's hands, worn with craft work as much as calloused from holding a stylus. The look and the feel of her smooth fingers were intensely pleasing, as were her words.

"My poor man," she said. "My poor, sad man." The lonely are infinitely vulnerable to kindness, and my emotions were so much aroused that I could not speak because in a kitchen reeking of fish, the scent of my wife's favourite perfume was in my mind, and I closed my eyes to dwell upon it.

I had enjoyed no intimacy with women since the fall of my city, even though women have always liked me. I make no foolish boast in this respect because a pleasing character is a gift of fate, like my gift of insight. There is no virtue in either, but each exists nonetheless. The

House of Scorteus was full of women, and many had smiled at me, and some had given physical comfort as food is given to a hungry man. But none had touched my feelings nor had I reached out for theirs.

And now I was transported into delight by the feel of Allicanda's hand, while confused with the memory of my wife, and hardly daring to breathe for fear that Allicanda would take her hand away. Which of course she did, being an intelligent women who doubtless saw the disturbing effect her simple gesture had worked upon me. So she spoke and I opened my eyes.

"I suppose you want to know about the dominus?" she said, and I sighed and reminded myself why I was here.

"Yes," I said. "Who'd want to kill him? What are the slaves saying?"

"Nothing. He was a good master, gods save his soul,"

"Doesn't anyone know anything?"

"Well, he had a couple of mistresses."

"Everyone has those."

"You don't."

"Pah! What about business rivals?"

"Everyone has them too."

"Anything else?"

"He was deep in city matters. Trying to get on the Civic Council."

"And?"

"And he always wanted to be a citizen. But you know all that."

"Anything else?" I said. "Anything at all?" She thought hard.

"No," she said, and shook her head. She did not know. Nobody knew.

At last, on the third day, I heard from Teutonius. I was summoned at dawn to the podium overlooking the Field of Mars, the vast parade ground next to Government House. It was cold, but fresh, after days indoors. I stood behind Fortunus and Badrogid who had been summoned, as my owners, while Petros the Athenian stood beside me with his six slaves, and all of us keeping to the left rear of the Governor and his military staff in full dress armour, with red cloaks, and parade plumes on their helmets.

There was a major military review in progress, and the whole world pulsed to the rhythm of marching men. There were three thousand heavies and six thousand auxiliaries in a rigid geometry of helmets and spears, armour and shields, and heavy, tramping boots. It was a fine spectacle which I watched, but Petros did not because he was working; him and his six slaves, plus swift runners who constantly came and went, or stood by awaiting duty. Thus the six shaven heads conferred, discussed and scribbled notes, some for the records and some for Petros, who nodded approval or shook his head or signed orders that were sped away for action. He was right next to me and I could not help but notice. He was issuing marching orders for the troops: all the complex organisation of wagons and horses, grain and fodder, and the numberless variety of stores and planning that enabled an army of nine thousand men to advance into hostile territory, everything from hard-baked campaign bread to six kinds of shot for the artillery machines.

"They're going north then?" I said, in a moment when I caught his eye.

"Yes," said Petros. "To the troubles." He nodded at the marching men. "Fourteenth Legion: Cohorts Four to Ten. The vanguard has already marched."

"Has it?" I said.

"Yesterday," he said, "So it's final inspection for the rest. Then it's two weeks hard slogging to reach Caledonia."

"Is it?" I said, though I knew already. The arithmetic was simple. Caledonia was just under three hundred miles to the north, but the Roman Army was world famous for its incredible sustained pace of twenty miles per day. This included the construction of a fortified camp built at the end of every day's march, before the men took a bite or a drop of drink. Even the Spartans never did that and certainly not the Athenians or my own people. It was inhuman. It was Roman. Meanwhile Petros nodded at the Governor.

"He'll see you when this is over," he said.

"Good."

"It's the only gap I could find in his schedule. I had to bring you here. Not an instant to spare. You don't know how bad things are in the north."

"How bad is it?" I asked.

"Bad," said Petros, then nodded at the troops. "Ah! Watch this bit," he said.

A single bugle sounded and the enormous formations surged forward at the trot, to the roar of massed chanting. In seconds the moving ranks were transformed into a vast, static, chequerboard of century squares. Then came rolling thunder, as thousands of swords beat upon shields, which stopped in a synchronous instant and utter silence followed, such that the birds dared not sing, and the dust dared not settle but hung in twinkling clouds. I had no love for the Roman army, but it was good at what it did.

Then the senior field officer marched forward. He looked to the podium and gave a formal salute to Teutonius, stretching out his right arm with the palm of the hand flat down. Then Teutonius saluted in return, and the thousands cheered. It was final approval and the troops were marching off, and Teutonius was approaching me followed by his officers. He stopped politely before Fortunus and Badrogid, blessed them in their bereavement, bowed briefly, then walked on past them. He wasted no time.

"Concerning the Silanianum," he said to me, "let it be known, that I shall not kill four hundred slaves for the act of one. It would bring disgrace upon my reign."

"Thank you, your Grace," I said and my legs trembled in relief.

"And you seek my help, Ikaros the Apollonite, to solve this matter?"

"May it please Your Grace, yes."

"Then you shall have it," he said. "I am fully briefed of the dreadful murder of Scorteus." He glanced at Petros. "And of your need, Apollonite, to become an inquisitor." He paused. "I have therefore appointed a representative to authorise your actions in my name." He smiled. "I cannot do this myself," he said, "as I shall not be in the city, but elsewhere!" and I could see his delight. He was going to war as other men go to the races, which surprised me. I would have expected dignified resolve from a Roman nobleman.

Then the audience was over. Teutonius marched off with his staff and Petros took charge. He bowed to Fortunus and Badrogid, left them standing, and set off for his office, surrounded not only by his six slaves, but by others: citizens, freedmen and slaves who had been waiting below and had ran up the podium stairs, shouting for attention because they were the tradesmen who supplied the army with everything that it needed. But first Petros looked at me, and spoke in plain Latin.

"It's all arranged," he said, already on the move with men tugging at his robes for attention. He pointed to one of his shaven heads. "Primus will take you to your man." He looked at me as if helpless and pointed to those around him. "Have to go! Sorry!"

"Would Ikaros the Apollonite be pleased to accompany me?" said Primus, when the rest had gone. He was an ugly little man. Or perhaps I remember him unkindly for the fact that he would tell me nothing about where we were going or who I would meet. Instead, he led me across the Field of Mars in the one direction that my bowels and liver did not want to take, the one that led to the legionary fortress.

It was a huge rectangle, with rounded corners, earthworks and ditches, palisades and towers, gates and artillery machines, and thousands of troops. The Fourteenth legion might be gone, but the Twentieth was still in barracks, and I was entering a Roman army world, which depressed me profoundly, for the memories it raised, and which jumped fresh out of my mind, prompted by what was in front of me.

I saw the Roman siege works outside my city; ballistas, towers and rams, and the untiring energy of Roman troops, working in their armour as they hammered and sawed, and dug. They worked for months to build and deploy the massive siege engines, that failed in the end to breech the walls of Apollonius because they were solid Greek masonry, forty feet thick at the base. And so, in their inhuman determination, working by the drill book, the Romans devoted more months to the plain, straightforward, tedious task of filling the outer moat and building an enormous ramp to carry a hard-paved Roman road right to the top of our battlements. Then they came charging up the ramp behind their shields, in the face of every projectile that Apollonite artillery could shoot; their artillery was the finest in the world, the fastest shooting, the hardest hitting and the most accurate. In memory I heard the Roman battle cry and the steel-headed bolts clattering into shields and thudding into men.

And so to the present, and across a drawbridge into a town laid out on a grid that made ordinary Roman cities look chaotic. I shuddered, but Primus marched up to the gate guard of a dozen men with bright armour, square shields, hard faces. Small as he was, and in a plain tunic, he showed no deference because they knew him, and stood back and made way, and Primus set off confidently down one of the broad streets.

"Here we are!" he said finally. "I leave you in the company of the Fighting Twentieth," he bowed and became suddenly talkative. "Since we are slaves, I must leave you here, at a soldiers' canteen. We may not enter the Optios' Mess, or the Centurions' Hall. And, as for the Tribunes' Club," he raised hands in pretend horror, "why they'd stab us on sight. Either of us."

"Where's my man?" I said.

"He has duties, but he will find you." Then he gave a final bow and walked off, leaving me alone, at which time I got the nasty feeling that I knew who Teutonius had appointed to be my guardian and the thought was profoundly depressing.

So I looked at the building where Petros had left me. Like all the rest it had one storey, a tiled roof, white-plastered walls. It also had unglazed windows filled with wooden grids that eloquently proclaimed the character of their makers. I studied the grids and shook my head in amazement. When ordinary folk made such a grid to fill a window, they use green sticks woven in and out of each other. They are sufficient for purpose, but not for the Roman army. The Roman army cuts *cross-halving* joints into perfectly squared bars, such that each bar slots into all the others, to make a smooth, flat, lattice of immaculate squares.

I went to the door, I heard noisy laughter and singing, I hesitated, then opened it and entered. Instantly the singing stopped, and they all looked at me. Over twenty soldiers in identical dress sat on identical benches at identical tables. At the far end, a bar ran across the room, with barrels of beer, amphorae of wine, and pans frying sausages. Everything smelt of stale beer and fish sauce, and older men stood behind the bar in long aprons, veterans out of their service time.

"So who are you, then ... *boy*!" said a soldier, sat with his friends around him.

"I am Ikaros of Apollonis," I said. "I am in the service of His Grace the Governor." I should have been polite, but it is hard to be patronised by the ignorant. Also I knew what would come next, because there is a certain aspect of Greek culture which never fails to exercise the minds of the ignorant.

"Ooooo-oo," said the soldier. "Lah-de-bleedin'-dah! Hark at him!"

"Dirty Greeks," said another.

"Arse bandits," said a third.

"So!" said the confident one. "On His Grace's service, are we boy?"

"There should be a man here to meet me," I said.

"Is he a pretty one? I know you Greeks!" More laughter. The confident one got up. He leered at his mates and walked across to me.

"Look at you, then," he said, and leaned forward and sniffed. "All sweet and perfumed." More laughter.

"Soap," I said. "Not perfume."

"Ooooo, soap is it boy?" He turned to his mates. "Ain't he lovely, eh?"

"Give him kiss!" cried a voice, to jeers and laughter.

"So it ain't perfume?"

"No."

"But you like perfume," he said. "And bum. You Greeks like a bit of bum."

"Perhaps you judge others by yourself," I said, and there was a pause while he worked that out. Then he cursed, and swung a hand to slap my face. He was almost casual, contemptuous of any defence that I might make. He moved as if chastising a hound. But my body remembered the military training of its youth, which included the discipline of unarmed combat. So the soldier ended up on the floor, tripped and calling for his mates, who came with a roar and a scrape of benches and threw me down, and kicked and stamped viciously, until suddenly they stopped and stood gasping all around me.

I had rolled into a ball with my hands over my face, and I looked through my fingers to see what was happening. Light shone through the open door and a man advanced into the room. The soldiers were looking at him, and standing to an attention so rigid that they nearly fell over backwards.

Chink! Chink! Chink! A jingle of harness and a pair of booted feet. I looked up and saw steel greaves, military belt, mail cuirass full of medals, sword on left, dagger on right, vine staff in hand, side-to-side swan-feather crest, and a big, grim face, lined with old scars. He stood with four men behind him, big, heavy men, muscled like stallions.

He was a centurion of utmost high rank.

Chapter 7

Stamp! Stamp! *Stamp*! The soldiers beat their right heels on the ground in unison. It was a salute, and the centurion nodded. Then he pointed his vine staff at me, as I got to my feet. He spoke quietly, without raising his voice.

"Who is responsible for the assault on this Greek?" There was silence. "I ask again, who is responsible?" he said. A man stepped forward. The one who had spoken to me.

"Honoured sir, O Leonius Morganus Fortis Victrix," he said. "It was me."

"And who are you?" said the centurion.

"Sub-Optio Trinclinus, honoured sir."

"Second Century, Fifth Cohort?"

"Yes, honoured sir."

"It is in my mind, Sub-Optio Trinclinus to speak to your commander."

"Oh," gasped Trinclinus.

"To tell him that I am displeased with you." The centurion looked around, "As I am displeased with all of you." They groaned. It was astonishing. They groaned and hung their heads. I looked at the centurion, with his quiet voice and scarred face. What kind of officer was this, whose mere displeasure caused dismay among his men?

"Thus I expect the truth," said the centurion, "for the gods are watching us."

"Yes, honoured sir," they said.

"How did it start?"

"It was me, honoured sir," said Trinclinus.

"And who else took part?"

"Me, honoured sir!" said the rest, in chorus, even the bar staff.

"Did any man *not* take part? If so, let him speak." But there was silence.

"This Greek is in His Grace's service," said the centurion. "Did he not tell you?"

"He did, honoured sir," said Trinclinus."

"And yet you attacked him?"

"Yes, honoured sir!"

"Why?"

"Dunno, honoured sir."

There was a long pause.

"In that case," said the centurion, "it is my judgement that you should all come before the Greek, and that you should kneel and kiss his feet in apology." He looked at Trinclinus, "Starting with you, sub-optio." Thus a mournful parade followed. Every man knelt and endured the disgrace of kissing the feet of a Greek slave, and doing it with his mates looking on. They would have preferred a flogging.

"So!" said the centurion. He spoke to all present, but looking at me, "I declare this matter to be ended." It was a definitive statement, but I thought it best to agree.

"Yes," I said.

"Then follow me!" he said, and the room stood to attention as he walked out. Chink! Chink! Chink! I followed him, and his four men followed me. Outside he stopped, turned and looked at me, inviting me to speak.

"Honoured, sir?" I said, "Were you sent by Petros?"

"Yes," he said. "I am First Javelin of the Twentieth Legion, the senior centurion." He paused. "And are you Ikaros the Apollonite Greek? Property of the late Fabius Gentilius Scorteus?"

"Yes, honoured sir," I said, and he nodded and stared at me again. He had a hard stare that made men blink. So I did not. It took great effort, but I did not. I was a slave, but once I had been a soldier.

"Huh!" he said. "In that case, Ikaros the Apollonite, I am required by Petros the Athenian, in the name of His Grace the Governor, to give authority and support to your investigations into the murder of your master." I closed my eyes and sighed at another surge of relief. I had convinced myself that Teutonius would slip away from his promise, by appointing the lowest-ranking, duty-dodging, baby-faced centurion Marianus to assist me. But the First Javelin of a legion was the mailed fist of Rome! On the other hand, there was a vast difference in status between a Greek slave and so powerful a man. So I chose polite words.

"Leonius Morganus Fortris Victrix," I said, "I pray blessing upon your legion, upon your rank, and upon your house, and I rejoice at this opportunity to walk in your shadow, for it is indeed an honour," He nodded, accepting the words as his due, which indeed they were.

"You may address me as Morganus," he said. "And you may thank the German pussycat for the honour."

"Ah," I said, "You know about her?"

"Yes," he said.

"Morganus," I said. "Can we talk?"

"Indeed we can. And we must. Come with me."

He marched off, and wherever he went, men leapt to attention and stamped their feet. He acknowledged them with a wave of his staff and went straight to the headquarters block, where he had a house next to the Commander's quarters and the Holy Temple of the Legionary Standards. We went in, and Morganus took off his helmet and sword and sat in a chair, by a table and rubbed his fingers through, short-cropped grey hair, as I stood watching him.

"Well sit down, then," he said, and pointed to a chair opposite him. "Count yourself fortunate, Greek, because Petros the Athenian speaks well of you and *he* speaks for His Grace." So I sat down and Morganus clapped his hands and four women entered. I knew the army kept no slaves and reasoned that these were his family.

"Will the Greek gentleman take wine?" said Morganus's wife. She was plump and comely, far younger than him and obviously a Celtic Briton with fresh skin, black hair and expensive clothes with gold clasps and more gold round her arms. Three pretty daughters stood behind her as she poured wine for the guest, me, a slave! And, the girls held dishes of bread, and pots of olives and cheese.

All the cups and vessels were of silver and the house was richly furnished, but then it would be because a First Javelin was exceedingly well paid. The big room looked out on a walled garden, where two off-duty soldiers were busy weeding, and Morganus's four bodyguards sat on benches, helmets off, mugs in hands, watching the workers.

The woman filled two cups. She put down the flask. The girls put their dishes on the table and stepped back.

"So, Lord-my-husband, I leave you with your guest," she said.

"Thank you, Lady-my-wife," said Morganus, "You may go," he said, and she went out with her girls. They closed the door and Morganus looked at me and took a sip from his cup. I drained mine and he refilled it. I was thinking hard, my head was full of things I wanted to do, and which now I could with his help. But, if I was going to work with this man, then I needed to know more about him.

"I suppose you want to get started," he said. "But if I am to work with you, I need to know more about you." I smiled at that.

"I know," I said, and he frowned.

"You knew, did you?" he said, and we considered one another, judging, measuring and wondering, as any man does who meets a stranger. In that long moment, by the unfathomable alchemy of two very different minds, and very much to our surprise, each found that he liked the other.

"Huh!" he said. "Petros says you're the cleverest man in Britannia."

"He said that?"

"Yes, and he says you have the magic to read men's thoughts."

"It's not magic."

"Is it not indeed? Then how did you just read mine?" I shook my head. How could I explain? And, there were more important matters.

"Morganus," I said. "There's something urgent. The torturers are working on a man I must speak to, Scorteus's barber."

"The one that killed Scorteus?" I shook my head.

"No. I don't think he did it. And he's not a strong man, and I'm afraid they might kill him. Can you make them stop, and give him to me?"

"Yes," he said. "I'll send a galloper." He stood up and looked into the garden, where his four men leapt to their feet and put on helmets.

"Good," I said. "And can we go too? I've got to speak to the barber." He went out and spoke to his men. They saluted and one ran off. Morganus came back and I began to worry because he looked as if something smelt bad.

"Do you need me for this duty?" he said, and I guessed the problem at once. It was the torturers. They were among the *infami* of Roman society, those who do things that Romans think vulgar or indecent, and there is a hierarchy even among them. At the top there are racing drivers and actors, who might be millionaires and famous throughout the empire. Going down, you pass prostitutes, gladiators and pimps and right at the bottom you find torturers. They are like the night-soil men who empty the privies, useful but disgusting, and you do not sit next to them at the theatre. So torturers are not even allowed in the city. They work outside and downwind, and Morganus did not want to go anywhere near them. They might make his swan feathers turn brown.

"Do you actually *need* me?" he said. "Me personally?"

"Will torturers listen to a Greek slave?"

"No," he said, and sighed. "So I'll come with you." He frowned, and I guessed that he was no great horseman, and was not looking forward to the ride. "But we'll take our time. We could never keep up with a galloper. They are Batavians, madmen on horseback." He frowned. "I suppose you *can* ride?" he said.

"A bit," I said.

We went out into the fort's busy forum, and I shook my head at the sight of a town populated exclusively by young men; no women, no children, no old people, just soldiers. We waited for the horses and I looked at Morganus. I am taller than most men, but he was even bigger especially with the helmet and crest. He was the power of Rome, which I was already wielding through him. For it sounded as if I was indeed about to save a man from legally-authorised torture. It was so utterly different from my painful manoeuvring with Dolbius and Badrogid that I could hardly believe it. But, it was exhilarating. I was coming out of the dark and into the light, which soon grew still brighter.

A troupe of horses arrived; a dozen auxiliary cavalrymen, with shields, mail-shirts, spears and helmets, riding fine young horses, all sleek and well fed. They trotted up with an optio leading, who held the bridles of two spare horses while guiding his mount with his knees. They were good horsemen who wheeled smartly into line and saluted Morganus with their spears. He acknowledged them with his vine staff, and looked at me.

"Are you *sure* you can ride?" he said, and I said 'yes' because it is not only mad Batavians that can ride. So first I chose a horse, then I took his head and placed my brow against his, and closed my eyes and sought calmness. Soon he snickered and snorted and gave permission. So I fell back three paces and leapt aboard; an easy trick when you are raised up to it, for in my family everyone could ride, and my father put me on a horse when I was three. The name of my clan was *Philhippos*, lovers of horses.

And so I sat on a horse for the first time in ten years, and my heart sang with such joy that I became foolish. We took a turn around the forum, the horse and I, leaping and galloping and doing tricks and raising dust. I should not have done it because it was showing off. But I could not help myself, and the half-savage Batavians cheered loudly for they were horsemen born and bred and they understood.

One thing I must say, the Roman military saddle is superb, having four pommels, one at each corner, to grip you and keep you steady. You can strike in all directions and not lose balance, which is important because the easiest thing *on* a horse is falling *off*. So, finally, I reined in, came back beside Morganus's horse, and patted my animal's neck and smiled at Morganus.

"*Huh!*" he said and shook his head, and mounted steadily. He mounted like a Roman, needing a man to give him a leg up. But then he smiled at me, the first time he had done that.

And so to the torturers, half a mile from the East Wall, just off the military road. There were three torture shops, clustered together in flat Britannic land, ever green, ever wet, within sight of the broad, slow river Thames and the lakes to the south of Londinium. Our galloper had long since arrived, and was waiting outside one of the shops, which was enclosed in whitewashed walls and heavily gated. He stood with his horse, keeping well clear of a man and a woman and a dozen slaves who all wore leather aprons. As we rode up, the trouper saluted and the aprons fell to their knees and bowed. We stopped and Morganus and I dismounted and men took our horses.

"Oh the honour! Oh, your worship!" said the master torturer. But his eyes constantly flicked to the cavalrymen, whose opinion of himself and his trade was shown in their scowling faces. He gave another deep bow, a squat, fat man with powerful hands and a powerful smell. He had a wet mouth and a pig's nose. But he was a mere beast and said nothing more, because his wife spoke for both. She was thin, shrivelled and heavily made up, with black dyed hair worked into vastly-complex curls, and bright red lips and cheeks. She had a clipped, nasal voice, trying to sound like Roman gentry.

"Oh, your worship," she said, gurning at Morganus. "We withdrew the subject from treatment the instant your worship's word arrived. We …"

"Shut up!" said Morganus. "Speak to the Greek!" He was within touching distance of the scum of the infami, and did not like it. But the woman gave a boot-licking smile, and bent hard over, and her husband and slaves went with her. I had never seen such grovelling, and the fear in their eyes gave explanation. They were terrified of the army, the all-conquering power which had never before touched them in their dirty little corner. They had just been ordered to spare a victim, and they knew not why nor even what they might have done wrong. At the least they feared for their licence, and maybe their very lives. They were positively shaking with fright.

"Where is Mettorus the barber?" I asked. "Is he alive?"

"Oh yes, your worship! We took him off the machine at once, and applied every known relief. And we were only at the third stage, which involves neither burning, nor removal of …"

"Shut up!" I said. I thought Morganus had been curt. But he had not been curt enough. These creatures sickened me..

"Yes, your worship," they said, and down they went again.

"Take me to him!"

"Yes, your worship," she said. They got to their feet and with much bending and fawning they led us inside. I will not describe the workshop in detail. I will not describe it because it was vile. It was an abomination. But there were *subjects* behind bars awaiting *treatment*, and there was equipment that was both ingenious and dreadful, for it shrivels the soul to see how resourceful men can be in such a cause, and women too. But the barber was not there. He was in their best bedroom, on the upper floor. Like other tradesmen, the torturers lived over the shop.

The bed was good, with fresh sheets and blankets and Mettorus was bandaged and clean and very much alive. But he was mad. They had broken his mind. Having come this far, I tried to speak to him, but it was no good. He just whimpered and twitched. I turned and looked out of the window and Morganus spoke to the woman.

"I am confiscating this boy as property of the Twentieth Legion."

"Yes, your worship."

"He must not be damaged, and he must stay where he is. Understand?"

"Yes, your worship."

"Good. Your lives are on it!" The woman bowed. She gathered courage and whispered to a slave. Then she took something from him and offered it to Morganus. It was a wax tablet.

"Would your worship be pleased to inspect our findings?"

"No! Give it to the Greek!" I took it. It was a list of names, dozens of them. I threw it on the floor. Then we rode away with the escort following.

"Perhaps he will get better," said Morganus.

"Perhaps."

"What next, Greek?" I sighed. The light was going and I was depressed again.

"Can you get him out of there?" I said, looking back at the torturer's workshop. "Get him back with his family? I wouldn't leave a dog in that place! I ask with all respect to your rank and status, honoured sir, but will you please get him out of there?"

Morganus was surprised. "If you want, yes. I'll send word to his family to come and get him."

"Will you do it now, honoured sir?" This time he was amazed.

"What for?" he said. "Why are you so bothered about an old slave?"

"I'm a slave myself." He shook his head, but sent one of the Batavians galloping ahead to take word to the House of Scorteus.

"Thank you, honoured sir," I said.

"You're a strange man, Greek," he said. "So what next?"

"The Syrian," I said. "I'll talk to him. He knows something for sure."

"Who is he?" said Morganus, and I explained.

So I turned my mind to the Syrian. He could not hide from me now. If necessary I could smash locks and break doors, Morganus would see to that; and, I could take all the time I needed to pick out the guilty secret that was hiding in the Syrian's mind. Which thought entirely lifted the depression off my back. That and the joy of riding a good horse over open ground, even in Britannic weather. Thus hubris precedes nemesis, because when we arrived at the House of Scorteus we found that the Syrian was gone where nobody could pick his brains, not even me.

Chapter 8

The Syrian had never been a popular man. He was mean in personal matters, he had no wife or family, and was ever ready to use the rod on his slaves. But the indifference of the house folk towards his fate was remarkable. On the other hand, it was only natural that they were far more concerned with my news of the Governor's word that the Silanianum would not be invoked.

Agidox and the other senior slaves were waiting for me in the vestibule, just inside the citizen gates by which I entered, being in company with Morganus. As we entered, the auxiliaries outside the house stood to attention and stamped out their salute, while the slaves shook in terror to see a senior army officer, fearing that he had come to carry out a mass death sentence. But then came hysterical delight and relief as I repeated the Governor's promise, and was kissed, embraced and praised, as slaves ran in all directions shouting the news with abandoned joy. Who could blame them?

"Where's the Syrian?" I said to Agidox, raising my voice over the din.

"Oh!" said the major domos. "Haven't you heard?"

"Heard what?" I said.

"Ah," he said, embarrassed. "I thought you knew." But his was the only solemn face. Everyone else was celebrating. They had already found wine, and there was laughter all around. It was like Saturnalia, and getting worse.

"Can we have order here?" I said.

"Yes, your worship," he said, and clapped his hands and shouted.

The other seniors did the same, and years of ingrained servility stopped the noise and confusion and, finally, there was a proper silence, even if the slaves still smiled.

"What's happened?" said Morganus, "to your Syrian?"

"I don't know," I said, and turned to Agidox. "Where is he, the master's secretary?" He blinked. "He's dead. Did nobody tell you?"

I sighed. "Show me!"

The Syrian had, *had* had, a private apartment like my own, a living room, a bedroom, a big office, an even bigger storeroom for his records, and a centrally-heated bath chamber. He had all that and a corridor leading to a side door to the house for business visitors whose status did not permit their entry via the great atrium. I had seen the office, but not the other rooms, and now I was examining them while Agidox stood by gazing nervously at Morganus who was watching me.

It was strange seeing the Syrian's personal things and I prickled with a growing fascination as I examined his robes and jewellery, his pens and books, and a shrine in one wall to Dagon the fish god, with incense still smouldering in a pot on the small altar. Naturally I raised hands and made a bow to the shrine, and Morganus and Agidox did the same, because you can never be too careful with the gods.

Shrines like that were common throughout the Roman world. Every home has its shrine to the household gods: *Lares* the Romans call them, and every shop and place of business or office have their little altar. But I was still surprised to see one here, because I had never thought of the Syrian as a man with beliefs. I had never even used his name, not that anyone else did. He was always *the Syrian* and I shook my head as I glanced at a document and, for the first time, saw his signature. It was written twice, once in Latin and once in the East-Semitic language of his homeland. Thus I learned that he was Eblos, son of Ishtath the Scribe, now gone to his ancestors.

I glanced at the bath chamber door. It was half open.

"Well?" said Morganus, "Are we going in?"

"Soon," I said, and turned to Agidox. "Who's been in here?" I said.

"Just the Syrian's boys and me. I kept everyone else out."

"You did well," I said. "Now will you get his boys back in here please?"

Agidox went off and I looked round the room again, and the fascination grew and grew. It was like drinking a good wine which improves with every drop.

There were papers on a desk, all neat and correct. There was a wine flask and some cups; one used, the rest clean. There was some bread and olives and two apples on a dish. They had not been touched and everything was tidy. I picked up the cup and smelled it, and I touched the dregs and put the finger to my tongue and realised that all these signs were mine to read. I shook my head in wonderment. This was better than wine, it was intense satisfaction.

Then I knelt by the desk and looked at a mosaic floor, patterned with dolphins, tritons and shells. Very Mediterranean, very warming in cold Britannia. So I stared hard. I put my nose to within inches of the tiny coloured stones and a vast contentment fell upon me as I saw faint streaks of cloth and leather, strands of hair, flakes of skin. They were skid marks running towards the bath chamber. They stopped and started several times, and were the past written down. It was a wonderful puzzle, crafted from the actual events of the living world. Then I stood as Agidox came back with the Syrian's four boys, who were sunk in terror, expecting to be blamed for their master's death. Even the youngest was over thirty, and the others older still. They were Gauls, highly-educated slaves used to book keeping and accounting.

I questioned them as to the Syrian's normal routines, and what had happened the previous night, and established to my satisfaction that none of them was responsible for what had happened. I told them so, to ease their terrors, but this caused them to bob up and down before me, chanting tearful thanks. It was embarrassing and I pushed past them and went into the bath chamber, followed by Morganus and Agidox.

It was almost identical to my own. Even the mosaics were the same, being standard patterns from the manufacturers. There were cisterns, glazed windows, a drain with a wooden grid for douching, and a deep plunge bath sunk in the floor, some three feet square and five deep, with an integral seat, so a man could sit comfortably in the warm water. As in my own bath chamber, there were pipes running in from a boiler room to fill the bath and the cisterns. I looked inside the boiler room, studied the plumbing, and returned to the bath chamber where everything was warm, gaily decorated, and bright and cheerful, except that it smelt like a kitchen where cheap meat was being boiled.

The plunge bath was brimming over with water, still warm, that ran all over the floor. The Syrian's thin legs, with boots on the feet, stuck out of the water, with the rest of him head down at the bottom. I looked down into water, faintly stained with blood and saw a distorted head and shoulders jammed into the conical recess at the bottom which led to the drain. Perhaps I was becoming accustomed to such horrors, because it was not as bad as seeing Scorteus dead. In any case I had seen worse, in other days and other places.

"Who found him?" I said to Agidox.

"I did," said Agidox. "His boys called me. You'd already gone. I didn't know what to do. I just kept everyone out."

"Did anyone hear anything?"

"No," said Agidox.

"What's happened here, Greek?" said Morganus.

"With your permission, honoured sir, there is more to see." I beckoned to the Syrian's boys, who were hovering by the door. "Get your master out of there, and lay him down," I said. It was a nasty business. The corpse was slippery, its skin beginning to peel, and it made an awkward load that took the combined strength of these four, bookish men.

Then I was on my knees beside the Syrian, looking for anything other than the obvious fact that the body had been immersed in scalding water and, even confronted with such ugliness, the fascination came upon me again as I read the signs, looking particularly at the hands, arms and legs. I took a gold sealing ring from one of his fingers. It was the sort used to sign formal letters, to endorse a signature. Then I emptied his belt pouch and found a few coins, a small knife, a pen in a case, a gold toothpick, and a key. I gave these objects to Agidox for safe keeping, and then tried the key on several doors with Morganus, Agidox and the boys watching.

Finally I turned and looked at them all and knew that, in these investigations, I had found such employment that I had never dreamed of before, and it was fascinating beyond expression. Compared with this, the translation of the Jewish mystery books, which had so much entertained me, was no more than banausic tedium. Now I was rebuilding the past through evidence of the present, such that every scratched tile, every cracked fingernail and every empty cup were talking to me. It was wonderful, and I sighed with satisfaction as the whole pattern formed in my mind.

"So!" I said.

"Well?" said Morganus.

"He was drugged," I said. "In there." I pointed to the office. "Then he was pulled into here, tipped into the bath, and the bath filled with water to finish him off because he was still alive." I paused. "It was done by someone with no great strength. Someone not of this house, and someone with a most sadistic mind."

"How, by Heracles, do you know all that?" said Morganus. I turned to Agidox.

"Were the rooms locked?"

"Yes. His boys couldn't get in. I had to use my key."

"What key?" said Morganus, and I explained, drawing on what I knew of the Syrian's duties and responsibilities, which facts were common knowledge.

"The Syrian did late-night business for the Dominus, using a side door," I said. "Anything that was special and private. He always locked the other doors against the rest of the house to keep out ears and eyes. So nobody of the house could have got in."

"Yes," said Agidox. "Nobody except the Dominus. He had a key, and me, of course, ... *oh!*" he said, and as he realised he was making himself a suspect.

"Yes," I said.

"What about the rest of it," said Morganus, "him being alive, and the killer not strong?"

"The Syrian was dragged across the floor with some effort. A strong man might have carried him, or dragged him in one go."

"And why sadistic?"

"The Syrian was alive when he went into the bath."

"How d'you know that?"

"Because his finger nails are broken, and his shins wounded." I sighed. "The boiling water woke him up, and he struggled to get out of the bath. He clawed at the tiles and kicked the edge of the bath."

The four boys began to moan.

"Shut up!" said Morganus, and turned to me. "So why didn't he cry out?"

"He was head first in the bottom of a bath with a narrow, conical bottom, which fills very fast. If he tried to draw breath to cry out he'd have inhaled boiling water."

"Ugh!" said Morganus, because even a First Javelin is horrified by some things.

"Yes," I said, "Come and look at this."

As with my own bath chamber, there was a boiler room next door, with two big iron tanks with lead pipes running through the intervening wall. Under one tank there was a furnace, hot from the previous night's charcoal. It was a cramped space, full of mechanism.

"This is the cold tank," I said, and it boomed as I tapped it. "And this pipe runs the cold into the bath, and this one runs in the hot." I looked at Morganus. "Filling the bath is slave work and the boys have to be careful, because the hot tank gets very hot." I pointed at the feed from the hot tank. It was a big pipe, three inches in diameter. "But, look at this. The hot tap's wide open. The killer did that, and he chose hot water not cold." I looked at Morganus. "That's sadistic!"

"Perhaps he made a mistake?" said Morganus.

"No," I said. "The hot tap is *behind* the cold tap. You have to lean over to reach it, and you can easily tell hot from cold, even in the dark. Feel them." He did, and nodded. "And that's when they've cooled!" I stood back. "When the furnace is going, the hot pipe is *really* hot. So somebody chose to boil that poor devil, rather than just drown him."

Morganus looked at me and shook his head. "You're a strange man, Greek," he said. "You've got a mind like a ferret. It runs round corners and down holes." I took that as a compliment and thanked him. Then we left the boiler room, and went back into the bath chamber and looked down at the distorted corpse.

"What do we do with him?" said Morganus.

"Does anyone know the traditions of his people?" I asked.

"He was in a burial club," said Agidox.

"Then send for them. Let him be buried in the name of his own gods."

Agidox nodded and, falling deep into my own thoughts, I wandered through the Syrian's rooms again, the boys bowing and making way. I ended up in his store room. I must have stayed silent for some while because Morganus shook my arm.

"What now, Greek?" he repeated.

"Ah!" I said. "There you are!"

"Huh!" he said. I blinked and gathered my thoughts.

"Three things," I said.

"Yes?"

"First, how did anyone get into the house when it's supposed to be guarded?"

"How indeed," said Morganus. "I shall speak to the optio of the door guard."

"Good," I said. "Second thing, get him to search the street, outside the door. Him and all his men."

"What are they looking for?"

"The key to the side door. I can't find it, and the key in the Syrian's pouch is for the doors leading into the house."

"So what?"

"I think the killer used the street door key to get out, walked off with it and then quickly threw it away because he wouldn't want to be found with it."

"So?"

"So if it's in the street, it's proof that the killer wasn't someone from the house." I lowered my voice, "Such as Agidox."

"Oh," he said. "I'll send word." He beckoned one of the boys, gave orders and the man ran off.

"Third thing," I said.

"Yes?"

"We're going to need a special kind of man."

"What kind?"

"Men we can trust. Men who are literate and numerate and accustomed to documents. Does your legion have men like that?" Morganus frowned heavily.

"How d'you think we keep records?" he said. "Scratched on bits of pot?"

"I meant no offence," I said. "But look here." I pointed at the racks all around us. There were hundreds of scrolls and tablets and boxes. "Someone's got to go through all this, and I can't do it. I have other priorities."

"What do you mean *go thorough it*?"

"Morganus, honoured sir," I said, "two murders in one house in four days? And such murders as these? That's not coincidence! Somebody killed Scorteus for a reason, and I think the Syrian was killed because he knew the reason. So we need men who can search his records for anything that might lead to this reason." Then I paused, startled, "Gods of Hades!" I said, as I recalled my meeting with Dolbius the lawyer when his expression told the Syrian to keep his mouth shut. I told Morganus.

"So Dolbius knows the reason?"

"Perhaps," I said, "and may be in danger himself."

"I'll send a runner," he said, "to warn him."

"No," I said. "Don't warn him. Ask politely for a meeting, without urgency, and tomorrow." Morganus scowled.

"Do you dare to give me orders, Greek?" he said.

"I could say 'may it please your worship' if your worship pleases?"

"Bah!" He said. "*Greeks*! So why not warn him, this lawyer?"

"I don't trust him. I don't know what he'd do."

So a runner was sent and I took the opportunity to send Agidox to Caradigma to request that Morganus and I might see her. With Morganus beside me, I had power to do as I wished in the house; but it would have been needlessly insolent to ignore her, and only a fool gives offence when it can be avoided. Caradigma agreed to a meeting, and we were taken to her favourite atrium, built for her by Scorteus and decorated in swirling Celtic curves, with nothing Greek or Roman in sight.

The mood was icy, with Caradigma sat in a big chair, supported by a dozen female relatives and slaves in their finest robes and jewellery. A slave stepped forward, bowed low and offered translation, but Morganus spoke fluent Britannic. Learned from his wife I supposed. We left as soon as we could, with Caradigma still in her chair, straight backed and condescending, displaying her contempt for Rome with every word and gesture. I feared that responsibility for this might splash upon to me, so I apologised to Morganus, on behalf of the house.

"No need!" he said. "I've seen it thousand times. The old nobility hate us. It's the same throughout the Empire."

"Nobility?" I said.

"Yes!" he said. "Didn't you see the leaping horse on the domina's cheek?" He tapped his own cheek. "The Lady Caradigma is a princess of the Iceni. Only they have that mark."

"Holy gods!" I said. "I never knew. So Scorteus was ..."

"An Iceni nobleman, at least by birth. Why do you think we never made him a citizen?" I frowned. That was news to me. I thought Scorteus was a Silure, the son of a tanner from the mists of Wales. Nobody had ever mentioned the Iceni, which perhaps was not surprising. They were monsters of the night, the murderous warrior tribe who'd burned Londinium and slain its people with hideous atrocity.

Then there was a commotion as a man came running through the house, knocking slaves out of his way. It was an auxiliary optio who fell to his knees before Morganus in a clash of armour and gear. He held out something, not daring to look Morganus in the face.

"Most Honoured, Sir!" he cried. "O Leonius Morganus Fortis Victrix!"

"Yes?" said Morganus.

"We found this, most honoured sir, down the alley!"

"Jupiter, Juno, Minerva!" said Morganus. "You were right, Greek!"

He took something from the optio's shaking hand. Morganus was deeply impressed.

Chapter 9

"You really do have a ferret for a brain," said Morganus, looking at me with amazement. "This will be the side door key. Right where you said!" He gave me the key, then turned on the optio kneeling at his feet.

"So," he said, "I assume you were in charge of the guard to the side door?" His voice was full of menace and I feared for the man before him, who replied without looking up.

"Yes, O most honoured sir, I am Optio Simonis Lartis, fourth century, Second Cohort of Numidians."

"And were you and your men ordered to let nobody in or out?"

"Yes, most honoured sir."

"So how did someone get in, commit murder, and then get out?"

The optio said nothing, but bowed his head until his helmet was all but touching the marble floor. Morganus started to speak, but noticed that slaves were peering nosily round every corner.

"Get up!" he said to the optio. "And the rest of you be gone!" The slaves fled. "Follow me!" said Morganus, and marched off, trying doors until he found an empty room; a small study with wall paintings of fruit and flowers, and exquisite ivory furniture. "Close the door!" he said. The optio obeyed. He was a North African Berber, slim, and brown skinned with a thin nose and straight hair.

"So," said Morganus, "how did someone get in and out of the house last night?" The optio said nothing, but his legs shook. Morganus repeated the question, the optio stayed silent and Morganus moved to within an inch of his nose. "What happened? Was it a bribe? Did you fall asleep? Get drunk? Did some tart open her legs?"

The optio still said nothing. Morganus stepped back and tapped his left palm with his vine staff. A centurion's vine staff is more than a badge of rank. It is a yard long and an inch-and-a-half thick, and with it a centurion may beat any soldier he wishes and none may strike back, nor even raise a hand in self-defence, not on pain of death.

"Right!" said Morganus. "Take off your helmet and gear." The optio gulped, unbuckled his helmet, laid it on the floor beside his sword and dagger. Then he reached for the straps securing his mail. Morganus swished the air with his vine staff. The optio pulled his mail shirt over his head, folded it carefully and put it down. "And the jerkin!" said Morganus. Auxiliaries wear leather under their mail, and the optio began to undo the lacings. Even *my* heart began to thud.

"Honoured sir?" I said, "May *I* try?" Morganus turned and glared at me.

"What are *you* going to do?" he said. "What *can* you do?".

"I can give you the truth." I pointed at the optio. "And he cannot."

"What in the holy name of Mithras do you mean by that?"

"Trust me, honoured sir. You can always flog him if I fail."

Morganus thought about that.

"Bah!" he said. "Go on then. Let's see how clever you really are."

I bowed, and turned to the optio.

"Soldier," I said. "Do you know who I am?"

"Yes," he said. "You are the Greek that sees men's thoughts."

That was unexpected. I was more famous than I knew, and it was useful. I could build on that.

"Then I will tell you *your* thoughts," I said. "You are afraid of this honourable officer." I indicated Morganus with a polite gesture. "But you are more afraid of someone else, the man who made you betray your duty." He staggered as if I had hit him, and he looked at me with dread. His eyes were round as coins and his jaw gaped open. Like many auxiliaries he was a savage in uniform, an illiterate, superstitious savage. He probably came from a stone-age, mud-hut village where nobody went out after dark for fear of the wizards and goblins, and he was wondering which of those I might be. I had guessed his thoughts precisely, and now he was terrified and even Morganus was impressed.

But it was not that clever, not really. He had obviously betrayed his duty. But, when Morganus reeled off the standard list of soldierly iniquities, the optio's face told me that he was innocent of every one of them. And what else could counter his fear of flogging, than fear of something worse? Which meant *someone* worse.

"Listen to me, Simonis Lartis," I said. "If you tell me the truth, you will be excused all further punishment and blame."

"*WHAT*!" yelled Morganus, and stepped forward. I raised a hand. "Please, honoured sir, I must ask for your promise too."

Morganus's face worked furiously. He pondered a long while. Then, finally, he spoke.

"You may bless this day, optio," he said. "For I give my promise likewise!"

So I began my interrogation of Simonis Lartis, which I will not report in its meticulous, question-and-answer, face-watching detail, except to say that, eventually, the optio walked off with his helmet, arms and armour and his back unflogged, while Morganus stared at me in amazement.

"Do you really expect me to believe that you don't use magic?" he said.

I shook my head because I was tired and could not be bothered to argue.

"Who cares?" I said. "What matters is that someone powerful ordered that the side door be unguarded between the tenth and eleventh hours of night, and threatened his family if ever he spoke of it." I frowned. "Family? I thought auxiliaries aren't allowed to marry?"

"They aren't," said Morganus. "But most of them have local girls on the side. They're well paid, you see, by native standards. It's the same all over the Empire." He nodded. "So who was he? The man who did the threatening? Even you couldn't get his name."

"I didn't try," I said. "As long as the optio thinks he's kept faith, he won't warn him, and we don't want him warned. And, anyway, how hard do we have to look? It's got to be someone senior to have that sort of power. So who commands that optio's unit?" Morganus frowned.

"There'll be a Numidian centurion. He'll do the dirty work when the Lord Justice pronounces death." His eyes went wide as he remembered my involvement. "Oh," he said, "Sorry Greek. It may never happen. Probably …"

"Never mind," I said. "Go on."

"Well. Above the auxiliary centurions, there's a military tribune." He ran through lists in his mind. "That'd be Publius Julius Severus," he said. "And he's a knight, an equestrian." Morganus looked at me. "If he's involved, it could be nasty, Greek. It could be political." That made me think of Dolbius the lawyer, who didn't know if the Governor's authority was enough for my investigation.

"Morganus," I said, "what happened to your runner? The one we sent to Dolbius?"

"I didn't send a runner. Agidox did." So we looked for Agidox and found him in his office surrounded by his clerks and writers. I had never been here either, and I looked round. It was big, with many desks and a large staff. That was not surprising, because Agidox was running the biggest domestic establishment in Londinium, with considerable financial and clerical responsibilities. What *was* surprising was the lavish decoration including a collection of exquisite Chinese pottery displayed on shelves round the walls, and Agidox sitting in state, in a chair like a throne, wearing a robe dangerously like a toga, and his two best boys beside him with their notes.

Obviously Agidox had money, a substantial peculium, thanks to Scorteus's generosity. Thus Agidox was a great man in his own little world, and not such a little world either. But he stood and bowed with all the rest, as Morganus entered with his swan-feather crest.

"Where's the boy you sent to Dolbius the lawyer?" said Morganus.

"Here, your worship!" said Agidox, and waved a hand at one of his clerks, a youngster who stood up, with his ears blushing.

"It was me, your worship," said the boy.

"So?" said Morganus. "What reply? When can we meet the lawyer?" The slave stammered and looked at Agidox.

"Speak up! Go on!" said Agidox.

"No meeting is possible, your worship," said the boy. "The honourable and learned Tullius Quintillius Dolbius had this very morning left the city and gone to take the sacred waters at Aquae Sulis." He bowed three times and looked at Agidox, who searched his mind nervously to seek best explanation of why he had not passed on this information.

"I thought it best not to disturb your worships with a negative reply." His face fell at Morganus'ss expression. "Not while you were busy, your worships."

"Bah!" said Morganus, and looked at me. "What now, Greek?" I paused. I needed to think. And everyone was looking at me. I suddenly realised I'd been on my feet all day without rest, food or drink, and needed some peace.

"Agidox," I said.

"Your worship?"

"Find a quiet place …"

"Yes, your worship!"

"And serve food and wine for this honourable officer and myself. Good wine. Good food and …" I was tired. I was flattered by being called *your worship* and was about to tell Agidox to be quick about it. But I did not need to. Just as Perseus slew Medusa, so had I slain the Silanianum. I was a hero and the house was eager to oblige. Soon we were in Scorteus's fabulously luxurious winter dining room, which faced south for the sun, looked out over the best of the garden, and was fitted out like a Pharaoh's palace, even if it was one imagined by an interior designer who had never left Britannia. Morganus laughed at it, but then he had been to Egypt. So he laughed and shook his head as he put aside his helmet and sword. Then he sat down at a table laid out for our meal, with goblets, flasks, plate and cutlery all of pure gold. Suddenly I was living the life of a Roman millionaire. I was living the life of Scorteus, here in his own favourite dining room. Of course it could not last. Scorteus's son Fortunus must eventually take over the house he had inherited, and I might not forever share the status of a legionary First Javelin. But for the moment it was astonishing.

There was just one moment of embarrassment. It was like sitting at table in Morganus's house, because no slave may ever dine with citizens on formal occasions, and even for informal meals, if any citizen be present; a slave must wait for permission to be seated. So when Morganus sat down, I stood and waited. Morganus looked at me with a puzzled expression and I saw that he had forgotten that I was a slave.

"Oh!" he said finally. "Sit down. Sit down b …" He was going to say *boy*, but turned it into a cough and I pretended not to notice, and the food and wine were excellent, swiftly served by the house's prettiest girls, who smiled and bowed then swayed their hips out of the door and left us alone. Thump! The door closed and the only sounds were the song of the birds and the splashing of fountains.

So we ate and drank most congenially, and talked over the investigation, and especially the possibility of a political involvement. Morganus was very interesting on the subject of provincial government, a typically Roman structure that avoided giving absolute power to any one man.

"At the top is the Governor," he said. "Next is the Lord Chief Justice who is head of the law. He's always a senatorial nobleman like the Governor. Then comes the Imperial Financial Procurator. He's only an equestrian, but he is responsible for money, and he can report wrongdoers directly to the Emperor himself."

"Could he even report the Governor?" I asked.

"Especially the Governor! That is what he's there for." I knew this already, but I had never had the chance to discuss it with a high ranking Roman officer whose attitudes were very different to my own. Thus he stressed that the nice sharp edges of these responsibilities were blurred by personal, family, and political rivalries. "They all spy on one another through their slaves," he said. "Anything one knows, all the rest soon know by slave gossip. That's why we don't have slaves in the army!" He laughed, but I was thinking over these political realities.

"Can you get me to see these men?" I asked.

"Yes. His Grace is only a day's march up the Great North Road, with the Fourteenth Legion."

"Yes, but not him. I meant the Chief Justice and the Procurator?" He thought about that.

"The Procurator, yes. He'll see me any time, and you too." Then he wagged his head from side to side. "The Chief Justice would be difficult. He hates Greeks. Really hates them."

"Can you try?" I said.

"Yes, certainly. But why do you want to see them?"

"Because I'm worried about what Dolbius said."

"You mean the Governor not having enough authority?"

"Yes. We already know these aren't ordinary murders."

"Not with a military tribune involved."

"And others," I said. "The Tribune Severus might have taken away the door guard, but I doubt he killed the Syrian."

"Never!" said Morganus, emphatically. "Severus is a soldier. He would have gone under the ribs with a dagger, quick and quiet." He mimed the act of catching a man by the mouth from behind, and stabbing at the kidney. I nodded.

"Then we really do need to see Dolbius the lawyer," I said. "He may know why Scorteus was killed, and he certainly knows about the authority problem." I frowned. "We'll have to go to Aquae Sulis. Can we do that, Morganus? Leave the city?"

"Yes," he said. "My orders are to expedite your inquiries by all means."

"Thank you," I said. "Meanwhile, this authority problem. We could work *up* the hierarchy. We could question this tribune. What's his name?"

"Severus!"

"But I think we'd do better to start at the top and work down. That way nobody lower down could refuse to see us or pull rank. And, if the authority problem is real, let's meet it at the top, head on, while we've got the Governor's support!"

Morganus liked that. He thumped the table with his fist and the plates rattled.

"Yes!" he said, "Always charge the enemy. Never stand while he comes to you." He nodded. "And we'll see the Lord Chief Justice first. I'll find a way."

Then another thought struck me. "Who's His Grace's deputy?" I said, "while he's away?"

"Ah," said Morganus, "that's His Grace's nephew." He chose careful words. "A poet and a scholar of the most noble blood." I looked at him, and was surprised to see that he was not telling the full truth. There was more that he was not saying. He proved it by changing the subject. "Look," he said. "We've talked till lamp time!"

I looked out at the garden. It was getting dark and slaves had come in to light the lamps. They moved so quietly that I had not heard them. But that is normal with well-trained slaves; you do not even know they're there, which is why slave gossip knows everything. And now they were sliding glazed panels along silent, well-greased channels to shut out the night air. We had been talking for hours, Morganus and I, and I was very tired.

"Honoured sir," I said.

"*Morganus!*" he insisted, and I bowed my head in acknowledgment.

"Morganus. With your permission, I've got to sleep. Go to my rooms, go to bed, and let my mind rest. Can we see the Lord Chief Justice tomorrow?"

"I'll do my best," he said, and stood and reached for his helmet. "I'd better be off," he said. "There's a lot to do, starting with finding a corps of clerks to search the Syrian's papers." He grinned. "We of the Twentieth, *do* have men who can read and write!" I smiled and he continued. "And, I must tell the Second Javelin that he's in charge until further notice, then make arrangements for a journey to Aquae Sulis, and send a runner to the Lord Chief Justice, in His Grace's name, seeking an urgent meeting." Morganus nodded. "His Lordship works late, so I'll do it this night. And if he agrees to see us, I'll be here tomorrow morning with an escort, and I'll take you to him."

Which he did, and I duly met His Greek-hating Lordship and received some extremely bad news.

Chapter 10

Dozens of citizens in togas waited on the first floor of Londinium's basilica, the biggest civic building outside Rome. A marbled giant of awesome size, occupying the entire west side of the forum. They waited with their lawyers, their grievances and their slaves, in a long, columned antechamber before a pair of huge, oaken doors smothered in gold leaf. They jostled constantly for precedence, as others arrived, whose rank and status dictated their place in the queue.

But they all made way for Morganus, who went straight to the front, as of right. They clapped with polite, fixed smiles, even as slaves swung open the doors, and Morganus marched forward into the Temple of Ordinance, where sat the Lord Chief Justice, supreme head of the law in the Imperial Province of Britannia.

Of course Morganus did not march alone, for nobody does anything alone in the Roman Empire, not if his business is serious or formal. Even I had two boys for such occasions; the Syrian had four and Petros the Athenian had six. That makes twelve between two slaves and a freedman, while Scorteus was followed by enough men to form a procession all by themselves. So Morganus came with the legionary elite, the First Century of the First Cohort of the Twentieth Legion, in full dress complete with buglers, signallers and standards. They were all big men, chosen to impress, except for two grey-haired legionary clerks, and myself hidden among the rest.

It was an impressive turnout of nearly two hundred men in steel, brass and bronze, with boots crunching synchronously as they marched.

But even this retinue was nothing compared with what stood behind the Lord Chief Justice.

He sat, draped in a senatorial, purple-striped toga, on a golden throne, on a dais, in a great echoing hall, where the floor was granite and marble, the walls were historical paintings of the blood-soaked Roman past, and a bright stab of light shone through the oculus in the centre of the coffered dome above. But that was mere architecture, just concrete, stone and paint.

That was not the power of the Lord Chief Justice, for six imperial freedmen stood behind him, each backed by ten imperial slaves, each a specialist in his own field. And behind them stood the real power, the full body of Roman law, plus commentaries and judgements, in rank upon rank and tier upon tier of book shelves, carved in black granite with golden lettering. Every slave knew where everything was in his own field, such that when his Lordship called for the written word, it was in his hands in seconds or should his Lordship be in doubt he would swiftly be advised and the proper text found.

And thus did Rome drill every act of humanity, and made it march in line and wheel to the word of command. All life was regulated here: contract and theft, marriage and murder, slander and charity, and whether a man might pass water in the streets at night, which he might if the public latrines were locked.

Before the majesty of the written law, the First Century of the First Cohort blew a salute of bugles, dipped its standards, then stamped to attention and stood, heads up, like lines of steel statues. But respect did not flow one way, and I saw the remarkable extent of a First Javelin's status, because the Lord Chief Justice beamed like a lighthouse on sight of Morganus.

"Leonius Morganus Fortis Victrix!" he said, and rose from his chair.

"Gaius Julius Domitius!" said Morganus, greeting His Lordship by name. Morganus smiled and two freedmen helped His Lordship down from the dais, so that he might embrace Morganus, who removed the swan-crest helmet to be kissed on both cheeks.

The assistance of the freedmen was practical, because Domitius was very short, with stumpy limbs and fingers. So the six-inch rise of the dais was a modest hazard. But he was also a remarkably young man, very young to rank second in an Imperial province, which meant either superlative talent, a powerful family, or probably both. But his youth was an embarrassment in one who wished to be perceived as wise. So he wore a beard for gravity, moved slowly to suggest the dignity of age, and he smiled sadly, as one does who bears afflictions without complaint. And, of course, his toga displayed the broad purple stripe that proclaims the rank of a senatorial nobleman.

"Morganus!" said his Lordship, beaming.

"Domitius!" said Morganus.

"My dear boy!" said the legate, to a man old enough to be his father. It was ridiculous, as was the disparity in height between himself and the big, grey veteran, which disparity Domitius himself perceived with all the bitterness of a small man cursing cruel fate. I could see it in his eyes. Then he looked at his throne and the height of the dais, and beckoned his freedmen and affected infirmity.

"Help me up," he said with his sorry smile. "I am not a faun. I cannot do it alone!"

The freedmen heaved him up and sat him down. They smoothed him and tidied him, and stood aside. He folded his hands over his belly and linked short, thick fingers. He sighed and sniffed and got himself comfortable. And then, his face set grim and clever. He was an affected, pompous little poseur, but a very clever one.

"So!" he said. "I smell the stench of a Greek. Where is he?"

"Here, O Domitius!" said Morganus, and pointed to me. I stepped forward.

"Come here, *Greek*!" said Domitius. I did, and I bowed, and spoke as politely as I could.

"May gracious blessings bejewel your house, O most noble and most learned Lord Gaius Julius Domitius!"

He looked at me steadily, nodding to himself as if perceiving clear proof of cherished prejudice, in which respect, and for all his undoubted intelligence, he was as morbidly ignorant as the soldiers in their canteen.

"There you have it!" he said, to the world at large. "Greeks! Lovers of words, lovers of learning, lovers of boys, and inventors of everything. Everything, that is, except heterosexual intercourse," he paused, and gave a sour smile: "Five hundred years ago we copied the Laws of Athens, having none of our own, and Greece has never ceased to feel superior."

"True, my lord," I said, "and Rome has never ceased to feel inferior." I could not help it. I could not resist it. It was so obvious. But all present gasped. Domitius glared at me in hatred, and then, and fortunately, intelligence conquered prejudice and he chose to laugh. It was a nasty laugh, but still a laugh. He laughed because he recognised truth when he heard it, and I had just spoken a great truth. I had proclaimed the profound unease felt by Romans when confronted by Greek learning. Because, in their hearts, they *do* feel inferior, and they all know it, and to deny it is to deny that the sun rises in the east, which to his credit, Domitius did not attempt to do.

"So!" he said, looking me up and down. "This is the mender of broken Germans?"

"Yes, O Domitius," said Morganus, and Domitius nodded.

"Clever. Always clever," he said, "Greeks!"

"Yes," said Morganus. "But it is the Twentieth Legion that brings him before your Lordship, and the Twentieth stands for Rome."

"Indeed!" said Domitius, and smiled at Morganus. "I have read your message, O honoured-soldier-my-friend," Morganus bowed, "Though I was already aware of the murder of Scorteus the native merchant," he sneered, and continued, "so what brings you before me, Morganus? You and your Greek?"

"With your gracious permission, O learned and noble Domitius, it is my wish that Ikaros of Apollonis should speak for himself." Morganus bowed, stepped back and stood to attention, vine staff in his right hand, left hand on the pommel of his sword, and battle honours gleaming on his chest. He was the military might of Rome, and he was giving me his full support. He was treating me as an equal.

"Hmm," said Domitius, and looked at me. "Then speak, Ikaros of Apollonis!"

Thus I enjoyed the privilege of a brief conversation, face to face with the second most powerful man in Britannia, and I found him exceedingly well informed. Whether from slave gossip or his own sources, he knew every detail of the two murders, and everything that I and Morganus had done so far.

"But why do you come here, Ikaros the Greek?" he said, eventually.

"To ask if your Lordship sees any impediment to an investigation of the death of Scorteus by the honourable Leonius Morganus Fortis Victrix and myself."

"By himself, and *yourself*?" said Domitius.

"Yes, your Lordship," I said, "because I would wish to ask many questions of many people. I would wish to ask them myself." It had to be said firmly and clearly, for Morganus's legionary clerks were taking shorthand transcript of the conversation, as were slaves behind Domitius. It was an important moment. This is what we had come to find out. Was Domitius the *authority problem*? I watched him closely and his face answered even before he spoke. He had no interest one way or another.

"If you keep within the law, you may proceed," he said. "It is as simple as that."

"I am grateful for your Lordship's clarification of this matter," I said, as indeed I was, and was preparing to go away happy. "And now I will trouble your Lordship no more." He nodded at these words and smiled a sly smile

"Indeed you will not, Ikaros of Apollonis, provided you cease your inappropriate statements about the Senatus Consultum Silanianum," he said, and the muscles of my stomach tightened.

"I beg your Lordship's pardon?"

"You have announced to the slaves of the House of Scorteus, that they are free of the threat of the Silanianum, have you not?"

"Yes, my Lord. Because His Grace the Governor promised that he will not invoke the Silanianum."

"Gods save His Grace!" cried Domitius, instantly.

"Gods save His Grace!" cried all the room, and Domitius nodded.

"But His Grace's word is not the last in such a matter," he said.

There was a silence. No man spoke. I gathered my courage.

"Then whose word is the last, my Lord?"

He smiled again.

"The last word is His Grace's word, as advised and instructed by myself, and as subsequently regulated by the wisdom of the leading jurists of Rome, to whom I have sent express letters, with my own advice appended." My feelings must have shown in my face, because he gave a short, spontaneous laugh, then he controlled himself and continued. "Therefore, Ikaros of Apollonis, one so clever as yourself will appreciate that the matter is complex, and by no means decided."

Later, outside, in the Forum, Morganus cleared a wine shop of customers, for privacy, sent most of his men to barracks, and sat down with me, while his four bodyguards stood at the door. It was a smart, expensive tavern, with excellent furniture, bright-painted walls and good view of the life of the Forum through proper glazed windows. The proprietor swiftly changed into his best white apron and served us himself, with humble courtesy. At first he politely refused payment, but Morganus offered silver, which was taken with a swift hand.

It was good Gaulish wine, rich and strong, and I took a full cup straight down and poured another. Morganus looked at me and took a tiny sip from his own cup.

"We have no slaves in the army," he said. "So we know nothing of the law on slaves." He took another minute sip of wine. "So. This *Silanianum*."

"The Senatus Consultum Silanianum?"

"Yes. Is that really, truly Roman law?"

"Yes."

"Then it's butcher's law. A disgrace to the Empire!" I sighed as guilt settled upon me.

"Maybe it was me," I said. "Maybe he'd not have mentioned it if I hadn't tried to be clever with that remark."

Morganus shook his head. "No," he said. "He hates Greeks. I told you so."

"But what I said about Romans being ..."

"Inferior?" He smiled, as if amused by some odd, but unimportant, matter. "There's some truth in it." he said. "A little. You Greeks are clever at clever things. But we beat you on the battlefield." He nodded calmly. "That's what matters."

I took another cup of wine. It stopped my heart thumping.

"We have to see the Vice Governor," I said.

"Why?"

"We need to know the limits of the Governor's power," I said. "We may be facing the authority problem, after all. I thought it wasn't Domitius, but I'm not sure now."

"Why? He said he *saw no impediment* to our investigation, did he not?"

"And then he threatened me with the Silanianum."

"That is not the same thing. Is it?"

"I don't know. And it's not just me he's threatening, There's four hundred others in that house." I emptied my cup, while Morganus took another small sip. "We'd better see the Vice Governor quickly."

"Why?"

"To check what Domitius said about *the last word*!"

Morganus nodded.

"And do you want to see the Imperial Procurator next?"

"Yes," I said. "And what about Aquae Sulis?"

"We're going the day after tomorrow. I've booked a legionary lightning."

"What's that?"

"A high speed army carriage with four horses. We use them for express transport down the great roads. I have an army pass to change horses at the way stations and we can stay at the Imperial Post hotel, half way, to break the journey. You can do it in one go, but it's twelve hours, and it flogs the sense out of your butt."

"Thank you," I said, and reached for the wine flask. "The First Javelin of the Twentieth is most efficient." Morganus smiled.

"We manage these things in the legions," he said, "thus you will be pleased to learn that I have found a corps of readers and writers who are marching through the Syrian's documents, even as you drink yet another cup of wine." I pushed the cup away.

"So," I said, "When can we see the Vice Governor?"

"We should be able to do that today," said Morganus. "I have more influence there. You'll see him today, Greek. But don't be surprised at what you find."

"What do you mean?" I said.

"You'll see when you see."

Chapter 11

His Grace the Vice Governor met us at Government House, in the map room where real estate ownership documents were lodged. It was a large, plain hall, full of desks holding filing cabinets, and citizens consulting maps and talking to the imperial slaves in charge. It was a busy workplace, with a steady drone of conversation, a rustling of documents, and entirely dominated by a giant master plan of the city of Londinium, painted on the plaster of one wall. It was huge, at least twenty feet high by sixty feet long, and so detailed that every property was labelled with the owner's name, date of purchase, and taxable value. Thus it was constantly under amendment as properties were bought and sold, or demolished and rebuilt, and there were painters working on ladders even as Morganus and I entered.

I looked at the map.

"Impressive!" I said, seeking to repair any insult regarding inferiority.

"That's nothing," said Morganus. "You should see the one in Rome."

"Morganus!" said a voice, and a group of men came down the room towards us, led by a young man in elaborate robes who had called out Morganus's name. He was smiling and followed by his body slaves, and behind them came Petros the Athenian with his six shaven heads. Others in the room bowed to the young man, and made way, while he waved a leisurely hand with palm turned inward.

"Your Grace!" said Morganus, and bowed as the young man came up to us and stopped. He was the Vice Governor, Teutonius' nephew, Marcus Ostorius Cerealis *Horatius* Teutonius, an adopted name based on Teutonius' own, since Teutonius had no son, and Horatius was his heir. Horatius was a smiling, good-looking man in his late twenties, with smooth skin, make up on his eyes, rings on his fingers and beautifully curled hair. He extended a hand to Morganus, who kissed it, and there was a contented purr from the slaves behind him, Gaius' slaves that is. Petros had his usual, smirk, and his six boys kept their stone-faced silence.

"We could receive you only here," said Horatius. "We are so busy today."

"Ahhhh," said his slaves, a soft respectful sound fading gently into nothingness.

"With my noble uncle gone forth to crush the Caledonians."

"Ahhhh," said his slaves.

His boys echoed his words with round eyes and a soft gasp, as if he were Socrates preaching. There were five of them; young, very smooth, very handsome and intelligent. They were a hand-picked team, working together. But Horatius chattered on, asking after the health of Morganus and his family. Then he turned to me with utmost good nature, and began to enquire after my own health, but I had no chance to reply because Petros the Athenian stepped forward and, slave as he was, he laid a hand on Horatius's arm and spoke.

"Your Grace," he said. "Why don't you go to the baths? Have something to eat? Have a massage and a swim? Yes?" Petros glanced at the boys behind Horatius, and gave a tiny twitch of his head towards the door at the far end of the room, and the boys closed up around Horatius and gently eased him towards the door. Horatius beamed happily.

"Oh?" he said. "What a good idea! We can all swim together!"

"Ahhhh," said the boys, and off they went, leaving a trail of perfume in their wake. I looked at Petros and he made a small, dismissive gesture with his hands.

"What can I do?" he was thinking. "What can anyone do?" I turned to Morganus, but he was staring fixedly at the big map. Then Petros cleared his throat and spoke.

"A most charming young man," he said.

"Is he?" I said.

"And very biddable."

"And he's the Vice Governor?" I said.

"Oh yes!"

"So who's running the province?"

Petros said nothing to me, but spoke to Morganus.

"Honoured sir," he said.

"Yes?" said Morganus, at last bidding farewell to the map.

"I've got things to say to Ikaros, and I'd like to use Greek."

"Go ahead!" said Morganus, and glanced at me, "He'll tell me later."

So Petros took my arm. He led me to a quiet corner and switched to Greek.

"Horatius is not quite a moron," he said, "but approximates to that condition."

"Does he truly reign as Vice Governor?"

"He believes so, and we pretend so."

"So who administers the province?"

Petros said nothing but gave a small bow.

"Oh," I said. "So how are things contrived? How do you manage him?"

"Last month," said Petros, "when he disliked the ending of a play, he made the actors extemporise repeatedly until they got it right. He wanted this done on stage before an audience of two thousand, but the boys persuaded him to remove the players to his house." He gave a tight little smile. "They are excellent boys," he said. "I chose them myself."

"But do they not talk? Do they not gossip?" Petros laughed. He laughed as a wolf does when a lamb pleads for mercy.

"No," he said, "They know me too well."

"I see," I said, "Then did *you* receive Morganus's message to the Vice Governor?"

"Yes. Horatius receives no communication. Everything comes to me."

"Then what of Teutonius' promise not to invoke the Silanianum?" I sighed as I saw the look on his face.

"Domitius is correct. The Governor does not have the final word."

"Then why did he offer me his assurance?" Petros looked round to check there were no ears listening. Then he turned back to me and was about to speak, but paused and frowned.

"Do not contemplate me like that," he said. "It is disturbing."

"Is it?" I said.

"Yes. You discern men's thoughts. You encroach upon the privacy of their minds and it is most unwelcome." He sighed, and continued, "Listen, Apollonite, I shall admit you into my deepest confidence. I shall do this only because I am convinced that you will eventually discover the truth by yourself. Yes?"

"If you say so."

"Then, as one Greek to another …"

"Yes?"

Petros paused, sighed as if bearing sorrow, then spoke.

"His Grace the Governor, my master Teutonius, is a classic Roman gentleman. He is honest, honourable, decent, generous, brave and I am very fond of him, because he is a very good man."

"But?" I said.

"But his intelligence is not greatly superior to that of his nephew's."

"*What*? That cannot be."

"I assure you that it is so, Apollonite, and exhort you to believe it."

I thought about that.

"But how can he lead armies? How can he be a general?"

"Bah!" said Petros. "The centurions run the army. A general need only make speeches."

"What of this present campaign?" I said, "against the Caledonians. Can he deal with them? Has he the necessary skills?"

"I have already told you. All such matters are for the centurions. They are life-time professionals of consummate ability. The tribunes and the generals – most of them – are rich men dabbling in the army. They serve a few years, then return to their native habitat, politics!" But, as he said that, and for the first time, I saw shiftiness in Petros's eyes. So I asked some careful questions, and he let something slip.

"And in whatsoever case," he said, "it is imperative that the Caledonians be defeated, because the family in Rome demands a victory, whether or not it is real." He blinked as he said it, and a door slammed in his mind. So I shifted the conversation, and put aside his words for future study, *whether or not it is real*.

"What about the other duties of a Governor?" I asked. "If Teutonius is not competent, then who manages the province? Who deals with patronage, appointments, tribal relations?" Petros smiled.

"I have been Teutonius' man for over twenty years," he said. "I have travelled the Empire with him, from province to province." I nodded.

"But I perceived no lack of intelligence when I spoke to Teutonius." I said.

"And what *did* you perceive, with your capacity for augury and divination?"

"An upright man, enchanted by a slave girl, and who speaks mellifluous Greek."

"Naturally," said Petros. "He has the manners and bearing of a nobleman, the girl is pulchritude incarnate, and he learned our language as a child when learning comes easy. But he is *lead* dipped in *gold*; lustrous on the outside, dull on the inside."

We did no more work that day. The Imperial Procurator could not see us until the following day, so Morganus and I parted; he going home to the fort and his family, and I to my rooms where eventually I locked myself in. The Lord Chief Justice's views on the Silanianum had been heard only by his imperial slaves and by Morganus's men. This was fortunate because the imperials sneered at gossiping house slaves, while the army, having no slaves at all, was immune to their chatter. But it was only a matter of time before the news got out, and I did not want to be questioned on the subject. I could not bear my fall from the hero's pedestal.

I made one exception to this self-imprisonment. Ignoring all others, I went to the fish kitchen and spoke to Allicanda. It was dark by then, with a couple of lamps making more shadow than light in her little office. She offered wine and I took it, and sat looking at her, with the kitchen quiet and her staff gone to bed. It would have been a pleasant moment except that now I spoke with the Governor's voice. I had power and I feared that she might be friendly only to seek advantage. But still I wanted to talk to her.

"What do the slaves say of Publius Julius Severus?" I asked. "A military tribune who commands the Numidian auxiliaries."

"Tall. Good looking. A nice lad," she smiled.

"Anything more?"

"He's aiming high. He could have *any* girl, but he's after someone special."

"Who?"

"Nobody knows."

"What does the girl's mother say?"

She laughed. "Don't know. I don't know who she is, do I?"

"Hmm," I said, "Of course it'd be her prerogative …"

"*Pre-rog-ative*!" she said. "That's a big word. What does it mean?"

"Her decision," I said. "Her choice. That's the custom." She nodded. "What about Severus himself," I said, "the tribune?. Have you heard anything else?"

"Such as what?"

"Anything unsavoury or dishonest?"

"No. Nice lad. Nice family. All the girls like him," she smiled, and looked at me. "Women like some men," she said, and leaned towards me and stretched out her hand. "Come with me," she said, "and let's see what's your pre-rog-ative, you silly man."

"It's whatever I want now that the Governor is my patron," I said. "As you well know." It was one of the most stupid things I ever said in all my life, and Allicanda drew back her hand.

In the morning, Morganus came with his four bodyguards and a half century of men, a number deliberately less that he had taken before the Lord Chief Justice, and reflecting the lower rank of the Procurator. But for me it was a new experience, because a slave has to watch his step in the public streets. He has to walk humbly and with care. But not when going at the quick march with scarlet shields all round. In that case, all those who do not get out of the way, get *knocked* out of the way.

So we marched almost the entire length of the Via Principalis to a great edifice which lay between the Temple of Jupiter Maximus and the Temple of Hercules, both of which were illuminations of the city's pride. But our destination outshone both of them, because people build biggest that which they value most. For Romans that means *first* the stadium for the chariot races, which is always colossal, *second* the theatres and amphitheatres, which are merely enormous, and *third* the offices of taxation and revenue.

Thus the official residence of the Imperial Financial Procurator was not only the tallest building in the city, it was not only marbled and pillared in exotic, imported stone, but it was lavishly decorated with huge statues of divine beings, each covered in gold leaf, crowned with fresh laurels, and bejewelled with coloured glass for eyes. I must admit that, in Londinium, the Basilica was actually bigger but it was nowhere near so gorgeously decorated.

The Residence was a vast counting house as well as a palace, and was staffed with hundreds of imperial slaves, working in dozens of offices that used up enough ink to float a war galley. Morganus was received with honour, by a guard of regulars found by the Twentieth, since the building, and especially the gold in its cellars, was heavily defended. The guards stamped to attention at sight of their First Javelin and summoned slaves to lead Morganus, myself and the bodyguards, upstairs to meet His Honour the Procurator.

It was very much upstairs. The building rose to a full five levels, and we came out on to a flat roof, with a dome rising in the centre, taking up about half of the space, to leave a broad, balustraded promenade all round. It had the most magnificent view of the entire city, and the lakes, fields and hills beyond. It had that, and a biting Britannic wind that whistled the ears and tugged the hair.

His Honour was awaiting us on the other side of the dome with his slaves, and something novel, something highly fashionable and desirable. He had the usual retinue that followed any great man, including a group of six imperials exactly like those that followed Petros, with the same disdainful noses raised as if against a bad smell. But there were some common house slaves, and a two strange little men with weather-beaten faces, leather clothes and caps stuck with bird feathers.

His Honour stepped forward and held a hand for Morganus to kiss. He was Quintus Veranius Scapula, a narrow-faced, thin man in his fifties, with fading hair and missing teeth that made him embarrassed to open his mouth. From the look of him, he'd earned his post by merit, and his conversation was intelligent, apart from his obsession.

"You come at an auspicious time," said Scapula. "As Horace says, *Seize the day! Put not trust in the morrow!* And I have done likewise, investing in the future!" He gave a closed-lip smile and indicated an elaborate wooden structure, like a big shed with lattice windows, firmly anchored to the roof and surrounded by its own, neat little fence. The birds wheeling above it in tight circles proclaimed its function. It was a pigeon loft, and a big one. Copied from native Britannic culture, it was now a rich man's fashion which had spread throughout the Empire, with cock and hen pairs of pigeons selling in the markets of Rome itself for more than big, male slaves. Scapula gave his wizened smile again and looked at me.

"And is this Ikaros the Apollonite? He who has recently become chief inquisitor to His Grace the Governor, gods-save-him?"

"Gods save him!" echoed the company.

"I am Ikaros," I said, and bowed.

"Then what does Greek learning say of these?" he said, and snapped his fingers at the two little men with feathered caps, who knelt, raised the lid of a wicker box at their feet, and each took out a pigeon, and stepped forward holding the birds in gentle hands. I stroked the feathers and felt the warmth of the small bodies.

"They find their way home," I said. "Even if taken hundreds of miles away, and even across rivers and seas. The male will fly home in a few hours if his mate is left behind. It is a wonderful mystery because no man knows how they do it." I smiled as one of the birds gave a soft, pleasant call, like a buzzing in the throat. "They can carry messages," I said. "The Egyptians, Carthaginians, and my own people, all used such birds for this purpose."

"Ah!" said Scapula. "So says Greece! And as Aristophanes has it, *The wise learn many things from their enemies*!" I looked at his tight little face and guessed that he knew of my conversation with the Lord Chief Justice, which he proved by lecturing me in great detail about his pigeons and the two little men in leather, who were Celtic pigeon masters from the Catuvallauni tribe. He was thereby making clear who was superior and who was inferior. He was trying to, anyway. He went on at length until finally, stupefied with the subject, Morganus shuffled his feet, coughed loudly, got Scapula's attention and asked, with minimal politeness, if Ikaros the Apollonite might ask a few questions.

The narrow face smiled and nodded, and I was able to establish very quickly that His Honour the Procurator had no special interest in the murders of Scorteus or his Syrian secretary, and did not mind who I spoke to about them. All he asked was that any inquiries within his own offices, or involving his staff, should first receive his permission, which was perfectly reasonable. Later, as we walked down the first of five flights of stairs, Morganus glanced upwards to make sure nobody was listening.

"Gods of Hades!" he said. "One more word about pigeons and I'd have out sword and gutted him!" The bodyguards nudged each other as Morganus looked at me. "And is that really the latest thing? Homing pigeons?"

"Oh yes," I said, "Scorteus had a loft somewhere. Not that he took much interest. He just had it because it was the fashion." Morganus shook his head in disbelief.

"Let us hope we do better in Aquae Sulis," he said, "with Dolbius the lawyer."

"What time do we start tomorrow?" I said.

"Dawn. Outside the fortress stables."

"I'll be there."

Which I was, for a remarkable journey, followed by a surprising disappointment.

Chapter 12

A legionary lightning moves at the astonishing rate of twelve miles per hour sustained, average speed, day and night, over long distances, including time for stops. A feat only possible on Roman roads, with Imperial post stations, every ten miles, where tired horses can be changed for a fresh team. And not just any horses, because those that pull the lightnings are specially bred and, unlike other horses, have iron shoes nailed to their hoofs to withstand the strain of pounding the hard road. Even the finest animals last only a few years under such strain; but, by these means, a lightning covers in less than two hours what a marching legion covers in a whole day. This enables persons with leather buttocks, or those on journeys of utmost urgency, to travel the barely-believable distance of two hundred and eighty-eight miles between one dawn and the next.

The lightning we used for the journey to Aquae Sulis was typical of its kind: a large, light, four-wheeled vehicle with a collapsible, canvas cover on iron hoops for bad weather and room for Morganus and myself, side-by side on the first bench seat, the four bodyguards on two others behind, our luggage under our seats, and an army driver in front, flogging speed out of the four-horse team. And flog them he did, such that the wheels roared over the road stones, obliterating any chance of conversation, while the whole structure creaked and groaned, and a dust-laden wind rushed into our faces.

So it was fast, but not comfortable, and the speed inspired devilment in the driver when the road ahead was full of people, which often it was. This surprised me, as a town dweller, because I'd never realised the extent to which the military roads are used by country folk, drovers, and others who must travel on foot.

"*Go* on! *Go* on!" the driver cried, at first sight of a black mass of cattle and people on the road, and he put his bugle to his lips and blew a loud warning blast.

"*Go* on you buggers!" he said, and stood up in his seat laying on with his whip and the horses galloped and the lightning rocked forward.

"What's he doing?" I yelled into Morganus'ss ear. "He'll kill someone!"

"Pah!" said Morganus and waved the matter away with a big hand.

He was right. The people and beasts parted like waves before the prow of a ship. They cursed and scowled, but they got out of the way then closed in again behind us. I looked back and saw it, and also the grinning faces of the four bodyguards sitting behind.

"They're used to it!" said Morganus, and so was I by the third time, and by which time even a padded seat was beginning to feel like a beating with clubs; so I was more concerned with my own troubles than those of others. Also, once we passed beyond the rich farm land around Londinium, there were no more folk on the road because, outside its cities, Britannia was mostly unkempt, unfarmed and uninhabited. Thus the lightning sped through dark forest, rolling hills and wide plains with just the barest, occasional sight of smoke rising over a thorn-fenced, round-house village which was a mere speck in the vast and savage wilderness. It was threatening and depressing. It was easy to imagine the ancient, local gods grinding their teeth in anger at the desecrating road that Roman engineering had cut through the heartland of their dominion.

So it was a great relief to stop for the night, half way, at one of the post hotels: *mansiones* the Romans call them. These are placed about fifty miles apart down the great roads and very comfortable they are too, with good rooms, good food and the blessed relief of a bath house where we could soak our aches in the hot pool. I think Morganus had suffered most, and he dozed, sitting comfortably in the hot water, while the four bodyguards sat respectfully to one side, looking very young without their clothes and armour, like huge, overgrown children, all pink and perfect. Beyond them, still lower in the hierarchy, the army driver sat by himself. But at least he was in the hot pool.

The bodyguards pointed out Morganus's scars to each other in hushed voices, so as not to disturb him.

"That big one on the shoulder?"

"Yeah?"

"Is that what he got off the Jews, in Palestine, in their first war?"

"No! It's an axe cut off the Iceni, in Boudicca's time."

"Is he that old?"

"Yeah! Joined up at fifteen. Everyone knows that!"

"So what's those two on his arm there …?"

Then I fell half asleep myself, only to be woken sharply by what they were saying. They were talking about a siege.

"There was a big ramp built up to the wall, and the assault team ready to go. But they was shooting our officers. First they got the tribune, and then the centurions."

"What, aiming at them?"

"Yeah. They had special artillery. Really accurate."

"Bloody Greeks!"

"Yeah. So finally there was only him left."

"Morganus?"

"Yes. Last officer standing, and all the men was looking over their shoulders ready to run away. Then *he* got hit. A ballista bolt through his cheekbone and the point sticking out the back of his helmet. It knocked him flat!"

"But it didn't kill him."

"Course not. He got up with the sodding thing still in him."

"Cor!"

"And he walked up and down the lines making a joke of it."

"Cor!"

"And, when the bugles sounded, he led the charge and was first over the wall."

"So that's where he got the Corona Muralis."

"Yeah. Highest award for bravery in all the Empire."

"And they took the city?"

"Oh yeah."

I closed my eyes and later drank more wine than a philosopher should, and by that means managed to sleep.

Next morning we left at dawn on the final run to Aquae Sulis, which lies far to the west of London, in the ancient territory of the Belgae, a tribe with strong connections in Gaul. The new Roman town was built over hot springs sacred to the Belgic god Sul, recently conjoined with the Roman goddess Minerva, as *Sulis Minerva* patroness of the modern bath complex which is famous throughout the Empire. It is famous because it centres on a huge stone pool, miraculously filled from unknown depths below, by a constant stream of natural hot water that is universally recognised as being of divine origin.

Perhaps even more remarkable is the fact that the town, which is quite small, is entirely unfortified, which shows how thoroughly the Romans had pacified the local people. But the town had a strong garrison, the Fourth Cohort of the Second Legion, the so-called *Augusta*, and our driver pulled up outside the main gate of their fort, a standard Roman earthwork just outside the city, where he gave an enormous shout to announce his distinguished passenger.

"Give honour! Give honour! Give honour!" he roared, "to the First Javelin of the Twentieth Legion, Valeria Victrix! Give honour to the noble, valiant, and ever-victorious … *Leonius Morganus Fortris Victrix!*"

I saw men's jaws drop at the name as Morganus climbed down from the lightning and put on his swan-crest helmet. The optio of the gate guard instantly sent a runner into the fort, the man yelling to everyone as he went, while the guard threw themselves to stiff attention. Morganus's four men swelled with enormous pride. Then there followed the nearest thing to chaos that I have ever seen among Roman troops, as the barrack blocks emptied and hundreds of men rushed forward, including an equestrian tribune and six side-crested centurions who had to push through the press to get to the front.

But what I noticed most was the expression on their faces. It was the same as is seen on those who meet famous racing drivers, actors or even gladiators: the round-eyed, awestruck, happy look of those in the presence of their idols. Even the officer commanding the cohort, a military tribune who out ranked Morganus, had the same look on his face and kissed Morganus's hand with reverence, while the centurions lined up in order of seniority, and bowed to the waist as they were introduced; while the troops behind, drew swords, clashed blades and chanted the name Morganus over and over again.

Shouting happily over the din, the tribune ordered that the garrison be paraded for inspection. He proclaimed a dinner that evening in Morganus's honour, and insisted that the fort's womenfolk, the tribune's and centurions' wives, plus sons and daughters too, be presented in the headquarters block, while the fort's best accommodation was made ready for its guests. Finally, he begged that Morganus might give blessing upon the fort's most honoured veterans, those who had lost precious limbs in the Empire's service and were kept on the books for light duties, and which group of unfortunates was duly brought out to bow their heads before him.

All this took hours, during which time I followed Morganus and the bodyguards, hardly noticed, much ignored, and much jostled by beaming soldiers trying to get a glimpse of *the big man*, as they called him, not so much for his height but for his esteemed status. I had arrived in the fort not knowing the extent of Morganus's reputation within the army, and now I was being educated.

It was dusk before I was able to talk to Morganus. We were in the drill hall, next to the fort's forum, which had been transformed by army cooks into a buffet for the wives and children, with little rolls, sweetmeats and sauces on tables tastefully decorated with fresh flowers in pots. The Roman army never ceased to amaze. But now the proud fathers, in their armour and crests, were filing out of the room with their families, and leaving Morganus with the tribune, the two senior centurions, the tribune's personal clerks, Morganus's bodyguards, and myself still very much at the back.

Morganus looked dazed, having received non-stop adulation for hours, which is not natural for a soldier. He blinked when finally I was noticed and the tribune, Sextus Lartius Rufinus, asked about me.

"And whose boy is this?" he said. "Is he a Greek?" Rufinus smiled. "Surely we have no slaves in the army, honoured Morganus?"

"Ah!" said Morganus, and introduced me, not making an especially good job of it, because he tried to explain my talents. I could see the politely-hidden disbelief in Rufinus' face, while the two centurions and the clerks looked away in embarrassment, not wishing to hear the big man talking such nonsense. So Rufinus was visibly relieved when Morganus explained our business in Aquae Sulis, because that was a plain, decent job involving no mind-probing, magical slaves. It was simply a matter of locating one Tullius Quintillius Dolbius, a Londinium lawyer visiting the city to take the waters. The tribune nodded eagerly, and at last I could bless the efficiency of the legions.

"Find him!" said Rufinus to his centurions.

"Yes, honoured sir!" they said, and the clerks reached for their note books.

"Send men to the hotels, inns and taverns," said Rufinus, "and to any private houses which might receive a gentleman of his rank. Take as many men as you need, and use your initiative." He looked through a window at the approaching night. "Do it now! By torchlight if need be!" The centurions nodded, the clerks scribbled. "Tell the men they do this for Leonius Morganus Fortis Victrix."

"YES HONOURED SIR!"

"And tell them the work continues until they find the lawyer!"

Then Rufinus, himself, led us to a suite of rooms in his own house, the commanding officer's house, which as usual in Roman forts was large and well appointed with plenty of extra space for visitors. He left us in a fine suite of rooms, generously giving us first use of the bath house and ordering fresh robes to be sent to our rooms. There was wine too and, after we had bathed and changed, I helped myself to a few cups while Morganus took his usual sips. The bodyguards were in an adjoining room and Morganus was silent, avoiding my eye as he fiddled with a lamp, supposedly to adjust the wick.

"What is it?" I said. He fiddled some more with the lamp.

"It's a formal dinner. They've invited guests. It's a reclining dinner."

"I see," I said.

"It's in my honour," he said, "I can't refuse."

"And you can't take me?"

"No. You can't even be in the room." I was surprised to see that he was embarrassed. "What can I do, Greek?" I smiled.

"You can go and enjoy your dinner," I said, and jabbed a thumb at the other room. "I'll eat with your bodyguards. No doubt they'll bring in some food for us if we ask."

"Oh no!" said Morganus, "You'll be eating in the k ..." He stopped short.

"In the kitchen?" I said. "With the slaves?"

"Not slaves! They're cook house men: soldiers."

"Cook house men?" I laughed "Go and enjoy your dinner," I said. "I'll manage."

He smiled.

"Thanks, Greek."

Later, when a polite orderly was sent to give word that dinner was served, Morganus left wearing the soft, elaborate dining robes and slippers that the tribune's men had provided. The orderly added that there was food in the kitchen for the rest of us, and I went downstairs with the four bodyguards. It was an especially large, noisy kitchen with a big table cleared for eating. The bodyguards were under orders to make sure I was treated properly, which they did, but the company was entirely men, entirely soldiers, with no women in sight. So there was much drinking and shouting, singing of obscene songs, and telling of dirty jokes, and then the senior bodyguard beat the table with his mug, and challenged all comers to arm wrestling, which he won every time.

This was not to my taste. It was already bad and then it got worse. Halfway through the meal, a man came back in from the latrines, hitching up his breech clout and shouting out the news.

"Here!" he said, "Know that lawyer, Dolbius, that everyone's looking for?"

"Yeah?" said someone, and I looked up sharply.

"I just met one of the medics doin' a piss."

"Yeah?"

"He said one of the lads came in with twisted ankle, silly sod."

"And?"

"He said they can't find the soddin' lawyer. And they looked everywhere."

"Have they told the tribune?"

"No. They're still looking, and they don't want to spoil his soddin' dinner."

I sighed and wondered what that might mean. I was still pondering when things got *even* worse. An orderly came into the kitchen and yelled for attention.

"Where's that Greek boy?" he said, and everyone looked at me.

"Here," I said, and stood up.

"Come here, boy!" said the orderly, beckoning, "Here, boy! Over here!"

The four bodyguards stood up and scowled at the orderly, who gulped.

"He's with us," said the senior bodyguard, "and his name's Ikaros of Apollonis!"

"Yeah, well," said the orderly. "Tribune's orders, he's got to come with me."

"D'you want us to come with you, Greek?" said the bodyguard.

"No, thank you," I said, "Thanks a lot, but finish your dinner."

"You sure?"

"Yes."

I followed the orderly upstairs, along lamp-lit corridors towards the noise of a dinner party in the main dining room: the *triclinium*, which had armed guards at doors which were whisked open to reveal a hot, bright-lit chamber packed with people, and a rolling, wafting odour of food, spices and perfume.

"Ah!" they said, as I entered and bowed, and the merry red faces told me that much wine had been drunk.

It was a big room, nowhere near as elaborate as those in the House of Scorteus, but it was smart in an army way, and well designed. There were couches set for nine guests on three sides of a square, which was filled with low tables for the food and which looked out into the body of the room, where the cook-house men came and went, bringing food and wine and removing empty dishes.

Thus I was squarely on the menial pathway from which not only service was given, but entertainment too. I was standing where singers, poets, jugglers and conjurors would perform, and I guessed at once what they wanted. Indeed, I should have been used to it because I had done the same thing so many times for Scorteus and his guests.

So I stood looking at the elite of Aquae Sulis, such as they were. Them and their bejewelled wives, lounging at ease and staring expectantly at me. I saw that in Aquae Sulis, for all the building and development, we were on the frontier, because the guests were not the aristocrats and millionaires of Londinium. The tribune Rufinus, and his wife were sophisticated people, but the rest had the look of traders and artisans, and all were happy and smiling, except for Morganus in the place of honour beside the tribune's wife. He looked at me with a huge apology upon his face. He looked miserably glum.

"So!" said Rufinus, "Welcome Ikaros of Apollonis!" I bowed again. "We have heard much of your skills!" The company grinned at each other and took more wine, while Morganus gritted his teeth. "So we have summoned you, Ikaros of Apollonis," said Rufinus, "asking for your wisdom in a matter which we have much discussed."

"Yes!" they said, and they laughed, and all looked in a certain direction such that, in all modesty, I had the answer to the tribune's question even before he asked it.

"Therefore, Ikaros ..."

"Of Apollonis!" they all cried.

"Therefore, perhaps you can use your magic." He looked at Morganus. "As we know you can!" And, they all laughed "To tell us what problem it is that we have been discussing, and how would you solve it?"

There were roars of laughter, much applause, and much raising of goblets to toast Morganus, who now looked utterly miserable.

"Shhh!" said the tribune. "Give him a chance to think!" There were a few giggles, then silence. I could have spoken at once, but I waited until the moment was right. Then I turned to one particular man.

"Honoured sir," I said, "may I respectfully ask for your name?"

"Lucius Petillius Nepos," he said.

"Then, O Lucius Petillius Nepos, if you can be more precise concerning your difficulties in extracting gold from the mines at Colcauthi, I will do my best as an engineer to help you."

There was a huge gasp of amazement. Some of the women were frightened and clutched at husbands for support, and every sound and movement stopped in the chamber, such that we could clearly hear the chatter of the staff in the corridors beyond the room. A slow drop of red wine formed itself on the chin of Lucius Petillius Nepos, and hung, and dropped to the floor below.

"Huh!" cried Morganus and laughed out loud. "What did I tell you?" he said, and leaned across to nudge Rufinus the tribune, who gaped like a fish in a pond.

But it was not that hard. The company had given me the man as a gift, by looking straight at him, with his worried face. His hands, even washed, had the grey, rough fingernails of a technician, in his case a miner, since he had brought a piece of gold-veined ore to show off over dinner. It was in plain view, in front of him, on one of the tables. The rest was easy, since all Britannia knew that the army was trying to get gold out of the old Celtic mines, and the most famous one in Britannia was at Colcauthi, only four miles from Aquae Sulis.

"Honoured sir?" I said prompting Nepos to speak.

"Well," he said, licking his lips uncertainly.

"Go on!" said Morganus. "Tell him!"

"Well. We want to use hydraulic mining."

"Ah!" I said. "Diverting a stream to wash soil off the land revealing the ore?" That was a simplification. In fact the water would be stored in a huge reservoir, then tapped with gates, sluices and hoses, and used in high-pressure jets to attack promising areas which might contain ore. It was technology unknown to the native peoples, and powerfully effective. Nepos nodded at my few words, and went straight to his problem

"Yes!" he said, "That's it. But there's a mountain in the way of the stream."

"Then tunnel through the mountain," I said. Nepos looked at Morganus.

"You told him that, didn't you!" said Nepos.

"No!" said Morganus.

"And so?" I said. Nepos turned to me again.

"We need to pierce the mountain before winter, and we're going too slow."

"So tunnel from both sides," I said, "and meet in the middle!" Nepos thumped a table with his fist.

"You *did* tell him!" he said to Morganus, who laughed.

"How could I?" said Morganus, "I haven't left the room!"

"Oh," said Nepos, and I easily guessed the rest of the problem.

"I take it there is difficulty with the method," I said. "Of making two tunnels meet in the middle?" I looked round. I had them by the nose, now. It was not only Morganus that thought I worked magic. They all nodded, with big round eyes, and Nepos spoke.

"Well, yes," he said. "We've never done that before."

He had not, but others had, inspired by the Greek engineer Eupalinos of Megara who, seven hundred years ago, tunnelled through a mountain on the island of Samos to bring water to the capital city. He worked from both ends drilling two tunnels which ran for a total of a thousand yards and met in the middle. The geometry he used to align the tunnels was elegant, clever and simple. Simple, that is, to those who already knew it.

"Honoured sir," I said to Rufinus. "Might I have a wax tablet of the largest possible size, and a stylus?" There was a sudden roar of conversation in the room, Morganus laughed out loud, Rufinus clapped his hands and an orderly was sent running. He brought me a good, big tablet and I thought for a moment, then started drawing. When I was done I bowed to Nepos and gave him the tablet.

"Honoured sir," I said, and he looked at it, studied it, ran his finger over it, muttered to himself, then shook his head in amazement.

"Holy gods of Olympus and Rome!" he said, and had the decent, mannerly good grace to smile, to get up from his couch, and come forward and offer me his hand. "If ever you want work as a miner," he said, "then come to me!" and the company cheered.

But some of them threw money at my feet, and I still was not allowed to dine with them. I had to wait outside, until the dinner party ended, before I could give Morganus the news that Dolbius the lawyer probably was not at Aquae Sulis. Unusually for Morganus, he was fuddled with wine and wanted to wait until morning to discuss the matter further. Which we did, and were duly disappointed, until a fresh door opened to compensate for the one which had just closed behind Dolbius.

Chapter 13

"We use three basic instruments," said Nepos the miner, "The chirobates, the dioptra, and the good old groma." He smiled nervously. "But I'm sure you know all these already."

I did, and so did Morganus, but the bodyguards stared uncomprehending at these technical wonders in the workshop of the cohort's fort. Nepos blinked, still not knowing quite how to behave towards me. He was full of gratitude, but nervous of Greek learning, and afraid of being shown up as ignorant of his own profession, and by a slave at that. Likewise, the engineer centurion, the engineer optio and some leather-aproned legionaries were staring grimly at their instruments, as if already resenting some patronising remark. Given that, I thought it best to be tactful, though it was easy to do so. The instruments were beautifully made and in excellent condition.

"This is first-class equipment," I said. "Exactly what would be expected of the Second Augusta." The centurion and his men relaxed. I went first to a row of huge, beam-like instruments, some of them over twenty feet long, and every one polished like fine furniture. "The chirobates," I said, "for obtaining levels." I went to a row of complex brass discs gleaming like jewels and mounted on tripods. "The dioptra for measuring angles." Then I went to the last row, of wooden staves with horizontal iron crosses hanging from outriggers, and cords dangling from the tips of the crosses, with plumb bobs to keep them true. I smiled. "And here is the faithful groma, by which Rome defines the grid-pattern camps which have conquered the known world!"

They liked that, as I had intended that they should. Yes, it was sycophantic greasing, but sometimes even that is appropriate and, in any case, it was true, and who knows that better than a Greek?

"Thank you for coming," said Nepos, awkwardly, not knowing whether to address me or Morganus. "I wanted to check that we had everything necessary." He smiled at last. "It's an army project you see, using their gear and manpower. It's really his honour the tribune Rufinus who's in charge. I'm just the technical expert ... oh ..," he said, and the smile died as he reflected on his inadequacy regarding tunnels.

"Honoured sir," I said, "with this fine equipment you had already done everything possible. It was mere chance that I had come across this ancient knowledge." I touched the tablet he was clutching to his breast. "This knowledge is a great secret, known only to a few men in the entire world."

"Is it?" he said.

"Yes!" I said, which was a polite lie, because every schoolboy in my city was made to study the tunnel of Eupalinos. On the other hand, my city is gone and its schools gone with it, so perhaps the lie was true after all? More important, I could see that Nepos wanted to say something, and I was curious to know what it was, and I would not find out if he were constantly expecting a snub.

Once we had left the workshop, he spoke freely, having first asked me and Morganus to walk back with him to the legionary stables where he had a horse. He did not have much to say, he just wanted to thank me properly, which was kind of him, and he wanted to do it privately for fear of seeming obsequious to a slave. However, this led to more as he became relaxed because, in his nature and when comfortable, he was a sociable, talkative man.

"So you are investigating a murder?" he said.

"Yes," I said.

"With this honoured officer?" he nodded to Morganus.

"Yes. It is a great privilege."

"I hear that His Grace himself appointed the honoured officer."

"He did. It was a great kindness by His Grace." Nepos smiled innocently.

"Hmm," he said, "did you know that *Her* Grace was here last y ...?" His face fell like a stone. He actually put a hand over his mouth and nearly dropped his precious tablet. My heart began to thump.

"Oh?" I said, "that's interesting," which indeed it was. The Lady Tertia's movements were eagerly followed by the fashionable world, and were a constant feature of slave gossip. So everyone knew that she spent much of her time in visits up and down the province in her role as patroness of the arts. So why should Nepos be nervous that he had mentioned such a visit? Obviously he knew something that the world did not, and wanted to keep it quiet. So I said nothing and left him to worry for a while.

"Ah ... er ... er ...," said Nepos, and eventually I took a breath, smiled at the sunshine, and looked around the busy purposeful camp, and saw that we had a good, long walk of hundreds of yards before we reached stables. My methods are not fast, but there might just be time with a man so thoughtless as this.

Later, Morganus and I watched him ride off, with the tablet in a saddle bag.

"We'll see him this afternoon," I said. Morganus shook his head.

"I don't know how you do it," he said. "So what now, Greek?"

"I think we need a word with the man in command here."

"Yes."

"And then we'll go to see this *brother*." Morganus frowned.

"Are you sure about this, Greek? It could be dangerous."

I laughed.

"With you there? And the bodyguards?"

He said nothing. He just looked away.

"Anyway," I said, "We can't to come to Aquae Sulis without seeing the sights."

So we went to the cohort headquarters' block, and found the tribune Rufinus, with his senior centurions, reviewing plans for the defence of the town, should the northern troubles get worse. Rufinus beamed at Morganus as he and I were shown into his office, and he most kindly agreed to give us a conversation in private, which kindness he soon regretted.

"Honoured Sextus Lartius Rufinus," I said, when his men had gone out. I bowed politely and Rufinus looked at Morganus, clearly puzzled that a slave had spoken first. Morganus simply looked at me. "Honoured sir," I said. "We are here on a matter of great secrecy." Rufinus looked again to Morganus.

"The Greek speaks for me," said Morganus.

"Oh," said Rufinus.

"And we speak for His Grace the Governor," I said, "who has charged us to inquire as to what progress has been made at the mines since Her Grace's visit last year."

Rufinus all but staggered. He was afraid. He gulped and spoke. He spoke at length.

Later, Morganus and I walked into Aquae Sulis with the four bodyguards behind. At my request he and they had taken off their battledress and were in tunics and robes like any other citizens. That way nobody stared at us.

"How do you manage to get truth out of lies?" said Morganus.

"Telling Rufinus that we spoke for His Grace?"

"Yes! I nearly fell over when you said that!"

I was flattered. Perhaps I smirked, because even a philosopher likes to be thought clever.

"You can often get the second half of a secret if you pretend to know the first," I said.

"But how did you know Tertia threatened Rufinus?"

"I built on what Nepos the miner told us. Tertia was in Aquae Sulis to open the new Theatre of Pantomimus. That much is public knowledge. Slave gossip."

"Is it?" he said, "And what's Pantomimus?"

"It's death by boredom," I said. "A show given by a single artist, the pantomimus, backed by a chorus and musicians. He acts all the roles, in mime, using masks, costumes and dance."

"Oh, that," said Morganus. "I've heard of it but never seen it."

"Lucky man!" I said, "Those that *have* are never the same again."

He smiled and prodded me with sarcasm.

"It's supposed to be very intellectual," he said. "I'm surprised you don't like it."

"Pah!" I said. "It's for aesthetes and poets, not engineers. But it's certainly the sort of thing that Her Grace would patronise. So that's why she was here. But she also did a couple of secret things, such as telling Rufinus to get the Colcauthi mine working, or lose his rank."

"No great surprise in that," said Morganus. "The Empire always wants gold. If she was here, she might as well put a fright up Rufinus to get him moving."

"She certainly put a fright up him, but she only met him once, so let's see what Her Grace was *really* here for last March. Let's meet Nepos and his brother." And so into Aquae Sulis, which I found very strange, although not unique, having years ago seen the Temple of the Holy Oracle at Delphi which was exactly the same mixture of sacred faith and venal commerce.

The town was quite small, but bright, sharp and new, with splendid buildings, broad streets and the huge bath complex dominating everything other than the numerous temples and shrines. These were mostly to gods other than Sulis Minerva, so that the faithful could honour them as well as her. So there was a constant drone of chanting and prayers from the various temples, with lines of pilgrims shuffling to get in. There was a great lowing of sheep, grunting of hogs, and bellowing of bulls, as garlanded sacrifices were led to the altars outside the temples, and swiftly slaughtered, and a tithe of the flesh burnt on ritual flames, while the rest went to the cripples, lepers and wounded who creaked and limped forward for the free food. So the whole town stank of wood smoke, roast meat and the sick corruption of illness, for most of the pilgrims were there seeking a miraculous cure, although others had come to seek darker favours from the goddess, and still others had not come for the gods at all.

"This way, your honour, this way!" cried a man in a tall, multi-coloured hat, grabbing my arm. He lifted up his voice, crying in a singing, ringing, far-carrying tone, "*I cure the bursteren, the blisteren, the blind-eyed and the twisteren!*"

Followers in his wake sounded gongs and bells and rattles as he tried to drag me off to a little, wooden doctor shop, gaudy and bright painted, with patients inside undergoing treatment in full view of the street. There were lines of these nasty sheds crammed up against the big, stone temples and public buildings.

"This way your honour!" cried the hat man, but the bodyguards stepped forward.

"Gerroff!" they said, and put a boot up his breech and sent him staggering, after which we were left alone. This was useful since nobody else could move without being grabbed and pawed by the chorus of eye doctors, wound doctors, mountebanks and pox doctors that worked the streets in lurid robes, followed by their rolling-eyed, howling acolytes. It was bizarre in the extreme, and there was more to come.

For one thing, the town was full of priests, most being the normal Roman citizen officials, serving as priests alongside other civic duties like running the libraries, law courts and aqueducts. In typical Roman fashion, they regarded the gods as gentlemen much like themselves, and offered them ritual and sacrifice in return for patronage. They were honest men doing an honest job.

Then there were cult priests who were honest charlatans, extracting money from pilgrims' purses in exchange for cant, gibberish and fraud, but who were otherwise harmless since all they took was money. But there were other priests, fortunately few, who were steeped in baneful faith, who wielded powers of the mind, and who were profoundly sinister and dangerous.

So, following the directions I had got from Nepos the miner, we walked towards the baths, where priests of the middle kind blew horns, struck cymbals and bellowed a welcome at the gates in the name of Sulis Minerva, while noisily rattling their collecting boxes. They had white beards, fat bellies, floral garlands and short robes that showed their skinny legs. The bodyguards could have knocked them down with ease, but it was a matter of propriety. So Morganus produced a gold piece, held it up for their holinesses to see, and dropped it into one of the boxes.

"That's for all of us, right?" he said, and the bodyguards stepped forward and the priests fell back.

The bath complex itself was nothing special, much like the same thing in any other Roman city. But the Great Bath of the Sacred Waters, a rectangle over thirty feet wide and a hundred feet long, was something else entirely, because of the obviously-magical nature of the up-welling hot water. And here there was blessed silence as sad, damaged folk offered their bodies to the healing warmth of the waters. Still sadder was the sight of anxious parents praying for the mercy of the goddess, while gently bathing their sickly and wasted little ones, some of whom were clearly on the threshold of the next world.

I regret with sorrow that my own capacity to respond to this, the most poignant of life's sorrows, is cauterised by experience, while the bodyguards were too young to understand. But I saw the tears run down Morganus's face at the sight of these tragic children.

The holy of holies, most silent of all, was the well spring from which the magical waters flowed into the Great Bath. It was contained within its own domed shrine where green and floral plants of every kind were cultivated in troughs to give the impression of a natural grotto. While the spring itself had been disciplined by Roman engineering to fill a deep, wide, pool of steaming hot water into which pilgrims could cast offerings to the goddess, from a marble platform reached by steps. But some who climbed the steps did not give offerings, they gave something dark.

Nepos the miner was waiting for us by the marble steps. He came forward, bowed to Morganus and looked nervously at me.

"I came," he said. "As we agreed."

"Yes," I said, "So where's your brother?"

"There," said Nepos, and pointed to one side of the hot pool, an area of shadow where plants the size of trees arose. Several figures stood there, men and women in long robes, with head and shoulders covered despite the hot humidity. They stood and waited, and would occasionally be approached by a pilgrim, who would kneel, give a coin, and be raised up and led off down a tunnel hidden in the foliage. One of these hooded figures was beckoning Nepos with white fingers that had long, untrimmed nails. His movements were slow, his face was hidden in the shadow of his hood, and the effect was repellent in the extreme.

"Greek!" said Morganus. "I'm worried."

"It's all right," I said. "Come on."

"No!" said Nepos, wide eyed and trembling. "Not them. Only you."

"Oh no!" said Morganus, "all or none!" Morganus was nervous and the bodyguards had outright fear on their faces. More than that, they had all reached inside their robes. One of the many virtues of the Roman army sword is that, slung from its baldric, it can be hidden under a cloak.

"Morganus," I said. "What danger can there be?"

"You don't know the Celts," he said. "Their priests can do things."

"But we must be safe here. This place is famous throughout the Empire."

"I don't care what it is. You don't understand." He looked at the hooded figures in the grotto. "They might be ... something old ..." He made the Mithraic bull sign that wards off evil. He raised his right fist to represent a bull's head, with first and last fingers stuck out as horns. The bodyguards did the same, for Mithras was a popular god with soldiers.

"There's no danger here," I said. "There can't be."

"You think so?" he said, and a hot, short argument followed. But finally he stood back. "Go on then!" he said. "But remember, we leave no comrade on the field of battle."

"No!" said the bodyguards fiercely.

"Thank you," I said. "Can you lend me a coin? Better make it gold."

"*What*?" said Morganus. He sighed profoundly and fumbled in his pouch.

"Comrade?" I thought. That was something new.

Nepos and I went over to the hooded man. I bowed. Nepos got down on his knees and the hooded man placed a clawed hand on his head and muttered in Britannic. As close as this I could see the priest's face and the resemblance to Nepos was clear. But, he was older, white haired and wrinkled. At this stage even I began to feel nervous because I had thought of Nepos as being a Roman and a citizen, which perhaps he was. Although, I did not know for sure and had not taken time to find out. He certainly looked Roman, But this brother, in his priest robes, was pure Celt, and I began to wonder what mixture of native and Roman blood there might be in such a family, in such a frontier town as this, and just exactly where the family's loyalties might lie. Meanwhile Nepos nudged me.

"Give him the offering," he said in Latin, without looking up. I passed over Morganus's coin, which instantly went into the priest's mouth to be checked for any taste of brass. Then he grunted in satisfaction, put away the coin, and stared at me, waiting for something. Then he scowled and spoke in Britannic which Nepos translated.

"My reverend brother asks why you do not kneel in respect of him."

"Because he stinks," I said, which I should not have. I needed his cooperation, not his antagonism. But his smell filled my nose and his hands were filthy. He was disgusting, and my temper overcame me.

The priest scowled again, but at the thought of the gold, he sniffed and raised up Nepos, and turned and beckoned us to follow. He led us into a dark, low, winding tunnel that sloped sharply downwards as if descending into a cellar. It was utter black at first, then light showed ahead and I heard a chanting and wailing, that grew louder as we went, and which made me regret the absence of Morganus and the bodyguards.

Our destination was another domed grotto, but a natural one deep underground, lit by torches set in walls that gave off sweltering heat from the mother rock itself. It was roughly circular with a levelled floor, and several big holes in the walls like cave mouths. A ragged figure, each one nastier than the last, crouched before each hole, fiddling with bits of bone and fur, and taking pinches from dirty little pots to throw into charcoal braziers that reeked of foul smells. There were visitors crouched before some of these caves, whispering furtively while the cave creatures scribbled with styluses. It was an arcane and mystic place, foetid and reeking with menace.

"This way," whispered Nepos, and got down and crawled across the stone floor towards a cave mouth decorated with intricate carvings of entwined serpents. I went and sat beside him, as did the priest, and the two of them rocked forward on their knees and chanted, summoning a creature that crawled out from the black cave. The figure was quite different from the others. It was a young girl, extremely well formed and shapely, and entirely naked, but covered in tattoos and with live snakes tied to her arms and legs. She moved on her belly and writhed and hissed and flicked her tongue in and out of her mouth. It was a forked tongue divided into separate, wriggling points. Nepos and the priest shuddered in holy dread, and I did the same, for the gods are everywhere and appear in strange forms. But then nothing happened. The girl hissed and stared, threw handfuls of powder into a brazier that swirled with smoke, while Nepos and the priest looked at one another and I looked at them.

"Well?" I said shifting uncomfortably in the heat.

"Tell him!" said Nepos, to his brother, in Latin.

"I cannot," said the priest, likewise in Latin. "My oath forbids!"

But then the girl suddenly spoke. She spoke to me.

"Who has wronged you?" she said. Her words were mutilated by her cleft tongue, but she too spoke Latin. She stared at me and cast more powders into the hot charcoal. She had the look of lunacy, or possession, and she stared without blinking, and sweat began to trickle down my temples.

"Tell him!" said Nepos, again to his brother, and lapsed into intense, whispered Britannic. His ease with the language was worrying. Morganus spoke fluent Britannic, but not like this. Nepos was uttering his mother tongue. The words were totally obscure, but I read the faces with ease. The priest stood superior and outraged, while Nepos stabbed his brother's chest and turned constantly to me, arguing a debt of gratitude and family obligation. I watched and tried to concentrate. It was dreadfully hot and the snake girl leered at me with lascivious eyes and flicked her tongue. She moved her body like a courtesan, she was lusciously curved and it was hard not to stare. So I stared for some while. Then the argument of the brothers was ended and Nepos nodding in satisfaction.

"He will tell you," said Nepos, and I shook myself and turned to the priest. He had supposedly given way, but had a satisfied look that I did not like, because *he* very obviously did not like *me*. He whispered to Nepos, who nodded. "He will tell you, but first you will be honoured." The priest chattered in Britannic to the snake girl, who took a small cup and a flask from a leather pouch on the floor. She gave me the cup, which was very old and very dirty, and she filled it with a thick liquid from the flask.

"Drink!" said the priest. "Then we shall talk."

"Drink!" said Nepos. "It is a great honour!" He, at least, believed that. But, the priest was leering and the snake-girl was mad and the bargain, the blackmail, was clear. The priest would talk if I drank the liquid. So I peered into the cup, while Nepos, the priest, and the snake girl waited to see what I would do. Eventually I thought of the Senatus Consultum Silanianum and knew that I was dead anyway if I did not find Scorteus's killer. So I drank the liquid, which was foul, and the priest giggled.

"Now then," I said to the priest. "The Lady Tertia, when was she here?"

"In March, " said the Priest, "of last year."

"Yes," said the snake girl. "The great lady was here." And she and the priest smiled at one another.

"For what purpose?" I said, now soaked in running sweat, and the priest and the snake girl laughed at me. But they began to talk; especially the snake girl who gazed at me and talked and talked. I tried to concentrate as the heat sunk into my blood and I began to feel dizzy I gripped hard to my purpose and asked more questions, and I saw the two of them sneering, but still answering, and the girl's eyes grew huge and I could hear, I could actually hear, the flickering of her tongue. She laughed and laughed and my head grew enormous and the stone floor attempted to rise up and smite my brow, which it would have done had I not gathered what was left of my reason and hauled myself, groaning and straining, to my feet and staggered off with the laughter loud behind me. After that I remember vomiting horribly, heavily and repeatedly, and the rest was all confusion.

Chapter 14

I was sitting in a wine shop, which not a bad place in which to wake up, although it was a grubby, shabby example, and I was soaking wet and covered with a blanket. I looked round. Morganus and the bodyguards were standing over me, and the shop staff were peering around them, and some of the shop's clients behind them. It was quite a crowd.

"Ah!" said Morganus.

"Ah!" said the bodyguards, and the people behind nodded to one another. I was still dizzy, and I gazed at them, wondering why I was there. Then my memory awoke, the facts paraded in my mind, and I sat still for a while and listened to voices discussing me as if I were not there.

"Is he alright, sir?"

"I think so."

"Where's the wine?" I said.

"Water might be best," said Morganus, and snapped fingers at the staff. A jug of water and a cup appeared at great speed. Morganus sat down.

"Get rid of them," he said, looking at the sightseers, and the bodyguards hustled them out of the shop, then came and sat beside us. I took a long gulp, felt better, and looked at the anxious faces.

"Why am I wet?" I said.

"We had to clean you up," said Morganus.

"How did I get here? I said.

"You walked out of the tunnel, we grabbed you, we brought you here."

"Thanks."

"You looked like the living dead, and you were stinking with sick."

"Thanks again."

He nodded.

"I told you," he said, "we leave no wounded behind."

"What about that wine?" I said.

"Tell us what happened, Greek!" he said, so I told them.

"You actually drank it?" said Morganus. "That girl's potion?"

"Yes."

"What was it?"

"I don't know. But my guess, my hope, was that they were more mischievous than malignant. I didn't think they'd dare kill me. I think it was my punishment for being rude to the priest."

"Yes," said Morganus. "Sometimes you need to watch what you say."

"Perhaps."

"So," he said, "what was Tertia doing there? *Was* she there?"

"Yes! They were proud of it. Boasting!"

"Why?"

"They're curse-makers. Them and all the rest down there."

"In the cavern?"

"Yes. It's a nasty secret. Aquae Sulis is supposed to be a sacred shrine of healing. But people come here to lay curses, as well."

Morganus and the bodyguards looked uneasy.

"Is this safe?" said Morganus. "Talking about such things?"

"I don't know?" I said. "Can I have some wine?"

A flask was brought. I drank a cup. It was African gut rot, but it was better than water. Morganus and the bodyguards looked on with big eyes as I explained.

"This is what happens," I said. "Someone like Tertia goes down to that cavern."

"Yes?"

"She tells them who has wronged her, in this case it was her husband's German girl. The slave he's in love with." I looked at the bodyguards, then at Morganus. "Do they know about her? The German girl?"

"Everyone knows," said Morganus. "But, we keep quiet."

"Oh. Anyway, Tertia wanted the girl cursed in the head, in the heart, in the breast, in the womb, in the liver, and in the bowels. The lot! And she paid heavily for the most powerful ceremony that could be delivered. Usually the snake girl writes the curse on a small sheet of lead, but it was *gold* for Tertia, and that was just one detail." I paused and took another cup of the vinegary wine. "And then," I said, "as is the custom, Tertia threw the curse, folded up, into the sacred pool."

"Ah!" said Morganus. "That explains the German girl's fistula."

"No," I said. "That was caused by a difficult labour. By straining in childbirth."

"Yes," said Morganus, "and the curse caused that!" I gave up arguing. Maybe he was right. Who knows?

"But why did she keep it secret?" said Morganus. "If you curse someone, you want them to know it!" The bodyguards nodded.

"Not in this case. Think about it. She's a senatorial matriarch of Imperial blood. She comes of Clan Uplius, same as the Emperor."

"*Gods bless him*!" they cried.

"Quite," I said. "So she's supposed to think nothing of slaves. She's supposed to think that if her husband copulates with a slave girl, it's like riding a horse. It's no cause for jealousy. It's beneath her dignity. But she's still jealous!"

"Ah, I see," said Morganus. "So that's why she came to Aquae Sulis?"

"Yes," I said, and reached for the wine flask.

"Will you drink it all?" said Morganus. "By yourself?"

I smiled

"Send for some more cups, then." Which he did, and more wine, but I noticed that the bodyguards drank as sparingly as he did, just sips and nips. Perhaps Morganus chose them for it.

"What about the forked tongue?" he said, later.

"It can't be natural," I said. "Done to her as a child probably. By her owners or parents, to make her useful."

"*Bastards*!" said Morganus, with a fierce intensity. It was one of the very few times I ever heard him swear. Indeed I can remember the individual occasions.

And that was our trip to Aquae Sulis. We spent the night at the tribune Rufinus' house and set out for Londinium at dawn the next day, aboard the lightning. Rufinus paraded the cohort to see us depart, and they cheered Morganus lustily. But Rufinus was glad to see us go. It was written on his face.

The return journey needed two nights on the road, because the foul Britannic weather threw dense, white fog over the road, such that we could move only at a walking pace, and were penetrated even unto the bones with damp and cold and misery. When we eventually reached another post mansion with food, warmth and decent beds, we stayed the night and reached the legionary fortress at Londinium after only a short journey the next day, which was as well because urgent work rushed out to meet us.

Our plan had been for Morganus to report to the officer commanding the legion, to check for urgent legionary business, and for me to go home to the House of Scorteus, to check what progress had been made by the team reading the Syrian's papers, then to meet at noon at the house of Dolbius the lawyer to discover just where that slippery gentleman had really gone. But another priority took precedence.

One of the bodyguards came running after me as I walked across the fortress drawbridge accompanied, at Morganus's command, by four auxiliaries who carried my small luggage and cleared the way before me. I was getting used to such treatment and feared the unavoidable day when it would cease.

"Ikaros! Wait!" cried the bodyguard. My escort stamped to a standstill and saluted him, because he was a regular and a citizen, while they were not.

"Yes?"

"Severus the tribune!" he said, "Him that took the guards off the side door?"

"Yes?"

"He's sick. Real bad. The honoured Morganus says we're going to his house, and we need you to come with us right now. The honoured Morganus said to say *please*." He paused, then added, "Oh! And there's news from His Grace and the Fourteenth. They're seven days march up the Great North Road. They've crossed the River Ouse and are advancing on the fortress at Durobrivae. They'll pick up two squadrons of auxiliary cavalry there, then and march on."

"Oh," I said, far less interested in the progress of Teutonius's expeditionary force than in the fact that Morganus had said please.

The house of the military tribune Publius Julius Severus was surprisingly modest. Equestrians are supposed to have a certain minimum wealth to sustain the dignity of their rank, at least four hundred thousand in the family strongbox and better half a million. For, as Romans say, *nullae opes nullae nobiles*, no money no rank. But the house was a first-floor apartment with only half a dozen slaves, and a mother and three younger children who'd come out from Rome to share the posting with Severus. This meant there was not much back home, because nobody would live in Britannia who had a house in Italy, not with Britannia's climate.

The apartment was modest, but the family was not. They were straight-backed equestrians, behaving with dignity in the face of oncoming tragedy because the Tribune Severus was gravely ill. The household domina was Severus' mother Aggripina, who received Morganus and me in the vestibule, with two small boys and a daughter standing behind her, and slaves behind them. They all wore formal robes, dressed for sorrow, but not yet mourning.

"Gods rest and thank you Leonius Morganus Fortris Victrix," said Aggripina, and offered her hand. Morganus bowed and kissed it. "I take it that you are come to offer the support and prayers of the Twentieth Valeria Victrix." Morganus blushed.

"Yes, most honoured lady," he said, "And … ah … I also bring the Greek Ikaros of Apollonis, who is … a most learned man." Morganus was extemporising. This was not the time or place to mention side doors and guards dismissed. Aggripina looked at me, but spoke to Morganus.

"Ikaros the Apollonite? Is he not the engineer owned by the late Scorteus the trader, gods save his soul?"

"Gods save his soul!" echoed her household.

"He *was*, honoured lady," said Morganus. "But now he is in army service."

"Most noble lady," I said. "I ask with respect that we might see his-honour-your-son. I do have some skill in the healing arts." That was not quite a lie because I have read numerous medical works. Neither was it entirely true, but it was expedient because Aggripina took us immediately to the sick room, where I was rightly stabbed with guilt for raising the hope that I saw in her face. There were four physicians working on Severus, at what cost only the gods might know. One pair was busy chanting, with raised hands, while the second pair was turning the patient to apply a line of brass cupping vessels to his back *to withdraw the foul humours*.

The technique involves holding a small cup, usually of glass or metal, over a lamp flame to heat the air inside. Then the cup is placed on the patient, the hot air contracts as it cools, and applies powerful suction which can draw blood through the skin. They were having to do this to Severus' back because his belly was already covered with mauve, circular bruises and no room was left for more.

Severus the tribune, commander of the Numidian auxiliaries, was a big, young man, now limp and sweating, muttering in his delirium and weakly trying to fight off the doctors. There was not the slightest chance of conversation with him, and the room stank of sickness and the smoke of the lamp used to heat the cupping vessels.

"We pray for his delivery," said his mother.

"What were his symptoms?" I said.

"Four days ago he fell ill with cramps in the stomach."

"Yes?"

"He took to his bed, and got steadily worse, and then he seemed to get better." She described the illness in much detail. I asked some questions and came to a tentative conclusion.

"Noble lady," I said, "I fear your son has eaten something bad. May I see your kitchen and your kitchen staff?" That caused outrage. Aggripina drew herself up still straighter, and fierce scowls came from her children and slaves. But, she looked to Morganus, who nodded, and so she took me to the kitchen with her retinue in her wake. It was a small cramped space at the back of the apartment, with no running water, and just one cook slave, an elderly Lombard with knobbed finger joints and a thin beard. He had come out from Italy with the family and had been with them all his life. He bitterly resented any suggestion of slackness in the kitchen, pointing out the scrubbed pans, the scoured surfaces and the neat, gleaming rows of knives and utensils.

"Everything done proper!" he cried, jabbing a finger at me. "In my kitchen there ain't no dirt, no roaches, no mice, no nothing, *only good order*!" He shouted the final words in my face, in his quavery old man's voice. He was shaking with anger and Aggripina stepped forward and put a kind arm round him. Like some old slaves, in some families, he was family himself.

"We know, we know," she said, quietly.

"As if I'd do harm to the young master," he said, and wiped his eyes.

It was very difficult and I had more to ask.

"Has the honoured Publius Julius Severus eaten mushrooms recently?"

"Of course!" said the cook slave. "He loves mushrooms, does the young master!"

"And who bought them?" I said.

"Me," he said. "Who else?" He turned to Aggripina, "I say *who else*, mistress?"

"Of course," she said. "Who else?"

"See!" said the old man, glaring at me as if some point had been proved.

But then I had to ask to speak to the other slaves privately, and to look over the rest of the apartment, which Aggripina indignantly refused, causing me to invoke the power of His Grace, as represented by Morganus, who promptly refused the duty.

He dragged me aside and whispered ferociously in my ear. "She is a Roman matriarch in her own house. *Look at her*!" I did.

She was standing bolt upright with her children and slaves clinging to her. They were terrified and she was on the limit of her courage. Morganus grabbed my arm and shook it. "She is a mother with her family behind her," he said. "As a soldier, it is my most *sacred* duty to defend her, and you ask me to insult her? To lay hands on her?" He glared at me. "Listen Greek, I would give my life for that noble lady!"

"Morganus," I said, "What about the lives of four hundred others?"
"What do you mean?"
"The Lord Chief Justice will enforce the Silanianum."
"You don't know that."
"Yes I do. I saw it in his face."

"Then it is your fault for saying Romans are inferior!"

I groaned aloud. He was right. I should have kept my mouth shut. But what could I do? I couldn't unsay the words.

"Morganus," I said. "If we don't pursue this investigation. If we don't prove the barber is innocent, then four hundred will die, and they are undoubtedly innocent, and you know it. It's as simple as that!"

So we searched the apartment, which was a truly awful thing to do. The family was poor, some of the rooms were shabby, and Aggripina was deeply ashamed of it. But worse things are done in the cause of justice. So I looked in every cupboard of every room and under the beds and in the corners. In the end it was not only Aggripina who was ashamed, I was too, and Morganus could not bear to be beside me.

Thus died my innocence in being a detective agent. It had all been joyful until then, but now it was shame, it was prying into the lives of decent people. But still I persevered. I did so because it was my duty to save four hundred lives, but also, I admit it and I record it here, for the perverse reason that the practice of detection had gripped me as an addict is gripped by his drug. Never in my life had I felt such total intellectual fascination; that and the power of being something like a god, in looking down upon the actions of others and passing judgement.

So I took the slaves, one by one into the kitchen and spoke to each of them, and when it was done I tried to make amends. I went to Aggripina and knelt before her, taking the hem of her robe in my right hand, as a supplicant.

"Most honoured and noble lady," I said, "I humbly ask your forgiveness, for I can now give you my assurance, before Apollo, patron god of my fathers, that no harm befell your son from anything or any person in this house."

"I knew that already," she said, just those few words, while looking sternly away from me and withholding any absolution. But it was her right to do so, and I was lucky that she did not pronounce a curse on my head. Such spite was beneath her dignity. So I touched my brow to the floor at her feet, and got up, searching for something else to say.

"At least get rid of the doctors," I said. "Cupping is absolutely useless, and any prayers come best from those who love your son, not those who must be paid."

The bodyguards were still waiting outside in the street, although we'd been hours in the apartment.

"I suppose you will want a wine shop?" said Morganus, full of anger.

"No!" I said, although I did.

"That was a true Roman lady," he said, accusingly.

"D'you think I don't know it?"

"So what will you do now?" he sneered. "Drink another gallon of wine?"

"Oh, come on," I said. "Let's walk."

Which we did, side by side with the bodyguards at our heels. It was late afternoon, the streets were busy, but people bowed and stepped aside on sight of the swan crest. I headed back towards the House of Scorteus and we walked in miserable silence. Finally, Morganus sighed and spoke. "Well," he said. "What did you learn from all that?"

So I told him.

Chapter 15

A Roman city's water supply flows non stop, with public fountains at every corner sending a constant overflow down the streets and into the drains. This cleans the city, but means that the gutters are always wet. So the pavements rise high and there are stepping stones at intervals so citizens can cross with dry feet, while still leaving room for the wheels of carts to pass between the blocks. This is very Roman, very systematic.

So I stood aside as Morganus stepped the blocks from one pavement to another. He looked back as I followed him. "Severus was poisoned with mushrooms," I said. "Probably death caps. They're native to Britannia."

"How can you know that?" he said, scowling. He was still angry, and guilty, at our treatment of Aggripina.

"Severus fell ill with diarrhoea and vomiting, then he got better on the third day?"

"Yes."

"He sat up smiling and everyone was happy?"

"Yes."

"Then next day he got worse again. Much worse."

"So?"

"That's typical of poisoning by death cap mushrooms."

"Is it?"

"Yes."

"Could it not be something else? Some fever or ague?"

"No. He was fit as a fighting dog, he hadn't been near anyone with any sickness, and it certainly wasn't one of these filthy Britannic fevers with coughing and sneezing and the rest."

"Well could it not be some other poison?"

"Possibly, but the cook said Severus loves mushrooms, and I think someone knew that, and took advantage of it, which means this is another one."

"Another what?"

"Another murder."

"But he's not dead yet!" said Morganus, and I sighed.

"He soon will be, and that's sad. He was all the hopes of that family."

"Was he?"

"Yes. The slaves said so. His father was no good at business. He lost a fortune then took his own life. Severus was supposed to make that right with an army career. And he was definitely trying for a good marriage."

"Who was the girl?"

"I don't know. None of the slaves knew."

Morganus thought about that and we walked on a while.

"If it was death caps," he said, "couldn't it have been an accident? A mistake?"

"No. That cook slave's an expert. He knows mushrooms from death caps."

"Well, a deliberate act then? By someone in the house?"

"Never! They idolise him. You must have seen it. All of them!" He nodded.

"So why did you search the house?" he said.

"Looking for something, anything. Some sign of disorder or guilt."

"And what did you find?"

"Nothing, which means there's no guilt in that house, which means that the guilt is somewhere else. Because, somebody poisoned that lad, and if we've heaped shame on his mother ..." I glared at him. "... you talked about sacred duty, didn't you? Sacred duty to defend that lady."

"Yes," he muttered, not looking at me.

"Then how about this for sacred duty? We have a sacred duty to find out who killed her son and make sure he gets punished!" But

Morganus was not properly listening, and suddenly he stopped dead in the street. The bodyguards skidded the hobnails of their boots to stop from bumping him. Morganus gaped.

"Gods of Olympus!" he said. "If someone else killed him, do you realise what this means?" I did, but it was not the time to be too clever by saying so. "Someone is ahead of us, Greek. Someone knows what we are doing, he knows about Severus taking the guards off the door, and he got to the lad before we did!" He was right, and we talked about it until we reached the House of Scorteus, with its guard of auxiliaries. These stiffened to attention and saluted Morganus with their spears, and their optio roared out Morganus's name to announce him. This brought Agidox the major domos at the run, with his boys behind him, and all fell to their knees before us, and that was to me as well as to Morganus, which felt odd. This house had been my home, for I had no other, and now I was being received with the formalities of an honoured stranger.

More formal still, we were invited to the great atrium, to be welcomed by the dominus, the *new* dominus, because Scorteus's son, Fortunus, was at last in residence. Obviously Scorteus's will had been opened and the succession proclaimed. Thus Agidox begged, with embarrassing humility, that I and Morganus would consent to be received.

"Honoured sirs," he said. "All Londinium knows of your efforts to find the wicked murderer of out late and beloved master."

"May his soul find rest!" said the slaves.

"And the new master would be honoured to greet you himself."

Agidox feared a snub to himself and his master, I could see that, and the fact that he was looking more towards me than Morganus. Obviously my reputation had grown and I was now feared by those who had been my family, which hurt. Yet, at the same time, I stood taller, for such is the perversity of mankind. I turned to Morganus because we had not come here for a social event, but to chase the investigation of the Syrian's files.

"Honoured sir," I said.

"Whatever you think, Greek," he said, and I turned to Agidox.

"The noble officer and I would be honoured to meet the new dominus."

It was as well that we did. The meeting in the great atrium was short and formal. No more than polite words, but it was interesting to see the immature Fortunus, draped in a man's robes, sat on his father's chair, and stumbling over his words, while his uncle, Badrogid, stood huge and prompting at his side, dressed in the pick of his late brother's wardrobe. Badrogid had on the very same Chinese silk gown that Scorteus had worn when he told me about the German girl, and that gown was worth a thousand acres of farmland. Whoever might legally be the dominus, it was obvious who was the power in the house and I wondered what else might have found its way into Badrogid's possession, with or without the permission of Scorteus's will?

Cui bono, as the Roman lawyers say, when seeking guilt: *who gains?*

And in that moment I realised how much I had changed, because I looked at Badrogid, whom once I had addressed with humble words, and who now I saw as a greedy delinquent to be questioned. But that would be later. There were other priorities, and we left the great atrium as soon as we could and went to the Syrian's rooms.

Morganus's clerks were waiting, stood to attention at their desks: neat collapsible structures brought in to spread papers for easy attention. In typical army style they were ranged in a grid pattern, each one a measured distance from the rest, with a stool behind it, papers stacked on it and an excused armour clerk stood smartly beside it.

"Well?" said Morganus to their optio, a greying veteran.

"We found something, most honoured sir," he said.

"Ah!" said Morganus and I together.

"This is it, honoured sir," said the optio, and offered a tablet folder: five wood-framed wax sheets, bound together to make one unit.

"Show it to the Greek," said Morganus. He did. He put the book on a desk, and looked at me. He was pleased. I could see it. He was showing off a job well done.

"Well?" I said, and the optio waved a hand at the racks of shelving, now empty of documents.

"We completed the first pass, honoured Greek," he said. "Our plan was a quick read through, looking for anything that stood out."

"Good!" I said.

"And all such were set aside for special attention later."

"And?"

"Most proved to be ordinary letters, receipts or ledgers, and some property deeds and contracts. Perfectly ordinary commercial matters."

"Go on," I said.

"But this one," he said, "we don't know what to make of it, and it was hidden in a cupboard." He gave a little shrug, trying to be modest. "Well actually, honoured Greek, it was at the *back* of a cupboard behind a false board. I told the lads to tap everything to see if anything was hollow." He smiled. "And it was!"

"Well done indeed!" I said. "What's your name, optio?"

"Silvius, sir."

"So show me what you found, Optio Silvius."

He smiled and opened the folder. I looked and I smiled too, because there were no words: not proper words, just groups of letters seemingly put together at random, and the nonsense words were lined up in ranks and files like a legion on parade.

"Ah!" I said.

"What is it?" said Morganus.

"A cipher, honoured sir," said the optio, and I turned to Morganus.

"A cipher is ..."

"Letters jumbled up to make a code," he said. "I know what it means."

"Of course, honoured sir," I said, and stared at the figures scribed into the wax, and I noticed that in several places the wax was indented with ring seals. I thought of the ring the Syrian had worn. "I will need time for this," I said to the optio. "Bring the folder with you. Don't leave it here." Then something jumped to my attention, as I closed the folder and saw the writing on the cover. The Syrian had used the language of his homeland, assuming that nobody would understand it, and he was almost right. But I understood because the language was Aramaic. So I put my finger on the writing and looked at Morganus.

"This says '*the business of shields*'." There was an awed silence in the room.

"Does it?" said Morganus.

"It could mean the *commerce* or *trading* of shields," I said.

"Honoured sirs," said the optio. "They do deal in shields! They make them. For the army." He beckoned to one of the clerks who picked up a folder of tablets and put it on the desk beside the other four. "Look!" said the optio. We looked. It was a ledger in plain Latin. Scorteus's company was manufacturing the big square army shield: the *scutum militaris*. They were making them for export: thousands of them at a factory in Londinium.

I looked at the ledger. I was getting tired and needed to think. This time we did not ask Agidox for a quiet room, we just sat in the Syrian's office among the papers and desks, and got rid of the army clerks. They had done their job anyway, and done it well. But I did ask for wine and cakes. I was getting used to my privileges, just as Agidox was getting used to delivering them. He sent his best girls again, hurriedly crammed into their best robes and jewellery and their best pretty smiles.

"Oh," I said, as they came in. "Ask the honoured Agidox if he would send me the ring we took from the Syrian's finger."

"Yes, your worship," they said, and went out. One of them brought the ring later, and I put it in my belt pouch.

"Well?" said Morganus, sat with his helmet on a table beside him. He looked as tired as I did. "Are you keeping track of all this?"

"I think so," I said, and picked up a goblet of wine. It was made of gold. Agidox was still seeking to impress, and, it was top quality wine. I saw Morganus staring at me with a disapproving look. So took a small sip and put down the cup, and stared at him.

"Oh go on!" he said, so I took a proper drink.

"The matter grows and grows," I said. "But the next two priorities are to see this shield factory, and to go to the house of Dolbius the lawyer." Morganus nodded.

"Which first?" he said.

"The factory! We still have the chance to take them by surprise. So, if there's anything to hide, they don't get a chance. But it's different with Dolbius' slaves. They probably had a tale perfected from the moment their master left." I drank some more wine. "Can we take your clerks with us to the factory?" Morganus nodded. "And some troops? There'll be hundreds of slaves and staff at the factory, and an armed presence might be useful in case they try anything behind our backs."

"Such as what?"

"I don't know. I'm just being careful."

"I'll bring men," he said, and looked out of a window. "It had best be tomorrow, at dawn." He paused, and corrected himself. "I mean the day after."

"Why?" I said, and he looked at me as if I did not know what day it was.

"There's a festival this afternoon, and a *dies nefastus* tomorrow."

"Oh," I said, not wishing to admit I did not know. But I did not. I can never remember the Roman festivals. There are too many of them celebrating things that do not interest me, and all with *dies nefasti*, dead days, after them, when the banks and law courts close and nothing is done, so the revellers can sleep off their wine. So I nodded, and then a thought occurred to me.

"Would it be possible for me to sleep at the fort tonight?" I asked, "and could a runner be sent for my notes?"

"What notes?"

"My master notes of this case. I keep notes on any project I'm working on."

"Do you?" he said.

"Yes," I said. "It's a discipline of the mind," which indeed it was, and still is.

"And where are they? How does our man find them?"

"My boys know where they are," I said, and he nodded.

"I'll send a runner," he said, "and there are spare beds in my house."

"Thank you," I said. "It will save time if I'm already in the fort."

That was true, but it was not why I wanted to sleep at the fort, nor why I did not myself want to fetch my notes. The sad truth was that I could no longer be comfortable in the House of Scorteus where I had become an even stranger creature to the house folk that I was before. I was an alien being with great powers. Also I felt that slave gossip would soon know, if it did not already, that the Silanianum was out of its tomb, and I did not want to be asked about it, not even by the unspoken question behind fearful eyes. So we went back to the fort, which took far longer than I had expected, because the festival procession was going down the Via Principalis with floats and music, and cymbals and gongs, and everyone decorated in bright colours and floral crowns, and a great deal of skipping, and dancing and singing.

"Huh!" said Morganus, as if in disapproval. "It's the *Bona Dea*." The bodyguards groaned in sympathy because this was strictly a women's event. It celebrated the nameless *Good Goddess* responsible for the welfare of women, especially as regards the monthly troubles that afflict their loins. Consequently it was usual for men to affect disdain for the festival, but it was remarkable how many of them would line the streets, grinning at the city's women all dressed in their best, especially the young, unmarried girls who did all the dancing in short, bright, skimpy robes that showed off their legs. So Morganus and the bodyguards pushed their merry way to the kerbside, through a growing press of laughing men, and I went with them, of necessity, to watch the parade go by.

It was a good show. The floats were smaller than usual, being carried by women, but were beautifully decorated with flowers lovingly grown and prepared for weeks past, and arranged in fierce competition by the various women's cults, guilds and sisterhoods who took part. All the city's bands and musicians were out, blowing and clanging and whistling, fit to lift the tiles off the roofs. As ever, the Emperor was represented in the place of honour, in the centre of the procession. Today he was represented by the Lady Tertia, the Governor's wife, and her four daughters, who marched within a giant, circular, floral wreath, carried by twenty slave girls in matching robes, who sung a holy anthem as they danced in slow and graceful progress.

The effect was extremely lovely, as were the Lady Tertia and her daughters, whose ceremonial robes displaced naked arms and necks and their right breasts exposed, bringing roars of applause from the male onlookers and a huge drumming of heels on the pavement, and ribald requests that still more flesh might be displayed. But there was an oddity. Among all the beauty there was a flaw. There was a dark woman long past her best, who danced with sagging breast exposed, and lank hair worked into ringlets. It was the same old-young slave woman who had stood behind Tertia when His Grace the Governor received Scorteus, and now she kept close to the side of the Lady Tertia, who constantly smiled upon her and caressed her cheek.

Such was the fondness between Tertia and this slave that I made the natural assumption that there was some relationship of passion between them. Women, just as easily as men, may become infatuated with their slaves, and since love is of the spirit not the body, the absence of beauty may be overcome by the presence of truth and kindness. But these speculations were driven from my mind by the realisation that only four daughters danced with Tertia, while I had seen five at the Governor's reception for Scorteus, and I wondered where the other one had gone.

Later, in Morganus's house, I was greeted by his own wife and daughters, who smiled upon me as if I were a citizen, and I was given a good room and a good bed. Morganus even brought me a flask of wine. He brought it himself. They were all very kind, they made me comfortable and, with the aid of the wine, I probably would have slept well, except that I spent most of the night re-living the memories of that day, and for some reason worrying about Tertia's missing daughter. So I slept badly as usual.

But at least I did not have to get up early the next day, and when I did it was for pleasing work.

Chapter 16

The next day no business was done throughout the city, including the manufacture of army shields, which perhaps was a blessing because it gave me a full day with the Syrian's cipher tablets, which had been brought back to Morganus's house, to my huge delight at the opportunity to attack such a problem. There are few things that I love more than the solving of puzzles.

I took the folder out into Morganus's garden, the day being bright and sunny, as can happen by rare chance even in gods forsaken Britannia. Morganus's wife took command of the bodyguards, clapping her hands and giving orders as if to children, while the four big men heaved a heavy stone table into place, and set a chair behind it. Morganus stood back and watched, looking very different in his civilian tunic and robe, and the scar from the ballista bolt stood out plain on his cheek, where usually it was hidden by his helmet. Then he caught my eye, nodded at his wife and smiled. He was proud of her.

"No! No! No! Not *there*!" she cried, "The Greek gentleman will have the light straight in his eyes!" She stabbed a finger. "Over *here*!" And the table moved again. And again. In fact moved several times before she was quite happy. Then Morganus had to go to the Centurions' Hall, which was their club room, and accustomed meeting place on dies nefasti. He even apologised before he went.

"It's expected, Greek," he said. "It's tradition. I'll be there all day."

"That's fine," I said, not really listening, because my mind was already deep into the task ahead. He saw that and smiled. After that, the family left me alone, which was exceedingly kind. They left me alone all day, bringing food and drink from time to time. No wine though, which was just as well. But after some hours, as sometimes happens with an intellectual task, my strength gave up before my will. The cipher was just too complex, and as much as I wanted to go on working, I was exhausted. So I sighed and gave up and pushed the Syrian's folder aside. Then, seeking for something different, some easy task to clear my mind, I was pricked with temptation. There was someone I wanted to see. Someone from whom I had parted badly, and while my mind had given up on the cipher, there were other matters to pursue, matters important enough to overcome any embarrassment or need for apology.

So I found my outdoor cloak and went into the city. I went to the House of Scorteus, where the auxiliary guard commander saluted me with a full, formal, right arm salute, as if I were a Roman centurion. He did so because he was Optio Simonis Lartis, the man I'd saved from a flogging by Morganus. But having done that, and with great politeness, he stood firmly between me and the door.

"Honoured sir," he said, with a bow, "are you going in on your own?"

"Yes," I said, "Why not?"

"Best if I come in with you, honoured sir. Me and a couple of my men." So he did, and he was probably right to do so. The slaves appeared in great numbers as the word went round, and they stood and stared at me, and muttered to one another, in surly antagonism and fear. They were not actually hostile, not with the auxiliaries behind me, but they obviously knew I had failed in my promise concerning the Silanianum, and I was ashamed.

Obviously, someone had betrayed the privacy of the conversation between myself and Domitius, the Lord Chief Justice. Perhaps the Imperial slaves were not so averse to gossip after all? But by whatever route, the slaves knew, and I was Perseus the Gorgon Slayer no longer. Not to them.

Allicanda was not in her kitchen. She was at the ice-well behind the formal gardens at the back of the house. She had to be sent for and I waited outside her little office, fiddling with the brooch of my cloak, with my guards beside me, while the slaves murmured to each other, and looked at me like an enemy, and I began to wish I had not come.

Then she appeared and my heart jumped. She looked tired, she was in a plain, slave tunic with her usual white apron, but still my heart jumped. There were two slave women behind her, carrying baskets of broken ice, and they and she bowed low. They bowed to me because I was now a powerful man. So I bowed low in return as if seeking to be one of them again, which was impossible and ridiculous.

"I give you good day, Allicanda," I said. "Can we please talk?" So we sat in the small office, while Simonis Lartis and his men waited outside. Wine was offered. Small pasties were offered. But no smile. Only politeness and reserve. But at least I was sitting with her, in private, and close enough to touch her. So polite phrases were exchanged, and then I fell silent, wanting to say more, but finding no words. But she spoke first to keep the meeting formal.

"And what does your worship want?" she said. "How may I be of service to the Empire and the common good?"

"How are you?" I asked. "And how are things in the house?" I was disturbed by seeing her, and my words were badly chosen. She sneered at me.

"How d'you think we are?" she said. "When the law is going to kill us all? How are you, yourself, because you will die with us!" She drummed her fingers on the table in front of her, and looked away. Then she turned her green eyes on me. "Do you know what they're doing? The slaves? Those with children? The grown children?"

"No," I said.

"They're shaving them. Shaving the hair between their legs, and they're telling them to stand small and act young so they'll be spared. They're terrified! Everyone is! What d'you expect." I think my face showed the misery of my feelings, because she sighed and reached out her hand and put it on mine. "Oh, never mind. It's not your fault. It's the Romans not you. So what do you want from me?"

I forced myself to concentrate

"I need to know about the daughters of the Lady Tertia."

"Gods save Her Grace!" she said.

"Yes," I said. "Now I must ask for your help." She nodded. "The Lady Tertia has five daughters," I said, but yesterday only four were dancing to the Bona Dea." Allicanda instantly raised hands.

"May the blessings of the dear goddess be upon us," she said, and she said it with feeling, because the Bona Dea was much loved by women.

"Yes, yes. But where was the other daughter?" Allicanda considered the question. Gossip was her fascination and she relaxed a little.

"That would be Velia. She's the middle one. Sixteen years old and reckoned to be the prettiest. She's ill. She's been sent back to Italy for the sunshine." She smiled for the first time. "You should appreciate that." I smiled in return, but something stirred in my mind. My questions about Tertia's daughter had been an excuse to see Allicanda. But now I was interested.

"When was she taken ill?" I said. "And sent away?" Allicanda pondered.

"Not long ago. A few days? It's fresh news, all the girls are talking about her. As I said, Velia's the pretty one and her clothes are ..."

"How many days? Do you know?"

"Well, it all happened suddenly, and Tertia's physicians said she had to go home for the sunshine." Allicanda frowned, "It would have been about five days ago. Maybe six." She looked at me, almost in the old way, almost as a friend. "You're thinking, aren't you? In that deep mind. What is it?"

"I don't know," I said, and as I concentrated on Velia and Tertia, a light shone on something else. "And who's the ugly woman that danced beside Tertia? The slave woman. What is she to Tertia? Are they lovers?"

Allicanda laughed. "No, you silly man. That's Merloura, Tertia's favourite. Almost her mother. Tertia loves her like a mother. Treats her like a mother, and Merloura treats her like a daughter. Even cooks for her. All her favourite food." She looked at me with her head on one side, "Don't you know? Don't you know how Tertia grew up?"

"No," I said, and indeed I did not. The home lives of the Roman aristocracy were of even less interest to me than the dates of Roman festivals.

"Well," she said, "Tertia comes from clan Ulpius, same as Emperor Trajan, and more than that she's a close blood relative. Trajan was nothing special when he was born. He was just one of a Roman clan in Hispania. He only became emperor through his army service."

"I know that," I said. "But what's this to do with Tertia?"

"They grew up together. Her family were noble but had no money. They had too many children and they didn't want Tertia and they begged a place for her in Trajan's family." I nodded. "So she had a hard time as a little girl. She was just a poor relation, and she was alone among strangers, and she had only one possession, the slave Merloura, who looked after her, fought her battles, and protected her, and wiped away her tears when she fell down. And Tertia has never forgotten it. She treats Merloura as her mother."

"I see," I said. "So how did she rise to where she is now? Tertia?"

"That was Trajan. He fell in love with her."

I frowned. "Doesn't he prefer men?"

"Oh yes, but when Tertia grew up a bit, she flowered. She was very dainty, very pretty, and he loved her as a sister, as *my little bird*. That's what he called her. He'd do anything for her. Still will. Anything legal, that is. And as Trajan rose, he took her with him, and did his best for her, and he married her to one of his best generals when she was fifteen. That was Teutonius. It was a very good marriage and she's never looked back. It was even a love match."

"Was it?" I said.

"It was on her part. She really loves him."

I thought about that. "A good marriage is a fine thing," I said, and looked at her.

"For those who are free." she said.

"Who knows what I may achieve with Rome behind me?" I said, and reached out for her. "Perhaps I might buy a slave into safety." I meant myself, but she thought I meant her, and she pulled her hand away. Perhaps it was the will of the gods? There are some things they forever deny. So I took my leave, I wrapped my cloak about my body and went back to the fort, feeling desperately sorry for myself.

That night when Morganus came home, we talked in his big living room and shared a flask of wine.

"What's wrong with you?" he said as we sat down, "You look like you've lost a gold piece and found a turd."

"It's nothing," I said. "It's this island. The grey sky. It depresses me."

"Does it though?"

"Yes."

"Anything else? Anything you want to talk about?" There was nothing I wanted to talk about. It was all vanity. The vanity of dreams that can never be made real. So I reached for the Syrian's folder.

"I did some work earlier," I said. "And this is a *book* cipher."

"Which means?"

"The letters refer to words in a book."

"What book?"

"I don't know. But the Syrian would have had one copy and someone else would have had another. That way, assuming the copies are identical, the cipher letters direct you to words in the book."

"How does that work?" said Morganus.

"Can you find me a book?" I said. "I'll show you." Morganus opened a cupboard and took out one of a number of books.

"My library," he said, and smiled with a slight nervousness. "Won't be like yours, of course." He put the book on the table. It was Caesar's *Gallic Wars*, so obvious a choice for a man like Morganus, that I fought hard not to smile. I took the book and unrolled it. As in all scroll books, the text was written in sections at right angles to the long axis of the scroll, so if you held the rolled-up ends, one in each hand, with your hands comfortably at your sides, the text read from top to bottom in front of you.

"Each of these sections is a page, right?" I said.

"Yes," he said.

"So you can number the pages. Then you number the lines of text on each page, and you number the words on each line.

"I see," he said. "So with three code letters you can point to any word."

"That's it," I said. "Basically, anyway," and he frowned.

"But there are only twenty-three letters in the alphabet and books can have lots more pages than that."

"Doesn't matter. The first twenty-three are enough."

"You mean they have enough words?"

"Yes." Morganus nodded, and pointed at one of the open tablets.

"But I can see four- and five-letter groups, and longer, in the code. Why do you need so many if you can identify a word with just three code letters?"

I smiled. "It's a bit more complicated than that. You can crack a plain book cipher by inference and by utility of words, common words that is."

"If you say so," he said.

"But there's all sorts of ways to make things harder. You switch words round according to a table or plan, and move letters to new places. That's the fun of it!"

"Fun?" He shook his head. "So can you read any of it, without the book?"

"A bit," I said. "This sequence means shields, this one is a number, and I think these here refer to hides, and nails, and I think this one may mean …" But I stopped, because he was not listening. He was gazing at me with an awestruck expression.

"How can you know that?" he said. So I explained the principles whereby a cipher may be broken. In my city, every schoolboy was taught ciphering and deciphering, and Morganus was no fool, so he nodded.

"Yes," he said, "I understand when you explain it, but don't ever ask me to do it." Then he sat bolt upright in his chair, struck with a sudden idea. "Listen Greek. If it's all based on a book, why don't we set the clerks to working through all the books in the Syrian's library, using this code, the way you said, to see which one is the right book?" Then he paused and looked at me. "Oh," he said, "You thought of that."

"Yes, and we could do it, but I think we'd be wasting our time."

"Why?"

"We know we're not dealing with ordinary murders, don't we?"

"Indeed!"

"We're facing something systematic and thorough, right?"

"Yes." I paused, not entirely certain of myself.

"Well, I'm guessing that whoever killed the Syrian would've removed the book we want, to prevent anyone reading these tablets."

"So why didn't he take the folder?"

"Because it was hidden and the book was not."

"What about the ring?" said Morganus. "The Syrian's ring?"

"Oh yes," I said, "It was used to sign the book. It was used four times and another ring, a different one, was stamped into the book beside it, each time."

"What does that mean?"

"It means the Syrian and someone else were signing something off. They were displaying agreement."

"Agreement of what?"

"Goods received? Payment made? I don't know." This was as far as our discussions went that day. Next morning, at dawn, we left for the shield factory, with the bodyguards, the clerks and a century of the Twentieth such that we were marching into a huge, stone-paved courtyard just as the factory was getting into full operation for the day's work.

This expedition also proved a treat, being intensely technical, and greatly appealing to an engineer. There were carts and oxen, horses and mules, stacks of timber, barrels and pots, the scent of sawdust, the stink of glue, and the smoke of industry rising from huge soot-blackened chimneys in a furnace house to one side. There were round eyes, and bowing, and much falling back, and a small group of well-dressed citizens hurrying out from the office block in nervous politeness, with their freedmen and slaves behind them. These were the senior management, surprised and alarmed at the unexpected appearance of the army.

"We are here on His Grace's authority!" said Morganus.

"Gods save His Grace!" cried the management, eyeing the legionaries.

"My men will secure the works so that none shall enter or leave," said Morganus.

"Yes, honoured sir."

"While I tour the works, with this Greek gentleman."

"Yes, honoured sir."

"And my clerks will inspect your books!"

A pause. A silence. A great looking at one another, then a most reluctant ...

"Yes ... honoured ... sir."

"Otherwise, all work shall continue as normal," said Morganus.

"Yes, honoured sir."

That was our agreed plan. The clerks had done well with the Syrian's papers and were the best men for the same job here. Meanwhile Morganus watched the management bowing politely and likewise he watched the glances and frowns they shot at each other, for these were substantial men, with position and power. Morganus whispered to me.

"Is this legal?" he said. "What we're doing?"

"I haven't the slightest idea," I said, and he laughed.

So we toured the works, which was fascinating.

"This is the splitting shed, honoured sirs," said the head slave. "We cut the timber into baulks and then shave it into thin rectangular strips." He saw our puzzlement and explained in more detail. "We use plane benches" he said. "Come and see!" Which we did.

The shed was full of benches and slaves and sweat, and the steady buzz of sawing and the hiss and scrape of timber being sliced by blades. Men were cutting tree trunks with huge two-man frame saws, over saw pits, turning out heavy planks with neat, squared sides. The planks were taken to trestles and sawn into standard, straight-grained baulks, precisely three feet long, and three inches wide by six inches deep. These baulks were taken to the plane benches, and the slave showed me how these worked.

The benches were long and narrow, with a channel running down the middle that just fitted the three-inch width of the timber baulks. Half way along the channel there was a blade set into a slot, as if in a huge carpenter's plane turned upside down. So when the baulks were slid along the slot, a thin strip was planed off the bottom of the baulk at each stroke. With several benches working, the strips were falling out of the bottom of the benches at great speed and into baskets below. It was all very neat and convenient.

I picked up one of the strips by the middle, and the ends bent down under their own weight. It was so thin, that I could see light through it, yet still fibrous and tough.

"And so to the glue shed, your honours," said the head slave, and we moved on.

The next shed was hot and stinking, with lines of long, iron glue baths bubbling on charcoal braziers, and rows of big, half cylinders, flat on the floor round side up. These were made of staves like barrels, each one carefully smoothed and exactly the size of an army shield.

"These here are the *formers*, your honours," said the head slave.

The process was self-explanatory. Slaves brought in baskets of strips from the saw shed, soaked the strips in glue then laid them on the formers. Each former received several layers of strips, the second at right angles to the first, and the third at right angles to the second and so on. Then the strips were pinned in place with brass nails tapped into the edges, such that the layers were forced into the shape of a shield.

"From here they go into a baking house," said the head slave, "to dry them."

The wooden formers with their glued strips were already mounted on stretchers so they could be carried to the next process, which was baking in a stone-walled, stone-floored hot house, with underfloor central heating like a bath chamber, but hotter. It was stifling hot and we looked in as half-naked slaves, with clogs to protect their feet, ran in and stacked the formers into rows and then piles. Next we saw the dried contents of other baking sheds taken out, and into a *tipping shed* where the rough shield shapes were unpinned, tipped off the formers and stacked.

"Don't the strips stick to the formers?" I asked. "With all that glue?"

"No, honoured Greek," said the head slave, "the formers are greased."

There were other questions, with other answers, for there were many tricks of technique, worked out over long years. Thus, in other sheds, the shields were cut to precise shape, then pierced for the metal shield boss that holds the hand grip, then covered with leather, trimmed with brass edges, and finally they were painted with the insignia of whichever unit they were destined for, or left unpainted according to the client's needs.

"Nice to see them made," said Morganus, when we emerged from the final building, and he stood as if taking guard behind a shield. "A shield's the most important piece of kit in the army!"

"More than a sword?" I said.

"Oh yes!" he said, with great emphasis. "You might get off the field alive without your sword, but not without your shield." I nodded. The soldiers of my own city had famously voted to abandon Greek equipment and copy Roman arms, especially the Roman shield which gave excellent protection, was remarkably light for its great size, and above all gave tremendous confidence to the user. I know. I had fought behind one.

"So!" said Morganus, and looked round the courtyard where we had first come into the works. There were guards posted at all the doors, the managers stood shifting and surly, and smoke boiled busily from the factory chimneys. "That was interesting," he said. "But what did you learn, Greek?"

"Nothing," I said. "Except that the Roman shield is a technological marvel."

"It is indeed," said Morganus, and I looked at the office building from which the managers had emerged when we arrived.

"Shall we see if the clerks have found anything?"

"If there is anything wrong they will find it," he said. "They know this factory. They buy shields for the legion."

"Excellent!" I said, "Presumably the trade is highly regulated?"

"Very much so! These are vital munitions. The number of shields made is checked by inspectors from Government House, and the records stamped. And no shield can be sold, or loaded into a cart or a ship without stamped records, and the carriers and shippers are licensed and inspected themselves, and the numbers sold are checked against master files, and so on, and so on."

"Good!" I said. "So let's see."

So we went inside and received a disappointment. Our clerks were in a huge, open office with slaves stood in one corner whispering to one another, and staring narrow eyed at our men as they busily went through the company's documents. On sight of the swan crest and the bodyguards, the slaves nudged each other, shut up, and stood straight as we entered, with the management crowding in behind us.

"Sir!" said Silvius, the clerk optio, and stepped forward and saluted.

"Well?" said Morganus.

"We found nothing, honoured sir."

"Do you need more time?"

"Well yes sir, indeed sir, we've hardly started. But ... em."

"But what?" said Morganus, and the optio glanced at me.

"It just don't look like they're hiding anything, sir." He nodded at the slaves. "They're angry and they're rude, but they're helping us. Like they've got nothing to hide and want to rub our noses in it."

"Very good," I said. "Very observant."

"Thank you sir!"

I took Morganus aside.

"First of all, that optio, Silvius, he's a good man. He's been looking at faces, not just books, and that's good."

"So what?"

"So now I'm going to have a go at *them*." I looked at the managers standing glowering nearby.

"Tread carefully, Greek."

"Bah! They've already decided to make trouble. Look at them."

"Still tread carefully."

Which I did not. I approached the senior management and bowed politely. They nodded back. It was easy to pick out the leader.

"Might I have the pleasure, most honourable sir, to have a few moments private conversation?"

"Take care, boy!" said the man. "I am a citizen, and so are all my colleagues."

"Yes!" they said, all together, and their freedmen and slaves nodded angrily..

But he walked a few paces with me and I whispered to him.

"I am investigating three murders with the full authority of the army and of his Grace the Governor!"

"Gods save Him," said the manager nervously.

"Men will die to answer for these crimes," I said and stared straight into his eyes looking for his reaction to my next words, "and I know exactly what you are doing here."

"Nothing!" I said later, as we marched back to the fort.

"Not from any of them?"

"No. You saw me put the same challenge to all of them, didn't you?"

"Yes."

"Optio Silvius is right. There's nothing going on here. Not a twitch or a flicker did I see. Well ... they're fiddling their taxes, but everyone does that! No. They weren't guilty, not of anything serious." I sighed. "They make shields. They export them all over the Empire. It's big business, it's licensed by the state, their records are clean, and now they're all going running to their patrons to complain about us."

"I warned you," said Morganus.

"I know. It can't be helped," I said. "Come on, let's find out where that lawyer went. *He's* certainly up to something and he may know why the Syrian was killed." So we sent the legionaries and clerks back to the fort, and went to the house of Dolbius the lawyer, with just the bodyguards.

This house too was an apartment, but as different as could be from the house of Severus. It was set in a huge, exclusive block of the most modern design. It had a vast, ground-floor atrium, entered by wrought-iron gates, guarded by liveried, gold-collared slaves, and opening out into a hall that rose three storeys high, with a huge, open compluvium in the roof, letting in light to a noble stairwell of imported marble, with spouts at roof level in the shape of native Britannic herons, to send rainwater through their long beaks into the impluvium below. The impluvium was of marble, furnished with bronze frogs and more herons, constantly sprinkled by a fountain.

The inside walls bore elegant lamps in brackets, and mirrors and paintings all fitted out in the most immaculate taste. It was obviously designed by Greeks, it was entirely lacking in vulgar ostentation, and it was immensely pleasing to the eye. Meanwhile the janitor was bobbing and bowing and leading the way to the house of Dolbius, which was one of the biggest, on the first floor. The doors to the apartment were polished teak with bronze fittings, also heron shaped, and the doors were already open with slaves bowing as we came up the stairs.

Just before we went in, I looked round the first-floor landing, which was most beautiful. There were three other apartments, one in each side of a square, and the architects had lavished yet more care on an entirely different shade of marble for each wall, with scented plants in huge Samian pots beside the doors. The plants were roses, imported from the far east. The place was magical, and I realised how wrong I had been to become an engineer and not a lawyer.

We were shown into an atrium, somehow contrived to have its own compluvium, open to the sky through the floors above, and furnished in entirely different, but harmonious taste, to its big brother down below. But the apartment was very obviously closed up and empty. Just a dozen slaves were in residence, and dust sheets were everywhere, and the furniture chained and locked. The slaves stood in three rows of four, repeatedly bowing in unison, like a stage chorus, until Morganus told them to stop.

"Now what?" said Morganus.

"Just to be sure," I said. "Can we get the lads to search every room? Just in case we're being made fools of and Dolbius is still here?" He nodded at looked at the slaves.

"You will speak to them, I suppose?"

"Oh indeed I will!" I said, and turned towards them. "Which of you is the senior?"

A woman bowed. A fat, neat-faced creature with extremely good clothes, silver bangles and an elaborately fashionable hairstyle. Even her toe nails were gold leafed, and gleamed brightly out of her expensive sandals. There were many citizen wives in the town not half as smart as her.

"I am Justinia, your honour," she said, in clear, classical Latin. "I am housekeeper to my honoured and learned master, Tullius Quintillius Dolbius."

"Gods keep and save him!" said the rest.

"Gods keep and save him," I said. "And now, be so good as to follow me Justinia the housekeeper, while the rest of you stay here and do not move."

"Yes, honoured sir."

I found a room, closed the door, and stood Justinia where plenty of window light shone upon her. She was rather younger than I had first thought, and perhaps more plump than fat. She was quite a well-formed woman. I let her stand for a while, until she blinked and shifted, and nervously touched her hair as if to straighten it. Then I tried as before.

"Justinia," I said. "You have lied to others. Do not lie to me. I know exactly where Dolbius has gone, and why he has gone there. I offer you now the chance to tell the truth."

I stopped. I needed to say no more, not for the moment, because I could see in her face that I had struck a vein of gold finer than any that Nepos the miner would discover with his high-pressure jets. Justinia the housekeeper was full of lies and secret knowledge.

"Will you sit down, Justinia?" I said, finding a chair for her and another for myself. I settled down with my most bland and harmless expression, and a small, quiet, unchallenging voice. "Do make yourself comfortable," I said.

Chapter 17

"Cogidubnus," I said.

"Cogidubnus the third," said Morganus. "It was his grandfather, Cogidubnus the first who built the palace." I frowned.

"Palace?" I said, "What sort of palace were the Celts building in those days? That must have before the invasion." Morganus smiled.

"It was," he said, "and it was a proper palace, because *we* built it!"

"What? Romans? Before the conquest?"

"Oh yes. And Greeks. Engineers like you."

"Sixty years ago, in Claudius' time?"

Morganus frowned and corrected me.

"The deified Tiberius Claudius Caesar Augustus, Britannicus," he said, respectfully.

"With his stammer and his feeble mind," I said. Morganus frowned.

"Can you not control your tongue?" he said. "But yes. Him."

I reached for the wine and Morganus looked at me, irritated. So, I took a piece of bread instead. We were sitting in the atrium of Dolbius's apartment, with refreshments provided by his slaves. The bodyguards and the slaves were in the kitchen, the atrium was beautiful and, once again, I was living like a millionaire; and this time one with good taste.

"So even *before* the invasion," I said, "you Romans were over here cultivating the local tribes, making friends, and building palaces for them?"

"Yes. It's amazing how the tribes like central heating, with glass windows and baths," he grinned. "We had the Regni and the Artrebati on dog leads before ever we put boot on beach! We had their leaders anyway. They were the ones in the palaces."

I nodded. It was like rebuilding a shattered vase. Morganus was adding the pieces I had not picked up from Justinia and the other slaves. The visit to Aquae Sulis was fiction. Dolbius had left suddenly, without warning, and gone to the palace of Cogidubnus, King of the Regni tribe, near the town of Noviomagus Reginorum, sixty miles down the Great South Road.

A thought came suddenly.

"Were Dolbius' family in the construction business?" I said.

"They were and are," said Morganus. "They are well known for it."

"So his family could've been doing business for three generations with the family of Cogi … Cogid …" I stumbled over the word. "Cogidubnus?" Morganus helped me out.

"It's Cog Iprog Dub Ellianos, in the original Britannic," he said. "It means *the shining, faithful and powerful lord*."

"Hmm," I said. "Cogidubnus will do nicely."

"But you're right," said Morganus. "Just building a palace isn't enough. It has to be maintained. And the tribes can't do that for themselves. They can't make glass or sewer pipes. And, of course, they'll want to expand and develop. The Regni are very wealthy, they have copper mines, corn and cattle."

"And Dolbius' wife? Would she be a Celtic aristocrat?" I asked.

"Yes. If she really is Cogidubnus' sister."

"That's what Justinia, told me,"

"Then she has royal blood," he said, "as do his children."

I spoke carefully.

"But, to Romans, to *some* Romans, having a Celtic wife means…" I hesitated. "It means you've gone native," he said, looking me straight in the eye. "But, in my own case, the-lady-my-wife, who was born of the Artrebates, is now matriarch and domina of a Roman household who wears the stola and honours the Emperor!" He brushed the matter aside. "So why did Dolbius run? Him and his wife and children and their body slaves. *And* their family strongbox."

"Well," I said, "the slaves he left here don't know, so I'm afraid we'll have to go and ask him. Just when my backside has recovered from the ride to Aquae Sulis. Can we order up another lightning?"

"It will take a day or two," said Morganus. "They are in constant use." He looked at me seriously. "And, you should know, Greek, that if we go to this palace we are outside Roman jurisdiction."

"Oh," I said. "Is it a client state down there?"

"Yes. All foreign policy is in the hands of Rome, and they must ..."

"Honour the Emperor, pay taxes, and raise no army."

"Correct."

"But they may keep their laws, enjoy their traditions and worship their gods."

"Yes," he said. "I see you know the words."

"I do. My own city was a client state. In Graecia Minor."

"I know," he said, and he looked away with much unsaid, which I already knew, and which I did not wish to raise at that moment.

"So," I said, "it'll be a few days before we can have a lightning? Never mind, there's plenty still to do in Londinium. To start with I want to speak to Badrogid again."

"Why?"

"Because he's stepped straight into Scorteus's shoes, with or without being named as the heir; and, of everyone we've met, he had most to gain by Scorteus's death. Apart from Scorteus's son of course, and I don't think he could kill a mouse."

"Oh? Do you think Badrogid killed Scorteus? His own brother?"

"He wouldn't be the first one," I said. "Not where the brother stands in the way of an inheritance." I thought about it. "But no. Not him personally. I can't imagine Badrogid creeping in and out of a bath house without being seen. But who knows? Maybe there are others involved."

So we went to the House of Scorteus where, as before, we were received by Agidox and his boys, I asked for a private meeting with Badrogid, speaking as politely as I could to Agidox whom I was still trying to treat as a colleague. But, I should have known better. With Morganus and the bodyguards behind me, Agidox took my request as a command. So he trembled and I soon discovered that it was not just me that he was afraid of.

Badrogid received me in Scorteus's study, which by comparison with recent experience fairly shouted at me for its over decoration, being crammed and jammed with priceless ornaments and rare books, and nothing matching anything else. It was pure Scorteus. He had loved it.

Badrogid scowled fiercely as I entered. He never moved, nor did I expect him to for neither protocol nor good manners oblige a man to stand to greet a slave. But the look on his face went further. It said that he would be damned across the Styx and beyond before he would acknowledge a thing like me. Obviously he was offended at being summoned and, from his point of view, who could blame him? I was a slave and he was a millionaire. Or at least he looked like one. He was dressed in the silk robe again, and sat in Scorteus's favourite chair behind Scorteus's desk. Meanwhile I closed the door on Morganus and the bodyguards, having already warned them that I must see Badrogid alone, because he would never speak freely in front of Romans.

"So what is it *boy*?" he said, and put massive hands on the garish mosaic of the desk top in front of him. "It's bad enough having Roman spears at my door, without taking orders from an arse-licking Greek." I ignored the insult, concentrating on the fact that he'd said *my* door, as if *he* were the dominus, not his nephew. Which told me how I might sting this proud, arrogant and self-righteous man.

"Was that silk gown left to you in the will?" I said.

His eyes bulged, his fists clenched and he was half out of the chair with rage.

"Watch your tongue, boy" he said, and I stabbed again.

"Did you not get anything at all? Were you very disappointed?"

"You crawler up Roman bumholes!" he said. "Do you think I don't know about you? Going round the town as if you were one of them?" He was sweating and blinking. He was dangerously near the brink already, which was too soon, and I had to damp down the fire. So I bowed low, stood in a humble, shoulders-bent posture, with my hands clasped before my breast, and spoke in a gentle voice.

"Honoured brother of my late master, gods-rest-his-soul."

"Huh!" said Badrogid, "rest his soul," and he sat down again.

"What I was seeking to say, O honoured uncle of my new master, was …"

"Get on with it, boy!"

"… was that, perhaps, my late master, entirely by some unintentional error or omission, *perhaps* did not provide for you quite, entirely, as a beloved brother might have expected?"

"Huh!" he said. "You can say that again!" After that it was like fencing with sharp swords, only more dangerous, as I stung him repeatedly to make him rave, then cooled him down, fired him up again, and kept the words pouring from his mouth, which indeed they did, leading step by step into utmost indiscretion, because it was childishly easy to get him to talk. The difficulty was controlling his temper.

"So tell me, again, what did you expect," I said, "from the will?"

"Huh! That bugger promised me the lot!" he cried

"What bugger would that be?" I said.

"Don't you swear at me you bastard Greek! I mean him! My brother!"

"Scorteus?" I said.

"Yes! Said I should have it all. He promised me!"

"But he preferred the young man. A son beats a brother does he not."

"Go to hell! It wasn't that. Nothing to do with it!"

"So what was it?"

"None of your business, boy."

"Think I can't guess?" I said.

"You smarmy sod. You Greek. What do you know about the old religion?" That made me jump. We had skidded, as if on ice, and were sliding in a new direction, way beyond mere family matters.

"But you kept this … er … *faith*?" I said.

"Don't you tell me what I did and what I didn't do, you cock-sucking Greek! What d'you know about faith? Faith to the oak and the mistletoe?"

"If it's that important then why didn't Scorteus keep the faith?" I said. "Wasn't he the eldest son of a princess of the Ic …?" I never quite said the word. It was a hot iron in Badrogid's flesh and he was ranting in Britannic, fists clenched, eyes rolled up, and head back, and then suddenly it was not ranting but clear speech. It was paced, deliberate, rhyming speech, although highly idiomatic in the Britannic language. Such that I completely failed to understand him and translated only later, by remembering the sounds, and with Morganus's help. Morganus's most uneasy help, since he suspected the words were powerful in the old Britannic faith, most likely some invocation, or statement of faith.

"*Oak and ash, hart and hind, fox shall bark and ivy bind,*" said Badrogid, and having declaimed these sacred words, he looked at me and his anger boiled. "Iceni?" he said in Latin. "You say Iceni? Then hear me, for I am no Silure. I am no tight-fist traitor like my brother. I am Iceni, and I will bathe in Roman blood!"

Then his face went white and his lips went black as he realised how much he'd said, and who had made him say it, and the desk flew over as he leapt forward, charged like a bear, and seized my throat, yelling spit and fury into my eyes as he strangled me with mighty hands. Which task he very nearly accomplished, with me flat on my back, crushed under his weight, with lungs heaving in futile agony and eyes bursting. Then the doors slammed open, the bodyguards charged, and they heaved and battered Badrogid off me, and he went completely manic and tried to fight the four of them in a tumbling, hurling mass of limbs that smashed a fortune in ornaments and ripped the Chinese gown from neck to hem.

Inevitably it ended with Badrogid unconscious on the floor and Morganus calling off the bodyguards, who rose staggering, gasping, heaving and dripping sweat on to the floor, and painfully getting their breath back. Which I thought that was the end of the matter, but was not.

"What do you want to do sir?" said one of them. Morganus reached down and pulled me up from the floor, where I was sat rubbing my neck.

"What do *you* want, Greek?" he said. "We'll say he pulled a knife. There's nobody here other than us." I looked at Badrogid, on his back with the blood bubbling out of his nose, and I looked the senior bodyguard as he picked up his sword which had fallen from its scabbard in the fight. He took a good grip of the hilt, felt the point, and looked at me. I felt sick.

"Leave him!" I said. "And, in Hades' name, I want some wine."

This time we did find a wine shop, a good one with good wine, and I did order a large flask and helped myself, whatever Morganus thought. But Morganus was puzzled. He sat looking at me and made no attempt to take wine. Not even a sip.

"Why not?" he said. "That was a capital offence, attempted murder."

"No," I said. "Criminal damage."

"Oh," he said, "Of course."

"*People* get murdered. Slaves get broken. We're property."

"Sorry Greek," he said. "I keep forgetting."

"Never mind," I said, "Because there are five citizens and one slave to give witness that Badrogid wilfully attacked Roman soldiers wearing the Emperor's uniform, and that constitutes high treason, which *is* a capital offence!"

"Ah!" said Morganus.

"Ah!" said the bodyguards.

"I'll write and tell him," I said, "so that he knows when he wakes up. I think we'll be going back to that house and we'll need to control him, which now we can. We can have a knife permanently at his throat."

"Good," said Morganus. "So let's drink some wine." Which we did. "So what did we learn?" he said later. "From Badrogid?"

"How much did you hear?" I asked.

"Most of it, once he got shouting."

"Yes," I said. "And what worries me is that he's so full of anger that it might cover the guilt."

"What guilt?"

"I can't tell. That's the problem."

I thought about it. Badrogid was angry at me for my rudeness, which was not surprising. But he was also angry at his dead brother for breaking faith. As I have said, my gift seldom makes me happy and now it told me that Scorteus had broken a solemn promise to his own brother, which was not something I wanted to know. But my feelings were irrelevant. What mattered was that Badrogid was so angry at Scorteus, whom he saw as a traitor to family, clan and religion, that he might feel no guilt in acting against his brother.

I told Morganus all this.

"But Scorteus was only acting sensibly," he said. "He feared that Badrogid might use his fortune," he paused, and lowered his voice, "in some evil cause."

"You mean rebuilding the Iceni nation?"

"No," said Morganus, and took a real gulp of wine. "He can't do that."

"Why not?" Morganus refilled his cup. He sat quiet, thinking deeply. Then he spoke.

"When we were on the lightning going through tribal land."

"Yes?"

"We were safe."

"Were we?"

"Yes. And do you know why?"

"No."

"Because of what Rome did to the Iceni, as an example to the tribes."

"What was that?"

He paused again for a long while.

"There are no Iceni. Not any more."

"I know you defeated them in battle."

"So do I," he said. "I was there!" I could see there was more, but I didn't ask, for fear of learning something else I did not want to know. But Morganus told me anyway.

"After the battle," he said, "we went from village to village and house to house." He looked at me. "Do you understand?" he said, and I nodded, but he sat with head bowed. "It was done for the good of the Empire," he said. "For the peace of the Empire and it was the right thing to do." Those were his words, but the truth was plain on his face. He was ashamed. "I was young then," he said. "I had no family. No understanding, and I did as I was told."

"But what about Caradigma?" I said. "Doesn't she have the tattoo mark of an Iceni princess?" I touched my cheek. "And Scorteus and Badrogid? They're her sons. So aren't they Iceni?"

Morganus thought about that.

"Some survived," he said. "Some few. But those that did had to hide. That's why Caradigma and her sons pretended to be Silures from Wales." He took another drink. "But believe me, Greek, the Iceni nation is gone."

"So why are you worried?" I said. "What's this *evil cause*?" He took a breath, he gathered strength, and deliberately made the bull sign as he had in Aquae Sulis.

"I mean," he said, and whispered a word that made the bodyguards shudder, "I mean *druids*." I had seen this before. The demon reputation that the old Britannic priests have with Romans, as if something vengeful is hidden outside the cities, beyond the Roman world; something primeval that springs from the lakes, the forests and the soil. I knew that Roman civilians felt like this, but not their soldiers. Yet here were five of their finest: armed and armoured, conquerors of all the world, in broad daylight in a busy, chattering wine shop with the bar girls giving them the eye, but afraid of a word.

"Why do you fear them so much?" I said.

"Listen," said Morganus. "Forty years ago we thought we had wiped them out. We levelled the sacred groves in Anglesey which were the heart of their religion, and we killed every one we could get hold of, for the vile things that they did. You read history, you must know that." I nodded. The druids practised large-scale human sacrifice, among other atrocities; thus, the druidic faith was banned under Roman law, and all persons supporting or encouraging it were punished with death.

"Yes," I said. "I know all that."

"But," said Morganus, "we never got them all, and we still have teams hunting them down even now, and I doubt very much you knew *that*!"

"No," I said, and neither did the bodyguards, who looked on with round eyes.

"And listen to this, Greek, and listen well. There was a time, many years ago, when I was an optio, and we had one of them." He lowered his voice. "A druid. We had him in a cell, ready for a neck stretching in the morning. And do you know what happened?"

"No," I said.

"No," said the bodyguards.

"He walked out of the camp in army kit."

"What?"

"A soldier took him his last meal. That soldier stabbed the two jailors, let the druid out, took off his kit, and stabbed himself. Then the druid walked out of the camp, in the soldier's kit, straight past the guards. I saw that myself. I saw a man in full army gear walk up to the guards, and talk to them, and then walk straight on." He paused and took another big gulp of wine. "And yet, when I challenged the guards, they said nobody had passed out of the camp!" He looked at me. "Ikaros the Apollonite, you are the cleverest man I have ever met. You may be the cleverest man in the world. But don't tell me not to fear the druids." The others made the bull sign with shaking hands. But Morganus wasn't done. "So," he said. "What if Badrogid wanted his brother dead? What if he had the help of druids and had a pact with them to use Scorteus's money in their service?"

"Go on," I said.

"Well in that case we have the answer to our first question. How did somebody get into Scorteus's bath house and cut his throat and get out again without being seen?"

"Yes?" I said.

"Yes?" said the bodyguards.

"It was a druid," said Morganus, "and druids can make themselves invisible."

Chapter 18

So, once again, we were talking of magic. This time druidic magic, which profoundly horrified Morganus and the bodyguards, but fascinated me because it offered an explanation of the conflicting facts of Scorteus's murder. Although this had to be set against my personal opinion that magic works, if it works at all, only in a strange way, in a dark place, in a corner. But that was only my opinion, and most people believed in magic. Morganus certainly did, and he had travelled the world, learned by experience, and had undoubtedly told the truth about the druid he had seen walk past the sentries.

"You're magic yourself," he said, when I pressed him in the matter. "Right?"

"No!" I said.

"Listen to me!" he said, raising his voice. "I know your magic isn't like a conjuror's magic, or old witches howling the moon, or even girls with cloven tongues. It's not mumbo-jumbo magic, it's engineer's magic."

"It's not magic," I said "It's …"

"Listen! Imagine the world is like an artillery machine, wound up and ready to shoot. Right?"

"If you wish."

"Well. I've seen barbarians stand amazed at our machines, not knowing what to do with them. And I've seen them smash fingers and break limbs in trying to work them. It's easy to do if you're not careful, especially with the big machines, believe me! But along comes an artilleryman, presses the right trigger and the machine shoots. It does what he says, right?"

"Yes, but so what?"

"Well. You're the artilleryman. You know the triggers to press, and that way you make the world do what you say. You can do it ... and so *can the druids*!"

I gave up further argument and, anyway, what if I were wrong? What if druids could make themselves invisible? And how *do* pigeons find their way home if not by magic? And what is magic anyway?

The thought stayed in my mind for the next two days, which I spent at Morganus's house, while we waited for a lightning to pursue Dolbius the lawyer, and which welcome interval of peace I used to work on *The Business of Shields* in the Syrian's cipher tablets. But, the possibility of invisible druids was like a man whispering in my ear and who would not go away, which is my excuse for not breaking the cipher, though perhaps that is vanity? But I did get some idea of numbers, the numbers of shields involved, because most of the tablets were coded ledgers and the numbers were highly repetitive, leading to intuitive guesswork.

My estimate was that some thousands of shields were involved. Presumably sold by some means that got round the licensing and inspection procedures, although that was the least of all puzzles. I had no doubt that between them Scorteus and the Syrian could slip round any such defences, either by bribery or by cunning. This made me wonder why I had not been asked to solve this problem, and I was smitten with the risible, nonsensical, vanity of jealousy. If Scorteus faced a problem, the problem of getting round the army's licensing system for shields, then why had he not come to me? Why had he gone to the Syrian?

I smiled, having at least enough sense to laugh at myself. But then my question found an answer, and took the smile from my face. I guessed that Scorteus saw me as the clean side of his life, and the Syrian as the dirty side, which meant that Scorteus had a dirty side and was less honest than I had thought. So, what with that and his broken promise to Badrogid, I understood that my image of Scorteus was idealised and naïve, and the pain of disillusionment was yet another punishment for being too clever. It served me right for asking questions.

But I kept asking questions, because there were four hundred lives at risk. Indeed I moved on to an even bigger question. What had Scorteus done with these thousands of shields? What benefit could he have gained from an illegal trade, when he was already making a good profit selling them legally to the Roman army? And who would he have sold them to? Certainly not Rome's enemies, not when he had spent most of his life trying to become a citizen.

So I puzzled away until finally a lightning was ready and Morganus said farewell to his family, who most kindly said farewell to me as well. We took our luggage, seated ourselves in the big four wheeler and suffered the journey down the Great South Road. The road we greeted with ceremony as we rode out through Londinium's southern gates, and crossed the busy Thames bridge.

There we pulled to a stop, where the road began, beside the first Imperial milestone, and Morganus and the bodyguards dismounted while the driver sat to attention, holding the reins. Morganus and the bodyguards drew swords and raised them high, and the people on the road in their carts, and on foot, nudged one another, took off their hats and came to a stop, in respect of the army and the swan crest.

"Hail Claudius Britannicus!" cried Morganus and his men. "Imperator and Conqueror of the wastes beyond the seas!" Then they smiled, sheathed their swords and climbed aboard again.

"Drive on!" said Morganus, and the lightning moved off, as did the people on the road.

"What was that for?" I asked, over the clatter of hoofs and the grinding of tyres.

"Tradition!" said Morganus, with pride, and pointed ahead at the straight white line cut through the green countryside. "This road is historic. It was the first road ever built in Britannia, the one that took the troops inland from the invasion beaches. The army always salutes this road and the emperor who built it."

"Clau-Clau-Clau-Claudius?" I said, mocking the famous Imperial stutter. Morganus looked at me and sighed.

"Why do you say these things?" he said. "What's the matter with you?" And, he looked away.

Six hours later, not counting stops to change horses, we reached Noviomagus Reginorum, site of the original Roman invasion base, near Britannia's southern ocean. It was now dignified as a *Civitatis Capital*, a favourite Roman device to civilise the heathen. There was a dozen of these in Britannia, one for each major tribe, and built as its centre of government and taxation. This was all very neat and very Roman, except that some tribes, those whose souls were in the pastoral wilderness, saw no use in towns at all, and left their capitals as dust-blown, empty streets, whose few inhabitants were despised as traitor collaborators.

But not Noviomagus Reginorum, which was one of the most successful, being dedicated to the Regni, a tribal branch of the Artrebati who'd long since adopted Roman ways and delighted to live in grid-pattern cities with theatres, law courts and gladiatorial games. So we stayed that night at a decent post mansion and next morning drove on to the palace which was our destination, and which proved to be more astounding than any druidic magic because it was magic that worked in a wonderful way, in broad daylight on an open plain.

It was a wonder from the first sight of it, five miles down a side road, which curved around a low hill covered with mature trees that blocked the view ahead. I wondered why the army engineers had not cut through the hill in usual Roman style. But then we came round the bend and I saw that the curve was deliberately contrived to give sudden sight of what was beyond, such that even the horses gaped.

I know now that, if I were transported to Olympus and saw the Heavenly Hall of the Gods, I would be disappointed because I had seen better. I had seen the Palace of Cogidubnus, beside a river with its own, white-stone harbour full of dainty, painted pleasure craft. And, beyond that, the most enormous work of human labour had transformed an entire landscape into a garden, where trees grew like graceful dancers, where the land rolled in artful symmetry, and where granite and marble pylons gleamed against an utterly artificial, yet utterly pleasing, improvement on nature.

And that was only the surroundings. The palace itself sat in easy harmony with its landscape, which surprised me because I had expected the palace of a wealthy Celtic king to be flashing with glitter like the House of Scorteus. But not this palace, it was the soul of good taste. And second only to that was the surprise of its enormous size. It must have been nearly two hundred yards from wing to wing, with a superb pediment on marble columns in the centre, and adorned from side to side with tall and graceful statues. It was huge, dwarfing not only the Londinium Basilica but quite possibly any other building in the Empire, including even those in Rome. Morganus certainly thought so, and he knew Rome well.

"Gods of Olympus!" he said. "It's bigger than Nero's Golden House! And that nearly broke the treasury." He paused and shook his head. "And it's *better* too."

I had never seen Nero's notorious palace, but I could have guessed why the one in front of me was better. The design was Greek, pure Greek, and I who loved my own city will further admit that it was *Athenian* Greek. For while Sparta excelled in war and Apollonis in science, Athens had, and has, no equal in the arts. The palace shone white, silver and gold, a dominating yet harmonious part of its wide, green parkland.

I don't know how long we would have sat and stared, because the palace grew more lovely at every glance. But, one of the bodyguards leaned forward. "Honoured sir?" he said, and pointed.

"I know," said Morganus. "Drive on!"

"Yessir!" said the driver and shook the reins.

"Look!" said Morganus, to me. "There, and there." There were horsemen, tiny in the distance, one on either side of the white palace. One was waving a sword over his head. Then a distant rumble of hooves came to us over the shaven grass, as a troop of cavalry, about thirty horses rode round the corner of the palace and stopped beside the waving man. There was a faintly-heard, shouted conversation, then a horn sounded, the troop formed up in a double line, the horseman from the other side of the palace galloped to join them, the horn sounded again, swords flashed from scabbards and the whole troop charged towards us with screams, whoops and war cries.

"Stand fast!" cried Morganus. "Do NOT draw!"

"What are they?" I said. "I thought they weren't allowed an army?"

"They're allowed a house guard."

"Oh," I said.

"Don't worry," said Morganus. "I'm First Javelin of the Twentieth." He nodded They dare not kill me. Or my men." Thus the rumble of hoof beats grew louder and the bodyguards and the driver kept hands on swords, looking at Morganus who sat calmly looking at the horsemen.

"Then what do they want?" I said.

"To know our business," he said. "We came without notice."

They were nearly on us. Screaming mouths, staring eyes, kicking heels.

"We had to," I said, "or Dolbius might have run!"

Morganus laughed. "You just tell *them* that!" he said, shouting over the din.

Then the horsemen were whirling round us in a flashing circle of noise, horseflesh, gleaming blades and hard faces. It was dizzying and terrifying, which was precisely why they did it. It was the classic horseman's trick, to daze unmounted opponents. You cannot hit them with an arrow or spear, because they are moving, but they can hit you because you are not.

But there was no attack. A horn sounded loud in our ears, the troop wheeled off and formed up in front of us, blocking our path to the palace. Then a man rode forward and, in a swaggering gesture, he threw his sword flashing and tumbling into the air then caught it by the hilt with barely a glance, and ran it back into its sheath. He was bare chested in Celtic style and much tattooed in whirling flourishes. He had long, unbound hair and was close shaven with a large, drooping moustache and a young, handsome face.

"*LACHANIG!*" cried his men, calling out his name in an explosive, guttural shout, and sheathed their own swords. He came alongside the lightning, saw the swan crest and spoke to Morganus.

"I am Lachanig, Captain of my Lord Cogidubnus' war band," he said. "And who are you that comes armed, without permission, into my Lord's domain?" It was slow, ponderous Latin, because he was thinking in Britannic and then translating.

Morganus stood, and bowed politely, and replied in fluent Britannic, too fast for me to follow. Captain Lachanig showed surprise at this, and a conversation followed, which ended with our being escorted to the palace, with Lachanig ahead and horsemen trotting on either side of us.

"What did you tell him?" I said to Morganus.

"The truth," he said. "Isn't it you that says *the truth is invincible*?"

"Oh," I said, wondering when I had said that to him. Soon we were dismounting before broad steps of white marble, leading to an entrance like that of a temple, guarded by six massive columns, and yet more men in arms. This time some thirty foot soldiers who reminded me of Badrogid, because they were kitted out in a millionaire's dream of Celtic gear: long swords, oval shields sheathed in bronze, horned helmets studded in precious stones, thigh-length mail, and elaborate arm bands and neck rings, plus the inevitable long moustaches. Captain Lachanig chattered loudly in Britannic at the commander of these men, presumably passing on what Morganus had told him about us. The officer nodded, then gave us a surprise. He roared out a command in Latin, and these Celtic warriors came to attention like legionaries. They stamped three times and gave honour to Morganus, with a snapping, simultaneous eyes-right. Then the commander stepped forward and kissed Morganus's hand.

"Leonius Morganus Fortis Victrix!" he cried, with a beaming smile. He was older than Morganus, equally scarred, and he was fat and walked with a heavy limp. He wore the same kit as his men, but he was pure Roman.

"Aulus Magrix Drusillius!" said Morganus, and embraced him like a brother. Then they stood smiling at each other and shaking their heads. "What billet is this then for an old soldier?" said Morganus, looking at the palace.

"A very good one for an old cripple!" said Drusillius.

"What cripple? I see only the drill master of the Twentieth!"

"Long ago," said Drusillius, and looked admiringly at Morganus's four bodyguards. "Useful lads!" he said. "Wish I had men like that!" Then he saw me. "And whose is the boy?" he said, "Surely not yours, Morganus?" I was getting used to that from Romans, and tried not to be insulted, as did Morganus, because he seemed more irritated than I was. But he explained me with careful politeness, which was just as well because Drusillius proved a great ally in dealing with the torturous protocol of a Celtic court, the first requirement of which might otherwise have stopped us right there at the door.

"I'm sorry old comrade," he said to Morganus. "But I must ask you and your men to surrender arms before you enter the palace." The bodyguards gasped, seized sword hilts and looked to Morganus, who frowned and looked closely at Drusillius.

"Is this necessary?" he said. "You know who I am." Drusillius shook his head with much embarrassment and regret.

"I can't let you in with blades," he said. "It'd be my head on a stick."

Morganus took a deep breath. "Do you give your word for our safety?" he said. Drusillius stood to attention and made the bull sign.

"I swear on the blood of our faith," he said, and Morganus slowly nodded, and unbuckled his sword and dagger. He gave them to Drusillius, who kissed them and passed them to one of his men.

"You too!" said Morganus to the bodyguards and the driver, who followed his example with utmost reluctance. Then Drusillius showed true Roman efficiency. He got rid of the horsemen, dismissed his guards, found a slave to take our driver and vehicle to the stables, and led us through acres of magnificent, marbled splendour filled with exquisite works of art and an army of slaves; then across fairyland gardens to his own quarters near a huge and elaborate bath house. Drusillius asked about our mission as we walked, and finally he led us into a suite of rooms with excellent furniture and a staff of slaves waiting to serve. He lived in great luxury and boasted of it.

"We've got it all here," he said, "Central heating, wine from Gaul ..."

"Oh?" I said. Drusillius said nothing but looked at me and his face said, "*What's it to you, boy?*" Morganus saw the expression.

"As I mentioned," he said, "Ikaros the Greek is my colleague. He sits with us, eats with us, and drinks with us." Drusillius nodded, and smiled at me.

"No offence, Greek," he said, "If it's all right with Morganus, it's all right with me." Which indeed it was not. His expression told me that. So we sat round Drusillius' table, all of us, and the wine was indeed from Gaul, and Drusillius explained how he would help us.

"You'll have to see *Himself*," he said. "Cogidubnus! He'll know all about you by now, 'cos the slaves have seen you and they'll have told him. But you can't just go straight in. You're not even *here*, properly until you've received hospitality. That's slept the night and been fed, see? And then you have to pass messages in and out, in proper ceremony, and Himself has to reject you three times, and then you get in. But, don't worry, I'll do all that for you."

"Thank you," I said. "And what about Dolbius? Is he definitely here?"

"Yes. He's here, with my-lady-his-wife, and the little 'uns."

"Good!" I said. "So when can we see him?"

"Not today," said Drusillius. "As I say, you have to sleep the night before anything. But I'll get you to see him tomorrow." I frowned.

"Will Dolbius know about us? From the slaves?"

"Oh yes," said Drusillius. "Everyone'll know." I looked to Morganus.

"We've got to stop him running," I said.

"Can you do that?" said Morganus. "For me and the Twentieth?"

Drusillius nodded. "Yes," he said, "I can do that, 'cos there's politics here you wouldn't dream of. Like in Nero's time or Caligula's. Himself thinks all his relations are trying to kill him to take the throne, and he's right because they are! That's what I'm here for. He can't trust one of his own to lead the house guard, and there's a constant cavalry patrol around the house, so nobody can sneak up with a few likely lads and some daggers."

"What about the cavalry?" I said. "Their commander was a Celt."

"Pretty boy, Lachanig? The ladies' darling? That's himself's nephew. His security in case *I* turn bad! But pretty boy and his men aren't allowed inside the palace without permission and, if do they come in without it," Drusillius mimed a sword stroke, "then *my* men chop *his* men!" he said. "That's Celts!"

"So how does that help us?" said Morganus. Drusillius grinned.

"Easy! I tell pretty boy there's another plot in progress, and he'll believe it 'cos it happens all the time, and nobody's to leave the palace till I say they can. And that's the job done, see?"

Which it was. So we spent the rest of the day being shown round the palace, with slaves bowing and scraping, and ourselves being watched constantly, at a distance from windows and corners by curious persons, women as well as men, in elaborate Celtic dress who observed protocol by covering the lower part of the face with their robes.

"That way they haven't seen you, see?" said Drusillius. "Remember you're not really here yet, see? But they've all had a little look, haven't they?" He nodded. "Himself'll be one of 'em."

"Cogidubnus?" I said.

"Yeah. He always has a look."

Later we visited the baths and had an excellent meal with excellent wine in Drusillius' quarters, and slept comfortably in a large bed chamber, except for the four bodyguards. They each produced a small dagger routinely carried hidden, and proceeded to bind blankets round their left arms as improvised shields, preparing to stand watches through the night. Morganus tried to stop them, but the senior bodyguard dared to argue with the First Javelin. The driver was with us, and he stared in amazement at the sight, his eyes flicking from Morganus to the bodyguard and back again, as if he were watching a play.

"There's no need for this," said Morganus. "Drusillius has given word."

"But, honoured sir, we're responsible for your safety." The others nodded.

"If they want to kill us, they will," said Morganus. "We're greatly outnumbered."

"But how could we face the legion, if you were killed, honoured sir?"

"You wouldn't have to. You'd be dead!"

"Of course, honoured sir, but we'd be bound in duty to leave a decent number of *them* dead too." The other three bodyguards nodded, as if at a statement of the obvious.

"Huh!" said Morganus, and gave up. Perhaps he gave them this small victory, knowing that a greater defeat would follow. Drusillius had already explained, privately, that the bodyguards could not possibly accompany Morganus and me about the palace.

"That'd be political, see?" Drusillius had said. "Any: *formed body of Roman troops*, even four of them, would be: *a demonstration of Roman occupation*. And that's banned under the treaty."

"Who says so?" said Morganus.

"Himself!" said Drusillius, "And you're standing on his ground."

So, next day, just Morganus and I met Dolbius the lawyer, and then His Majesty King Cogidubnus III and, for two entirely different reasons, my gift failed to work with either of them; while someone else, every bit as skilled as me, worked his own gift upon us.

Chapter 19

Dolbius agreed to meet us in one of the many gardens inside the palace grounds. The building itself consisted of four wings, laid out like the sides of a square, enclosing a huge open area lined by colonnades. This open area was filled with fountains, statues, hedges, and mature trees, artfully laid out to form a complex of small private spaces. Drusillius led us down the maze of pathways, and stopped at a gate in a high hedge that enclosed the garden we wanted.

"He's, in there," he said quietly, then bowed and left. He seemed a good friend, helpful but not getting in our way. So I forgave him his attitude to slaves, which was quite normal after all, and not some vice particular to him.

Then, as we entered, I thought of my conversation with Morganus about men with Celtic wives, because Dolbius had really, seriously gone native. He was sitting on a bench eating nuts and apples from a bowl, wearing full Celtic dress, even including trousers which Romans regard as the quintessence of barbarism. He looked up and smiled at us, perfectly comfortable in his clothes. He was telling us that he was at home in this puppet state, while we were foreigners and interlopers.

To make sure this nail had been comprehensively knocked in, he had his wife and children on display. Three little boys, aged about two to five, were playing with bright-coloured wooden toys, while his wife sat rigidly on a stool to his left rear. She wore rich, Celtic jewellery and had a small tattoo on her cheek. Not an Iceni horse this time, but something else, and she was thin, hostile and plain. She had certainly not been chosen for beauty.

"Leonius Morganus Fortis Victrix!" said Dolbius, formally, and he stood and bowed.

"Tullius Quintillius Dolbius!" said Morganus, and bowed in return. Whereupon Dolbius sat down again and nodded briefly to acknowledge me. I expected him to introduce the lady, but he did not, not from first to last. Celtic custom I presumed. She just sat on her stool and followed every word with sharp intelligence. I never even found out if she spoke Latin, but I suspect that she did.

So we held a most odd and unsatisfactory conversation. Morganus and I spoke standing, Dolbius spoke sitting, and he munched through his nuts and apples without offering them to anyone else, including his family. Perhaps it was rudeness, perhaps the normal behaviour of a Celtic paterfamilias. I did not know. He tried to speak to Morganus not me, which may be because he knew my reputation. Or perhaps he just did not want to speak to a slave. In any case, Morganus would not have it.

"You know my colleague?" he said.

"Colleague?" said Dolbius, raising eyebrows. "Yes. We have met. He is Ikaros the engineer, once owned by my late patron, Fabius Gentilius Scorteus, and now owned by his son Fabius Gentilius Fortunus."

"Ikaros speaks for me," said Morganus, "and for his Grace the Governor!"

"Gods save His Grace!" said Dolbius, and looked at me. "So?" he said.

And so I tried, and so I failed. I failed because Dolbius was a lawyer, and a very good one, and he had behaved as lawyers do, taking fastidious care to know nothing that he should not know. Thus a lawyer who interviews his client, before defending him in court, never asks the client if he is guilty. He may ask 'why were you seen holding the knife?' He may ask 'why were you in the house where the murder took place?' But he never asks 'did you stab your wife's lover?' So it was with Dolbius. But that was merely his first line of entrenchment. The second line was a carefully constructed story which left his client, and himself, saved of all blame. He was so good at it, and had been doing it for so long, that whether or not he actually *believed* the constructed story was irrelevant.

I could see that from his face and responses, but I could not see what he had chosen not to know ... because he did not know it! As I keep saying, I do not work magic. So all I got was his well-prepared, finely-polished responses to questions he had long since anticipated.

"... no, I never intended to go to Aquae Sulis. My slaves mislead you.

... my visit here was long planned. Again, I apologise for the error of my slaves.

... I know nothing of Scorteus's business that is not public knowledge.

... I have no special connection with the unfortunate Syrian.

... I feared no danger in Londinium. I came here only to visit my family.

... yes, His Majesty is the brother of-the-lady-my-wife."

The nearest I came to success was early on in the conversation with an exchange about the Syrian's hidden tablets. I went straight into this without warning.

"Oh, about *The Business of Shields*," I said, "I've broken most of the cipher. If you'd give me the book, the one it works from, it'd save me a lot of trouble." His eyes widened and his smile faded. Just that and no more, and the trick did not work again. He had not thought of that one. But he had thought of everything else.

Later we tried to find our way out of the garden. This proved difficult because it was indeed a maze.

"Drusillius said *just keep turning left*," said Morganus.

"Hmm," I said. "We've seen that tree twice before."

"So what about your famous geometry?" said Morganus, "drilling through mountains?"

"As useless as my mind reading," I said. But we got out in the end, and stood in one of the long, elegant colonnades.

"So what did we learn?" said Morganus, looking at the lovely gardens.

"Nothing we didn't already know," I said. "Except that Dolbius knows about the shields and the cipher. Or maybe just the shields. I don't know." So we found a slave to direct us to the guard room and rejoined Drusillius, the bodyguards and the driver.

Then we waited, while Drusillius sent messages in and out of His Majesty's chambers in our name, and we were rebuffed the statutory three times before being granted an audience at dusk.

"That's good," said Drusillius. "Dusk is auspicious, see? They worship the sunset do this lot. It means Himself likes you." We nodded. "So what d'you want to do for a few hours?" He turned to Morganus. "I could show you my lot drilling. They'd like that. I've told 'em about you." And then I thought better of Drusillius, because he thought of me, "And you could see Himself's library, Greek. It's s'posed to be good."

Which indeed it was. It was one of the most interesting private libraries I have ever entered because there were books in Britannic Celtic. A wonderful revelation because the Celts were supposedly illiterate before the conquest. But this library had books written in ink on parchment, using characters that were entirely novel to me, and distinct from any other language I knew. Thus Britannic was not set down in phonetic script like Latin, Greek or Hebrew, but in pictographs like Egyptian or Chinese. It was tremendously exciting and a tragedy that I had not time to study the books properly, since some of the characters, for instance those for man, horse or water, were obvious in meaning in contrast to the alien *sounds* of Britannic words which, as I have said, give no clue to the Mediterranean ear. I was still deep in fascination, trying to understand more, when a house slave entered, whispered in the librarian's ear and the librarian politely reminded me that the time of audience with His Majesty was approaching.

Soon after I was in Drusillius' quarters, where the bodyguards were buckling Morganus into his armour which they had been polishing all afternoon.

"Here," said Drusillius. "Real special honour from Himself!" He handed Morganus his sword and dirk. He smiled. "But it does mean I'll have to be all round you with some of my lads." Morganus nodded approval.

"We'd do the same," he said, and Drusillius smiled gratefully. They were getting on very well these old comrades.

"Now here's how it works, see?" said Drusillius. "I take you in, you get announced, see? You stand where I tell you, and you don't look straight at him, see? You *never* look at Himself. You stand to his left and look past him"

"You mean Cogidubnus?" I said.

"Yes," said Drusillius. "You never, never, look him in the eye, see?"

"Then how do I speak to him?" I said. "*Can* I speak to him? As a slave?"

"No," said Drusillius, "Not you or anyone."

"What?" said Morganus. "Can I not speak?"

"No! Nobody speaks to Himself. You speak to Maligoterix."

"Who's he?" said Morganus, and Drusillius paused as if searching for words.

"We'd call him," he said, "we'd call him," he blinked, "the Lord Chief Justice, probably. Yeah." I glanced at Morganus, because Drusillius was not telling the truth.

"Is that his actual title?" I said. "Lord Chief Justice?" Drusillius affected not to hear, so I repeated the question and Drusillius looked at me reluctantly.

"He's head of law and tradition," he said, "and he's chief adviser to Himself."

"What does he do here?" I asked, "Maligoterix?"

"He speaks for the king," said Drusillius, "and you speak to Maligoterix, and . Maligoterix speaks to Himself. Then Himself speaks to Maligoterix and Maligoterix speaks to you. See?"

"That's not what I meant," I said. "Morganus, I don't like this." I felt that something was wrong and Drusillius confirmed it by looking away and saying nothing.

"Is this man an enemy?" said Morganus. "Are we in any danger?"

"No!" said Drusillius instantly. "You've been given hospitality. That means your lives are sacred in this house." That was true, I read it from his face, where I also saw that Drusillius had wriggled around the real question. But Morganus was satisfied. He smiled at me.

"Brace up, Greek!" he said. "What are they going to do? Butcher us and start a war?" He turned to Drusillius. "Do they know the legion knows we're here?"

"Oh yes," said Drusillius.

"There you are then," said Morganus. "So let's get on with it."

So Drusillius took us out into a big courtyard, in the fading light, where two dozen of his Celtic guardsmen formed up and led us, at a very Roman quick march, tramping across the marble and mosaic floors of long corridors and great halls, to the gates of the throne room where another dozen guardsmen levelled spears and gave challenge. We stamped to a halt while Drusillius bawled out the formal words that stood the gate guard at ease and swung open the great doors.

Then we marched in, with the guardsmen around us, and we halted some ten feet in front of a man who stood alone in long white robes, belted with a length of plain, white rope. He had white hair and a white beard, which were beautifully combed into waves over his shoulders and chest. He stood with hands clasped within the depths of sleeves, with cuffs so long that they draped to the floor, and he wore a crown of plaited oak leaves.

He stood in the middle of a surprisingly plain room, lined with pillars of oak trunks, still with bark attached, under a dome with an occulus that let in the light of the setting sun. Other guardsmen stood by the oak pillars and others to our right where we must not look directly. There, on the edge of my vision, I could just see the figure of King Cogidubnus sat on an great chair, with slaves, favourites, and more men in white standing round him. Even if we had looked straight at him we would hardly have seen him, for he was enclosed in a ring of courtiers and there was an active, busy murmur of conversation among them as they pointed at Morganus and me, and spoke behind their hands as if in secret.

There followed another long and formal challenge in Britannic, with Drusillius giving the responses and proclaiming our names, Morganus'ss anyway, and then there was silence but for the shifting sandals and rustling robes of the courtiers.

Then the old man in white stepped forward. He came very close. All peoples have their chosen distances at which one man is comfortable speaking to another, and these differ considerably. Thus Celts step far closer than a Roman or a Greek, and I saw that the old man was not old at all. Indeed I spotted that as soon as he moved, for he did so with the vigour of a man in his prime. He was not old, but one of those who is born without colour in his skin or hair, and whose eyes are pink. He was a man of great physical presence, confidant, dominant and bold. He came close enough that I could hear him breathing and, to my astonishment, I heard Morganus take a deep gasp and shiver in fright.

I am Maligoterix," said the robed man, speaking directly to Morganus in excellent Latin. "I am the voice of My-Lord-His-Majesty-the-King, and you are the spear of the Twentieth, hero of legions, who is joined with an Artrebate, bound to a slave, and was pierced by the Greeks … *here*," he said. He raised a finger and pointed towards the ballista scar hidden within Morganus's helmet. Then he turned to me and spoke excellent Greek. "And, you are the magician." He gave a tiny smile at the word. "You look behind eyes, bring sleep, cut mountains, drink from a snake, and who failed this morning, and who fights for a house of four hundred."

Then he looked back at Morganus and said the same things over and again, putting a distinct rhythm to his words, before switching to Britannic and declaiming as if reciting poetry, with a pulsing, soporific metre and rhyme, such that, soon, Morganus was standing with his mouth gaping open and his eyes closed. Had he been awake instead of asleep on his feet, he would have declared that Maligoterix was working magic.

But I knew better because, in my city, there was a temple dedicated to the goddess Panacea, where medicine was practised on the Hippocratic principles of observation and experiment. It was here that the drug had been invented which I prepared for the German girl. But the temple had another technique which blocked surgical pain, and which was also used to treat despair, depression and illnesses of the mind. The technique was named after Hypnos, divine incarnation of sleep, and was called hypnosis.

So, when Maligoterix turned his attention to me, which soon he did, he failed because this technique works only by consent or by stealth, and it works far better on some individuals than others. Thus, it works very well on a man who has never even heard of it and perceives no threat, but it does not work at all on one who knows exactly what is being attempted, and fixes his mind against it.

So that is what I did, and I claim no special distinction in resisting Maligoterix, whose face first showed impatience, then puzzlement that my eyes did not close, and then anger when pride and vanity overcame good sense and I grinned and shook my head. It was a foolish and intemperate thing to do, but I could not help it because he was so puffed up in his arrogance. My guess is that he was a master of the art who had never failed before, and seeing my little smile he reacted with an explosion of temper.

He stopped his chanting, stamped his foot, snarled in rage and cursed me in Celtic, with the spittle running into his beard. But then he stood straight, looked me in the eye and amazed me with an honest, outright bow of respect. It was pure Celtic, because Celts are the very opposite of Romans. Celts give unhindered expression to their feelings, and they rant and rave and weep and sigh. They love their friends and damn their enemies and shout it to all the world. Which is exactly how Scorteus behaved, so it was very important indeed to remember that such open display of emotion did not make a Celt any less clever, any less formidable, or any less dangerous than a Roman nobleman with his rigid control.

Thus Maligoterix pondered briefly, glared at me with his red eyes, then snapped his fingers, summoning two men in white from the King's side. They were robed and bearded like Maligoterix, but their beards were black and they were young and muscular. They were like Morganus's bodyguards.

"Bring him!" he said, in Latin, then looked at the throne and without the least deference or respect. He beckoned sharply with one hand, and went out through a small door on the far side of the throne room. He did not even look back to see who was following him. But, King Cogidubnus leapt up from his throne and ran after Maligoterix, while the young men in white grabbed my arms and hustled me through the door. I fell into dread that I was being taken for something far worse than hypnosis. But the room I entered was not a torturer's workshop. It was merely a private place where private matters could be discussed.

It was also a very strange place to find in so modern a palace, because was a traditional Celtic roundhouse, about sixty feet across, complete with thatched roof, wattle and daub walls, a beaten earth floor, and a fire glowing in the centre.

It was built right next to the Palace, joined by a short passageway, and it was another idealised, fancified version of Celtic reality. Thus it was all immaculately clean, with perfectly-squared roof timbers, a copper hood and chimney pipe over the fire, and the fire itself laid in a beautifully-crafted wrought-iron basket, while the walls were whitewashed and painted in some modern artist's conception of Celtic hunting scenes. It was brightly lit by totally-incongruous Roman star lamps hanging from chains. It was a playroom where King Cogidubnus could pretend to be like his ancestors, without the fleas, hogs and smoke of a genuine roundhouse.

But, just now, His Majesty was not playing, because he and Maligoterix were standing next to the fire, yelling at one another. Cogidubnus III was a gangling, awkward man of about thirty, with elaborately braided hair, a wispy moustache and an odd mixture of dress. He wore several Roman tunics, each cut to reveal the differing colour of the one beneath, belted over baggy Celtic trousers of checked woollen cloth, and he was burdened with a greater load of golden ornaments that I had ever seen on one man. He wore three Celtic neck rings, bracelets up to the elbows, hordes of broaches and rings, plus a sword and scabbard that jingled and rattled with gold chains and ornaments.

And so he stood, stabbing a finger at Maligoterix, while Maligoterix yelled right back at him and stabbed in return with a long finger. I had no idea what they were saying because it was all in rapid Britannic, but I could see that it was a very personal argument between old enemies, with much past history and old scores to settle. Or perhaps they were old friends, because they finally fell silent, glowering at each other, and certainly never came to blows.

"Bah!" said Maligoterix, and he pointed at me, said something curt, then advanced towards me with Cogidubnus at his side. They came together, as equals, proving, if ever it had been in doubt, that Maligoterix was something far more than a Lord Chancellor.

As before, Maligoterix came right up close, as did Cogidubnus who smelled strongly of perfume, and the men holding my arms kept me fixed to the spot. Cogidubnus yelled at me. He was red faced and sweating and I did not understand a word.

"Latin!" said Maligoterix.

"Oh," said Cogidubnus, switched languages, and jabbed a finger at me. He did not hold back as he had with Maligoterix, but jabbed right into my chest with vicious force. "You! Slave!" he said. "We can't touch the others, but you're no more than a horse. We can do what we like with you. Do you understand?"

Chapter 20

"No!" said Maligoterix. "You cannot say that, and you cannot do that. Not if he were a horse or even a dog. Not when he has eaten your bread and slept under your roof."

Cogidubnus stamped and growled. He ignored me and yelled at Maligoterix.

"I say different!" he cried, "and I am King!" But Maligoterix sneered and mocked.

"King, he says? And when his time comes, and the king enters the tomb of his ancestors, does he cherish hopes of the joyful life beyond?"

"Yes!" roared Cogidubnus, and Maligoterix smiled.

"And who shall perform the rites to pass you beyond the tomb? Who shall save you from the loathsome pit where serpents writhe and spiders crawl?"

Faced with that truth, Cogidubnus lost his temper and yelled at Maligoterix, while Maligoterix calmly stood with his hands in his sleeves and waited until Cogidubnus had exhausted his rage, and had groaned and sighed, and finally admitted by reluctant, resentful looks, that he had lost the argument. For such is the power of faith and such is the fear of hell.

Cogidubnus hardly spoke after that, but stood chewing his knuckles and uttering sighs. The rest of the conversation was between myself and Maligoterix, and it was a most fascinating conversation since, having failed with his own method of interrogation, Maligoterix was intuitively using mine. He was a clever and perceptive man and studied my face as intently as I studied his. It was a match between two gladiators.

Maligoterix spoke first.

"You have heard my truthful words," he said. He said it in Greek, and Cogidubnus who could not follow, objected and seized Maligoterix's arm. But Maligoterix gave a Gorgon stare, and Cogidubnus let go the arm, with profuse apology, which Maligoterix accepted with a sneer, and wagged a finger to indicate that Cogidubnus should fall back a pace.

"So!" said Maligoterix and looked at me, and continued in Greek.

"You and your Romans are guests of this royal house," he said, "and will leave tomorrow, safe and unharmed." I nodded, but said nothing, because silence is very persuasive in causing a man to say what is hidden in his mind. So we stared at each other for a while and Maligoterix stepped so close that his nose almost touched mine. He was worrying and wondering.

"What are you?" he said. "Are you a holy man among your own people?"

"No," I said. "I am an engineer."

"Yes," he said, impatiently. "We know all that," and he stared harder. "But engineering is mere mechanics. You have greater powers. You are a necromancer. So what creed do you serve? What doctrine do you worship?"

"I try to be a Stoic" I said. "And what creed do you serve?"

"Ancient truth," he said. "Ancient power," and he nodded in profound satisfaction, confident in his faith, and secure in his determination to tell me nothing of it. So I quoted Badrogid. I quoted him in the original Britannic.

"*Oak and ash, hart and hind, fox shall bark and ivy bind,*" I said, and Maligoterix jumped as if stabbed, for he was caught out twice, first in surprise that I had spoken Britannic, and second that I knew words which, to him, were sacred, such that in his anger, he said a lot more than ever he would have chosen to.

"Do not try to be clever," he said. "Do not call on what you cannot understand. You do not know our power. Not when our faithful eyes and ears are everywhere, and our speech flies swift on the wind. Thus we know of the murders in the House of Scorteus, for he was a man to whom we had long since offered our hand, and who finally showed a true heart." Then he blinked and sniffed, and put a hand to his mouth, as if to stop his tongue, and he breathed deep and took control of himself.

"So, Ikaros the Greek," he said, "what are you doing here all unexpected?"

"I am here to question Dolbius the lawyer," I said, "about the death of Scorteus."

"Dolbius?" said Madrogid, sneering. "That go-between? That know nothing who takes care to know nothing? Do you expect me to believe that in order to drink from an empty pot you came accompanied by the First Javelin of a Roman legion?"

"Yes," I said. "The honoured Morganus is my mentor. Did you not know? You who know everything?" He snarled and turned nasty. "Now listen well, slave. We may not harm you here and now; but, if you lie, we will know and then we will come for you. We will hang you from a tree, and we will open your belly and remove your bowels with infinite slowness."

Thus began a long conversation with Maligoterix checking and cross questioning my every word, searching me for some hidden motive that would be a threat to himself or his king. But, as he did so, he unwittingly passed back information to me, because I turned my answers into questions whenever I could and because, clever as he was, Maligoterix was a Celt who showed his emotions very clearly, and was surprisingly easy to read.

Eventually Cogidubnus got bored, sent out for food and drink, sat down at the table and single chair brought in by servants and, like Dolbius with his nuts and apples, he consumed the whole lot himself. Soon after that they let me go because Maligoterix had long since concluded that I was telling the truth, and had persisted in his questions only until he was sure that the fact had sunk into the lesser brain of his majesty King Cogidubnus III.

So they led the way into the throne room. I was pushed after them, and there was a great rustle and clatter of men jumping to their feet, who had been sat on the floor for hours. Morganus, who was already standing, was blinking at me in fearful anxiety, and I tried to reassure him with a smile, as Maligoterix gave orders, and Drusillius and his guards stood to attention before leading Morganus and me back to his quarters.

But there Drusillius left us. He left us quickly, scuttling out with hasty and mumbled excuses, with the guilt plain written on his face for taking us before Maligoterix without proper warning, and Morganus glaring at him for the traitor that he was. Or perhaps Drusillius was a loyal servant of a new master? Who can say? But he never dared look at Morganus, while the four bodyguards and the driver, were on their feet, staring at the haggard face of their First Javelin and wondering what had happened to him.

As soon as Drusillius left, I put my hand to my lips, found a tablet and wrote the words: '*Say nothing. Spies listening*'. I showed it to Morganus and the others, and he nodded. But they frowned, and I saw they could not read cursive script. So I wrote the words again in plain capitals which they understood, except the driver who could not read at all, but the eldest bodyguard whispered in his ear and he nodded. Then Morganus reached for the tablet. He wiped out my words with the flat end of the stylus and scribbled swiftly. '*Are we in danger?*' he wrote, and put a hand to the pommel of his sword, which he still wore because Drusillius had not disarmed him, probably too ashamed to do so.

'No,' I wrote. '*Celtic laws of hospitality.*' Morganus took the tablet.

'*Will they let us leave tomorrow?*'

'*They will insist that we leave.*'

Morganus sighed and looked at me, and I could see how much he wanted to talk, and how much he distrusted everything here, including the laws of hospitality. Because, by signs and example he put us on guard: him with his sword, the bodyguards with their daggers and the driver with a stolen kitchen knife. Finally, Morganus offered me his *pugio*: his military dirk. It was a serious weapon, almost a small sword, with a blade a foot long and three fingers broad.

"Here," he said. "You were a soldier once." I looked at him and hesitated. Under Roman law we were about to commit a capital crime: him by giving a weapon to a slave and me by accepting it. But I took it because here we were not under Roman law and, more important, it would have been unthinkable to refuse so vast an expression of trust.

And so we spent a miserable night, sat on stools looking at one another to keep awake, with no peace, no rest and no wine. The only grace was that it was a short night, with few hours left until dawn, at which time the House of Cogidubnus sent us on our way. We did not see Drusillius, Cogidubnus or Maligoterix again, although doubtless they were peering from their Celtic corners. Instead we were politely hustled out by slaves backed by guardsmen. The lightning was ready outside the front steps of the palace, with our horses rested and fed, our remaining weapons aboard, and the vehicle surrounded by Captain Lachanig and his riders. As a final courtesy we were given food for the journey: meat, bread and fruit, and a cask of beer, and were escorted off His Majesty's land, and back to the Roman road.

Lachanig and his men took us around the hill that hid the palace from the road, and there he led them forward in a thundering gallop, then wheeled them round to come back past us with swords drawn in salute, before disappearing round the hill in a cloud of dust and war cries, while our driver looked to Morganus for orders.

"Get us away from here!" said Morganus, and the driver thrashed the horses, while Morganus stared at the road and said nothing. The bodyguards stayed silent behind us. After a few miles, and safe on the Roman Great South Road, Morganus put a hand on the driver's shoulder.

"Stop here," he said, "For breakfast."

"Yes, honoured sir!"

"You five may eat while I talk with the Greek gentleman."

"Yes, honoured sir!"

So we stopped and the bodyguards and the driver got out the food and sat on the grass beside the road, which in usual Roman fashion was cleared of shrubs and trees for a hundred paces on either side against ambush. Then Morganus led me far enough away that nobody could hear us, and stood looking at me, doing his Roman best to control the fear and guilt within him.

"What did he do to me, Greek?" he said, "and did anyone see it, other than you?" He paused and spoke with hesitation. "My honour is stained," he said, "and that of the legion with me." He bowed his head, then looked back at the bodyguards and the driver, "What do they know?"

"Nothing," I said. "They weren't there, were they?"

"No," he said.

"So what did he do to me?" he shuddered. "He was a druid wasn't he?"

"Yes," I said, and Morganus made the bull sign. He was deeply troubled by what had happened and deeply ashamed.

"I remember looking at him," he said, "then nothing else until I was standing in that room with the oak trees, and everyone else was sitting on the floor." He sighed, and took off his helmet with shaking hands. "And how did he know about this?" he said, pointing to the scar in his cheek. I got it from …"

"I know how you got it," I said. "The bodyguards told me."

"But how did *he* know?" Morganus frowned desperately. "What happened in that room, Greek? And where did you go? When I woke up you'd been somewhere hadn't you?"

I nodded and I told him everything, and tried to reassure him. He listened very carefully and tried to understand. But, in the end, he shook his head.

"It's magic, whatever you say, druid's magic."

I sighed. "But do you believe me when I say that he can never do it to you again?"

"Do you give me your word on it?" he said, and I smiled.

"He tried it on me and failed, didn't he?"

"Only 'cos your magic is better than his."

"Just believe me," I said. "And if ever he tries it again, him or anyone else, then say a poem, or sing your legion's battle anthem, or count to a thousand. Anything."

"Ah!" he said. "As a drill? I can do that!" He smiled, and I felt as if I had exorcised a demon, which feeling I almost believed because superstition is an easy bed of dreams, while rationality is a mountain to be climbed. But, in any case, the demon was gone and Morganus was immensely relieved.

"Give me your hand."

So, we shook hands, then Morganus put on his helmet, straightened his back and took refuge in another drill, the drill of familiar words. "So what did we learn?" he said.

"A great deal," I said. "First of all, the druidic faith survives and flourishes in Cogidubus' kingdom."

"Which it won't be once I've reported back to the legion!" said Morganus.

"I'm not so sure," I said.

"Why not? I could take that palace with a cohort, never mind a legion."

"I don't think they'd let you."

"Who?"

"The Provincial Government. Rome itself."

"Why? The druids are illegal. It's death even to deal with them."

"Morganus," I said, "you can't be the first Roman to visit that palace. Anyone who goes there must see what's going on. They weren't even trying to hide it. I think Rome allows it because there is political advantage in having a tame Celtic state that's loyal to the Empire."

He thought about that and nodded. "You could be right," he said, "It's an example to the rest of them."

"Let me talk a bit," I said. "And think as I go."

"Go on then," he said, and I tried to arrange facts into patterns.

"Maligoterix is a druid and very great one," I said. "He knows a lot about you and me, he knows about Scorteus's murder, and he knew about it before we even got to that palace."

"How do you know that?" he said.

"Because he wasn't expecting us and had no time to find out about us. He already knew about us because he was already interested in Scorteus. I think they'd tried to recruit Scorteus through Badrogid who was already in their power. But they're not fools. They'll have seen what a sort of an idiot Badrogid is, and it wasn't really him that they wanted. They wanted Scorteus with his millions." I looked Morganus forcibly in the eye. "That means it wasn't the druids that killed Scorteus. They wanted him alive!"

"Yes," he said. "But *how* did they know about us? About what happened in Londinium and Aquae Sulis? And about my scar, and you meeting the snake girl?"

I took a guess. "I think there's an underworld of native Celts, all over Britannia, that are still loyal to the druids. I think they have spies listening behind doors and passing on information. It's just like slave gossip, except that it's being collected and channelled. Perhaps it's their way of still fighting against Rome."

"But how do they tell Maligoterix what they know?"

"How about pigeons with messages? He said their speech *flies swift on the wind*, and the Celts can write. I saw their own written language in Cogidibnus' library. It's not like Latin or Greek, but it's writing." Morganus frowned. He thought about what I had said.

"You're suggesting a system that works right across Britannia. But that would mean planning and organisation. How could they set that up behind our backs?"

"They wouldn't need to," I said. "I think it was always here. The druids have been in Britannia since time unknown, and ruled over the native tribes. I've read that a druid could stand between two armies and stop a battle. They've always had great powers."

"Jupiter, Juno, Minerva!" said Morganus, with a deep frown. " I saw pigeon houses years ago, when we burned the sacred groves in Anglesey."

"The druids' sacred place?"

"More than that. The centre of all their magic. They had pigeon houses there. Lots of them, just like the one we saw on top of the tax office."

"That's it then," I said. "That's how they do it."

"Yes," said Morganus. "And this magic of the mind, that you Greeks invented, well it looks like the druids have it too. So at least I know how that druids, years ago, walked past the guards." He shuddered. "And to think I actually saw him at it. I saw him speaking to our lads, working this ... this ..."

"Hypnosis," I said.

"Yes," he said. "I suppose he did it to the others as well, and it was him that killed them." He shook his head, then thought of something else. "What about Dolbius the lawyer?" he said. "What does he know, and what's he afraid of?"

"The honoured and learned Dolbius?" I said. "He was the go-between that contacted Scorteus for the druids, Badrogid too. Which, as you say, means death under Roman law. Which is why he ran to his brother-in-law's kingdom which is beyond Roman Law."

"What about the Syrian, and the business of shields? Does Dolbius know anything about that?"

"No," I said. "Maligoterix says he takes care not to know dangerous things, and I am inclined to believe him." But, there my imagination failed. I tried to take the next step in solving this complex matter, but could not.

"What is it?" said Morganus.

"I'm tired," I said. "I've not slept."

Morganus smiled. "Isn't that normal for you?"

"Yes, but I think there's something more. Something I can't grasp."

"Perhaps you need some wine?"

"We've got some beer," I said, and he laughed.

"Come on, Greek. Let's have breakfast."

We found the bodyguards sitting round a fire they had lit, with food carefully laid out for Morganus and me, and two horn mugs ready by the keg. They had eaten and cleared away, and they stood as we approached and stamped heels in salute. But they were young men who could not hide their bleary-eyed tiredness. Morganus looked all round. The view was clear for miles and the Caledonian revolt four hundred miles to the north.

"You may sleep by turns," he said to the eldest bodyguard, "with one on watch."

"Yes, honoured sir!"

So Morganus and I sat down to eat, and I forced myself to drink beer, because even beer is better than nothing.

"So how much did we really learn?" said Morganus, and I sighed.

"Very little," I said. "In fact we've hit a dead end. I was hoping for something useful from Dolbius."

"So what do we do?"
"Go back to Londinium and start again."
"What does that mean?"
"I don't know. I'm tired. We'll have to see."

Chapter 21

The bodyguards and the driver slept a few hours, as did Morganus, while I sat with a cloak around me and tried to find solace in beer. But it was not to be found, not from one end of the keg to the other. The thin liquid simply filled my bladder then stung me to get up and empty it just when I was falling asleep; not that I really could have slept in daylight sitting on grass. It is hard enough at night in a decent bed.

Then we were on the road again; the number-one, first-ever road in Britannia, and we drove without stopping, except to change horses, and were back in Londinium's legionary fortress by late afternoon. Then I had no excuse for not sleeping, not in Morganus's house, with Morganus's wine, and his family greeting me as if I were one of them. They were kind and friendly, and I fretted deeply that I was becoming used to their companionship, and I began to wonder how I would cope when I had to do without it, as surely I would in due course.

So I had my usual struggle when I tried to sleep that night, except that it was not quite usual, because things were bumping and knocking in the depths of my mind, trying to get out, and I was too tired to rest and could not compose my thoughts. But, as always with my perceived insomnia, I suppose I must have slept a little because a man dies if he is kept completely from sleep, and I certainly did not die. In the morning Morganus had the latest news from the expeditionary force. He told me as we took breakfast.

"A galloper came in last night," he said, "from His Grace."

"Anything special?" I said.

"Not really. It's routine. His Grace will be sending messages up and down the line throughout the campaign, and keeping Londinium informed."

"So what's happening?"

"He's two days march into Caledonia and sending out cavalry sweeps to locate the enemy. But no contact yet." I wondered what to say about these events. I was not a Roman. I came of a conquered race. Should I take sides in Rome's wars? But Morganus was looking to me for a response.

"Good," I said. "May fortune favour His Grace's endeavours."

Morganus smiled. He seemed relieved at my response. "So what do we do now, Greek?"

"I want to talk to Badrogid again about the druids."

Morganus sighed and shifted in his chair, uneasy as ever with the subject of druids. He shook his head.

"I doubt he'll talk about that," said Morganus. "I wouldn't if I was him."

"We'll have to find out," I said. "And I'll have certainly have to see him on my own again. I think he'll behave this time."

Morganus nodded. "Don't worry," he said, "I'll be waiting outside with the bulldogs."

I smiled, realising that that was what he called his four bodyguards. I had not known that before, because he never referred to them in conversation, probably taking them for granted as a natural privilege of his rank. But he saw my expression and frowned. "What's funny?" he said.

"Nothing," I said. "And we'll talk to Caradigma too. She may know something."

So we went again to the House of Scorteus, which of course was now legally the House of Fortunus. But it was the same house, with its same guard of auxiliaries, except that there were many more of them round the house than the last time I was there. The front-door guard stood to attention, in their mail coats, bronze helmets, and flat, round auxiliary shields, and they raised spears to salute Morganus. He waved his vine staff in return, and spoke briefly with their officer; the same Simonis Lartis I had met last time.

"Why so many guards, optio?" he said. "Is there trouble in the house?"

"Yes, honoured sir," said Simonis Lartis. "They are under great fear, honoured sir, and some of the young men keep trying to break out." He lowered his voice. "Some dozens of them tried last night, at the side door. They came armed with knives, all together like a charge of barbarians, with their women and children behind them with all their possessions in bundles, ready to run away." His face showed regret, even guilt, and I could see his sympathy for the wretched slaves. "So we did our duty, honoured sir. What else could we do?"

"Did any escape?" said Morganus.

"No, honoured sir."

When we went into the atrium. There was slovenly untidiness everywhere and the slaves were standing around in misery and dejection, or sitting in corners huddled together. They mostly ignored us, except for a few that showed open hostility, until Agidox appeared with his senior slaves, clapping their hands and shouting at the rest, and bowing to Morganus and me in obsequious humility. Thus the great mass of common slaves were sent off to whatever corners of the house they lurked in, and we were faced only with their seniors, who tried to behave as if everything was normal. Which it was not, because they had fear behind their eyes.

"Is Badrogid in the house, honoured Agidox?" I asked, when he stopped bowing.

"I regret, honoured sir," he said, "that the Honoured Badrogid has gone into the city with my young master Fortunus."

"Oh," I said. "What about the Lady Caradigma?"

Agidox bowed again and spread hands in apology.

"My-lady-the-Domina, is taken to her bed with the phlegm," he said, and I groaned at the mention of the Britannic phlegm, that hideous affliction that strikes every soul in that miserable island at least once a year. It is a debilitating disease, highly infectious, and especially dangerous in the winter when it kills off the old and the weak, and prostrates even the strong, inflicting harsh breath, a running nose, foul sputum and a burning throat. It exemplifies everything that is cold, nasty and miserable about Britannia itself, and I detest it as a frequent and highly susceptible victim.

Nonetheless, our journey was not wasted because I could see that Agidox had something to tell me. It was embarrassing at first, because Agidox, who now perceived me as a part of Rome's power, was trying to win my goodwill. It was a pointless and demeaning activity because I already liked and respected him, and it was depressing too, because it meant that he had so little trust in me that he could not assume I would do my best for him without persuasion.

"Your worships," he said, once he had explained about Caradigma. "Yourselves having graced this house with your presence, and my master being elsewhere, it would do me great honour to entertain you in my master's name." He said that with a graceful bow, reflected by the slaves behind him, then he blinked and looked at me like a delinquent hound pleading against the whip, because what he was proposing was highly irregular. The fact was that, however senior Agidox might be, he was a slave while Morganus was a Roman citizen of exalted rank. Thus the social gulf between them was infinite and they could never interact socially. The most that was proper was a formal conversation on matters of business.

I stress, incidentally, that while Agidox was speaking to me, I was irrelevant to this matter of etiquette because I was a slave and of no account whatsoever. I might as well have been in Africa or at the bottom of the sea. The only person who counted was Morganus, in his armour and swan crest, with his bodyguards behind him. He was Rome personified and, as Agidox of all people knew, if so prestigious guest were to be entertained while the dominus was absent and the domina unwell, then some kinsman of the dominus, or if all else failed a kinswoman, should have been found who could face Morganus with propriety.

Thus Agidox was taking a serious risk, especially as the real dominus of the house was not the meek and immature Fortunus, but his uncle Badrogid, who was a vicious, ignorant, abysmal snob. So Agidox displayed such nervous anticipation, and chewed his lip so hard, that I realised the half-baked incongruity of his invitation stemmed from his having taken a sudden chance. He had seized the unexpected opportunity of myself and Morganus being there such that he could talk to us in private. So I was curious. What did he want? I turned to Morganus.

"Honoured sir?" I said. "What is your pleasure?" But I gave a swift nod and Morganus saw the signal.

"We would be pleased to accept hospitality," he said. So Morganus and I took wine in Scorteus's library, where everything was tidy again and the broken ornaments replaced. That is to say Morganus and I took wine while Agidox stood back and bowed and smiled while his best girls, the ones with the swivelling hips, served us, from gold ewers, into gold cups and with napkins to wipe our lips. Then the girls were gone. Agidox, Morganus and I were alone, and the door was closed.

"So. Agidox?" I said. "Thank you for an excellent wine." He bowed. "But why are we here?" I prompted him with silence, and saw that he was working up courage. He had something to tell but was not quite ready. So I helped him. I stopped trying to be clever and just smiled. "Agidox," I said. "I have known you since first I came to this house, at which time I was in despair. You were very kind to me in those days, and I have never forgotten this. I cherish you as a friend and I respect you as a man. So how can I help you now?"

Agidox sighed. "I am not one who listens at doors," he said. "But often the dominus, the old dominus, would speak as if I were not there." I nodded at this obvious truth, and he continued. "For over a year past," he said, "there was a matter that greatly concerned the dominus and the Syrian. It was something dangerous," he glanced at Morganus then back to me. "I think it was something outside the law." He paused, weighing the possible consequences of what he must say. "And by that, honoured sirs, I mean seriously, dangerously outside the law. Do you understand?"

"Yes," I said. "Go on."

He nodded. "This matter had to do with Gentius Civilis Felemidus, who goes by the name of Felemid."

"Felemid?" I said. "Wasn't he Scorteus's greatest business rival?"

"Yes," said Agidox. "But then he became a friend."

"I know of him," said Morganus. "He's a Duovir of the Council of the Province, one of the two elected officials who lead it. He's deep in native politics, and enormously rich."

"Yes," said Agidox, "that's him," and his words came faster. "The dominus met him several times about a year ago, and after that he and the Syrian embarked on the business of shields."

"What?" I said, nearly jumping out of my chair. "What do you know about that?" Agidox gaped at my reaction and wrung his hands. "It's what they called it. The master and the Syrian. I wasn't listening. Not deliberately. I couldn't help hearing. And I don't know what it means. I just heard the name. It all started after the master met Felemid." I was fascinated and wanted to know more about the business of shields, but Agidox pressed on to what he thought was the important matter. "It was all connected with the main thing," he said. "Because the lady Caradigma and his honour Badrogid are faithful to …" He paused and his hands shook as he continued, "That is to say, Badrogid led the dominus …" His eyes went round and his voiced faded away. His courage was spent. But it did not matter. I knew what he was going to say because it was the mirror image of what I already knew. So I said it for him..

"Badrogid led him into the hands of the druids," I said, and he sobbed and fell to his knees. He went down with the ungainly, shuddering thump of a big heavy man whose joints carry a vast load, and he landed with his belly quivering and his head jerking forward, and he raised arms as if in prayer.

"I couldn't help it," he said. "And what could I do, once I knew? It would have been death or sending to the mines, and I have family. Help me! Help me!" He fell on hands and knees and crawled in his gross, fat awkwardness and tried to clasp my knees in supplication. It was horrible. I could have wept for the indignity of it.

We left the house soon after and I stood in a great muddle of emotions, outside the triple gates, looking at the house and its guard of auxiliaries who now saluted even me, let alone Morganus. I looked at Morganus and the bodyguards, who were awaiting my comments, which effectively meant my orders. After ten years of slavery I was behaving not just as a free man, but a man of power and influence. It was like being a senator again, in my own city, and the pleasure was unbearable because I knew that it would be taken away as surely as night follows day. Rome could not, and would not, allow a slave to behave like this, not for long anyway.

"Well?" I said to Morganus, "Aren't you going to ask what we have learned?" I said it with extreme bad grace. But he just raised his eyebrows.

"And aren't you going to ask for a wine shop?" he said.

"Yes," I said, defiantly. "But it had better be a near one, because we'll be back here later, but I need time to think first."

"Then lead on," said Morganus. "You're the expert on wine shops." So we found one, because indeed I did know all the good ones, and I sat down, and put my head in my hands until a flask and cups appeared. I looked up and saw Morganus facing me and the four bodyguards at the next table, sat up straight like good soldiers, carefully not paying attention to Morganus and me. They made me angry. Everything made me angry.

"So," said Morganus, "What have we learned?"

"Agidox wants us to save him," I said. "He knows Badrogid will kill him if he talks about the druids, but the law will kill him if he doesn't. And he's afraid I'll find out by myself, and he's a superstitious Celt who's terrified of druids."

Morganus looked at me and just about managed not to make the bull sign.

"Oh, go on and do it!" I said, and I made the sign. He shook his head.

"What's wrong with you, Greek?" he said.

"Agidox," I said. "He's a good man, and I was ashamed to see him grovel."

"Jupiter maximus! He wasn't grovelling, he was scared witless."

"Scared of what?"

"Scared of you! He nearly dropped dead when you guessed about the druids. Holy gods Greek, I nearly did myself, and I'm used to your magic."

So I drank wine until my mind steadied, and then we went back to the House of Scorteus-Fortunus, where I wielded the powers that had fallen upon me, by ordering Agidox to take me to Caradigma, in whatever condition she might be, just so long as she could draw breath.

Agidox bowed and led us to the women's quarters on the first floor, where he clapped hands and slaves threw open the doors to the domina's bed chamber. They did so without the least regard to their mistress's privacy, or what state of undress she might be in. I recalled that Scorteus had been just the same, showing no modesty even in his most personal moments because he, and presumably his mother, held the tribal belief that public and private life are the same.

As the doors swung, I looked into a broad, high room which, like Caradigma's atrium, was a temple to all things Celtic, where limitless money had deified a modest reality. Thus the room fairly shouted its wealth. The tall windows alone must have cost a fortune, being fitted with bespoke, bronze glazing bars that curled and curved in Celtic contradiction to Roman rectangles. The bright light of these windows illuminated a priceless display of ornaments which were dedicated to the organic wilderness of nature. Silver hares leapt, bronze stags fought, golden birds flew, and ceramic fish capered with flashing scales.

All this in cheerful innocence of the fact that Britannic art, without Roman industrial backing, could never have delivered artefacts on such a scale and of such complexity. Thus the effect, while beautiful, was fundamentally self-defeating because every Celtic item in the room had been made by Rome.

Furthermore, it was a great irony because the man who paid for it all, Scorteus, was more Roman than the Romans in the public areas of the house, while here in the privacy of his mother's chamber he was more Celtic than the Celts. Which made me think that perhaps this was not sentimental irrationality. Perhaps Scorteus was more loyal to his ancestors than I had thought. Perhaps more Celtic than I had thought.

And so we entered and were met by a wave of hot, damp, scented air, because all the beautiful windows were tight shut, while pots steaming of camphor and frankincense were bubbling over charcoal stoves to drive off foul humours and ease the sufferer's breathing.

Caradigma herself sat in a multi-coloured silken nightgown, propped up with silken cushions in a massive wooden bed. Slave girls stood attendance all around their mistress, bearing jugs and cups in case she should be thirsty, plates of food in case she should be hungry, plus a harp for music, towels to wipe her brow, and a large spitting sheet held ready to catch Caradigma's expectorations.

She was in the middle of a particularly, chest-wrenching evacuation as we entered, and hawked tremendously to empty her lung pipes, seemingly right down to her toes, before savouring the dredgings in her mouth, then discharging them with great force to hang like a yellow oyster in the sheet.

"Ah!" said the girls, and leaned forward to study what Caradigma had brought forth. Then they turned to look at Agidox, Morganus and me, then swept their heads back to Caradigma for her judgement upon us. They did not wait long because Caradigma screeched and pointed a finger at me and, throwing off her bed sheets, rose to her feet on the great bed and advanced towards me like one of the furies, albeit one with a red nose, watering eyes, and wobbling feet. Her girls darted forward to support her as she swayed, and she pushed their hands aside and stamped for footing on the soft bed and yelled at me in rapid and angry Britannic.

It was far too fast for me, but not for Morganus, who stepped forward and met her syllable for syllable, his voice steadily rising to tones of command, such that Caradigma plunged from anger to self-pity and sat down, and crawled back to her pillows, snivelled and wept, and allowed herself to be wiped over with towels and propped up, facing us, with a girl on either arm.

"What was that about?" I said to Morganus.

"Tell you later," he said, "Every insult imaginable upon your head for letting the Silanianum get out of its cage."

I sighed with remorse. I felt as if I were responsible. Morganus saw the expression. "Shall I tell her it wasn't your fault?" he said.

"If you like," I said, which he did. To my surprise the old woman calmed down, and nodded and chattered at Morganus.

"Huh!" he said. "She says she knows that, and she apologises."

"Tell her thank you," I said, "and will you please carry on translating for me?"

"Of course," he said.

"Good," I said, and looked at Agidox. "You may leave, and take the girls with you."

He bowed, beckoned the serving girls, and backed out of the room with them behind him, bobbing and nodding to their mistress as they went, all except for the two girls holding Caradigma's arms, because she whined like a child when they got up to go, and reached out for them with her voice rising towards hysteria. So I told them to stay, thinking it best to keep her calm, even with more ears present than I wanted. And in all these orders and commands I behaved as if I were the dominus himself, and knew for sure that such behaviour could not continue.

Then I conducted my first interrogation via translator, which proved surprisingly efficient. Morganus put my words instantly into Britannic, enabling me to concentrate all my attention on Caradigma as she reacted to the questions, then gave her answers which Morganus turned into Latin. It was at least as effective as a direct conversation, and possibly more so.

The only problem was keeping Caradigma's attention from flying off wildly to some subject of her own choice, because she was a strong-willed woman bred up to please herself. So there she sat, embraced in the arms of her two girls, who constantly cleaned her with towels as she sneezed and dribbled. And, all the while, she peered at me with wet and red-rimmed eyes, in snivelling self-pity intermingled with sparks of temper.

"Honoured mother of my late master," I began, and even before Morganus could translate, I received a spitting, froth of words in reply.

"She says ..." said Morganus.

"Never mind," I said, "I've got the general idea." Indeed I had, for she had obviously forgotten her apology and was accusing me again, using the word *Silanianum* repeatedly. "Ask her if she agrees with me that Mettorus is innocent," I said. He nodded, and spoke, then translated her response.

"She says she's heard what you think in the matter," said Morganus. "That's you Greek, and she says you're clever and she agrees with you." I took that as a compliment, and paused while Caradigma had another noisy, throat-clearing spit, and then I asked a series of bland questions about Celtic art, intending to put her at ease before coming to the legally-perilous matter of any connection between herself, Scorteus, and the druids. But I think Caradigma guessed where I was going. She frowned with alert concentration, and gave short replies to all my questions, as if seeking to be rid of the subject and move on. Then I came to my first real question.

"What do you know, honoured lady, of the ancient *faith* of Britannia?"

And, as soon as Morganus translated, I knew that she had secrets to hide, because she leaned forward with a smug smile and the same look of spiritual confidence that I had seen on the face of Maligoterix, and fairly poured out words which Morganus did his best to turn in to Latin.

"Faith?" she said. "What do you know of faith, and truth? Of the woods and fields and lakes?" Then off she went in a ranting mixture of poetry and rage, with Morganus barely keeping up, until she coughed and choked and stopped. But then she beckoned for a drink, which her girls gave her, then she snarled at me and picked up right where she had left off. And so she went on, with me barely having to prompt her.

Most of it was the rambling of a very old woman whose mind was irrational and prejudiced at the best of times, and who was now unwell and angry and afraid. But some of it, echoing through Morganus, was not nonsense. It was horrifying.

" ... they came to *us*. Not *us* to them ...

... he called them here. My son. It was him ...

... he said, we aren't many different tribes, but only one ...

... they blessed him for it, and I was proud of him at last ..."

With these few words I got my first clear insight into the business of shields, and my first evidence that Scorteus had been a traitor.

Chapter 22

I said nothing to Morganus until we were out of the house. I wanted to get outside, well away, and well clear of any ears other than his. I would have gone to a wine shop, but I realised that the wine shops would be useless for private conversation because they would be filling up with slaves guzzling cheap wine and native beer. I knew that as soon as we passed through the guard of auxiliaries at the triple gates and saw what was going on in the street.

"Ah," said Morganus. "Juno's geese." He stood to attention, removed his helmet and bowed respectfully, as a citizen in his toga went past leading half a dozen chickens by white ribbons round their necks and his family in their wake. The bodyguards and auxiliaries likewise removed helmets and gave honour, while the citizen, a local baker, acknowledged their salute with a wave of his hand and his nose in the air, because on this day with his birds in tow. He was the social superior even of a First Javelin, never mind boot-nailed grunts and auxiliaries.

I sighed in frustration as I saw other households emerging from their front doors on their way to the city's temples, to make sacrifice on yet another holy day. This one was in the name of Juno's sacred geese who had saved Rome five hundred years ago, when it was under siege by a Gaulish army. On one famous night, when the defenders lay exhausted, the enemy silently scaled the Capitoline hill, the last stronghold of the city, but the geese heard them coming and roused the Romans with their furious honking.

In eternal gratitude for this patriotic act, it could not be geese that felt the chopper on remembrance day, but only lesser fowl. Thus whole families were out. Paterfamilias with wife and children, and the slaves given the day off with enough money to get drunk, while paterfamilias himself drew the sacrificial offerings behind him, solemnly bowing to his superiors, nodding to his equals, ignoring the unworthy, and tugging at the flapping, clucking brood in his wake, because the greater the flock the more the honour. The whole thing looked hilarious to me, because of the contrast between swollen dignity on one hand, and strutting poultry on the other, pecking and squawking and shitting on the pavement. As I have said, I take no cognisance of Roman holy days, and they are a mystery to me. But Morganus, the bodyguards and the auxiliaries kept their helmets under their arms, and meekly fell back before the citizens and their fowls.

"Can we go somewhere to talk: where we can't be heard?" I said to Morganus, as he bowed to the latest clutch of birds.

"Where d'you want to go?" he said.

"There's a small shrine to Vesta the Home Maker, just round the corner," I said, pointing. "Nobody goes there anymore."

So we made our way round the growing procession and into another, larger street where there stood a small, brick-built temple, with cracked and rotting plaster, heavily scored with graffiti, and with weeds growing thick in its tiny precinct. The whole thing was not more than thirty feet square, with room for a mere handful of worshippers, and nobody paid it the slightest attention. The merry, noisy people who passed by on this festival day never even glanced at it.

"Sad, isn't it?" said Morganus.

"Three old freedmen paid for it," I said. "But they're dead now."

"You'd think someone would take over," he said.

"Can we go inside?" I said, looking up and down a street that was even more crowded than the last. People jostled past us, chattering and smiling and leading their chickens. "It's the business of shields," I said. "I know what it is, and I can't talk here."

Morganus instantly nodded and told the bodyguards to stand fast, while we trod a path through the weeds, where he stopped and looked at me.

"No," I said. "Right inside. Please Morganus." Probably I was worrying too much about eavesdroppers. But I was afraid of Maligoterix's informers, even if I could not see any, and I wanted stone walls around me when I revealed what I knew, or thought I knew. So we went into the shabby little sanctum, which smelt of damp and mould, and stale urine from all those disgusting persons who had used it as a latrine. The closed, brick space echoed and was lit only by light from the narrow doorway, since the eternal hearth flame was long dead from lack of tending. But the votive ornaments of silver stood before a sandstone image of Vesta, even if covered with spider webs, and the coins in the collection box lay safe beneath a shroud of dust. That was especially reassuring because, whatever other insults the temple had suffered, it had not been desecrated by theft, since stealing from a temple is an unthinkable abomination to all decent men, Greek, Roman or barbarian.

So Morganus and I raised hands and bowed to Vesta, and each added a coin to the box. Which is to say that he added two, one being for me because I had no money.

"Right," said Morganus. "What is it then, the business of shields?"

"It's Scorteus selling arms to the tribes," I said.

"*What?*" he said, horrified. "How d'you know?"

"Because Scorteus met the druids, here in Londinium. I think he met Maligoterix himself, and the meeting was Scorteus'ss initiative, his idea."

"Was it?" said Morganus.

"Yes. And he met them for a purpose, which must have been vastly important to him, because he was risking his life to do it, and I'll tell you what it was. When we were in Cogidubnus's palace, Madrogid told me that Scorteus *finally showed a true heart* and Caradigma's just told us the druids *blessed* Scorteus, and that Scorteus said the tribe – *aren't many different tribes but only one*. That's a declaration of loyalty, Morganus. It's a declaration of Celtic tribal loyalty. So, if the whole thing is called *the business of shields*, what else could that mean but Scorteus shifting allegiance and arming the natives?"

"Well that's it then," said Morganus. "It's an army matter now. We'll shut down that factory, put the slaves to the question, and arrest everyone else."

"Wait," I said. "I can't prove any of it. It's only my best guess. And worse than that, it makes no sense. Not when Scorteus spent most of his life chasing Roman citizenship. He was in paradise when he finally thought he'd got it. I know. I was there and I saw his face. So why should he betray everything he'd fought for?" Morganus sighed and shook his head.

"So where do we go from here?" he said.

"To Felemid," I said. "He's deep into this, according to Agidox." I looked at Morganus. "How soon can we see him? Can we just knock on his door or do we have to make approaches?" For once Morganus was unsure.

"I'll have to take advice from His Honour the Legate," he said. "Felemid is a big man in local politics. Celtic politics." He frowned uncertainly. "I know where I am with the Lord Justice and the Procurator because they're proper Romans. But Felemid? I don't know." He thought for a bit, and came to a decision. "We'd better see the legate," he said. "He's been asking about you anyway, Greek. I think he's impressed." So we went back to the fort, where I was presented to Nonius Julius Sabinus, Legate of the Twentieth Legion, which presentation was not an act carried out easily or lightly.

As ever, Morganus marched straight into the fort, with men stamping to attention on sight of him, and myself and the bodyguards following. Then we went straight down the main thoroughfare to the *Principia*, the Legionary Headquarters. The building dominated the main forum and was an absolute converse of the forlorn, abandoned little Temple of Vesta, because the Principia was huge and thriving and gleamed with worshipful attention. This because a Roman legion was a thriving community of thousands of men within whose ranks were found every mechanical trade known to mankind. There were masons, glaziers, plumbers, joiners, painters and the rest, and since they could not be fighting or training every hour of every day, they were kept purposefully busy in building. Then once they had built, they cleaned, polished and maintained.

In my opinion, indeed I proclaim it as obvious truth, the Roman army is the greatest civil engineering organisation in history, spending far more time on building than ever it does on conquest. Or perhaps the two are the same, since every inch of ground it takes the army stamps as Roman for ever, with walls, domes and arches built to last a thousand years. Furthermore, all those unfortunate souls who have had trouble with builders – builders who do not arrive on the promised day, builders who do not complete their work on time, builders who are rude and impolite – all those unfortunates who have suffered such pains, should contemplate builders who serve under military discipline, with centurions to kick their arses such that every task is completed to utmost perfection, because utmost perfection is the only way the Roman army knows how to build.

Thus the Principia of the Twentieth Legion was lavish and splendid. It was like a huge villa within tall, white-plastered walls and, being the heart and soul of the legion, even Morganus had to stop and be questioned at the heavily-fortified gatehouse. Even he had to bow low before the life-sized statue of the Emperor set in a niche above the entrance, with the letters LEG XX in gilded stone beneath His Imperial Majesty's feet.

Then a grey-bearded centurion stepped forward with a formal challenge, and a dozen men behind him, all twinkling and glittering in the dazzling polish of their kit, firmly blocking the gateway. They were men of the Legate's Guard, the elite of the elite, found from the first century of the first cohort. They were long-service veterans, scarred and decorated from at least twenty years service per man. Obviously they and their officer knew Morganus well, but there was a solemn exchange of passwords and questions until a runner could be sent into the building to beg an urgent audience with the legate. After that everyone relaxed and the centurion smiled.

"Will you join me in the guardhouse, O Leonius Morganus Fortis Victrix? It may be some while before His Honour replies."

Morganus smiled, the centurion led us through the gates, indicating the guardhouse door, where I suffered a moment of embarrassment because, while the bodyguards fell back, knowing the invitation was for Morganus and not them, I did not know what to do. But Morganus spoke.

"The Greek gentleman is Ikaros of Apollonis," he said. "He is in His Grace the Governor's service, and he goes where I go."

"Gods save His Grace!" said the centurion, but he did not like entertaining slaves in the guardhouse. Then he looked at Morganus's grim face and stood to attention and nodded.

"Be welcome, Ikaros of Apollonis," he said to me, although his eyes denied the welcome.

So we sat down and were entertained with tiny, formal cups of army wine, with tiny rolls and cakes, served by men of the defaulters company whose punishment included waiting at table, even waiting on a Greek slave. The guard centurion did not like that either, but he said nothing. Then as I raised my cup I felt the heavy pressure of Morganus'ss eyes on me to take no more than a sip of the wine. So I sipped and looked through the grid-lattice windows at the interior of the Principia.

There was a fine colonnaded courtyard, complete with fountains and a garden trimmed into geometric discipline, while at the far end the headquarters block itself rose to three storeys with a pediment and pillars like any great public building, except that everything looked brand new. It looked like that because limitless skill had kept it that way, and there were men busy even as I watched, with brooms and shovels and polishing rags. There was even one man, half naked and without his armour, standing in the fountain, scrubbing the bronze boar that incongruously spouted water into the pool, because a charging boar was the legion's iconic image. Meanwhile Morganus talked army small talk with the centurion. It was mainly about the latest news from the north.

"Have you heard they've made contact, honoured sir?" said the centurion.

"No," said Morganus. "I knew our cavalry was out. But that's all."

The centurion, glanced briefly at me and raised eyebrows to Morganus.

"You can speak freely," said Morganus. "The Greek gentleman is in His Grace's service."

"Gods bless His Grace!" said the centurion. "Well, they've found the buggers. Our cavalry burnt a few settlements and provoked an attack." He sniffed. "Quite a serious attack. We lost a lot of men."

"How many?" said Morganus.

"Most of a squadron. About two hundred men. They couldn't cut their way out because the enemy came in enormous numbers. Just a few of our Batavians got away."

Soon after that a runner arrived to summon us to the legate's personal office, and the guard centurion led Morganus and me to the headquarters block, past sentries on the doors, sentries on the stairway, and sentries at the entrance to a long corridor lined with small offices full of documents, cabinets and clerks. At the end of the corridor, I saw the legate and his staff in a big office spanning the entire width of the building. None of the offices had doors and there was a constant, loud chatter of dictation and discussion.

The guard centurion announced Morganus at the threshold of the big office.

"Leonius Morganus Fortis Victrix!" he cried. "First Javelin! Champion! And honoured hero of the Twentieth Legion!"

"Ah!" said the legate, and all those around him stamped their heels three times in salute of Morganus, while even the legate gave a brief bow, which Morganus and I respectfully returned.

Nonius Julius Sabinus, officer commanding the Twentieth Legion, and better known by his nickname *Africanus*, was very old. He was eighty at least, and his surprisingly dark skin, and tight-curled hair, instantly explained the nickname. He seemed frail, his face was disfigured by an old wound that had taken off part of his nose, and he peered fiercely through clouding cataracts, as if he would discipline his eyes to duty by sheer force of will. But he was dressed in the full dignity of a Roman general. He wore a heavy, muscled cuirass with mail epaulettes, a military kilt of hanging leather straps with golden chapes, elaborate boots, open toed and cross bound with gilded cords and topped with lion heads, and across the left shoulder, secured with a brooch, he wore a scarlet cloak of incredibly fine wool, draped gracefully into the crook of his arm.

He stepped forward and looked straight me. He stared with intense curiosity as if at some phenomenon that cries out for explanation.

"Hmm," he said, reflecting with great interest on what he saw. Then he turned to Morganus. "Greetings, O Spear of the Twentieth," he said. "So this is your special boy." His voice was oddly pleasant, deep toned and clear. It was strange to hear such elegant speech from so ugly a creature.

"Greetings Honoured Legate," said Morganus. "I present Ikaros of Apollonis who, in his own city, was a senator and an officer of cavalry." I was touched by Morganus's support, but his words surprised me. I had not known that he knew so much. I must have talked more about myself than I had realised.

"A noble knight?" said Africanus. "Were you indeed? But now you are the boy that reads minds." He came close and licked wet lips with a long tongue, as old men do, and I saw the brown stumps of ancient teeth ground flat by decades of chewing the miller's grit in his daily bread. "So what am I thinking, boy?" he said, which irritated me, because he saw me as a thing and not a man. So I was less than gentle in reply.

"You are cursing the need to stand long hours on tired legs," I said, "and you are longing for a hot bath to take away the pain where the weight of your armour cuts into the flesh of your shoulders."

"Uh!" he gasped. A sharp intake of breath indicating surprise and fright. But one look at a tired old man had told me most of it, and the absence of furniture in the office told me the rest, for the technique of standing meetings is common enough. It encourages focused discussion and swift decisions.

Africanus showed fear for only an eye blink, because he was a worldly patrician, calloused by long experience against the shocks of life. So he drew himself upright in distain for the physical discomfort I had recognised, then nodded to himself in satisfaction as a man does who has taken delivery of something useful. Clearly he regarded my talents as powerful and exotic, like the strength of an elephant or the ferocity of a lion, but it was nothing that could not be controlled and used by the Empire. He instantly proved that by speaking not to me but to Morganus.

"Well done," he said. "Well done indeed. I congratulate you."

Then he plunged into cross-questioning on the progress of our inquiries, of which he was so well informed that I became nervous in a room full of listening men. Morganus obviously felt the same, because he swiftly asked that we might speak in private. The request was granted, one of the side offices was emptied of its occupants and we spoke in there, in whispers, conscious of the absence of doors. There I explained what I believed about the business of shields and why we wanted to interrogate Felemid. Fortunately Africanus agreed with my reasoning, and for the first time showed some atom of respect towards me personally.

"Celts!" he said with a sneer, "*in* the Empire, but not *of* it." He nodded. "I believe you to be correct, boy, in your conclusions regarding Scorteus, and it was most proper that you came to me before approaching Felemid. So give attention, Ikaros of Apollonis, because I will now reveal truths that not all Romans know." He glanced at Morganus. "Be aware that I am telling you this only because His Grace has invested special trust in you, and I am His Grace's man."

I nodded, and he continued.

"Know first, that in Britannia we rule in large part by consent, because Britannia is a most difficult province. It is constantly at risk of rebellion, and while we are superior in military might, it is useless to Rome if we have constantly to fight the natives, killing the very young men who are the working hands of the province. Without them neither grain nor hides nor any other good thing will come out of this island." He paused briefly, as an obvious exception came to mind. "Caledonia is another matter," he said. "The natives there are beyond redemption, being incapable of any useful work." He waved a hand as if dismissing a fly. "They are sword fodder. Nothing more. But in Britannia proper we need collaboration, and that is why we recognise the kingdom of Cogidubnus, and others like it, and why at the extreme limit of our tolerance we suffer even the despicable, secret practice of the druidic faith." He paused. "Do you understand that, boy? Do you see it in my mind?"

"Yes, honoured sir," I said, "because the honoured Morganus and I had already come to that same conclusion."

"Had you now?" he said. "How very perceptive of you. Then listen further. This Felemid is a multi-millionaire as was Scorteus. But, unlike Scorteus, he comes of a safe and docile tribe. And so, after he had spent a sufficient fortune on public works, he was granted citizenship. But still he intrigues with the old powers, the tribes and the druids. He does so even as he advances the new powers of the Provincial Council, and hopes to make Roman citizens out of every free man in Britannia."

He saw the surprise on my face at this enormous political ambition. "Oh yes," he said. "Every free man! That is his stated aim. So, my clever Greek with your magic mind, can you tell me where his true loyalties lie?" He stepped forward and I smelt old man's breath in my face. "So. Yes, you may go to see him," he said, "and yes, you may ask your questions, and draw your conclusions. But you will make no trouble, do you hear? You will make no threats, and you will tread carefully, boy. You will disturb nothing political."

"Yes, honoured sir," I said.

"And by the same token you will make no more visits to Cogidubnus. You have been once, and come away safe with your clever conclusions." He nodded. "So! Well enough to that. But now you will keep away from him, and you will not seek to disturb the balance of powers within his court. Leave these matters to those who are born with the proper rank, who are granted the necessary authority, and have been trained in diplomatic skills. Do I make myself clear?"

"Yes, honoured sir."

"Good. Then know that I allow this investigation only out of love for His Grace."

"Gods save His Grace," I said, carefully, and I bowed.

"And know also," he said, "that I can tell you, right now, exactly what happened to your late master Scorteus." He stared into my eyes. "The so-called Scorteus," he said, "who was a prince of the Iceni, whose real name was Scortrogid son of Beltragnidos of the Broad Fist." He pounced on that as he saw my reaction. "Ah," he said. "The mind reader did not know that, did he?" His delight annoyed me.

"That is because you have only just called it to mind," I said. " I see what a man thinks, not what he has not yet thought." It was nonsense, and yet he believed it and fell silent, confounded in logic such that the shadow of unease fell upon him once more. Because, even in the strongest minds, superstition hides behind corners, waiting its chance to stab with an icy knife. But then the patrician discipline returned.

"Bah!" he said, and shook off the fear. "Listen boy! The fate of your late master is obvious. He was deep in some plot with the druids, and they quarrelled, and the druids disposed of him. But this knowledge will do you no good because you can never bring druids to a court of law." He spread hands to absolve himself. "I would help you if I could, boy, for His Grace's sake. Indeed I would. But, do you not see? We cannot even admit that the druids still exist. Not in public."

He paused and considered me carefully. I guessed that he was hesitating before revealing a confidence, and I was correct. "The best I can do for you," he said, "is to warn you that I have discussed this matter with Gaius Iulius Domitius, the Lord Chief Justice. Do you know that he has sent to Rome concerning the Silanianum?" I nodded. "Then let me add that he has received an express reply, because the Jurists and Senate believe this matter touches upon the security of the Empire." As he spoke, the sickness of dread fell upon me. "Thus Rome's instruction is to inflict the Silanianum, unless unequivocal proof can be given that the killer of Scorteus was not his slave." He spread hands again, this time in real sympathy. "An Inspector Plenipotentiary is on his way to enforce that judgement, and your cause is already lost."

Chapter 23

We spent a bad evening in Morganus's house, arguing endlessly over the druids and what part they had played in Scorteus's death. Morganus was once again convinced that the druids were the cause of everything, and was right back to believing that everything had been done by magic, with invisible assassins, curses and spells. On the other hand he surprised me with a forthright refusal to give up the fight, when I fell into a depression and drank too much wine.

"Brace up, Apollonite!" he said. "We're not done yet!" I blinked, and tried to sit straight and look him in the eye, which was difficult because his face was only shadows in his dark living room, where only a few lamps were burning.

"But you think we're fighting magic," I said.

"So what?" he said. "You're magic aren't you?" I just groaned. What use was denial?

"Anyway," he said, "I don't know about Greeks, but it's not the Roman way to give up. Did we give up after Cannae or the Teutoberg Forest? And those were dreadful disasters."

"No," I said, and drank another cup of wine. "You Romans never give up, do you? Even when you should." I said it with despair, not admiration, because I was very tired, and because something else was drawing me down. There was a soreness in the little passages behind my nose, and it was becoming painful for me to swallow. These familiar signs told me that I had caught the damned, accursed, detestable Britannic phlegm from Caradigma, and few things in all the world depress me more than that.

"Right then," said Morganus, who had either not noticed my tone or, more likely, chose to ignore it. "So, come on Greek! What do we do when we're knocked flat? We rally round the standard don't we? And we re-form and we fight on!"

"Oh, holy gods of Olympus," I muttered.

"And even if at last we fall," said Morganus, "let's fall like Romans with all our wounds in the front." He meant it. He meant every word. But he sounded like an actor in a drama. What did these fancy words mean to four hundred slaves? Would they fall with all their wounds in the front? Would the women and girls die like Romans? But then he saw my misery, and did an astounding thing. He filled our cups and put one in his hand and one in mine. Then he leaned forward, hooked his right arm in mine at the elbow, and made the Roman army's most sacred toast.

"Brothers!" he said. Just the one word, but a word of enormous significance. Compared with this, no other compliment he ever paid me was as great. For this famous toast was also an oath, it was a pledge from one to another, to be faithful unto death and beyond. To make such a pledge to a slave was unthinkable. It was unbelievable. And, I was profoundly moved.

"Brothers!" I said, and sniffed my painful nose and drank the cup.

It was no help at all to us in our troubles, but I was comforted. Later I even managed to sleep for some of the night. But I was up long before dawn, pouring buckets of hot water over my head in Morganus's bath house, to wash away the headache and the congealed snot. Then I sneezed several times and shuddered, and had to wash my face again, then spit into the drain.

Soon after, Morganus sent a runner into the still-dark city to make an appointment to see Felemid, the Celtic millionaire. For this important duty, the runner bore a white wand topped with a legionary eagle in miniature, a privileged symbol of the First Javelin's rank. This was such that the runner took precedence over all others and would instantly be let through the salutatio crowd at Felemid's door to place his message into Felemid's own hand, commanding an urgent response. The white wand did its job, and the runner was back even before we finished breakfast. He knelt, panting at Morganus's feet, as we sat at table. He bowed his head and handed over Felemid's message, which Morganus read.

"The *honoured* Felemid," he said, with cynical emphasis, "invites us to meet him at the Senate House at the third hour. He's done a careful calculation, has Felemid. If it's too early he ranks himself beneath us, and if it's too late, he's being rude."

"Is the third hour, about right then?" I said.

"Oh yes," said Morganus. "He's on his best behaviour." He looked at me and frowned. "Are you fit for service, Greek? You look awful."

"I'll do," said the Stoic within me. "It's the phlegm. It always takes me like this." I shook my head. "It's nothing," I said, in the depths of my misery, for I cannot abide being ill. Then we finished breakfast, the bodyguards came, and we left the fort and went into the city. We went just west of the forum, to the Senate House of the Britannic Provincial Council, an odd, square, plain structure some forty feet high, with a pitched roof and big windows set high up in the walls. It was devoid of the usual triumphal statures of Roman civic buildings, and had no decoration other than a cladding of white marble, and a modest portico running across the front, supported by eight, skinny pillars rising from an equally modest run of steps. It stood within its own iron-railed precinct, with officials and slaves manning the gate. As we stopped outside to look at the building, Morganus shook his head.

"I never know what to make of this," he said, pointing with his vine staff. "You know it's a copy of the senate house in Rome, don't you?"

"Is it?" I said

"Yes," he said. "The one built by Caesar the Great." It was typical of him to say *Caesar the Great*, because even though the contemporaries of Gaius Julius Caesar had comprehensively butchered him, he was revered by the Romans, and especially the army, as one of Rome's greatest generals even a hundred and forty-four years after his death. But that is politics too, since it was Gaius Julius' faction, in the person of his nephew Augustus, who won in the end and became Rome's first Emperor after yet another blood-drenched civil war. So I looked at this copy of Caesar's Senate House.

"So what's the problem?" I asked. "What's wrong with a bit of imitation?"

"If it is just that," he said, "and not something else."

"Such as what?"

"Well it's supposed to be a foot bigger in all dimensions than the real thing."

"So?" I asked, and he puzzled over his own attitude.

"I don't know," he said. "But that's the way the Celts built it, and I don't even know what it's for. Not really."

"Do you not?" I said, puzzled.

"Something to do with local senates, tribal senates I think."

Thus I found to my surprise that here was an aspect of Britannic politics that I knew better than Morganus. I knew better because Scorteus had always wanted a place in the Provincial Senate, although he never got one because senators had to be Roman citizens. But he had talked about it endlessly. It was a key part of his ambitions for the future. So I cleared my throat, blew my nose into the gutter, wiped my fingers on the hem of my tunic, and faced Morganus and the bodyguards.

"Well," I said. "It is indeed connected with tribal senates." Then I delivered a lecture, as if to visiting tourists, as we stood outside the Senate gates, with the gate officials whispering and looking at us, and occasionally bowing, just to be on the polite side of so senior a Roman officer.

"It's an assembly of delegates of the regional senates," I said. "Because each tribe has a senate at its Civitas Capital. There was one at Noviomagus Reginorum."

"Was there?" said Morganus.

"Yes," I said. "They've all got one. It's to encourage the tribal elders to be loyal to Rome. Or rather it's the other way round. Those elders who have proved loyal to Rome are given citizenship so they can serve on the local senate."

"So what's this one?" he said, pointing again with the vine staff.

"That's where the delegates meet. They meet once a year for a month," I said. Then added, "As you know." But he did not, because he shook his head in disdain.

"But what's it for?" he said. "The Governor's staff run the province, and the City Council runs Londinium. So what do they do in there?"

"They manage the Cult of the Spirit of His Imperial Majesty."

"Gods save His Majesty!" cried Morganus and the bodyguards together.

"Yes," I said. "Quite. They run the main shrine here in Londinium, and the local shrines everywhere else. They serve as priests of the cult, and they pay for all the ceremonies, games, athletics, sacrifices and whatever. Any man who gets in has to spend big money."

"And a good thing too," said Morganus.

"Yes. But they have other duties sort of semi-officially, including acting as a talking shop to bring local affairs and tribal affairs to public notice."

"That's not much good if they only meet once a year," said Morganus.

"Ah, but they have permanent officials, Duovirs and a few chosen senators, based in Londinium. So the local senates write to them."

"I see."

"And they have one special duty. When a Governor retires, the Provincial Senate passes a resolution in thanks for his service, and the resolution goes to the Emperor. It sounds like nothing special, but it is because they can word the resolution any way they like. So they could destroy the Governor's reputation if they chose to do so. They could even indict him for fraud and corruption."

"What? Celts could do that? A load of natives?"

"They're citizens remember. Every one is a Roman citizen."

"I don't like that."

"And there's more. They're constantly pushing at the limits of their power." I smiled, recalling Scorteus'ss enthusiasm. "My old master knew all about that," I said. "He was all for it. They claim to be constantly preparing and researching the farewell resolution, and to do that they keep a staff recording the Governor's activities at all times. And not just the Governor. They check up on lots of other officials too, supposedly looking for corruption."

"But that's the Procurator's job," said Morganus indignantly.

"I know," I said, "and he knows it too, and it's dangerous to cross someone as powerful as him. But that's politics. Scorteus used to say, *if your power isn't actively growing, it's actively shrinking. Politics is endless struggle, endless risk, endless danger,*" and then I fell silent.

"What is it?" said Morganus.

"I've just thought of something," I said. "Scorteus wasn't just enthusiastic for the Provincial Council, I think he was in it."

"But you said he couldn't be, because he wasn't a citizen."

"Well, no he couldn't," I said. "He couldn't be a senator. Not properly. But knowing him, he would have been preparing the way. I mean spending money, going to meetings, getting involved." I looked at the dull, plain building. "I think we've just found a whole new universe where Scorteus might have made enemies."

Soon I had evidence that I was right, at least about the politics. We went through the gates, with slaves and officials bowing and backing before us. They did not quite throw rose petals in our path, but it was close. They had been warned to expect us and took us straight inside the building, where one look made Morganus shake his head even more.

"It's just the same," he said. "It's like the real one, in Rome."

If so, I was impressed for once with the good taste of something Roman. The chamber was tall, deeply echoing, and austere, some eighty feet long by fifty feet wide, and it was lit with sombre dignity by its high, square windows that threw beams of light like golden pillars sloped against dark walls.

The only decoration was in the floor, where yellow stone was ruled into rectangles by inlaid green blocks, and each rectangle was full of curves, discs and cornucopias laid out in green and red stone that were almost Celtic in their animation. There was an altar inside the entrance with a huge winged statue of Victoria Goddess of Triumph. At the far side there rose three great steps, each ten feet deep and a foot high, that curved in successive semi-circles, bearing rows of seats carved from single blocks of black marble, one for each senator with his name in gold lettering in the back rest.

The rows of chairs were like an empty theatre, for the senate was not in session. But a handful of Provincial Senators were waiting beside the altar, all in togas, all standing like Romans, and I was surprised to see that their togas bore the broad purple stripe of the Senatorial Class. This must have been with Rome's approval because they could never have displayed such rank without it. They had even covered their heads with a drape of material, which Romans do on formal or sacred occasions. Nonetheless, they were so incongruously Celtic in their appearance as to make Morganus frown. Thus a few displayed plain togas and were short cropped and clean shaven, but most wore jewelled brooches, long oiled hair, and had full beards twirled into plaits that dangled and shone with gold ornaments. And before all else, their features cried Silure, Belgae, Parisii and the rest.

There was not one full-blooded Roman among them and, sensing their defensive hostility, I felt that right here in the centre of Londinium, in the very heart of civilised Roman Britannia, when these men faced Morganus we were staring across the gulf between the conquerors and the conquered.

One man stepped forward, one of those who looked most Roman. He bowed gracefully to Morganus, elegantly sweeping the trail of his toga behind him with his left hand, while he uncurled his right arm expressively towards us, palm upward, as if offering a gift. He was slim, and small. He moved like a dancer, and had obviously taken lessons in classical deportment.

"Greetings, O Morganus," he said.

"Greetings O Gentius Civilis Felemidus," said Morganus carefully, but the Celt smiled.

"No need for fancy," he said. "I am Felemid. That is what friends call me and I like you as friend. It is good to be friend." He spoke with smooth confidence, being a smooth and confident man, but he was one of those unfortunates whose ears are deaf to pronunciation and grammar, and he came from the far north of Britannia where a totally different culture flourished, such that even his native Celtic speech would be obscure to the Celts of Londinium. Thus Felemid might have looked like a Roman, but he certainly did not sound like one.

Morganus nodded curtly and said nothing. It was obvious that he disliked Felemid and distrusted his attempted familiarity, while I was surprised at Felemid's youth. He was much younger than I had expected; in his late twenties, with a high, bony nose, heavy brow ridges, thin lips and a yellowish-white skin typical of the Brigantes tribe of the north west, as was his slight, almost child-like, stature.

But while he was small in size he was large in character. He was intensely self-satisfied, and he stood smiling at Morganus as if they were equals, or even, just by a grain, perhaps he thought himself Morganus'ss superior. If so, it was extremely saucy of him to show it. Looking behind the smile on Felemid's face, and knowing that, like Scorteus, he had made his own fortune by his own hand, I saw a very talented and successful young man who believed himself to be better than others because their thoughts moved slower than his. Then he turned his smile on me.

"Ikaros," he said. "Magic Greek! You don't know the many times I try buy you off Scorteus!" He laughed. "But Scorteus never sell." He shook his head. "Is shame, eh?" Felemid was reminding me that he had the power to own me if my master would sell, and since Fortunus, which is to say Badrogid, would undoubtedly sell if the price were right, I was developing a considerable unease where Felemid was concerned. I think Morganus guessed this because he cleared his throat and raised a strong voice that reverberated in the high chamber.

"Ikaros of Apollonis is an inquisitor in the service of His Grace the Governor," he cried.

"Blessings be upon His Grace," murmured the senators, and bowed their heads.

"When the Apollonite speaks, His Grace speaks," said Morganus.

"Many blessings on him," said Felemid, and gave the ghost of a bow to me and raised his eyebrows. "So. What His Grace want know?"

I began my questions, as best as I could, because my throat was sore, my eyes were watering, and my voice croaked like a raven's.

"Who are these honoured and reverend gentlemen?" I said, looking at the senators standing behind Felemid, "And why are they here?"

Felemid waved a hand. "These men? Elder senators. From Civitas Capitals," he bowed to them, they bowed back, "They think like me, they vote like me." He bowed to them again. The senators nodded and stood on guard. Had they been armed they would have raised shields and shown steel.

"Does any reverend gentleman speak for the Regni tribe?" I asked. "For Noviomagus Reginorum?" One of them stepped forward.

"I speak for the free kingdom of His Majesty Cogidubnus III," he said, proving himself to be a man whom I wished on the other side of the Earth, because he would send my every word straight back to Maligoterix. As for the rest I had no intention of conducting an interrogation in front of them. So I gave a small bow to Felemid, and spoke. I spoke with considerable arrogance, taking full advantage of my temporary powers.

"I assure you, O Gentius Civilis Felemidus," I said, "that since, like all citizens, you are folded within the embrace of Roman law, you need no support against me. I also assure these reverend gentlemen, all of whom surely bear heavy responsibilities, that they have His Grace's permission to leave." I paused for effect. "In fact they may leave right now this very instant." It was like kicking an ant's nest. A great shouting and stamping followed, with red faces, loud voices and an open display of angry Celtic emotion. But I could almost feel the approval of Morganus and the bodyguards, who stepped up beside me and gripped sword hilts and glared in hostility at the senators.

The gulf had opened wide and, for a moment, I wondered if I had been stupid to pander so outrageously to Roman army prejudice against those whom they saw as uppity natives. It was dangerous, like throwing a firebrand into a field of dry grass, because these particular natives were men of special power within the Roman system. But I was suffering the torment of a Britannic sickness and was in the mood to hate all things Britannic. So perhaps my judgement was imperfect.

Fortunately, Felemid pulled them together, drew them aside, and argued with them in fierce whispers. Finally, with utmost bad grace, the senators withdrew and left the Senate House with not a single bow or nod to Morganus as they went. A most pointed demonstration of rudeness, by which they attempted to salvage their pride.

"Now, boy," said Felemid to me, "what you want know?" I was surprised to see a look of admiration on his face. I had a lot to ask him, and did my best to get through it all, until finally the chamber started to circle around my head, and the ache in my limbs grew unbearable. But I uncovered two important facts, the second being by far the more important, because it told me who it was behind the business of shields, and responsible for the deaths of Scorteus, the Syrian, and the Tribune Severus.

Chapter 24

Considering my wretched condition, the interrogation of Felemid went remarkably well, even though it delivered only negative information at first. Thus I learned nothing when I attempted to bounce unguarded comments from him by steadily discussing something bland, then suddenly slipping in a question on something important.

"By the way," I said, "what quantity of weapons were actually involved in the business of shields?" Later. "Out of interest, who was it that invented the cipher? Was it you or the Syrian?" These challenges certainly surprised him, but only in the sense that he did not know what I was talking about, and there was no spontaneous leakage of secrets because he had no secrets to leak, not on these matters anyway. It was only when I got to the subject of his friendship with Scorteus that I gained fresh knowledge. Or rather I stood back as it poured out in a stream because Felemid was a vain and socially-ambitions young man who stuffed names into his conversation, as a cook stuffs onions into a chicken.

"When do I make friend Scorteus?" he said, and basked in self-admiration. "Is when Her Grace come senate house, for supply water Imperial Baths." He smiled easily to give the impression that the first lady of the province was just one of many acquaintances. "They big friend of Senate," he said, "Tertia and Governor. I meet them many times."

"Do you indeed?" I said, politely, to keep him talking.

"Yes, yes," he said. "I Duovir, yes? And because Duovir, I Chief Priest of Temple of blessed Coventina." He raised his hands. "Goddess of springs and wells." He drew himself up in pride. "Chief priest *sacred* office, yes? Above *civic* office? I meet everyone, His Grace, Her Grace, His Honour Procurator, all big actors at …"

"Yes," I said. "But what about Scorteus?"

He frowned briefly at my interruption. But then he smiled indulgently, as if forgiving a lap dog for cocking its leg in the house. "You listen, boy," he said, "I Chief Priest springs and wells, yes? That mean I lead Council of Imperial Baths. I meet Scorteus. I meet Scorteus because he come Baths Council with plan." He nodded. "Your plan, boy."

"For pumps to raise water for the baths?" I said.

"Yes," he said, "Scorteus say you make small, little thing …" He frowned in frustration, "Give me word boy. What is small thing like big thing?"

"A model," I said, and he beamed with approval.

"Yes. Model. Scorteus say you make model."

"Did he?" I said.

"Oh yes," he said. "Scorteus talk about you very much. Like you very much."

His words were puzzling. He was saying things to please me, and his manner was friendly, almost ingratiating, and I could not think why. But it was good to hear what he said about Scorteus and I stored it away to comfort me on those occasions when I might learn even more things about Scorteus that I would not like. Meanwhile I had to concentrate on Felemid.

"Please continue, honoured sir," I said.

"So," he said, "Her Grace is Baths Patroness. She want plenty water for baths, because is bad for Londinium, is make fool Londinium, if Londinium have great baths where water come in like old man's piss. So," said Felemid, "Scorteus know I lead Bath Council. Scorteus come. Scorteus want favour. He want give pumps to Tertia. He want see her yes?"

"Yes," I said, and he gave a sly grin. "So we sit down, me and Scorteus, 'cos he want favour, yes?" Then the grin faded as he remembered what must have been a considerable negotiation. "He very good, Scorteus. Nobody twist him. Nobody beat him." Felemid nodded. "I like him," he said. "He clever, but he make me laugh and I like him very much." He thought for a moment, before adding the greatest praise of which he was capable, "Scorteus same as me," he said, "very same as me."

"So what happened when he met the Lady Tertia?" I said. "Did he present the pumps idea?"

"Yes," he said. "And she like, but then she forget, because she get wild bad angry. She get angry because big fool Belgix say big fool thing."

"Who's he?" I asked, "Belgix?"

"Elder Senior Senator Belgae tribe. Stupid Belgae people."

"So what did he do?" I asked.

"What he do?" he said, and looked round the great, empty chamber. "All this very different. All dressed for festival. Very fine, very nice, not like now," he said. "Flowers, dancers, music, all good things." He pointed to the plinth supporting the statue of Victoria. "Lady Tertia up there," he said, "with big throne, with girls behind her, daughters, slaves, all girls." Then he swept his arm round the room. "All people in fine clothes. All very good, very polite, very low bow." He mimed a deferential bow, and a courtly gesture of respect. "I stand to front," he said, "in white toga. In Roman toga. Duovir Felemid!" He sighed at the memory of it.

"Go on," I said.

"So. I call names and each people come forward. I give name to Tertia. She look down, she speak. They look up, they speak, yes?"

"Yes," I said.

"So. Scorteus come. He tell her about pumps. She smile, she pleased, he bow, he go. Is very good for Scorteus, yes? But next is Belgix, the stupid Belgae. He want be clever. He want crawl up arsehole. He tell great news from ship in harbour. He pay big money so no other man have news, yes? So he bow to floor, and he tell Tertia, General Urban have great victory over Thracians."

"Yes," I said, and I recalled Livius Fidus Urban's slaughter of a Thracian host, up beyond the northern borders of Greece, early in the previous year. It was a considerable victory and Urban got a triumph in Rome and a memorial arch.

"But big idiot Belgix make big mistake," said Felemid, chuckling merrily. "Urban is deadly enemy of Tertia husband."

"Is he?" I said.

"Oh yes," said Felemid, and I turned to Morganus for guidance, because I take even less interest in Roman politics than I do in their religious festivals. But Morganus frowned massively.

"There are no enemies among Romans," he proclaimed. And, while even Felemid dared not contradict him, there was a silence because the statement was laughably untrue. It was ludicrously untrue. It was catastrophically untrue, because Roman history for the last fifty years had been one, long, blood-wallowing slaughter of civil wars, and the worst enemy a Roman legion ever faces is another Roman legion. But Morganus was not going to admit that to a Celt, and I was not going to argue with Morganus in front of one. So I chose careful words.

"I see, honoured sir," I said, to Morganus. "But perhaps there may be honest differences of opinion, even of ambition, between these noble gentlemen?"

"Perhaps," said Morganus. "The two families do have differences because there are certain disputes inherited from ancestral times, and it is true that both His Grace ..."

"Gods save him!" cried the bodyguards. Morganus nodded, and continued in rigidly formal speech, so as to put Felemid in his place for speaking a truth that decent Romans do not mention.

"It is true that His Grace, Marcus Ostorius Cerealis Teutonius, and his Honour, Livius Fidus Urban, both seek the same appointment as their next step in the cursus honorum. Both these honourable and noble Romans seek the Governorship of Italia, the beloved homeland of our people. Since this most senior and sacred of posts bestows a rank second in importance only to that of the Emperor Himself, it is an inevitable consequence that, since only one of them can achieve this ambition, there is a certain rivalry between them, especially on the field of martial valour." Having completed this masterwork of understatement, Morganus fell silent and Felemid was too clever a politician not to take advantage. So he bowed low to Morganus.

"Honoured sir," he said, "You say everything perfect. You say what I think, but I have no words so good like you." Morganus gave a small, not entirely hostile, shrug.

"So," said Felemid to me, "Belgix tell Tertia of General Urban great victory." Felemid shook his head and puffed out his cheeks as he recalled a formidable event. "And Tertia, she stand from chair, eyes of flame, she lash him like whip. She say so bad things that nobody can look, and idiot Belgix fall to knees. He make tears. Then even I turn away." He frowned. "I am … I am …" He looked at me. "What is word boy?"

"Embarrassed?" I said, and he smiled and half reached a hand out towards me.

"Embarrassed. Yes. You clever boy," he said. It was all very interesting, but by then I was beginning to tremble and ache in my limbs, and badly wanted to take to my bed. So it was only an unexpected oddity of Felemid's character that brought vital information just as I was seeking to end the interview.

"Why you say shields?" he said. "You say shields, yes? When we first talk?" I gathered what strength I could. This sounded interesting.

"I asked you about something called *the business of shields*," I said. "The words are a code with special meaning. Do you know anything about it?"

He looked steadily at me and slightly raised his eyebrows and gave the briefest glance at Morganus. The gestures were unconscious. He was not even aware of them, but I read them. He had something to say, but not in front of Morganus.

"Honoured sir," I said to him, "I have some questions to put to this Reverend Senator, which might be of a delicate nature. Might he and I withdraw a few paces for this purpose?" This was my turn to speak nonsense, but I knew Morganus would understand, and he did. He knew my methods by now.

"No need," he said. "My men and I will be outside when you need us."

Felemid and I bowed as he marched off with the bodyguards behind him and the crunch of their synchronous footsteps echoing round the chamber. Then I was alone with Felemid, whose manner changed entirely as he looked at me with wondering eyes.

"Magic boy," he said. "You knew I want Romans gone? You see in my mind, like Scorteus say." For once I did not disagree, and Felemid reached out and clasped my arm. "So, look in my head, boy. You look and you see, that I make no stroke against Scorteus, yes? Someone kill him, but not me. You see that, yes?"

Indeed I could see it. It had been the very first thing I got from the interview. I already knew that he had nothing to do with the business of shields or the murders. I knew it because when I questioned him on these matters, he answered with a complete, open-faced readiness. Whatever capacity for deceit might lay within him – and I had no doubt that it was profound – I had already seen that, on this occasion, he was telling the truth because he had nothing to fear.

"Yes," I said, "I can see that." He gasped, as my seeming admission of magic powers, caused him first to blink with excitement and then to surprise me with something I had not seen, because he kept it so profoundly hidden.

"Greeks," he whispered. "I like Greek boys. I got three Greek boys. They do good things." He stood close, like a Celt, and touched my face. "But my boys, they don't see when I been bad." He paused and relished yet another thought. "And they weak. They soft." He nodded. "But not you! Before we talk, you don't want senators here. So you say go." He waved a hand towards the doors. "You say go, in big voice, and senators go." He shivered in delight. "I think you are boy who punish a man who been bad, yes? You know what I say?"

Of course I knew. His desires were nothing special. In my city there were mystery houses where those who enjoyed such services could receive them in complete discretion, to the accompaniment of music, and with dinner to follow. And as for Felemid's preference for male sensuality, it was flattering that someone with the pick of the slave markets was interested in me. Nonetheless, my heart sank at the thought of such theatricals and pretence as he would demand. After all, I am an engineer by profession and not a catamite. So I trod as carefully as a barefoot man in a field of serpents, because Felemid might, just possibly, become my next owner and I dared neither offend nor encourage him.

"The culture of Greece is ancient and sophisticated, reverend sir," I said. "Thus Greeks have many skills that others lack. But may I ask how my skills will serve you here and now? I see that there something that you wish to tell me?"

"Yes, yes," he said, with mystic awe in his eyes, and he licked lascivious lips. As I have said, if I deduce half a man's thoughts, sometimes he will tell me the rest. On occasions, with a gullible man, less than half will get him talking, and so it was with Felemid. Though in his case the motivation was pleasure in debasement, because he believed, metaphorically at least, that he was being stripped naked..

"After Tertia spit upon idiot Belgix," he said.

"Yes?" I said.

"Scorteus talk to me. We talk who won best battle, Teutonius or Urban, because big job in Rome go to him with the big battle. You understand?"

"Yes," I said.

"So, Scorteus, he say Teutonius need big battle, and he ask me why Caledonian tribes, they not fight no more."

"Why did he ask you that?" I said, and Felemid stood even closer, and became very confidential.

"I Roman, yes?" he said. "Not hairy-arse native outside Empire, yes?" I nodded, and he continued. "So now, I have big house in Londinium. I live here most times, yes? But where I born?" He pointed upwards. "Up north," he said, "I still got business. I got fur trade." He paused. "And Caledonian tribes are near." He put on an exaggerated expression of innocence, to show how harmless were his intentions towards Rome. "So I buy skins from tribes. I buy otter, beaver, bear." He lowered his voice to the briefest whisper. "So Caledonians come south to trade with me. You understand, boy?" I nodded. "I speak their words. I know their ways. We sit down, we drink beer, we talk." He looked at me closely. "I am Roman" he insisted. "But this is business. Is different. You understand?"

"I understand," I said. "And Scorteus knew this?" Felemid nodded.

"He knows. So he ask. He say why the Caledonians don't fight? He ask and I tell. I say they not fools. Each time they fight, Romans win. Romans win if Caledonians army is ten times Roman army, because Romans very fierce, and because Caledonians don't have arms for all men."

I nodded because I had heard that before, from Morganus.

"Yes," I said. "I believe that in a Britannic host the leaders may be fully equipped, but the poorest men fight with only clubs or stones."

"Yes, yes," said Felemid. "No factories. No big making. They live in hills. In forest. They make little bit iron. They make little bit spear, axe, bow. But not armour." He shook his head. "They don't want armour. They want move quick. They leap high, run fast. *But* they want shields! Roman shields! They cannot make, but they want. They give anything for shields. Sell children, sell wives." He nodded emphatically. "Then with shields: they fight!" He paused and frowned, and added something else with a slight shrug, as if he were not really sure of himself. "I tell this," he said. "I tell Scorteus, and he smile. He make nod of head, and I ask myself, why he ask me?"

I started swaying on my feet at about that time, and I do not remember much more of my conversation with Felemid, who presumably summoned Morganus to my aid, because I remember Morganus looking at me and beckoning the bodyguards forward to take my arms in case I fell over. He ended the interview with Felemid and there were formal bows, and then we left the Senate House with the bodyguards almost carrying me. But I shook them off. I had little dignity left, but what I had would not allow me to be carried like a child. So I sneezed and coughed in the cold drizzling rain which had come down from a typical Londinium sky, and myself without a cloak and feeling profoundly miserable. Indeed I think I was worse even than I usually am with the Britannic phlegm, because my imagination began to work, and I felt detached from reality like the time when I drank the snake girl's potion, and above all I was chillingly cold and soaked wet through to the bones.

But the army is efficient at everything, and they got me back to Morganus's house, where I sat in a hot bath for my aches and pains, and went to my bed, which Morganus's wife had made up with hot bricks wrapped in towels at my feet, and hot spiced wine on a table beside the bed. I was used to being waited on by my two boys, but they were slaves who were obliged to serve me. Thus the personal care I received from Morganus's wife and girls, pleasant as it was, was deeply disturbing because it stirred my emotions and made me think of my own house in my own city and my own family.

Later, at lamp time, Morganus came to see me. By then, I had managed a few hours of sleep, I had got several cups of wine inside me, and I was warm and comfortable. So the sneezing had abated, and I felt much better. Morganus was in his tunic, with armour and gear removed and he sat on a chair by my bed. He smiled.

"I've never seen anyone take the phlegm so bad," he said. "You look awful."

"It's this filthy island," I said. "Britannia. Everything here is grey. Where's the light? Where's the sunshine?"

"In the wine," he said. "There's sunshine in the grapes. You'd better drink some more." So I did. "Well," he said, "what did we learn from all that?"

I closed my eyes to bring concentration, and found that my thoughts had already arranged themselves as sometimes they do after a rest and a sleep.

"Morganus," I said, "I must ask you to trust me."

"I do!" he said.

"Wait until you've heard what I have to say."

"Well?"

"We knew that Scorteus was supplying arms to the natives didn't we?"

"Yes."

"And this endeavour was called *The Business of Shields*?"

"Yes."

"Well now we know that it was only shields he supplied, and that he supplied them to the Caledonians so they'd have the confidence to rise against Rome."

"We know that?" he said.

"Yes," I said. "Trust me. But here's the big news. We didn't know why he was doing it, because it was against all his interests in becoming a Roman citizen, yes?"

"Yes."

I paused. Even now I could hardly believe what logic dictated. "You're not going to like this Morganus," I said.

"Get on with it, Greek."

"Scorteus was a bold man," I said. "If he saw a big opportunity he'd take it, even if it was dangerous. He'd go forward where other men fell back."

"So?"

"So, I think the business of shields was just another project to get him Roman citizenship. He found out from Felemid, and from watching the Lady Tertia, that Teutonius needed another big victory if he wasn't going to lose the race to become Governor of Italia. Then he found out that the Caledonians wouldn't rise for lack of arms, lack of shields, so he supplied them with shields so ..."

"But that's madness," said Morganus. "What if the rebellion succeeded? What if the other tribes rose? Londinium might've had to be evacuated. There might've been another slaughter like in Boudicca's time."

"He'd have planned for that," I said. "He'd have money safe in Gaul, and a ship waiting at the docks to take him and his family out of Britannia if the worst happened. Believe me, he would. I knew him well. But above all he'd take that risk because everything else seemed to be failing, and because he judged that you Romans," I pointed to Morganus, "you would win in the end, and beat the Caledonians. Which is to say that Teutonius would beat them, and Scorteus wouldn't have to run."

"Wait, wait," said Morganus, "How would he gain? You said he did this, this insane thing, to get Roman citizenship. But how could he get it? How would we give it to him?"

"It would be given by someone powerful. Someone actually within Government House. Nobody else can grant citizenship. Do you agree?"

"Well yes, that's right, but ..."

"Listen! You know that His Grace is not quite the man he seems, don't you?" Morganus'ss face drained of colour as anger swelled within him.

241

"His Grace is a Roman nobleman," he said. "His honour is unquestionable. You are my pledged comrade, Greek, but if you seek to imply that His Grace is ..."

"No! No! No!" I said. "I agree with all that. He's a decent man, and I don't think he knows anything about this. But he's a puppet worked by others. He's no administrator, you must know that. And you know better than anyone that it's the centurions who run the army. Morganus, listen to me, you're a Roman, aren't you?" He frowned in anger. "'Course I am!"

"So you're loyal to Rome, right? To Rome itself, not to any one man?"

"Where's this leading, Greek? I'm loyal and the sea is wet. So what?"

"So you've got to face the fact that what we're doing might harm Teutonius, even if we don't mean to. But, if it does, it's done for justice. And it's done for Rome as well, if you Romans really do care about justice, with all your laws and law courts."

"'Course we do!" he said.

"So listen to me. Do you remember my telling you that someone told me *the family in Rome demands a victory whether or not it is real.* Well that someone is the man who Scorteus approached with a plan."

Morganus said nothing, but sank back in his chair and looked at me in horror.

"The plan was," I said, "that Scorteus would arm the Caledonians to give them the confidence to rebel, so that Teutonius could take an army north and win a victory. This is politics, Morganus, deep, dirty politics. Scorteus would get his citizenship, Teutonius would get his victory." Thinking of that, I cursed my gift of insight which had shown me truth of Scorteus's character, the man who had promised me freedom, the man who made jokes, seized hands, slapped backs, and ate with his mouth open, spraying crumbs. He was all that, but he was also the man who had set the Roman army on a race of wretched tribal savages who, by his considered judgement and Iceni tribal knowledge, would be slaughtered on the field of battle, then removed from history, village by village and house by house. How many dead Celts, to make one live one into a Roman? But Morganus was shaking my arm.

"Come back!" he said. "Who is he? The man who made the deal?"

I stared at him.

"He's the man that Dolbius the lawyer was thinking of when he said he didn't know if His Grace's authority was enough. The man who runs Government House, and runs His Grace, and His Grace's idiot nephew. He's probably the most powerful man in Britannia. He's Petros the Greek."

Morganus gaped. He did not know what to say.

"So we've got to be very, very careful," I said, "He knows exactly what we're doing, he'll have spies out everywhere to track us, and we can't risk warning him that we know that he's responsible for three murders and a colonial war!"

"So what do we do?" said Morganus.

"We carry on as before," I said. "We carry on until we've got so much evidence that we can take him to law."

"When will that be?"

"I don't know."

Chapter 25

I was still in bed after three days because the phlegm got worse not better, but I was very comfortable with Morganus's family fussing over me and bringing hot drinks and food. I confess, in all my miserable time in Britannia, I had never so much enjoyed being ill, nor even thought that it was possible to enjoy being ill, even with the shadow of the Silanianum upon me. Likewise, I had enjoyed another attack on the cipher books, and the pleasure of the task had set the hours running like greyhounds. I had never known time to pass so swiftly.

At first I worked surrounded by every tablet in the household bearing my scribbling and crossing out, because cipher breaking is not a task to be done in the unaided mind. The detail is overwhelming, like a flock of mad sheep that want to run in all directions, and as soon as you grasp one the rest are gone. Thus charts and diagrams are needed to act as a sheepdog that brings order out of chaos. But, on the second night, as sometimes happens, I was granted inspiration that soared like a songbird above the plodding mule of tedious labour. Such an experience seems magical, but a philosopher must insist that inspiration usually comes only after a period of intense work, such that, beneath and below conscious thought, the mad sheep are disciplined in the mind. Either that or it is indeed the gods who whisper in our ears. How should I know? How should anyone know?

So when Morganus came into to see me next day, I had the tablets stacked on the floor by the bed, with just one beside me, next to the Syrian's cipher book, and my master notes on the investigation. I smiled as he came in and he raised eyebrows as he sat down in a chair.

"You've cracked it, haven't you?" he said

"Yes," I said. "I was falling off to sleep and my imagination was free, so I saw a legion on parade, when every tenth switched with every thirteenth. The thirteenth fell back to the rear, and then each man lined up by height, with the tallest to the left and the shortest to the right. The centurions took all their names and wrote them down on tablets, and swapped tablets. So it was just a matter of transposing every tenth for the thirteenth, and then ..." But I saw his face. It was like telling Scorteus about the resurrection of eastern gods. So we laughed.

"What is it then?" he said. "What's in the Syrian's book?"

"Here's my translation," I said, and gave him the other tablet. "It's bills of lading for goods taken aboard ships. There were four cargoes, in four ships that set sail on the dates recorded. As you can see, the cargoes were not only shields. There were other goods, mainly ship's stores such as cables, blocks, tar and anchors, and there were some lead ingots and some copper, and some barrels of salt pork. But, between them," I tapped the cipher book, "this is a record of the shipment of over ten thousand shields, plus waterproof shield covers."

"Ten thousand!" said Morganus. "That's enough for two legions, maybe three!"

"I know," I said, "and there's more. Each shipment was paid for in gold, very large quantities of gold, and each shipment and payment were signed off by the Syrian and by someone else, using their signet rings as seals. And, look here at the amount of gold!"

"Gods of Rome!" said Morganus. "Who's got that sort of money?"

"Precisely!" I said. "The druids are involved in this for sure, and the poor damn savages up north, but I can't believe they've got that much in ready gold. Morganus, it's got to be the Province Treasury itself. There's nowhere else on this island that's got that much wealth. And you know what that means?"

"What?"

"It's got to be Petros that's behind this. There's nobody else that can authorise payments like that. Him or the governor himself."

Morganus frowned fiercely.

"I know, I know," I said. "I'm not saying its him, not His Grace. I'm just saying that if it's not him, it has to be Petros."

"So what do we do now?"

"First I want to see that clerk optio, Silvius."

"Why?"

"Because he's a sharp knife and he went through the books at the shield factory, and I want to know what's in those books." I frowned. "Ten thousand shields couldn't have been loaded on board ships without following the licensing procedures."

"No!" said Morganus. "Shields are strategic goods."

"Right," I said. "So I want to know what's in the shield factory's books, without giving more warning to the enemy."

"To Petros?"

"Yes. If it's him."

"Is it?"

"Yes," I said. "It's him."

I saw Silvius next day, when I was feeling sufficiently better after my morning bath, that I stayed out of bed and dressed myself. I dressed good and warm, in several tunics, thick socks, warm boots, and a soft cloak, all from army stores. Then I sat in Morganus's living room, by the window, with a foot warmer under my feet.

It was a device that Morganus's wife found for me. A wooden box, like a footstool, but drilled with holes to let through the heat from charcoal glowing in a little grate inside. She even gave me a stack of small spitting sheets torn out of old linen. They were about two feet square, and were not actually for spitting at all, but for blowing your nose. It was a novel and pleasing idea, very clean and tidy, and the little sheets could be boiled, laundered and re-used afterwards. It was Roman cleanliness. Even a Greek has to admit they are our superiors in some things, with their plumbing and baths and aqueducts. But also it was the kindness of the lady herself, who seemed to like me and was concerned about me.

"Have you got everything you want?" she said, bending over me in my chair, with her daughters behind her. She was younger than me, but was acting the role of a mother.

"Yes, honoured lady," I said. "You are most gracious." Which she was indeed. I hate illness, and I know that I make a fuss when I am ill. But never had I been so thoroughly looked after. Morganus was standing grinning to one side, as he had when his wife made the bodyguards move the stone table. He was in full armour, but without his helmet, and the bodyguards were stood behind him.

"You just let me know if you need anything," she said, then bowed to her husband and went out with her girls.

"So," said Morganus, "when you're quite ready, Greek." I sensed the hint of chastisement.

"Well," I said, "I've got the phlegm, haven't I?" and I shuddered, and blew my nose loudly into one of the sheets.

"So you have," he said, "as all the world knows. So I'll tell Optio Silvius to stand well clear of you."

"Have you got him here?"

"He's waiting outside." Morganus nodded, and one of the bodyguards fetched Silvius, who was fresh shaved, in his best military tunic, and who stamped to attention in front of Morganus and raised an arm in formal salute.

"Hail Leonius Morganus Fortis Victrix!" he said, and Morganus nodded.

"Greetings upon you optio," said Morganus. "You will speak to the Greek gentleman."

Silvius was in his forties and was fat by legionary standards, because legionaries are slimmed to within an inch of their lives by constant marches, drills and exercises. So, while legionaries are intensely tough, they are sinewy and lean rather than bulky, and such heavily-muscled men as Morganus's bodyguards are exceptional, and the excused-drill clerks are different again. They live a sedentary life, they put on weight, and they are very intelligent, because only high intelligence can justify their non-combat role in the legionary hierarchy.

So Silvius turned to me and gave a small bow and I was pleased to see no hint of surprise on his face that Morganus had referred him to me. There was none of the usual Roman suspicion of a slave acting a citizen's part, even if the slave sat like a paterfamilias in an armchair, with a foot warmer and a cloak, while the First Javelin and his bodyguards remained standing. Silvius had the sense to overcome ingrained prejudice and to do what made sense.

"Optio," I said. "I give you good day."

"And I to you, honoured Greek."

"You were in charge of the team that read through the books in the offices of the shield factory."

"Yes, honoured Greek."

"Then tell me what you remember of any movement of shields by sea. Anything at all."

He had an excellent memory and was a great asset to his legion.

And so to the Londinium docks, despite my utmost reluctance to leave the house. I went with a heavy, hooded outdoor cloak over my indoor cloak, my legs wrapped in woollen puttees, and a supply of nose sheets in my pouch.

The docks were on the southward, river-facing side of the city, outside the fortifications, and upstream of the long, timber bridge that crossed the Thames, linking the Great South Road with Londinium's First Avenue that went, broad and straight through the main gates to the forum. The bridge was huge, with a hinged centre span that could be raised to let through the giant ships, the five-hundred tonners or greater, that could not let down their masts. However, the greater part of the docks, where serious trade came and went, was above the bridge.

Before we went into the docks, I insisted that we go up on to the bridge which gave an excellent view of everything, and I wanted overall impressions first. Once on the bridge I regretted this decision, because we were very much out in the open and the Britannic wind came whistling over the waters and stabbed like daggers. It made me sneeze repeatedly and soak all my nose sheets. So I crammed them soggy into my pouch, and leaned out over the rail, and used my fingers to empty my nose into the Thames, which was some small revenge. Then I raised my head and looked about me.

The view was spectacular. The Thames was vast and slow at Londinium, and it was many hundreds of yards wide and flowed into shallow lakes to the south of the city, where it formed an archipelago of islands and marshes. It was a savage and wild place that not even Roman engineering could civilise and, looking at the wet vastness of it, with the sound of the wind and the calling of birds, I could understand the Roman fear of primeval powers that lurked beyond their city walls. I looked at Morganus and the bodyguards, who were silent and thoughtful as they contemplated such ragged wilderness, because Romans love order and straight lines.

But the view immediately to the south east of the city was far more appealing to them. This was the main dockyards with rows of great piers jutting far out into the river. Whole and enormous tree trunks had been trimmed and trued and thundered into the river bed by Roman pile drivers, then planked over massively with neatly-squared timbers and good Roman right angles. Then to the shore side of the piers, butting against the city ramparts, was a small town of wharves and warehouses, cranes and sheds, with offices, clerks, stevedores, citizens, freedmen and slaves, all of them as busy as the wheeling gulls above that called and cried and dived for anything edible that fell into the waters. The wet smell of the river and the sound of the gulls are in my mind even now, for I like dockyards. I love them. I love them for their energy and for being a gateway to the whole, wide world.

And there were ships, dozens of them, of every shape and size, mostly made fast to the piers, but some were anchored in the river, and others were coming in or setting out, with the mariners alow and aloft, and calling out in their arcane patois, for no man can understand the speech of a sailor. Not when every other word is *avast*, or *belay*, or *clew the fo'c'sl bitts through the yard arm*, whatever that might mean. The technology is fascination, but the language is impenetrable and is nowhere set down for a scholar to study. So I forgot the Britannic phlegm for a while, and wondered if I might ever find time to write a dictionary of the sea, along with all my other stillborn books. What pleasure that would be if I could!

Morganus and the bodyguards were happy too. They were staring and talking, and pointing out the different kinds of shipping. The eldest bodyguard was an enthusiast. He whispered politely at first, but Morganus encouraged him and he grew confident and spoke aloud.

"That there's the main kind, honoured sir," he said. "See that one there, with the red flag? That's a Veneti round ship, a merchantman, about a hundred foot long. Driven by mainmast and foremast, with a dozen crew, it's steered at the stern by twin rudders. We copied them from the Celts in the time of Caesar the Great, and then improved them. Ships like that can go all the way to Rome, or Hispania, or Gaul, or up to the German ports. They're very stout and strong; built for the northern seas."

"What can it carry?" said one of the other bodyguards.

"Anything! And it'll take two hundred tons or more. On land that would mean a hundred carts and two hundred mules, *and* someone has to build road for them in the first place. But a ship does that all on its own. Marvellous isn't it?"

"What about the Navy?" said the other bodyguard. "There ain't no warships here."

"No, you won't see them," said the eldest bodyguard. "The fleet, the *Classis Britannicus*, is based down river by the sea at Dubris. They don't get up here much, 'cos there's no need, is there? *We* keep the peace up here. Us! The proper army!"

The rest laughed.

When we had seen enough, we left the bridge and went into the dockyard, where Morganus was saluted by the auxiliary troopers who guarded the dock gates, and provided a force to support the authority of the harbour master and his clerks. The harbour master was responsible for permits, passports and all the other records that ran the docks, and a community quite distinct from the city. The docks were fenced all around, guarded day and night, and no ship came or went unannounced or without permission, or without paying the taxes required. It was all very Roman and regulated, for the obvious reason that it was the busiest port outside the Mediterranean. Thus the total volume of trade that passed through it each year was enormous, and the Roman state wanted its share of that trade.

Within the dock gates we were in another world. Londinium was cosmopolitan, but the faces, costumes and manners of those within the docks were almost alien. To begin with, all the mariners walked with that peculiar rolling gait that marks them out, that and their leather-tanned, sun-dark faces. And, they wore bizarre clothes, and they swaggered and roared and did not give way to others, but made a great show of bumping into each other and yelling the most foul and filthy abuse, and yet then they laughed and passed on without ill will. They are a most proud and arrogant breed, raised up from childhood to the sea life and despising all those who are landsmen.

Then there was the astonishing range of outlandish goods on display; spices, glassware, sauces, apes, parrots and leopards, as well as a few top-class slaves. They were pampered exotics, mostly in their teens, who walked past, fresh and beautiful, with noses in the air, following their owners. The mariners leered at them, and yelled out what they'd like to do to them. They were most imaginative in their proposals and it was very funny. A stone statue would have laughed and we certainly did.

The harbour master was waiting for us outside his office, with his freedmen and slaves lined up beside him, in all the bustle of the busy docks. One of the auxiliary guardsmen had very properly run on ahead to warn him, and the harbour master was standing ready to give honour to Morganus. He was an old mariner himself, retired from the sea with an excellent job on land. I read all that in his manner and bearing, and the fact that, like all mariners, he was familiar in his speech, believing that no man is his superior.

"Morganus the Javelin!" he said, with a smile. "Welcome to you and yours, from me and mine!" He bowed low, and waved a casual hand to introduce his followers. He was about thirty, which meant he could have been over twenty years at sea, because they start so young. He was handsome, he was carefully shaved, his hair was trimmed like a Roman, and his features told me that he was a Gaulish Celt of the Veneti tribe, which is not surprising as they are formidable seamen. He was well dressed, with good jewellery and had the look of a man used to luxury. This was not surprising either, because dockyards are notorious for the bribes that are passed so that goods might escape the rules for private profit, and who better to benefit than the harbour master?

"I'm Grannix Calindo of Darioritem in Gaul," he said, and jabbed a thumb at his chest. " I'm harbour master here, and I'm a Roman citizen, me and me dad before me. So, what I can do for you?"

I thought of the miserable torturers terrified by Morganus's sudden arrival, as compared with this cheerful, insolent man who boasted of citizenship while still using a Celtic name. One look at him told me that he was either a tremendous actor or had nothing to fear. But his informality irritated Morganus, so the bodyguards frowned and gripped their sword hilts, and Morganus was not polite.

"Grannix Calindo," he said, "I'm here with Ikaros of Apollonis, and you'll answer his questions and answer them truthfully." Grannix stopped grinning. He looked me over and frowned. He could not judge my rank or status because I had not been properly introduced. He could see I was a Greek, but was I a citizen or a foreigner? Was I free man? A freedman? Even a slave? And himself ordered to answer to me! Roman citizens are sensitive to that, even citizens with Celtic names. So I prodded him to see how he would respond.

"I am a slave," I said, and I paused to allow the frown to form on his brow. "But I am in Imperial service, and I am investigating the murder of my late master Scorteus. Him and several others."

"Oh?" said Grannix. "Scorteus?" And, a flicker of something showed on his face. It was not guilt, not quite, not exactly. But it was something he wanted to hide, and I wondered how best to drag it out into the light. It was a puzzle to be solved, and a pleasure besides.

"You knew Scorteus?" I asked.

"Certainly!" he said. "Scorteus was rich. He had lots of ships." He turned to his senior clerk. "How many was it?"

"Nineteen, honoured sir," said the clerk.

"There you are, then," said Grannix. "And I met him once or twice, and his secretary more often than that. I mean the Syrian." He raised a hand to his neck and made plucking motions with his fingers. "Him that picked at himself. Nasty habit."

"Can we go into your office?" I said. "There are things to be discussed. A number of murders have been done, and someone will have to pay with his life. Most probably by crucifixion." The implied threat was necessary. I felt already that he was innocent of blame, but I needed to knock the bounce out of him. So he showed us inside, and the bodyguards and Grannix's men waited in an outer room. I took a tablet from the senior bodyguard, and Grannix sent for wine and cakes and we sat down together.

As we entered the office, Grannix bowed slightly and raised hands to an altar in the wall. It was a neat little wooden structure, with a couple of incense burners, and a much-worn statuette in the middle. Morganus and I raised hands, but Grannix had a further devotion to perform. He stepped forward and embraced the image with both hands, and stroked it several times, and nodded reverently. Then he turned round, and sniffed, and flopped down into the office's only chair without first inviting us to do the same. He just sat looking at us. He was ready to talk, but he was still rough in his manners. So Morganus and I found stools and sat down.

I stared at him a while, then opened the tablet I had brought in with me, and looked at that too. My purpose was to disturb him into indiscretion, so I waited till he was suitably uncomfortable before I spoke.

"I need your comments on certain facts," I said.

"Go on then," he said.

"We know that Scorteus owned ships, and that he exported shields in them."

"All legal and proper!" said Grannix. "Always with the right documents."

"We'll check the documents," I said. "A team of legionary clerks will come to look into your records."

He did not like that. He frowned. But I could see that it was just annoyance. There was no depth of fear in his face, and by that I was convinced that there was no guilt in him, nor would we actually need to send for Silvius and his men. So what was Grannix hiding?

"Would you please look at this," I said, and gave him the tablet. "This is a list, taken from the records of Scorteus's shield works. It shows all his ships that set out loaded with shields during the last two years. Some of them were lost at sea and some were not. Is there anything odd in that?"

Grannix had a long, careful look at the list. Then he sent for his senior clerk, and the office's records were brought out and compared with my list. He and the clerk spent quite a time at it, and Morganus and I finished his cakes, and I finished most of the wine, which was superlatively excellent. But then, we were in the dockyard through which all wine must pass on its way to Londinium, so I presumed the harbour master had taken his dip. Finally Grannix looked up from the documents, with his clerk standing behind him.

"It all tallies," he said. "Your list from the shield works is correct, and we've got all the documents to certify that any shields went aboard with all the proper permits. And ships get lost all the time. Nothing special about that," he said. "The north sea is deadly, especially outside the safe months, and the sea gods take a ship from time to time." He respectfully raised hands. "It's their tithe," said Grannix. "It's the dues of the gods." He raised hands again. "So, you sacrifice before putting to sea, you sacrifice on safe arrival, and that's all there is to it." He nodded emphatically. "And, all those who can't stand it shouldn't go to sea!"

"So there's nothing exceptional in the number of ships lost?" I said. Grannix looked to his clerk.

"What d'you think?" he said. The clerk wagged his head from side to side.

"Maybe a bit high," he said, "six lost out of twenty sailings."

"Could be bad luck," said Grannix.

"Perhaps," said the clerk. But he was not sure, and that might have been all we got out of Grannix. But, I took a final look round his office and noticed something about the shrine. There were some letters cut into the pediment at the top. They were in the shade and hard to read, but I could just make out *D S TRAJANI I*, and I realised that I had misjudged Grannix, because I had not recognised the identity of who the shrine was devoted to. It was the Emperor, but I had not recognised Him in this much-worn little image.

This was unusual because the identity of the little statues that grace Roman shrines is meant to be obvious. They are mass produced in factories, made from soft stone or plaster. They are bright painted and have boldly-obvious signs pertinent to the deity: the Wheel of Beltranos, the Thunderbolt of Jupiter, the Crown of Minerva and so on. In the case of the Emperor, He was always depicted in a general's military cuirass, with right arm raised. But Grannix had been so devout with his stroking the image that the arm was worn to a stump and the cuirass was unrecognisable.

But *D S TRAJANI* stood for *The Divine Spirit of the Emperor Trajan*. The shrine was sacred to the Imperial Cult, which all citizens must respect, and to which all must pray on the Emperor's birthday. But not every citizen went so far as to put an Imperial altar in his office! Most folk chose from the usual pantheon of Olympic divinities, especially those that bring luck to commerce. So the presence in Grannix's office of such a shrine meant that Grannix was a serious patriot, and that offered an opportunity.

"Could we have a word alone?" I said to Grannix, and he looked shifty for the first time.

"What for?" he said.

"For privacy," I said, and Morganus, being the comrade and friend that he was, got up without a word, and put on his helmet.

"I'll be outside," he said, and the clerk leapt forward to open the door for him, then went out and closed it. I pulled my chair close to Grannix.

"I see you are a true Roman," I said, pointing to the altar.

"Gods bless His Majesty!" said Grannix. "My dad served twenty-six years in the fleet to earn his citizenship, and he raised me to be loyal."

"So," I said, "you should know that my inquiries are not only into murder, but into betrayal of the Empire." I paused for effect. "So I call upon you to do all in your power to help me. I call upon you in the Emperor's name!"

He sucked his lower lip. He blinked.

"So what is it about Scorteus and his ships that you haven't told me," I said, and he gasped, and joined the swollen ranks of those who believe that I read minds.

"How did you know?" he said.

"Just tell me," I said.

So he did.

Chapter 26

Grannix the Harbour Master looked at me. He looked at the door, as if fearing eavesdroppers. He looked at the window that gave a view of the dockyard through an unglazed lattice grid, such that the shouting of the mariners and the calling of the gulls came in loud and clear. Grannix sighed and shifted in his chair.

"I made a very good marriage," he said, "thanks to my father and the will of the gods."

"Yes," I said, and he frowned as he wondered how best to explain his thoughts. This often happens when a man is reluctant to speak, and the questioner must be patient. So I was patient and Grannix found the words.

"When my dad came out of his service, he got a bronze citizenship certificate, and a grant of money. He was a centurion by then, and the grant was a big one."

"Yes," I said.

"Well. Trouble was we were Veneti. And I don't know if you know, but there was a big war between the Veneti and the Romans in Caesar's time."

"Caesar the Great," I said, because I did know. I had read *De Bello Gallico*, his book on the Gallic Wars. It is lurid and self-praising, but fairly accurate for a work of propaganda, and the Latin is strong and elegant.

"Yes," said Grannix, "Him." He sniffed and fished in his past for old truths that stank. "Thing is that the Veneti don't like people who serve the Empire. Not then, not now."

"So?" I said.

"So when dad was out of his time, he brought me and my mother and the little 'uns over here for a new start. 'Cos they're not Veneti over here. And he bought a ship and he put me to sea, which I always wanted, and we made more money. Quite a bit. And just before he died, he got me a good wife. A real Roman girl from Italy. You know. Real Roman. Citizen's daughter. Cost a bit to smooth everything, but I married her, and my kids are proper Romans make no mistake, and my wife's family got me the job as harbour master."

"I congratulate you," I said. The life history was tedious, but he was leading up to something.

"So she's a Roman matriarch, my wife. And the marriage is a good one." He sighed and stopped, and I could see so easily what was coming next.

"So?" I said.

"So you know what it's like," he said. "Marriage is for business. It's important. But there's no spark in it. Not down below the belt. Know what I mean?"

"So perhaps you looked around?" I said.

He nodded and fell silent again. But this time I judged that he needed the goad, like an ox which dozes in harness.

"So who is this other woman," I said, "who is connected with Scorteus's ships?"

He gasped. His eyes went round. Sometimes it is pitiful to see the depth of human superstition and how easily a man can be persuaded of magic powers.

"You know, don't you?" he said, and all but fell on his knees. "Don't tell anyone," he begged. "She won't understand, won't the wife. And there's nothing in it with the other one. Nothing! I just shaft her now and again. She likes it! I like it! That's all there is to it!"

He said much more in the same style, as some do who are found out in this particular sin, and it puzzled me, as always, because if all he needed was to satisfy his lust why not use a slave or visit the brothels? That is what most men did, and kept their marriages intact; because, lust has nothing to do with marriage and a Roman wife understands that. The trouble with some men is that they want more than lust. They want the intoxication of enjoying a woman who gives herself to him because she *likes* him, and not for a slave's duty or a whore's fee. Unfortunately the mirror image of that, in a wife's eyes, is serious adultery, calling down the vengeance of herself and her family. For Grannix this meant serious trouble, because he was only a Veneti, one-generation citizen, while they were real Romans with ancestors behind them. They had put him into his job, and they could probably take him out of it. So Grannix was very afraid.

"Grannix," I said, "I give you my word that I will keep silent if you tell me precisely what is the connection between this other woman and Scorteus's ships."

"Gods bless you, Greek," he said. "Thing is, she's a widow. She's got a lad. He's a nice lad, and he wanted to go to sea. So I got him a ship."

"One of Scorteus's ships?" I asked.

"Yes. *The Lucky Eye*, one of them that carried a load of shields."

"And?"

"It went to sea. It was gone too long, and we thought it was lost. But then the lad came back on his own."

"What happened? To the ship with the shields?"

"Don't know. The lad won't tell me. Won't even tell his mother, 'cos he's scared shitless and he won't even come out of the house any more. He's frightened of something. That's all I know, Greek, before all the gods of land and sea." He was speaking the truth, and I nodded.

"You have my promise of silence," I said, "but I will need to know the name of this boy, and of his mother, and where she may be found."

Soon after that, Morganus and I went into the warehouse of a ship-chandler's warehouse, just fifty yards away from the harbour master's office. Grannix had not looked very far for his adventures. But that was no surprise. It is typical of adultery that men are lazy. They take what is closest and most easily on offer.

The warehouse was long and narrow, and packed with sea-faring goods, which not only lined the shelves and floors of the building but hung in great rows from the rafters. There were sails, anchor stocks, rope, sounding leads, pulley blocks, timbers, spars, flags, nails, carpenters' tools, and long rows of barrels. It was all very orderly, everything was labelled, and the whole place stank of rope and pitch, and it was tremendously busy, with mariners bargaining nose to nose with the staff slaves. Wheelbarrows and porters were going out laden with goods, and nobody was giving precedence to anybody.

Just inside, where the light came in from the main doors, there was a raised platform, fenced off with knee-high railings with a gate in the middle, and a big slave to guard the gate. The railings were a statement of authority because the mistress of the house sat behind them, at a table with another slave behind her, and rows of shelves for documents and a big, iron strongbox at her feet. This was the place where payment was made or credit given, and there was a noisy queue of master mariners outside the railings, yelling and chattering and laughing.

They nudged one another, as we approached, and they stared boldly at Morganus in his swan crest and gleaming armour. But they fell silent, at least by mariners' standards, and they gave respect with briefly bowed heads and made way when the bodyguards physically pushed them aside. I followed Morganus through the little gate and the woman at the table had the good manners to stand and bow properly to Morganus.

"Are you the lady Massilina?" said Morganus. "Widow of the late Decimus Otovi the Chandler?" She replied in good Latin, with just a touch of Celtic accent.

"I am the lady Massilina," she said. "And I ask in return, O centurion, if you are he who has been asking questions in the shipyard? You and your Greek boy." She pointed to the queue of mariners. "All present are all talking about you." She gave another small bow, and looked at Morganus. She was a bold, smooth woman, tall and well formed, with fine round limbs and hair elaborately dressed, and she wore good Roman clothes. Her outer cloak was pinned open with brooches to display the status garment beneath, the stola of a Roman matriarch. I was surprised. Having met Grannix the Harbour Master, I had expected that his mistress would be some scruffy trollop with an easy grin, not a fine woman like this. Morganus was clearly impressed because he gave a deep, formal bow.

"Honoured lady," he said, "I am First Javelin of the Twentieth. This is my colleague Ikaros of Apollonis, and I ask that you might speak directly to him." He bowed again, and then it was my turn. I stepped forward conscious that the warehouse was full of ears.

So I produced the tablet I had shown Grannix. I took the stylus from its holder, and I wrote out five words, *your son is in danger*. I showed them to her and she gasped as if I had struck her. It was an unkind shock, but it was the quickest way to get herself, myself and Morganus into a private place where we could talk. It was not a pleasant place, being the latrines at the back of the warehouse, with the bodyguards at the door to keep out those with full bladders. There I told her what I knew about her and Grannix and her son's survival from the wreck of Scorteus's ship. I added a promise as recompense for the fright I had given her.

"Lady, I have to say that your son is indeed in danger, and that this honourable officer," I bowed to Morganus, "can offer your son the army's protection. We can take him to the legionary fortress, where no assassin can reach him."

That did not have quite the effect I had hoped. She was wondering what was more threatening, assassins or the Roman army? So I took the risk of saying more.

"Lady, I must warn you that our investigations are being spied upon. A powerful enemy is following just behind us. He will learn of your son and come after him, if he is not in the army's protection."

That got us into Massilina's house inside the city walls. It was a good house, on a good street, and well staffed by good slaves who Massilina trusted. But still they were slaves, and slaves gossip, and I really did believe that her son was not safe there. Not now.

His name was Otovi, after his father, and he was sixteen years old, but looked much younger. He was small, and thin and pale, with a wispy moustache and beard. He had not been out of the house for over a year, and I met him in his bedroom on the upper floor. It was cluttered with board games, including *Tabulae*, as the Romans call it, but which we Greeks invented and is properly called backgammon. Massilina had to spend time reassuring him before I entered the room, while Morganus and the bodyguards waited downstairs, which proved to be good sense. Otovi would have jumped out of the window had he seen them, because he was fearful and damaged, and troubled in mind. I of all people could recognise the signs.

He was sitting by the window, rattling dice in a cup and throwing them on to a Tabula board on a small table. He did that over and over again, not looking at anyone, and certainly not at me, while his mother stood at his side with her hand on his shoulder and whispering to him, trying to comfort him as she had done when he was a child. But he was immune to a mother's comfort. Small as he was, he was no longer a child, because a mariner lives a man's life in a man's world. He faces storm and peril, and seas coming over the bow, and the wind blowing the ship towards death on a lee shore. All mariners knew such horrors, but I suspected that Otovi had known worse, perhaps much worse. His mother looked up as I entered. She shook him gently.

"This is the Greek gentleman," she said. He barely looked up, then he ignored me and his mother, and carried on throwing his dice.

"I see you play Tabulae," I said.

"Yes," he said, without looking up.

"Who do you play against?"

"Anyone. Slaves mostly."

"Will you play against me?"

"If you like."

I sat down opposite him and set out the pieces.

"My people played this game," I said, and I smiled, and reached for the dice cup. He gave it to me and I threw the dice.

So we played and so I let him win. I did so because if I play fair I always win at board games, unless the game or the players are new to me, and then I lose only at first but slowly overtake the rest until I become bad company to all concerned, including myself. It happens most markedly with games of skill, but even with dice I win more times than is natural. I suppose it is my gift of insight, or rather my curse. That and the oddity of mind that enables me, without effort, to think several moves ahead, and to perceive alternatives. Whatever it may be, it denies me the sociable pleasure that decent folk take in such games, because who wants to play with a man who always wins?

So we played, and little by little we talked. In the end he found a lot to say, and agreed, with many tears from his mother, to come back to the fortress with us. But we waited until dark, we wrapped him in a hooded cloak, and we went with the household slaves bearing torches, with two bodyguards to the front, two to the rear, and with the boy between myself and Morganus. Having lost two vital witnesses already, we considered the threat so great that Morganus gave me his pugio again, and the law on arming slaves was damned across the Styx to Hades. I hid it the weapon under my cloak in case anyone should see it, anyone not bent on killing us.

These precautions seemed sufficient, but they were not. We were attacked on the first street corner that we passed.

The monster came pattering out of the darkness, barefoot and fast, with a frightful and hideous face. Slaves gasped, torches wobbled, light flickered and the creature was on us before we could blink; naked, silent, and deadly. Two bodyguards leaped and drew and hacked and blocked, but the enemy slipped between them and fell upon Otovi, knocking him down between Morganus and me, gripping the boy in a lover's embrace of two legs and one arm, and stabbing and stabbing with the free hand. Even as Morganus ran it through with a sword, the bodyguards failed to haul it off, and I sank my pugio into the slimy back, hilt deep into the kidney, which certain death stroke did nothing to stop the attack. The thing did not finally die until the eldest bodyguard drove his sword two-handed into its head, and rocked the blade from side to side, to mangle the brain within and send the life force back into the underworld.

Then we stood and stared and gasped, and I fell to my knees and stabbed the thing two or three times more to make sure, then sheathed my dirk and tried to pull the dead monster from its victim, which was surprisingly hard to do because my hands kept slipping, and because even my mind, my rational, Greek, philosophical mind, was filled with the sure and certain belief that we were dealing not with mortal powers but a demon from hell.

"MITHRAAAAAAAAS!" cried Morganus, in a great shout at the full strength of his body, as he called upon his god in his foul moment.

"MITHRAAAAAAAAS!" cried the bodyguards.

"Bring the light!" I cried, still pulling and pulling at the slippery body.

"You boys!" cried Morganus to the slaves. "In the name of Jupiter, Juno and Minerva, bring those torches here!"

The slaves never moved. They just moaned and whined, and all I could see in the wavering light was Otovi's wide, dead eyes, and the naked body still on top of him.

"Help me!" I said, and I tried to grasp the body, which I could not properly do. But the bodyguards finally heaved him clear and rolled him on his back beside his victim.

"Bring the light damn you all!" cried Morganus. But the slaves hung back, hunched and trembling with hands over their mouths.

"Men of the Twentieth!" said Morganus. "To me! Bring the light!" The bodyguards snatched the torches from the slaves, and came close and we finally saw what had attacked us. Not a demon, not a monster, but a man, a very young man, pure Celt, but wild and dark with a strong animal smell. He was slender, but with exceptional muscular development. He was entirely naked. His head was shaved, his face and chest were painted with horrific black-and-white paint, he was armed with a dagger bound fast to his right hand, and his entire body was thickly coated in grease. I had never seen anything like him.

"What is he?" I said. "Does anyone know?" I looked round. The slaves were gibbering, and the bodyguards shook their heads, but Morganus knew. He had served many years in Britannia.

"This is bad, Greek," he said. "And we can't talk here." That was all he would say, but he gave swift orders, sending the youngest bodyguard running to the fort, with his armour thrown off for speed, to bring a full century of troops at the double. We took refuge in the house of the Lady Massilina, taking Otovi's body with us, but leaving the Celt because he was too slippery to carry. Massilina howled at the sight of her dead son, while her household slaves stood wringing their hands, and I read guilt in every face. Meanwhile, the house had doors and shutters, but it was only a house and not a fortress.

"Are we safe here?" I said to Morganus.

"No!" he said. "But it's all we've got, and they might send another one, and, if they do, I don't want to meet him in the dark and in the open."

"Another what?" I said. But he just shook his head.

"It's druids, Greek. It *is* druids after all."

So we barred all the doors, and stood guard, and waited with drawn steel, while Massilina and the slaves wept over Otovi's body, wailing and rending their garments. "What was he? That Celt?" I said, and Morganus sheathed his sword briefly so that he could make the bull sign.

"The Celts call them *cennad angau*," he said. "It means *messengers of death*. They're raised from children. Raised up by the druids. There were never many of them, and there aren't supposed to be any of them any more! They're fed special food, they do special exercises, they're kept apart from all other people. Their lives are devoted to prayers and sacrifice." He looked at me. "Which means human sacrifice."

"Does it?" I said.

"Yes. And they tell them, the druids tell them, that they're destined for paradise, and that no blade can cut them nor missile strike them. Do you understand?"

"I think so."

"And they're trained in tracking and woodcraft, and in all arms, and they're greased and naked so you can't get hold of them. They don't try to defend themselves, they just go straight for the victim and keep on stabbing until someone kills them." He looked at me, as if defying me to doubt what he said next. "Then they go to paradise."

"Do you believe that?" I said.

"Why not?" he said. "Didn't I warn you about the druids?"

"Morganus," I said. "Yes, it was the druids. Maybe Maligoterix. Yes, they sent a fanatic covered in grease. And yes, that was clever, and you Romans have got unfinished business with the druids. *But it doesn't mean the druids are magic and it doesn't mean they control the afterlife!*"

I think I actually shouted those last words. Morganus looked away. As far as he was concerned we were not dealing with crime or politics. We were dealing with druids. And perhaps he was right, because when the century arrived, and we set out under their protection, we looked for the body of the *cennad angau* and it was gone.

Chapter 27

We talked properly next morning, over breakfast in Morganus's house. We were safe there and the sun was risen, and Morganus's wife and daughters served us. They served good, fresh bread, and eggs and butter, and little cuts of meat from last night's table, with hot apple juice flavoured with honey and spices. And the fear of the uncanny, fear of the druids, was not so bad in the bright morning as in the dark night. Very few things are in my experience and, better still, the Britannic phlegm had run its course, and I was not sniffing and sneezing.

"So you think the slaves told the druids?" said Morganus, "Messalina's own slaves?"

"Yes," I said. "I think we were right about the druids still having spies everywhere. People who pass on important information." He nodded. "And more than that, I think they were already watching Otovi, and they had this, this death messenger."

"*Cennad angau*," said Morganus.

"Yes," I said, "I think they had him ready in case of need."

"How d'you know that?"

"Well I hardly think they breed them in the middle of Londinium! There must be a place, a camp, a settlement, somewhere in the wilds, and the cennad angau would have to be summoned from it and brought here, and they couldn't have done that in a few hours. He must have been kept here. Kept in case of need."

"Why not send anyone to do the killing? Anyone faithful to ... them."

"Because, from what you've told me, I would guess that a cennad angau would either die in the attack, or kill himself afterwards, or be totally immune to torture if captured, and would die without revealing who sent him."

"But why didn't they kill Otovi months ago?"

"I don't know, but I'd guess they have to be careful not to draw attention to themselves. Druids aren't supposed to exist, are they? And if they make too much trouble, you Romans might turn nasty and stop tolerating them. So I think they held back until they were sure that Otovi was going to pass on the truth about Scorteus selling shields to the Caledonians, because the druids were involved and they were afraid of what Rome would do if Rome found out." Morganus nodded.

"So what *is* the truth?" he said, "What did he tell you last night, that poor little devil?" He thought of Otovi and raised hands. "Gods rest his soul and bring him peace," he said, and I did the same, and we looked at each other knowing that Otovi had been murdered whilst under our protection. So I added a few words of my own.

"And may the gods bring peace to those who struggle in a righteous cause," I said, "those of us who do the best that we can. Which is all that men can do."

"So be it," said Morganus, and made the bull sign. Then he plodded on like a Roman. "So what did we learn, Greek? What did we learn from Otovi?"

"We learned that Scorteus was worse even that I'd thought," I said. "He was capable of mass murder and treachery."

"Oh," said Morganus. "I'm sorry. I mean, I know you liked him."

"I did. But didn't really know him," I said. "Not all of him."

"So let's hear it!"

I filled my cup and took a good gulp. It was not wine, but fruit juice is appropriate at breakfast.

"Otovi was an able seaman," I said, "That's a fully trained hand who's learned his craft. I know he's small, but he went to sea at eight years old, which is typical. More than that, he was a topman, ship's elite. They're the ones who go up the masts to trim the sails." Morganus nodded. "He wanted to go further, to train as a mate, that's a ship's officer, and Grannix got him aboard one of Scorteus's ships, *The Lucky Eye*, apprenticed to the Shipmaster." I stopped and filled my cup again, and Morganus's.

"Go on," he said. "I'm following so far."

"So. The ship took aboard a full cargo, including shields, five thousand of them with their waterproof covers, and you'd be surprised how little room that takes in a ship."

"Would I?" he said.

"Yes. Otovi was very informative. He said a shield weighs about fifteen pounds with its cover.

"That's right," said Morganus.

"So in a ton weight you'd get about 150 shields, and five thousand shields comes to about thirty-three and a half tons."

"That's interesting," said Morganus. "Those are standard army figures."

"He was told them," I said. "Or, rather, he heard the Syrian tell someone."

"You mean your master's secretary, the one that got boiled alive?"

"Yes. When the ship was loaded, the Syrian came aboard with a man in a cloak that kept a hood over his face. They came after dark, by lantern light. He was a small man with Celtic boots and plaid trousers, and a harsh voice. Harsh when he spoke, but he didn't speak much."

"Go on."

"The Shipmaster made a great fuss of the Syrian, because he was the owner's representative, and the Syrian and the little man were shown everything that had gone aboard, just as if the little man was checking it."

"And what was the cargo, apart from the shields?" said Morganus, and I couldn't help but smile in triumph.

"Exactly what I read from the Syrian's cipher books, a mixed cargo of ship's stores and metal ingots. A valuable cargo, and the shields had all the proper documents and were bound for Hispania, to go to a legion out there."

"That'd be the Sixth *Hispaniensis*," said Morganus.

"Yes. Them," I said. "So there was no need to falsify anything. The shields went out with the real documents."

"And?"

"Once the ship was well under way, and out of the Thames mouth, the helmsman didn't turn south for Hispania. He steered north, up the coast of Britannia, and the Shipmaster took Otovi aside for a little word. Grannix had dropped Otovi right down the bog hole and into the mire. Unintentionally, I'm sure, but he had. The Shipmaster and his crew had done a deal with Scorteus, or rather Scorteus had done a deal on them! The deal was that they take *Lucky Eye* up to an agreed rendezvous in the Firth of Tay ..."

"What's that?"

"A river inlet. A great big dent in the eastern coast of Caledonia. A sort of natural harbour, miles long and miles wide." Morganus nodded, I continued. "The agreement was that they'd give the shields to the druids. And then the Shipmaster could keep the ship and the rest of the cargo, with all necessary documents to give it a new identity, with bills of sale, certified ownership, the lot. The ship would eventually be struck off the books as lost at sea, and the Shipmaster and his men would sail away, to anywhere they wished, with a fine ship and more wealth than honest mariners would see in their whole lives."

"But why would they carry shields to the tribes," said Morganus. "That's fomenting rebellion!"

"They were Veneti. That's how Grannix knew them. He may be a citizen and proud of it, but they weren't. They hated Rome."

"Well, what was to stop them just taking off with the ship? They had all the documents didn't they?"

"No they didn't. They were to get the documents from the druids."

"Well, why did Otovi go along with them?"

"The Shipmaster told him it was that or they'd heave him over the side with a sack of ballast tied to his feet."

"So what happened?"

"They were betrayed. They anchored at the rendezvous. The Caledonians came paddling out in dugouts, whooping and yelling, and with a druid in the bows of the biggest one. They came aboard, seized the crew, and killed them by torture, one by one. Otovi didn't see it because he was hiding down below, but he heard it. He thinks it went on for days."

270

"Why didn't they find him? Didn't they look?"

"He ran below as soon as he saw the boats coming out. He was frightened by the war whoops, and he was right. And he's small. He crammed himself into some nasty little hole deep down in the dark. Perhaps the natives didn't look very hard? They had plenty else to play with. Anyway, they didn't find him. Then, eventually, it all went quiet, and he got the courage to come out of his hole and look round. And it was pouring hard with rain, there was nobody aboard, and the natives had tried to fire the ship, but the rain had put the fire out. The ship was swinging to anchor and in a vile mess, with everything broken open and looted, and all the cargo gone. The crew were hanging by their feet from the yard arms, and not looking human any more because they'd been skinned."

"So what did he do, Otovi?"

"He got aboard the ship's boat, that was towed behind. It was a big sea boat that they kept ready for emergencies, with a sail and some stores of food and water."

"Why didn't the natives take it? The boat?"

"I don't think they wanted it. They didn't want the ship, did they? They tried to burn that! They're not a seafaring race and they probably don't want ships, just as some Celts don't want cities."

"Could be," said Morganus.

"Anyway, Otovi waited till the tide was on the ebb."

"What's that?"

"Going out."

"Oh."

"And he cut the cable to the ship, drifted out to sea, and put up the sail. Then he went south down the coast to the first safe Roman port, hid the boat, kept everything secret, begged for food and shelter, and eventually got himself a berth on a coaster bound for Londinium. It took him months, but he got back home, and he hid away in his mother's house."

"Why didn't he report to the Roman garrison at this first safe port? Why did he keep everything secret?"

"Because he knew they wouldn't believe him! He was up against Scorteus, and Scorteus would make an invincible enemy. Otovi had the sense to see that. Believe me Morganus, I knew Scorteus, and the lad was right. He'd have denied all knowledge of what the Shipmaster said, and blamed everything on him, and on Otovi too probably. And, Scorteus was a millionaire and Otovi was nothing. Anyway, I don't think Otovi was entirely sane at the time. Not then or ever after. Remember he spent days in hiding, waiting for the natives to pull him out and skin him. He saw what they did to the others, and it turned his mind. But, he was right to be afraid of Scorteus, and he should have been afraid of Petros."

"Petros?" said Morganus. "Why him? It's the druids we're fighting now."

"No it isn't," I said,. "They're only half the problem. Less than half. Scorteus started this plot at the Londinium end. He conceived this plan and went to someone with it, Petros in my opinion, and *he* wanted the Caledonians to have those shields, and paid Scorteus with huge quantities of gold. The druids only came in later, when Scorteus needed to get the shields to the Caledonians. But the Londinium end is the important one, because the gold had to come from the Roman treasury, because it's only the Roman treasury that had more gold than Scorteus had already!" The thought stirred my imagination. I sat upright and blinked.

"What is it?" said Morganus.

"We're losing sight of the main plot," I said. "It's like a classic drama at the theatre, when you get so bound up in the characters that you forget the story."

"If you say so," said Morganus. "I prefer the races, or a good comedy." He smiled, briefly, but the rest of what I said was not funny.

"We're supposed to be finding out who killed Scorteus," I said.

"So?"

"Well we haven't done that. We haven't got anywhere near it. We don't even know how anyone got in and out of that bath chamber to kill him." I saw Morganus'ss expression, and almost groaned. "By all the Gods of Greece and Rome, let's not go back to thoughts of invisible druids! We've got to go back and start again. We've got to go back to the House of Scorteus: House of Fortunus as it is now. We've got to go over everything, again and again and again. We're supposed to be proving that it wasn't a slave that killed Scorteus, because if we don't then four hundred slaves will be executed, including myself." So we sent for the bodyguards and would have gone to the House of Fortunus.

But before we left the fort, another galloper came and all centurions were summoned to the Legate in the Temple of Standards. So I had to wait with the bodyguards until Morganus returned. This took some time and, while he was gone, bugles were blown throughout the fortress. There was a vast pounding of boots and jingling of military gear as legionaries turned out in arms and headed for the parade ground. I went to the door of Morganus's house, with the bodyguards, to see what was going on. I wondered if some disaster had occurred, but they knew better.

"Third level alert," said the eldest bodyguard, looking at the troops hurrying past. Only odd-numbered centuries, no marching rations, no baggage wagons, and they're not going at the double." He looked at me. "Nothing to worry about, Greek," he said, and Morganus returned half an hour later and confirmed that.

"News from the north," he said. "Teutonius has found the main body of the natives, and they're retreating in front of our advance. They're falling back in vast numbers into the mountains. If they're preparing to make a stand, this could be just what we want, or they might be leading Teutonius into a trap." He thought about that, remembering, from his vast experience, the realities of advance, counter attack, and ambush. Then he shrugged his shoulders. "Either way, we look like getting a battle."

"Is that serious?" I said. "Can you leave the fort?"

"Oh yes," he said, and pointed at the troops, "This is just a drill. Keeps the men on their toes." That is what he said, but I looked behind his eyes. He was a veteran of the Britannic wars, and nobody knew better than him how cunning the Celtic warriors could be; that no battle brought certain victory; and, that only forty years ago, a Celtic host had burned Londinium to ashes. But that was for others to worry about, so we went again the House of Fortunus, which was now unrecognisable.

The Numidian auxiliaries had been replaced by a full cohort of the Twentieth Legion, over five hundred men, with a command post in the great atrium, and a military tribune in command. The family had gone to their country villa. There were fully-armed legionaries in every room of the house. The slaves were under close guard, and the few that we saw looked broken in spirit, and given over to dread of what was coming to them. There was fear seeping out of the walls, and an awful silence, with none of the sounds of life that are the background chatter of a living, breathing house. If the Silanianum was a monster, it was already within the walls, holding every man, woman and child in its claws.

So we did what we could. We went back to Scorteus's bath chamber. We went for another look. At least I looked while Morganus and the bodyguards looked at me as if I were giving a performance, and they looked at the luxurious bath chamber.

"Very nice," said Morganus, "very nice indeed." Which it was, and scrubbed so free of all traces of the murder that I feared that I was wasting my time after all. I feared there was nothing to be learned here, and Morganus did too. He just looked round like a tourist in the Pantheon dome. I looked too. I looked and looked and saw nothing. Then I looked again.

Sometimes a puzzle may be solved by blessed inspiration, by clever calculation, or sometimes by chance or by luck. On other occasions there is a need for endless diligence and the absolute refusal to give up. So I walked round and round the bath chamber. I did so until Morganus and the bodyguards must have been faint from boredom. Then I began to feel my way round the walls with my fingertips ... and so ... and so ... Then, I noticed something. There was a big cupboard set into one side of the room. It was made with exquisite skill, and the doors were so disguised by the wall painting, and by decorative ridges worked in the wall plaster, that it was impossible to see it, which of course was the intention of whoever had designed it. It was a stroke of art, a work of delight. Also, on the morning of the murder, there had been rows of slaves standing between me and it. Here indeed was something that I had missed!

I stepped forward, found a superbly hidden catch and pulled open the doors and looked inside. There were three rows of wooden grids holding a great number of white linen bath towels where the central heating would keep them warm.

"Nothing there," said Morganus, looking over my shoulder. But, I was barely listening, and systematically pulled out all the towels and threw them on the floor, looking for I knew not what, until I found it. Hidden right at the bottom of a pile of towels was a bundle of filthy, black rags. They were greasy and nasty and smelt strongly of fish.

I guessed whose they were at once. It took no soaring flight of the intellect, but to be sure I sent for Agidox, and he called a few of his senior staff into his office, where everyone sniffed and waved away the stink of fish, and said, "*It's the Corvidics*." There were a dozen or more slaves standing round nodding in agreement, with Allicanda prominent among them. I made a small bow to her and she gave back a curt nod. Like the rest of these seniors, she somehow maintained her dignity in the face of the fear that hung over them all.

"So who are these Corvidics?" said Morganus, and Agidox turned to Allicanda.

"This girl is mistress of our fish kitchen," he said. "She will tell you." Allicanda stepped forward and bowed low to Morganus. I looked at her and was stabbed by the realisation of how lovely she was, how fine and white was her skin, how red her hair, and how wonderfully green and deep were her eyes. I realised how much I missed her and how much I wanted to enjoy her company and I wished that I could control my own stupid tongue. I wanted to speak to her, to say that I was sorry. But it was not, absolutely and completely not, the time for such a conversation, and she hardly looked at me. She looked at Morganus.

"Speak up, girl," he said.

"May it please your honour, the Corvidic sisters are mad old women," she said. "They're in here most days, one or another of them, trying to sell fish, whether or not I have ordered any. They're in my kitchen before dawn usually. Before morning calls." She bowed to Agidox. "Isn't that so, your worship?"

"Yes," said Agidox. "They are a harmless nuisance, if somewhat insolent."

"And sometimes you find them wandering round the house," said Allicanda, and all the other slaves nodded.

"What do you mean?" said Morganus.

"I mean they get lost, your honour," she said. "And go round the house muttering and cursing."

"Indeed they do," said Agidox. "With foul and uncouth speech."

"What about the morning the master was killed," I said. "Were they wandering around the house then?" Allicanda frowned..

"I don't know, your worship. I was in the kitchen all the time."

"What about the rest of you?" I said, looking round, "Did anybody see the Corvidics, even one of them, wandering round the house?"

"Yes!" said some.

"No!" said others, and some stayed silent and pondering.

So Morganus and I and the bodyguards went to see the Corvidics themselves. They lived in Fish Lane, by the fish market, next to the Londinium docks where everything stank so strongly that the nose soon grew accustomed to the smell and noticed it no more. So it was not a pretty or a pleasant place; but, by comparison with the House of Scorteus, it was sunshine and flowers, and all of us were lighter in heart to be there, and not back among the terrified slaves.

Fish Lane was narrow, and crammed with shops and shoppers, and with shopkeepers bawling their wares, and heavy cleavers thudding onto blocks as fish were decapitated, then gutted and trimmed on marble slabs. The red-faced, red-armed fishwives stood yelling and cackling to one another as they worked, with barely a glance at the darting, razor-sharp blades in their skilful fingers, nor at the handfuls of offal and tripes which they threw into the gutters, where a permanent stream of water from the street fountains washed everything into the sewers below.

Fish Lane was noisy, raucous and coarse, for it was exclusively run by the fish wives: tough, self-reliant women, used to long hours of hard work in the wet and the cold. They bowed to no creature, not man or woman, free or slave and they reacted to the arrival of Morganus and his men with hilarious amusement. They stepped out of their shops and stood on the crowded pavement, among their customers, and called out to each other, with fists on their hips, elbows out, and open laughter as hob-nailed military boots skidded on slimy paving slabs, where gobs of fish guts had not quite reached the gutters. It was the only time I ever saw Morganus and his swan crest received without respect.

The Corvidics were out with the rest, as if they knew we were coming, and they screeched and chattered and clapped their hands. They were particularly taken with the four bodyguards, especially the youngest, who despite his bulk and his muscles was smooth faced and beardless. He reacted to the massed shrieks and cat calls of the fish wives by blushing bright red, which only increased their focus upon him and the volume of their noise, while the Corvidic sisters nudged one another and pointed at him

"Ain't he lovely?" cried one of the old women.

"Look at his legs!" cried another.

"What you got up your loincloth sonny?" said a third. "A big cod or a wet sprat?"

There was more laughter, until Morganus finally enforced some semblance order on the crowd with a terrifying, parade-ground roar.

"SILENCE IN THE NAME OF THE EMPEROR!" he cried.

"Gods save him!" said the bodyguards instantly.

"Yeah," said one of the fishwives, "him and his boyfriend too," and there was more laughter.

"Get 'em inside!" cried Morganus, jabbing his vine staff at the low-ceilinged, hovel that was the Corvidic's shop. "In there!"

The bodyguards pushed the women into their shop, and blocked the doorway against any interference, so that Morganus and I faced the Corvidic sisters in an approximation of quiet and privacy, except that I found that I was wrong about my nose being used to the smell, because there were fish everywhere, on marble slabs kept wet with buckets of

Thames water. But that was not all. A vile smell came from the squalid living quarters at the back of the shop where the old women slept on a half floor built over the shop. Gods know what they had for a latrine, but the living quarters smelt like old urine festering in a bucket.

Meanwhile, inside their own shop, the old women grew great in confidence and had the unbelievable effrontery to fall upon Morganus himself, pawing and giggling and standing on tiptoe with horrid lips pursed in slobbering kisses which they tried to plant on his cheeks.

"Ow! Ow!" he cried, and leapt back. I had to laugh. Morganus was the bravest of the brave, the champion of the legions, who would have stood unflinching before a charge of barbarian warriors. But now he fled. "Get 'em off me!" he cried.

"Yessir!" said the bodyguards, and physically pushed the Corvidics back and sat them down on stools, all of which the old women enjoyed enormously, fondling the bodyguards' arms and cheeks, and running hands up their legs and squeezing their genitals.

"Stop that!" cried Morganus.

"Why? What you gonna do?" cried one of them.

"See this?" said Morganus, waving his vine staff. "D'you know what I can do with this?" He received a reply that I will not repeat, and his temper broke and he snarled and raised the vine staff.

"All right! All right!" said the old woman. "Like that is it?"

"Yes!" said Morganus, and she looked at her sisters.

"You heard him! So! Have we got one ready, girls?"

"Yeah!" said two of them.

"Hang on," said the third, and contorted her face in concentration before nodding. "Ready when you are," she said.

"Right!" said her sister. "Drop one!" and all four broke wind together with a thunderous, rolling stench, such that this time we all fell back. But they still were not done. When the air had cleared and we stepped back, the old women picked on the youngest bodyguard again.

"Does your mother know you're out?" said one.

"Are you a good boy, my little sunshine?" said another.

"Have you had it away yet, ducky?" said the first, and turned to her sisters. "Nahhh," she said. "Look at him blush!" Then she turned back to the bodyguard. "Never mind, petal," she said. "You come over here and we'll show you how to do it."

This time, even Morganus laughed. We all laughed, and the old women did too, which changed the mood. They sniffed and spat, and picked their noses, and looked at us and fell quiet, apart from muttering to one another. Then the eldest pointed at me.

"Is he with you, dear?" she said to Morganus. "Does he do tricks?"

"The Greek gentleman is in his Imperial Majesty's service," said Morganus.

"Yeah, but he's the funny one, ain't he? We know all about him."

"You will answer his questions," said Morganus, and stood back.

So I did my best, although mostly they ignored my questions or gave nonsensical answers. But it did give me the chance to study them, and I learned quite a lot. To begin with they were nowhere near old as I'd supposed. I'd put the eldest in her early fifties and the rest younger, much the same age as the Lady Tertia and many others who were celebrated as beauties. But the Corvidics had horribly lost their looks from rough living, and they acted old. Neither were they half so mad as they pretended. They were certainly eccentric, horribly unclean, and they were vulgar and aggressive too, but they had a sharp wit and they were intelligent in a reactive, intuitive way. My conclusion is, that faced by what they saw as a cruel world that had turned them into hags, they hit back by exaggerating their faults to rub them into the nose of the cruel world. Or, perhaps, I analyse too much. But I did find out something important when I produced the black rags that I brought in a canvas bag so I did not have to touch them too much.

"Whose are these?" I said. "Are they yours?" But they just laughed and made jokes about Greeks, so I threw the bundle at the eldest sister. She caught it, sniffed it and passed it to the others, who likewise sniffed at the rags.

"Not ours," she said. "They don't smell right, do they girls?"

"No," said the rest. The rags had caught their interest. They fell silent, stopped chattering, and for the first time I could read their faces plainly.

They were speaking the truth, because a household will often have a particular smell, which those within it seldom notice but strangers do, and the rags smelt foreign to the Corvidic sisters. The rags were not theirs.

All I had to do now was work out what this meant.

Chapter 28

We left the Corvidics, and Fish Street and the red-armed, loud-faced women. I gave the canvas bag to one of the bodyguards and we found a wine shop so that I could sit down to think. It was not a very good wine shop and there was sawdust on the floor to soak up the clients' spitting. But I needed wine to help my imagination. So we sat down and I looked at the half dozen, shabby patrons sitting with mugs in hand and gazing at Morganus, half in fear, half in wonderment.

"Could we clear the shop?" I asked him. "I don't want anyone listening."

Morganus nodded, and the four bodyguards hustled everyone out into the street, including the owner and his slaves. They even checked the rooms at the back to make sure nobody was there. Then they saluted Morganus and stood outside so nobody else could come in. They did all that without a word spoken, and Morganus nodded in approval.

"They're good lads," he said. "They're getting used to you, Greek," and he smiled. "So?" he said.

"So what did we learn?" I said, and swirled the cheap, nasty wine in the cheap, nasty, native-pottery mug. "Those black rags. The fake Corvidic rags? Let's suppose someone wanted to pretend to be one of them. The Corvidics."

"Yes," said Morganus. "Someone with a blocked nose!" But I did not smile because a great misery was approaching.

"Perhaps," I said. "But, more important, somebody put those rags into the hidden cupboard, which means somebody who knew the bath chamber very well. Look how hard I had to try to find it! You'd never know it was there if you hadn't been shown it. And only Scorteus used that bath chamber, and I can't believe it was him, so that must mean one of the household slaves." I paused to drain my mug. "So," I said, "if these rags are anything to do with Scorteus's murder then we're proving the very thing we don't want to prove."

"Oh?" said Morganus.

"Oh indeed," I said. "Do you realise that everything we've found out so far is either hearsay and guesswork, or testimony from people who are dead? And now, at last, we've got a real piece of actual, physical evidence."

Morganus nodded.

"This real piece of evidence is saying that a household slave murdered Scorteus. It's telling the law to invoke the Silanianum!" I reached for the wine flask and filled my mug to the brim. "I'm sick of it Morganus," I said. "I feel as if I've put my hand down a rabbit hole and been stung by an adder. I gave those slaves a promise that I'd save them, and I'm sick of it." I paused as black depression rolled over me. The deep, black depression that destroys the will and leaves a man fit for nothing. I looked at the floor and did not move. "I've had enough," I said. "I can't do this any more."

I remember Morganus looking anxious and telling me to drink less. And then I was struggling with him when I went to fetch another flask. I remember being hoisted out of my chair and carried. Then I was waking up in my bed in Morganus's house, the next morning, feeling very ill. After that I spent a long time in the bath house, drenching myself with hot water. Then I dressed and sat in Morganus's living room, while his wife and daughters fussed over me because I was too sick to eat anything. They were very kind, wonderfully kind, considering all my woes were self-inflicted. Morganus himself was out, on duties within the fortress. So, I sat exhausted in the garden until the afternoon when he returned. I felt better by then, and he came and stood over me, without sitting down or taking off his helmet, and with the bodyguards behind him. The birds sang, the sky was blue. It was a pleasant day by Britannic standards. But not in Morganus's garden. His face was grim.

"So," he said. "Are you yourself again?"

"Depends what you mean," I said, "and what am I anyway? What use am I?"

"Give it up, man!" he said. "I've seen men speared through the chest and they wouldn't give up."

"Romans I suppose. They *never* give up."

"Look, Greek, this business isn't done. It's down to you, not me. I'd do it if I could, but I haven't got that sort of mind. Nobody has. You've got it, and it's a gift of the gods, and it's your duty to use it."

"I've told you," I said. "I can't carry on."

"What about your famous love of justice? Isn't it you that believes the innocent must go free and the guilty must be punished?"

I blinked at him. "When did I say that?"

"You say it all the time. You say there has to be justice in the universe."

"I don't care. I'm a man, not a machine."

"I'm not asking you as a man, I'm asking you as a brother. I invoke the oath that we swore. And, by that sacred oath, I command you to get up and fight on." Thus spoke Leonius Morganus Fortis Victrix, First Javelin, Father of the Twentieth Legion, Hero of the Armies of Rome, Honoured Veteran of forty years service. All of which is very splendid, but is not the reason why, in the deep of my despair, I forced myself to stand up, and to offer him my hand. I did that because he was my friend and I could not bear the thought of letting him down.

"Ah," he said, "That's my Greek!" So we clasped hands and perhaps the sun shone brighter. "I've got something to tell you," he said. "Petros wants to see you."

"Petros the Athenian?" I said.

"Yes, him. He sent word to His Honour the Legate. You're to go to Government House at the eighth hour."

"Petros?" I said. "Now what can that mean?" Seeing Petros could be dangerous. What could he want? We had gone in fear of him; fear of alerting his suspicion that we knew what he had done. But, seeing him would be a blessing in one respect. I could question him and watch his responses, which might lead somewhere. More important to me, Petros represented the opposite end of the case, the other extreme to the practical actuality of Scorteus's murder. He was a thousand miles from the Corvidic black rags.

"Shall we go and find out what he wants?" said Morganus. "The eighth hour is approaching."

So we did. To fight off the depression I made the best of myself. I shaved, I trimmed my hair, I put on the best robes Morganus's house could provide, and we went through the busy city to Government House. Here I noticed the oddity that the Governor's Guard, in their antique gear, clearly felt themselves above regular legionaries, while the regulars looked down on the Governor's Guard as fakes and poseurs. Thus there was much clanking and stamping and challenging at the outer gates, and locking of shields in a wall to deny us access, and prolonged and pretended study by the Guard Centurion, of the written summons which brought us here. Likewise, Morganus roared out his replies, over loud, to the Guard Centurion's questions, and the bodyguards sneered, fit to sour milk, at the lined-up guardsmen.

"Toy soldiers," whispered Morganus to me, as finally we were led inside. "They never see action, and they're too fond of the baths and the boys in the massage booths."

This time we did not go to the audience chamber on the first floor. We were taken through the splendours of the entrance hall, and through a series of offices where clerk slaves were in furious activity, busy with documents, opening cupboards, shouting at one another and getting in our way. The guardsmen shoved through and the noise was tremendous. Finally we were taken into a particularly large office full of beautifully polished furniture, together with golden lamps, tablets, pens, ink and all the impedimenta of high bureaucracy. The guardsmen stamped and saluted and then left us and closed the door, shutting out some of the noise. I think it was Petros's own office, but he was not there. We were greeted one of his shaven-head slaves. He was a Greek.

He stood, blank faced, beside a great desk, and showed little emotion throughout our meeting. But neither did he sit nor invite us to sit, and he unconsciously tapped the polished woodwork with the index finger of his right hand which, for him, expressed what screaming hysterics did in lesser men. I could see that he was under mighty stress. Then he bowed, and I bowed back.

"I give you good day, O servant of Petros," I said.

"And I to you, honoured sir," he said, very correctly ignoring me and speaking to Morganus. "My name is Clarios, and I would also give greeting to Ikaros of Apollonis." He looked questioningly to Morganus.

"You may speak to Ikaros of Apollonis," he said. "Your master's summons was directed to him." Morganus looked round, because there were other doors to the room. "Where is Petros of Athens?" he said. "We were expecting to meet him." Clarios bowed again.

"My master is heavily involved in preparations for the coming visit, of which I would speak to Ikaros of Apollonis."

"What visit?" I said.

"I will show you," said Clarios. "And it will explain everything." Then he gave two very short and proper bows to Morganus. "Would the Honoured First Javelin permit that Greek should speak to Greek in his own tongue? To be more fully understood?"

"Whatever you please," said Morganus. "My comrade will explain to me later."

"Thank you, honoured sir," said Clarios, and switched to Greek. "So penetrating intellect as yours," he said to me, "will appreciate the enormity of labour that attends the impending presence of the Imperial House."

"Do we speak of the Emperor?" I asked.

"Concentrate your attention upon this document," he said. "And all will become manifest. With His Grace the Governor on active service, the document was opened by my master Petros the Athenian, but word has been transmitted to His Grace."

He handed me a massive and ponderous document, a hugely bigger version of the summons that His Grace the Governor had sent to Scorteus. It was rolled up on a pair of two-foot staves of rich African ebony, capped with solid gold finials displaying busts of His Imperial Majesty. The document was of the finest Egyptian papyrus, the broken wax seals hung by braided, red silk cords, and the calligraphy was of a distinct and elegantly-convoluted style that I guessed, from the context, was that of the Imperial House itself. The script was so twisted that it was almost impossible to read, but there were only a few words and the first few lines, giving Teutonius' titles, were abbreviations of things I already knew. So, with them as a guide, I drew out the meaning of the rest. They said:

To Marcus Ostorius Cerealis Teutonius Governor of the
Imperial Province of Britannia Chief Priest Conqueror of
the Teutonic Hordes Three times Consul of the Roman Senate
Greeting
   Be warned that Caesar Comes
   He comes at the 12th hour three days hence
   Josephus of Antioch Inspector Plenipotentiary
   Given at the Naval base of Dubris
   this 15th day before the Kalends of May in the year of Trajan
and Frontinius

I had never seen such a document before, but it was typically Roman, being formulaic, unpunctuated and leaving much to be inferred. Thus *Caesar* meant The Emperor, because it was the clan name borne by Caesar the Great, and it was not Trajan who was coming, but one who stood in his name, Inspector Josephus of Antioch. I looked at Clarios.

"So it's Josephus," I said.

"Yes. Josephus of Antioch."

"Josephus the Jew," I said. "Raised to the status of Imperial freedman, who previously was an Imperial slave." Clarios gave a small gesture of envy. He was an Imperial slave himself, and normally no Imperial slave was ever made free. But there were rare exceptions for men of supreme ability.

"His Imperial Honour Josephus of Antioch is famous throughout the Empire," he said, carefully.

"Yes," I said, and repeated the well-known verse: "*When Josephus passes by, flowers wilt and infants die.*" Clarios pursed his lips in prim disapproval.

"Even the greatest, tremble at the name of Josephus," he said.

"And does he come to enforce the Silanianum?"

"Josephus of Antioch is entrusted exclusively with matters of high concern," he said. "Matters vital to the Empire. Thus His Imperial Honour comes as the right hand of His Imperial Majesty."

"I see," I said, and I did see. Clarios was purging himself of any hint of disrespect for Josephus, any hint that others might report.

"So," I said, "for what cause am I summoned here, and where is your master Petros of Athens?" I asked. But, hearing the torrent of noisy activity going on in the offices behind me, I knew already.

"My master is ensuring that all necessary records are ready to hand which His Imperial Honour the Inspector, might need to see."

"Of course," I said. "And I presume that, even as we speak, a conflagration is in progress behind Government House of all those records that an inspector need *not* see."

Clarios frowned and ignored my question. "His Imperial Honour is expected tomorrow at the sixth hour. He sojourns in the naval base at Dubris, having safely crossed yesterday, gods be praised!"

"Gods be praised," I said, and raised hands. Although, perhaps I smirked, because Clarios frowned as he pressed on.

"He crossed over from Bononia in Gaul. His Imperial Honour made the crossing in a sea-worthy merchantman, but will ascend the river in a naval vessel of the first class, together with his retinue. His summons arrived this morning aboard a *liburnian*." He gave a patronising smile. "It is ..."

"A naval vessel of the fastest type," I said, "with a single bank of oars, and a light hull."

"Hmm," said Clarios, and I was pleased to see the smile fade away. Then he shrugged, and sniffed, and reached for another document. It was entirely different from the first, consisting of several, very thin wooden sheets, each about six inches square, the ordinary medium that Romans used for letters. Each sheet was punched with two holes so that the sheets could be wired together, and the sheets were covered in writing in ink. It was ordinary cursive script and the document was plain and cheap, with cheap lead seals. But the sheets were the drama for which the ebony-bound papyrus was merely the prologue.

I looked at the first page. It was addressed simply to *Governor Teutonius* and the writing was the ugly scrawl of someone who had much to say, and had set it down fast. Thus there were ink splatters where the pen had caught on the wood, and there were crossings out, insertions, and some underlinings for emphasis. I turned to the back and found the signature, the single word *Josephus*, in the same urgent scribble. The man himself had written the letter. So I had a good look at the front page, then would have turned to the next.

"Proceed no further," said Clarios. "Much of the letter is confidential." He snatched it back. Morganus and the bodyguards growled and stepped forward.

"What're you doing *Boy*?" said Morganus.

"It's all right," I said in Latin. "I've seen what I need." I had indeed. The front page was a list of the people who should present themselves to the inspector, a list of the great men of the province in order of precedence: the Vice Governor Horatius, followed by Lord Chief Justice Domitius, Imperial Procurator Scapula, the Consuls of the Londinium City Council, the Duovirs of the Provincial Council, led by Felemid, together with other gilded beings and prominent office holders. Only Teutonius was excused, being on active service, and Petros was summoned in his place.

And one other was summoned. One who, beside the rest, was an ant that crawls beneath the Roman boot. He was myself, the slave Ikaros of Apollonis, property of the late Fabius Gentilius Scorteus. To my very great surprise I was so high on the list, that my name was preceded only by those of the Vice Governor, the Chief Justice and the Procurator.

Afterwards I regretted my cynical assumption of what Petros had been doing, because in fact he was arranging the reception for His Imperial Honour, which had to be the utmost that the city of Londinium could deliver. It needed complex organisation of all the skill that Romans possess to decorate the city by turning out the soldiers and guilds and trades, and the sisterhoods, clubs and societies. Also the dancers, musicians, performers, and actors, the clowns, actors, tumblers and jugglers, and every slave in the city were to be put to the task of erecting vast floral displays along the Via Principalis, and in the Forum, the Basilica, the Capitoline Temple and, most especially, the docks. All this because Josephus of Antioch really did come in Caesar's name, and had to be received as if he were Caesar.

All this in three days! But, whatever crimes Petros had committed in raising a phoney war, and however much he lacked normal decent morality, he was a superb administrator, and the reception given to Josephus of Antioch was as magnificent as the ship Josephus came in. It was the biggest ship ever to come up the river Thames, and one of the biggest ships in the entire world: a quinquireme.

Chapter 29

Since the quinquireme represented His Imperial Majesty, protocol insisted that it must not dock at the civilian wharves below the Thames bridge. It had to go through the bridge to the Imperial wharf, where naval craft docked when in Londinium. But it was so big that the lift-up section of the bridge had to be removed, and three sets of piling and decking taken out, to widen the centre gap by thirty feet to allow for the huge sweep of the battleship's oars. But the engineers of the Twentieth Legion easily dealt with that, hundreds of them wielding axes, mallets, pulleys and cranes with typical Roman efficiency. Everything would go back to normal once the Inspector was gone; but, in the meanwhile, cross-river traffic reverted to the primordial days of ferries.

Even so, the huge ship only just cleared the bridge on either beam. I had an excellent view from the Imperial wharf, where the Governor's guard was drawn up, behind Africanus, Legate of the Twentieth, and the first century of the first cohort with armour polished like mirrors. Above and behind them, on a dais, swiftly erected and decorated in Imperial colours, were the massed, toga-clad dignitaries of the province, broad-striped senators to the fore, narrow-striped knights behind them, and prominent citizens behind them.

All these noble Romans were supposedly led by Horatius the Vice Governor, but Petros was at his elbow to control him, and behind them came Domitius, the Lord Chief Justice, Scapula the Procurator and the rest; while I stood to the right of Petros and just behind him. I was in this immensely privileged position, strictly and only because

Josephus had asked for me by name. Otherwise I would have been in the main mass of the London mob. Even so there were many who stood behind me who normally would have protested with utmost anger that a slave should stand where I did, because there is nothing that exercises Romans more than precedence. But, on that particular occasion, there was no great desire by any man to stand to the front, not when meeting Josephus of Antioch. So most of the citizens who stood shuffling their feet and adjusting the drape of their togas on that day were entirely happy if someone stood in front of them.

So I had a fine view, but I had it by myself because I stood without Morganus and the bodyguards who were on duty, below the dais, with their legion's first century, and I found that I had grown so used to them, and the dignity that they conferred upon me as a sort of surrogate citizen, that felt vulnerable without them.

I glanced at Petros, who was exhausted. He had greeted me curtly, hardly meeting my eyes, and exclusively pre-occupied with his labours, with runners constantly coming up to him with documents to sign and decisions to make. I saw nothing in his face. Nothing at all, neither guilt, nor threat nor anything else. So I gave up and watched the cormorants diving for fish in the brown flow of the river, and the army bands playing on the bridge to entertain the people, of whom there was an enormous number. The whole city had emptied and come down to the riverside, the docks, the bridge, and any point from which a sight might be had of the flotilla coming upstream. The press of humanity was enormous, noisy, cheerful and raucous. For the common folk at least, this was a holiday.

Then I heard the ships. I heard them before I saw them, since the bridge was in the way, and galleys do not move silently like sailing ships. They come onward to the beat of drums, the sound of bugles, and the deep-chested singing of the oarsmen, as they give a pulling shanty to keep the time of the oar beat. It is a sound to raise the hairs on the back of a man's neck, and make women go weak at the knees, because naval oarsmen are the elite of the service. They are the biggest men, the strongest men, the finest men, with famous appetites and a mighty thirst for beer. They sang the ancient songs of the sea; they sang with deep emotion, with bass voices, and with awesome, ponderous harmony.

Thus the first two ships of the flotilla passed the bridge, to a huge and brazen blaring from the military bands, and answering calls from the naval buglers. I watched in fascination, and wished that the eldest bodyguard were beside me to give explanation, because I knew much of the theory of warships, as did every schoolboy in my city, for we were taught the history of the navy of Athens. But my city had never had a navy, I had never been aboard a warship, and I wanted to know more. So I looked and did my best to understand.

The first two ships were long, low-lying libernians: narrow and light with only a single bank of oars, twenty pairs in total, one man to each oar, with forty men pulling in an open hull, and just a tiny fore deck for lookouts and buglers, and a stern deck for the helmsman and commander. These were the fastest ships in the fleet, even faster than legionary lightning in smooth waters. The pair came through the bridge, in line astern, with bugles sounding from their fore decks, banners waving aloft, and the dark-tanned oarsmen pulling in symmetrical teamwork that was wonderful to see. Another pair of libernians followed later, but no creature, including even the cormorants, had eyes for anything than the flagship, once it nosed through the bridge in its splendour, with its massive, triple-point, bronze ram, breaking the waters ahead.

It was magnificent, it was huge, it was scarlet and gold, it glittered in brass and steel, it was packed with marines, and it was armed with batteries of artillery machines. And, where most ships are well under a hundred feet long, the quinquireme was twice that, and was massively broad, and no less than four hundred oarsmen pulled a total of one hundred and twenty oars. Even I knew that, because the crewing in a quinquireme was three men to an oar on the bottom tier, two men to an oar on the middle tier, and just one to an oar on the topmost, and the whole crew was crammed into a space so tight that, to quote the old Athenian joke, each man who farts in the upper tiers, blows straight into a nose below him. Yet all these men moved like the cogs of a fine machine, to the massed singing that carried over the waters like the music of the gods, and you cannot even see the oarsmen, the ship being mostly decked over and the oarsmen buried down below. Nonetheless, the singing is wonderful. Or perhaps I romanticise because there is a part of me that forever sorrows that I never went to sea.

But if I romanticise, so did the entire population of Londinium. As the quinquireme came through the bridge there was an enormous crescendo of cheering and a sounding of horns, trumpets, gongs and bells, and a vast waving of banners and hands, and the yelling joyful faces of citizens and freedmen, slaves and foreigners, the fools and the wise, the dull and the clever, the civilised and the barbarian. Thus did the people greet Josephus of Antioch. The hierarchy might have been in terror of him, but not the people, because they had had no political power to lose and, therefore, no fear. They just loved a good show, because Romans love a good show and they have taught the conquered races to do the same.

When the flagship docked, displaying a masterly drilling of oars, that turned the huge craft in its own length to come alongside the wharf, Petros shoved Horatius forward to lead the province's rulers down a flight of stairs to the wharf proper. Here every man stood bowing in greeting, as the First Century of the Twentieth lowered a bright-painted, fresh-carpentered gangway on to the stern deck of the big ship.

"Josephus!" cried the troops. "Josephus! Josephus! Josephus!" as the man came ashore in the Emperor's name, with his staff who were very numerous and included many strange races, in strange costumes, plus the usual corps of shaven-head Imperials, which every great man of the Empire kept beside him, and who sneered at all other forms of life.

Thus Josephus came ashore and stood within ten feet of me, as he was greeted by Horatius. He was a small fat man, superbly dressed in silks and fine wool. He was pale skinned for a Jew, with black hair and bitten fingernails. I saw that, and I saw great force of mind, and an anxious impatience to get things done, that was shown in quick speech, quick frowns, and nervous gestures of the hands. He reminded me tremendously of Scorteus, but without the charm, and with eastern sophistication replacing the rough Celtic vigour.

Thus he affected to give attention to Horatius, but in fact ignored him, having rightly dismissed him as an idiot. Even as he nodded to Horatius' words, he was glancing in all directions at, and taking prompts from, one of his shaven heads who consulted a list. Josephus nodded to himself as he identified one man after another, including myself, whom he wished to interview.

There followed some hours of formalities, during which Josephus was led in procession through the city's cheering populace, first to sacrifice a bull in His Imperial Majesty's honour at the Temple of the Imperial Genius, then to the Basilica, to be saluted by the City Council, then to the Provincial Senate to be saluted by the senators, and finally to Government House. All these ceremonies were performed at such double-march pace as to be almost farcical, but that was clearly the way Josephus wanted it done.

Then there were more hours of waiting in the Great Hall of Government until past lamp time, while many citizens arrived who wished to make public display of their respect for Josephus, but showed in their nervous faces that they prayed not to be summoned before him. It was almost comical. Then, finally, I was called for, and soon after that I was back upstairs in the audience chamber with a line of guardsmen behind me and myself bowing to Josephus, who sat in the Governor's chair, with his shaven heads behind him, and Petros pouring words into his ear. It was a fearful moment because it was the perfect opportunity for Petros to extinguish any threat that I might present to him.

If Petros chose, he could easily persuade Josephus that the Silanianum should be invoked at once, with myself taken outside for a quick thrust of a guardsman's sword. I became convinced that such was his plan, and wished that I had been given time to say goodbye to Morganus and his bodyguards, and his family too. Then my heart began to thump, such that my hands shook, as I discovered that I wanted to fight. I decided that, when they took me outside, I would give a pretence of hopeless terror, then suddenly snatch a sword from a sheath that I might take an enemy with me across the Styx, and perhaps two. But then Josephus looked at me and whispered to Petros, who frowned, then bowed low and whispered back. Then Petros beckoned to me.

"Come!" he said, in Greek, and Josephus got up and waved away his shaven heads as Petros led us into the same office where I met the German girl. The lamps were burning and there were deep shadows in the corners and beneath the furniture. I looked around. Everything was quiet.

"You may leave us," said Josephus to Petros. He spoke Greek with a heavy accent. Petros looked at me and I read pure envy in his face, but nothing more. He bowed and went out and closed the door, and Josephus came and stood close. He was much smaller than me and he had to look up and, to my amazement, I read fear in his eyes. Although he was immaculately clean, I smelt fresh sweat. Then he launched into speech and, at first, I had no idea why he was addressing the topic that he chose.

"You must understand," he said, "that Britannia is of vital importance to the Empire. It produces minerals, corn and slaves. But that is not why Rome is here. Rome keeps Britannia as an example to Rome's enemies because, when Rome took Britannia, Rome moved off the map, beyond the edge of the world and planted civilisation in a barbarian wilderness in the face of ferocious opposition. You understand?"

"Yes, honoured sir."

"Even the German savages beyond the Rhine know about Britannia, and they know that if Rome could conquer Britannia, then Rome could conquer them. Yes?"

"Yes."

"So Rome will hold Britannia, at all costs, and Rome will do anything necessary to keep order, and Rome will relish the opportunity to do so, because that is why Rome is here. Do you understand?"

"Yes," I said. Although I did not understand why he was so nervous. He was reciting a piece of standard Roman policy. Why should he be uneasy? Even afraid?

"So," he said, "after due debate within the Imperial civil service, and with the sanction of His Imperial Majesty, it has been decided that the Silanianum will be enforced upon the slaves of Scorteus, because the shedding of their blood will send fear of Rome throughout the world." He had pronounced doom. He had signed my death warrant, which was dreadful for me, but not for him. This was a man who could pronounce a death sentence then go to dinner with a merry heart. There was something more. He was up against something in his own mind.

"Imperial sir," I said, with a bow. "I am honoured to receive such explanation, but I wonder what actions of mine might affect such lofty affairs?"

He stepped closer. "I have read much of you," he said, "your character, your abilities, your service to your late master, and your investigations into his murder."

"Your honour is most gracious," I said.

"Yes," he said, and I saw that, at last, he was coming to the point. He was ready to mention the thing that concerned him. He was ready to jump from safety into danger.

"With regard to your late master," he said.

"Imperial sir?"

"There were certain books brought into your possession."

"The books of the Jewish sect that practises symbolic cannibalism?"

"Communion," he said. "The rite is celebrated as Holy Communion."

"I am grateful for your correction, Imperial sir. But what of the books?"

He came even closer. "In what language were the books written?" he said.

"Aramaic," I said, and he shuddered.

"Who wrote them?" he whispered.

"There were three authors: Mordecai, Zoltan, and Matthew."

"Matthew!" he said. "The lost book!" Josephus closed his eyes in religious ecstasy, proving what was already obvious that he was a member of the cannibal sect. He opened his eyes and looked intensely at me,. "Forget the other books," he said. "They are apostasy. They shall be burned. But Matthew! When did he write his book?"

"He describes the trial of the rabbi Jesus Bar Joseph, "I said. "Which took place sixty-seven years ago. But he does not mention the destruction of the Temple of Jerusalem, thirty years ago, so it must have been written between those dates."

"Which makes it the earliest account of the life of Jesus!" he said, and he stared at me, and his lips quivered as his courage failed. "I have a question," he said.

"Ask, Imperial and honoured sir."

"It concerns the nature of Jesus," he said, and the smell of sweat was strong. He was under tremendous agitation. He had come to the matter that was twisting his soul in torment, but he could not go on. He blinked and gulped. There was a question he dared not ask. So I prompted him.

"Jesus, Imperial sir? He that believed himself to be the Messiah?"

Josephus all but fell over. He staggered, he gripped my hands, his face opened with wonder. I had answered the question of all questions, and given the right answer. He was weak with joy. His eyes opened wide.

"What does Matthew say?" he gasped.

"In the sixteenth chapter," I said, "Matthew describes the rabbi going to the town of Caesaria Phillipi, where he asks his followers what men say of him. One of them, Peter the fisherman, replies, '*You are the Messiah, the son of the living God.*' The rabbi praises him for it and accepts it as truth."

"I must have the book!" he said. "Whose it is? Where is it?"

"It is mine, your honour. At the house of my old master, in my rooms."

"I will send for it. You may name your price." He meant it, but only a fool would have bargained with him.

"Would your honour be so gracious as to accept the book as a gift?" I said. "With my translation into Greek." He all but twisted off my hands in his passion.

"Greek translation? *Greek*? Oh praise the Lord! Wonderful! Many in the wider community have no Aramaic." He smiled and smiled. He was drenched with relief. Obviously his sect revered the lost book, but feared it might show their founder to be less than they hoped. It is strange what trust men put in books, believing that if a book says that a god inspired the author, then a god truly did. They believe the words and seek no further proof. If engineers displayed such faith in hearsay then all the houses and bridges would fall down.

But now Josephus's manner changed completely. He stood back and stood up. He had great self-control and wrapped himself in it like a cloak.

"So," he said, "I bless you, boy. Not least because it was you that proved the Followers of Jesus do not eat the flesh of men." I bowed, he continued. "Rome has decided that Silanianum shall be enacted, and I am here to enforce that decision. The matter is closed beyond debate." He paused for effect. "Yet there is a way out," he said, "because everything must be done by law. So, if you can bring suitable evidence, I will preside as chief magistrate and I will strike down the Silanianum in court. The evidence must be the testimony of high-ranking Romans. We are talking of the narrow stripe at least, and better the broad stripe. Can you, therefore, produce such evidence?"

So I told Josephus what I knew. He shook his head over the business of the black rags and finally, he sighed, much disappointed by what I had said.

"A chair," he said. "Get me a chair, boy." I found a chair, he sat down. He motioned for me to sit facing him, and he chewed at his nails and closed his eyes in deep thought. Then he looked at me.

"It is lamentably insufficient," he said. "You have not even discovered how the killer entered and left Scorteus's bath chamber, nor who killed the Syrian or the Tribune Severus. You have a circumstantial case against Petros the Greek." He looked at me closely. "But, you should know that while Rome is aware of Teutonius' deficiencies, nonetheless, *as guided by Petros*, Teutonius is hugely esteemed. The balance between the ambitions of Teutonius and his rival Livius Fidus Urban are so finely balanced that I would hesitate to act against Petros, because it would be perceived as acting against Teutonius and for Urban!"

He fell silent and closed his eyes again, and considered these dangerous political matters, probably wondering which faction to back. Then he looked at me again. "Meanwhile," he said, "you have demonstrated that the druidic faith is active in the province, which Rome already knew. Your only real discovery is the continued use of druidic assassins, for which discovery Rome thanks you, and which practice Rome will suppress by appropriate action."

He rocked in his chair, bit fiercely at his nails, drew blood, wiped his fingers distractedly on his tunic, then fixed me with his eye. He had a tremendous intellect, but it was open to me, and I could see that he was telling me the truth, and that he was in great distress being faced with a dilemma.

"We who follow the Messiah are deeply in your debt," he said. "But, your case is so weak that I cannot risk myself in your cause, because I must carry the book of Matthew to our community within the Empire." He pulled his chair close to mine and lowered his voice. "Our community is at risk," he said, "because we cannot offer prayers to the Emperor."

I gasped. Roman tolerance became Roman outrage towards those who refused to give the one and only prayer that Rome required, a prayer to the Divine Spirit of the Emperor. Just one prayer, once a year, on His Majesty's birthday, to show patriotic loyalty. I wondered what religion could object to that, when they were free to worship their own gods all the rest of the year? Does Apollo mind that we also pray to Zeus? Does Heracles mind that we sometimes pray to Athena? It was beyond understanding, and it was deadly serious too, because it was high treason.

"Because of this we are discrete," said Josephus, "even secret. Thus I am one of few who know where all of the faithful are to be found." He sighed, and sat up in his chair, and spoke in a normal voice. "So," he said, "I shall take the book, and I shall admit your case to court should you find the evidence I need. In that respect I offer the advice that, if you cannot prove the killer of Scorteus was not his slave, you might, just possibly, prevent the Silanianum with proof that Scorteus, in the business of shields, caused major corruption within the body politic. But that would be a perilous step, risking serious repercussions." He gave a small gesture of apology. "And now, boy, I can do no more. I cannot meet you again. I can order no arrests, nor inquisitions, nor take any other action on your part. Do you understand me?"

"Yes," I said.

"And I can promise you nothing if the matter comes to court. My judgement will be strictly impartial because it will be picked over by those above me, especially by those of the Urban faction."

I nodded.

"Beyond that, all I can do is give you time, and ensure that nothing stands in the way of you and your centurion. I am under the strictest orders to enforce the Silanianum at once, but I will give you until the Kalends of May. That is the best I can do. The executions will take place at dawn on the Kalends. You have seven days."

Chapter 30

I asked Morganus if the bodyguards could hear what I had to say.

"Yes," he said. "They've fought the same fight as you and me." So he beckoned to them where they sat in the dark shadows at the other end of the long room, with their helmets on their knees, politely pretending not to pay attention to us. They put on their helmets and came and stood in the light, by the table in Morganus's living room, where he and I were seated.

It was night time of the seventh day before the Kalends of May and, by one last favour of Josephus, Morganus and the bodyguards were still assigned to me, because otherwise they would have been on ceremonial duties throughout Josephus' visit. So I told them all what he had said, and they listened. Finally, I said, "So I can't see the end of this business, and I want to say to each of you, that I might have to stir up major politics. If I go down, I don't want anyone to go down with me. So if any of you would like to be excused further duties in this matter ..." But, I was interrupted.

"Bollocks!" said Morganus. He turned to the bodyguards. "What do we say to the Greek gentlemen, lads?" They spoke together. "Bollocks, honoured sir."

"So," said Morganus. "What next, Greek?"

I was much affected. Great fears and emotions were working within me and I was moved to tears. So Morganus sent the youngest bodyguard to the kitchen to get cups and wine, and the six of us sat at the table as comrades should. "So what next?" said Morganus.

"I want to try another approach," I said.

"Yes?" said Morganus.

"We'll give up a direct assault on Scorteus's murder and go round the side. We need the testimony of senators or knights, right?" They nodded. "Well, the business of shields must have left a trail somewhere. Someone must know something. I can't believe any conspiracy is that tight."

"So what do you propose?" said Morganus.

"So we go in from the top again! We ask ourselves which senators and knights might know something."

"Go on," said Morganus. So I did. I had thought of nothing else for hours. I went down the list.

"His Grace the Governor comes first," I said. "But, he's on campaign and, with all due respect Morganus, we can't go to him, because the first thing he'd do is check back with Petros who works him like a puppet."

Morganus sighed and muttered, but said nothing.

"Then there's his nephew, the boy Horatius who thinks he's Vice Governor, and the same goes double for Petros."

They nodded.

"Then there's Domitius, the Lord Chief Justice. But, he hates Greeks and he'll do me no favours."

They nodded again.

"Then there's the City Councillors. Some of them are knights."

I looked at Morganus and his reaction was an education into the inner workings of Roman society. In my city, all free men were equal under the law, and any man's word was as good as any other's, whether in business, in science or in evidence. But Rome was very different. There was a hierarchy of credibility and respect, depending on social status.

"City Councillors aren't good enough," he said. "They're tradesmen, and some of them had freedmen for fathers or grandfathers, and those that didn't are tainted because they sit down with those that did."

"Right," I said. "What about Felemid and the other Provincial Council members? They're full senators. They wear the broad purple stripe."

Morganus sneered. So did the bodyguards. "Tell him lads," he said.

"They're natives," said the eldest bodyguard, "wogs in togas."

I remembered how they had reacted to Felemid's familiarity towards Morganus, and I gave up and moved on.

"There are others we might try lower down," I said, "but for the moment what about Scapula? The Imperial Financial Procurator? He's only a knight, but he's third highest man in the province, and he's in charge of the money, and Scorteus was paid out in gold."

"Much better!" said Morganus. "Just what we need." So we went to see Scapula, early next morning of the sixth day before the Kalends. We were well received, we were taken past layers of guards from the Twentieth, who stamped fierce salutes to Morganus, and ran before us crying out his name. Scapula received us in his place of work, a raised stage at one end of an enormous counting house, full of clerk slaves, filing cabinets, huge windows for light, and rows of tall desks with men stood working at their documents. There was a steady murmur of conversation, which fell silent as Morganus entered the room, then a deep rustle of tunics as more than a hundred men bowed in his honour, while Scapula stood fast on his platform, with his shaven skulls behind him who merely twitched their heads.

We advanced to the stage, climbed a short staircase, and a few words from Morganus had me speaking directly to the skinny, balding Quintus Veranius Scapula, with his bad teeth, and his pigeons, which fortunately we did not discuss that day. He began the conversation.

"All the city knows that you were summoned by His Imperial Honour the Inspector," he said. "I wonder what he may have asked you?"

I bowed. "Your Worship will understand that His Imperial Honour demands discretion from any man who meets him, let alone a slave."

He frowned, but made no further inquiry, and then, with nothing to lose and few days left, I jabbed him with a sharp stick. "I want to know who took the gold from the treasury," I said, " to pay Scorteus."

He gulped, and the same delight filled me as fills the hunter whose arrow thumps hard into a deer. I had hit the mark! He blushed and stammered. Then he was bustling me into a corner and waving everyone else away and wiping his mouth and sucking his few, brown teeth.

"Got you!" I thought. "You know, don't you?" But that was all

I found out, because he became so hysterical that I could not read his face.

"It was Petros wasn't it?" I said, and he shook his head as if he would shake it off. So I threw different questions at him, straining to the limits of my skills to spark off something more, by trick or by chance. But I failed. He just grew more and more incoherent.

So I gave up, and we left the Treasury and found a wine shop and sat down. It was very elegant, at the top level of establishments on the fashionable Via Principalis. Fresh water, ice-cold, in cups of expensive Italian glass, was served the instant we sat down, together with fine pastries and small, sweet biscuits, and the service was by girls with immaculate gowns and swivelling hips. They were like the girls who had served us in Scorteus's house, and the bodyguards grinned at them, and the girls smiled back.

"We'll have to try the City Councillors," I said, "and Felemid and the rest."

"Waste of time," said Morganus. "I told you they don't count."

"But they might know someone who does," I said. "We've got to try."

So we did. We spent three precious days going up and down the city, from one lavish building to another, speaking to dozens of the great and the good, including Felemid, who was so delighted to see me that he invited me to his private bath chamber, which I politely refused, and he joked about buying me, which was not a joke. It was not good to hear, because he really seemed to be smitten with me. He drew me aside and became confidential.

"You good boy," he whispered. "I do favour for you if you ask, eh? You come to me. You not same as Romans." He dropped his voice still lower. "Romans think Celt is like pig, like donkey." He came close. "I don't like Roman," he said, and planted a small kiss on my cheek. "I like Greek!" But that was all I got from him, because neither he nor anybody else knew anything fresh relating to the business of shields or to the murder of Scorteus.

That brought us to the evening of the fourth day before the Kalends, when Morganus and I sat at his table and drank a great quantity of wine. We were both very tired, we had slept badly and, with so few days left before the mass slaughter of the House of Scorteus, we were downcast, and stretched to the limit of our strength. We were stretched like the string of an over-wound ballista, just before it snaps. Thus our conversation wandered into grounds that, by mutual consent, we had not previously entered.

"You know I'm supposed to be guarding you as well as helping you?" he said.

"I didn't know it for sure," I said, but it would be logical. Logical for the legate and Petros to do that. To make you do it, I mean."

"Yes," he said, "'cos they'll want you as well. If it happens. The Silanianum."

"I know."

"Well, I've been thinking."

"Yes?"

"If you were to escape."

"No!"

"I mean when I wasn't looking."

"No!"

"Or, I mean, if you were to pick up a chair, or anything and hit me over the …"

"No, Morganus. They'd take it out on you. At the least you'd lose your rank and your pension. They might even want your head."

"Jupiter, Juno, Minerva!" he said, "is there nothing I can do?" and I realised that there was.

"If you want to help," I said, "there is something."

"What?"

"That boy. The junior centurion. The one that was sent to the house?"

"Marianus?"

"Yes him. Well, if it happens."

"Yes?"

"Don't let him do it. I mean organise it. Let it be someone who will do as clean a job as can be. I don't want people chased through the house screaming. Let it be done with dignity, if it must be done, and the poor souls assured that there will be no abuse of the women, and nobody thrown to the beasts in the arena. Do you understand what I'm saying? Let's have a good man in charge."

"Who do you want ?" he said, and I looked at him

"The best man in the legion," I said, looking him in the eye. "A man who will be kind to the children, and who will spare as many of the rest as he can."

"Oh," he said, and we sat silent together for a long time.

"One other thing," I said. "In my city the method of execution was by sword, a sword passed downward … just here," and I tapped the small depression between my neck and collar bone. "The victim sits and the executioner stands over him, and stabs down, aiming for the heart." I looked at Morganus. "It's instant, painless death. It's the most humane method, and it spills no blood, which will help to avoid panic and horror."

"Thus shall it be," said Morganus, and raised hands. "I swear it in the name of Mithras the bull slayer, and by all the gods of Rome."

That night I had another dream of my city, as it fell to the Romans. It had to do with women and killing. The dream was ugly, frantic and wildly confused. It would not settle into a narrative, not even the crooked narrative of dreams. Instead it leaped from image to image, always bad images, but I knew that I was coming close to a great truth. I tried to find that truth, but my limbs were paralysed and there was a door that I could not pass, and the truth lay beyond the door, which was my own front door. The door to my own house in the burning chaos of the final hours of the siege.

I do not believe that dreams predict the future, or that they are the voices of the gods coming to us in the night. But dreams are powerful. They leave a weight upon the mind, and nobody can resist trying to explain them, or at least I cannot. So I explained the dream as a re-working of the discussion I had had with Morganus, especially concerning the hideous act of killing of women. I believed that, and I was wrong. But the dream of the closed door, opened another door. I told Morganus at breakfast.

"There's someone we haven't tried!" I said.

"Who?" he said. "Who is he?"

"Not him, *her*!"

"A woman?" He looked at me as if I were deranged. Compared with the way the Athenian Greeks shut their women in the house, Roman women, especially rich matriarchs, are shameless creatures who stalk the streets, boldly looking men in the eye. Also, Roman women may hold any of a wide range of religious and semi-religious offices, as well as membership of sisterhoods and societies. But they have no place in public life, they may not hold civic office, they have no political power and, of course, Roman women have no vote. No civilisation on earth would allow that!

Nonetheless, like all the women of all the ages, they influenced their husbands within every shade of relationship between gentle submission and nagging dominion. So Morganus thought of all this. Perhaps he thought of his own determined and efficient lady. She was half his size, but who knows what went on between them?

"Hmm," he said. "Who've you got in mind?"

"Tertia!" I said. "The wife of His Grace the Governor."

Morganus whistled in amazement, and shook his head. Then he thought again. "I see," he said, and the more he thought, the more the idea appealed to him. "It's an odd one, Greek, but then you're odd," he smiled, "if you know what I mean. So go on, tell me. What can we get out of the Lady Tertia?"

"I don't know," I said. "But she must be one of the most powerful people in the province. She's kin to the Emperor, she's got the ear of her husband, and she's got massive influence in anything to do with art and culture, and even on building works. She was in Aquae Sulis opening a theatre, remember? A theatre that she'd commissioned?"

"What about her cursing the German girl?" he said. "Isn't she involved in all this business?"

"No!" I said. "That's a side issue. She hated the German girl, and she couldn't admit it, so she did something secret to get at her."

Morganus nodded.

"So I suppose you'd like me to arrange an audience with her?"

"Today! This very morning! Send your runner with the white wand. We can say that this touches upon the honour of His Grace her husband, which indeed it does, and she'll believe it coming from you, Morganus, because nobody's more loyal to His Grace than you."

So Morganus sent his runner. It was early in the morning of the third day before the Kalends.

When I met the Lady Tertia for the second time, I saw that I had been wrong in thinking of her as cold and lacking in beauty. I concluded that this was because she was a trained aristocrat, steeped in duty, and at the formal audience, when I first saw her, she was drawn up straight and severe, being His Grace's dutiful wife. In that respect she was an actress who delivered a role. But off duty she was a very lovely woman.

Of course, beauty comes in many forms, and I could not help comparing Tertia with the German girl, because in strict terms of perfection of face and figure, and in the exoticism of her golden hair, the German girl was her superior. But there are many aspects of beauty: grace, sophistication, purity of voice, elegance of deportment, sympathy of understanding, perfection of dress, and especially the magic that glows from a royal princess. It glows even for republicans like me, who claim not to believe in royalty; and, while Tertia was not quite a princess, she was of the Imperial clan, and she was tall and slender, with a perfect complexion and much younger than I had thought. On close inspection I saw that she was only in her thirties. She had been married at fifteen, and six daughters could have been delivered within ten years of marriage, after which time Teutonius presumably gave up hopes of a son, and looked elsewhere for satisfaction.

Morganus and I were led to the Lady Tertia's day room on the first floor of Government House, with the bodyguards left downstairs. Scented slave girls led us with many bows and smiles, their bare feet treading so softly as to be soundless, and threw open a pair of doors leading into a huge, high room decorated in the most immaculate taste that ever I saw outside of Athens itself.

The twin themes were minimalism and classicism. The room was light and bright and south facing. The furnishings were few and perfect, the statues were exquisite, the floor mosaics, the simplest and best I had ever seen, and the colour scheme was pure white, with thin lines of gold, fringed with acanthus leaves. There was a great balcony, entered through glazed windows which were thrown open to admit a cold Britannic wind. Even the cold enhanced the austere perfection of the room, while the view was rolling green landscape, beyond the disciplined lines of the Field of Mars, the legionary fortress and the city walls.

The lady herself was sat in a fine-draped, silken stola, with Merloura, the ugly, dark slave woman, standing beside her. Merloura was about forty years old, she was wizened and small, but looked intelligent, and had bright little eyes, and one hand, dark as a raven's claw, rested on Tertia's shoulder. Such presumption would have astonished me, except that I recalled Allicanda's explanation of her relationship with Tertia.

As we entered, the Lady Tertia rose from her chair, which was another miracle of craftsmanship. It was so finely wrought, with such slender, curving limbs that it looked incapable of supporting a human body. But that was nothing compared with the fact that the Lady Tertia had condescended to rise to greet us and to offer her hand to Morganus, and I looked at him from the corner of my eyed as I bowed. He was blushing. He was charmed out of his armour. He advanced, he took her hand, he kissed it with reverence and stood to attention.

"Hail to thee, O champion of the arms of Rome," she said, in slow and formal Latin, every word given perfect enunciation. Normally I do not like the sound of the Roman language. It is short and brutal compared with Greek, but not when spoken by the Lady Tertia.

"Hail to thee, O mother of the children of Marcus Ostorius Cerealis Teutonius," said Morganus. Then Merloura looked at me, and whispered in Tertia's ear, and Tertia nodded.

"And is this the magic Greek?" she said. "The kindly bringer of the sleep that banishes pain." I was astonished. She was making instant reference to the awkward matter of my part in the cure of the German girl, and seemed to be blessing me for it! This was puzzling in the extreme because it could not be reconciled with Tertia's curse at Aquae Sulis. So I wondered if I had missed something? Were there facts I did not know? It seemed that I had miscalculated and, in any case, she was clearly exerting herself to put me at ease.

"O mistress of the house of Teutonius," said Morganus, "I bring my comrade Ikaros of Apollonis, a noble warrior among his own people. I bring him before you and beg that you might hear his own words from his own mouth."

Merloura whispered at length in Tertia's ear, and Tertia nodded and spoke to Morganus. "O sword and shield of Rome," she said, "there is no man on this island or beyond who stands higher in honour than you." The voice was seductive. Even I was stroked by so sensual a voice, and Morganus blushed again. "Yet I would ask," she said, "that I speak alone with your comrade." Merloura whispered some more. "I ask because I am informed of the very delicate nature of the inquiries in which this Greek is engaged, under the authority of His Grace my husband."

"Gods bless His Grace!" said Morganus, and bowed. "Whatever your Ladyship wishes," he said, and bowed again. By now, he was well used to leaving me alone for confidential conversations, so he just nodded to me, then paused, expecting the slave woman Merloura to open the door for him, as any slave should. But she never moved, and Morganus gave a tiny shrug and did it for himself. Then, as the door closed, Tertia's manner changed. She stepped forward, held out her hand for me to kiss, and remained standing so close that her perfume enveloped me.

"Ikaros," she said, in ordinary swift speech. "I know why you've come here, I know you act in my husband's name, for the good of the Empire, and I'll do all that I can to help you."

I took a deep breath. With three days to go before the holocaust, I had found an ally.

Chapter 31

Tertia was wonderfully easy to talk to. She was highly intelligent, she paid close attention, and she made a great deal of wise comment on what I said. So I told her everything I knew. And why not? I was looking into the eyes of failure. If I could not gather some new and powerful evidence, deduce it by intellect, catch it by cunning, or just happen upon it by unworthy chance, then my execution and those of four hundred others would take place at dawn in three days' time. So I was mentally exhausted, I needed help, and I told her everything, even including my meeting with the snake girl beneath the magical spring of Aquae Sulis.

I stumbled over this because it revealed so sinister an act by Tertia. But two things made me speak. First I do profoundly believe that truth is invincible, in that having spoken the truth a man cannot be tripped, trapped or found out, as he can if he begins with a lie. But there was another reason. As I hesitated over the details of what the snake girl had said, Merloura came close to her mistress and whispered in her ear, and Tertia reached out her hand, and laid it on mine.

"Don't be afraid," she said. "I know why you hesitate, so you should know that I, and my mother," she smiled at Merloura, "are devotees of the goddess Perliphoni." I raised hands, even though I had never heard of this particular deity. But there are hundreds of them and no man knows them all.

"May the goddess smile upon you, lady," I said.

"And may Apollo smile upon you," she said. "Thus you should know that the holy Perliphoni teaches that jealousy should not be kept within, where it grows, but exorcised with a curse, and so discharged." I nodded.

"I understand lady, and I thank you for your confidence in me." And so we continued, until I was finished, when Tertia gave a practical summary of what could be done, and came up with a truly radical suggestion.

"It comes to a matter of power, Ikaros the Apollonite," she said. "The army is the ultimate power, and the army will arrest the guilty, at least in serious matters of politics. So! We consider first Badrogid, brother of Scorteus, and Caradigma the mother of Scorteus." She waved a slim, dismissive hand. "These are mere Celts, and a word from me to Africanus, Legate of the Twentieth, will see them imprisoned."

I nodded.

"Then there is Dolbius the lawyer, who is a citizen and a knight." She frowned, whispered to Merloura, and Merloura nodded. "I agree," said Tertia to her, and turned back to me. "Dolbius may be a problem, but I think Africanus will seize him at my request." Then she frowned. "But Petros the Athenian is in another category, as is Quintus Veranius Scapula, the Imperial Procurator. I doubt that Africanus would touch either of them, without written orders from my husband or from Rome." She hesitated. " I am not sure of this," she said, "I cannot predict how Africanus would act." She had a long whispered conversation with Merloura, and finally Merloura shook her head. They did not know. Tertia turned to me again.

"What I will do, Ikaros, is send word to my husband, and to Rome, by express messenger, laying your evidence before them and seeking arrest warrants for Petros and Scapula. It is the best that I can do."

"How long will that take?" I said, but the question was futile. There was not the remotest chance of a reply from Rome within three days, and it would be exceptional to get one from Caledonia, where Teutonius might be fighting a battle or under ambush, or even dead. Tertia looked at me smiled.

"I will do what I can," she said. "Trust me." I nodded. "Meanwhile," she said, "I have a suggestion." She paused. "Though you may find it surprising."

"What is it lady?"

"You need the testimony of someone highly placed in Roman society."

"Yes lady. One of the senatorial or knightly classes."

"How about a king?" she said, and I frowned.

"Rome has no kings," I said. "Not since ancient times."

"Rome does not, but the client states do, and each of those kings ranks ahead of senators in civic processions. It is a point of politics, and it is taken very seriously."

"Who are you thinking of, lady?"

"King Cogidubnus!" she said. "He will have detailed knowledge of the business of shields, and you told me yourself that there is intense rivalry between him and the druid Maligoterix, who is the centre of the business from the Celtic side. If you were to appeal to him to act against Maligoterix ..."

"But we can't bring him to court, lady, we can't even admit the druids exist. The Legate Africanus told me that." I frowned, as I remembered something else. "He said I mustn't go near Cogidubnus again, and specifically ordered me *not* to interfere in the politics of his court."

She laughed at that.

"Africanus is wrong," she said, "and I will support you against him if necessary because you act on my orders. And we are not talking about the law courts, but military power, because Maligoterix has sent an assassin into Londinium. He has exceeded the limits of Roman tolerance and Rome will act against him! Josephus said as much to you, so trouble is already on its way to Maligoterix. If you tell that to Cogidubnus, and assure him of the protection of Rome, he may be only too willing to come to Londinium, and testify in court, accusing Maligoterix by whatever name and title we choose, and never mentioning the word druid." She shook my arm. "Remember the other thing Josephus said. If we can't prove Scorteus's murderer wasn't a slave, we must prove corruption within the body politic, and Cogidubnus' testimony would be good enough for that!"

I was inspired. I kissed her hand and bowed.

"Now do not delay," she said, "Go to it, Ikaros of Apollonis!"

So I did. Whatever protocol may say about backing out of the Imperial presence, and Tertia ranked as Imperial, I just turned and ran for the door, and through other rooms and down the great staircase, shouting the name of Morganus. It was undignified. It was emotionally incontinent to run like a stupid schoolboy let out early from his lessons. But I was not my normal self. Who would be, who is under sentence of death to be carried out in three days' time, and suddenly thinks he has found the way to a pardon?

Morganus and the bodyguards were in the Great Hall, and curious citizens and clerk slaves peered at me as I ran by. I seized Morganus'ss arm, pulled him outside into the street, past Governor's Guardsmen who saluted, and we stumbled down the great marble steps. I cast around for some private place and, in the absence of anything better, dragged Morganus into the centre of the plaza in front of Government House. Then I looked in all directions, like any guilty conspirator, and realised that so open a place was ideal, since any eavesdropper would be obvious. Only Morganus and the bodyguards could hear me. So I told them what Tertia had said, especially concerning Cogidubnus. As I spoke I recalled their contempt for the testimony of Provincial Senators, and Cogidubnus was pure Celt, and I wondered if he too would be dismissed as worthless. But Morganus surprised me.

"By Heracles," he said, "that's clever and no mistake. I'd never have thought of him! I'd have put him in the front rank of our enemies."

"But is he all right?" I said. "Is his word good enough? As a native?"

"Well normally I'd say no," he said. "But this one's different. I told you his family have been in Rome's pocket for generations, didn't I?"

"Yes," I said.

"Well that goes two ways," he said. "Even *grandfather* Cogidubnus had friends in Rome, and they've been building alliances ever since. They've got money, remember, and that's what really counts, and I'd say that the present Cogidubnus is at least as well connected as a real Roman senator. He's certainly got honorary citizenship, and when he comes to Londinium, he's received at Government House, with full turnout of troops on the Field of Mars. I've turned out myself!"

"Morganus," I said, "can we get a lightning? Can we go to Cogidubnus? We've got less than three days."

"You know we can't take troops?" he said. "You know that, don't you? Even though Maligoterix might turn nasty and they have armed men in that palace?"

"I know," I said. "We have to take the risk. We're disobeying the legate's orders in going at all, so I suppose we can't call for an escort or someone might tell him, and then he'd stop us."

"Correct," said Morganus. "Otherwise I'd have taken every horseman in Londinium. But we can't. It's just us." So we went to the fortress and by the kind will of the gods there was a lightning in the stables, with fresh horses ready to go, and men were sent running in all directions for the stores and gear we would need for the brief journey.

"How quickly can we do it?" I asked, putting a hand on the driver's shoulder, as we crossed the south drawbridge. Morganus was beside me, the bodyguards behind, and the lightning fresh out of its shed, with greased axles, a clean hood, bright paint, and four good horses pulling hard.

"About seven hours to get down there, Greek," said the driver, "including changes every ten miles, and seven hours to get back up."

"Can we cut that down?" I said, but the rumble of the wheels on the drawbridge was too loud for proper conversation, so the driver looked back at Morganus.

"Fast as you can," yelled Morganus.

"Yes, honoured sir!"

"And through the night if need be!"

I nodded and did some calculations. We were in April, well past the vernal equinox in the middle of March, so there was more day than night in the sky. We should easily get down the Great South Road to Noviomagus Reginorum within daylight, and on to the Palace of Cogidubnus. The five-mile road to the palace was as good as a Roman highway, which it should be because it was built and maintained by the Roman army. Then, if our business with Cogidubnus was quick, and his stables could give us fresh horses, we could be back on the road by dawn on the second day before the Kalends.

It could be done! And the driver did his best. *He* did. But, the loathsome, weather of Britannia did not. It did its worst, and all the prayers to all the gods of the seven of us were ignored. I have never so much hated Britannia and its detestable climate. The clouds rolled over us as we drove the lightning onto the pontoon ferry that the army had running across the Thames, and the horses snorted and stamped in fear of the water, such I got down and caressed their heads and drove away their fright.

Then on the south bank, once we got back on the road, the clouds opened, the wind got up, and the rain came down like a volley of javelins, and bounced back two feet off the road. It was so intense, and the wind blew so hard, that the horses kept tossing their heads to keep the stinging wet from their eyes. The speeding lightning was reduced to a crawl, with me out of the vehicle again, in a dripping wet cloak, leading the front pair so they should not go off the road. A man can shield his eyes with his hand, but a horse cannot. I took turns at this with the driver. Sometimes he led them, sometimes I did, with the other at the reins. It went on for hours. We had to stop at night on the road, well short of the post mansion, or even a changing post, because it was too dangerous to go on in the dark. Even I could not see the edges of the road, let alone the horses.

So we spent the night in profound misery. We could not get a fire going. We ate cold food. We sheltered under the canvas hood, and we dripped and shivered and cursed, and still the rain fell, and the Kalends came closer and closer.

Then it got worse. The rain lifted shortly after dawn, and we pressed on to the next changing station. They are just sheds for stables and a little house for the station keepers. But we got fresh horses, and moved on at speed, until the rain came down even harder, and so it went on, with every one of us stupid with lack of sleep and groaning in frustration, and grinding our teeth in futile anger against the malignant Britannic gods that sent rain to close down the Roman roads. In my light-headedness from lack of sleep, and in my anguish at being prevented in what should have been a simple task, I saw clearly that it was indeed the ancient tribal gods of this barbarous land that were laughing at us. They laughed at the straight line of the Roman road across their green hills, and laughed at our technical superiority, with our carriages, our fine-bred horses and post stations, and our arrogant pride in swift passage across the face of the tribal heartlands.

So we staggered down the road, in stops and starts, in futile hope and in tortured despair, as the rain came and went. It was a dreadful, soul-burning journey, and the whole of the second day before the Kalends was wasted with long stops on the road. Thus it was not until just after dawn, on the last day before the Kalends, that the lightning finally came round the hill that hid Cogidubnus' palace, at which time the Britannic gods resorted to mockery. Just to show what they could have allowed had they wished, they pulled away their clouds to reveal a hot bright sun. The sudden warmth sent steam rising from our clothes, from the dank canvas hood of the lightning, and even the grass of the manicured parkland itself.

And it revealed us to those who were waiting for us. There were horsemen on patrol before the palace, and horns were blown as we drove down the road towards the enormous building. And, as on the occasion of our last visit, there came a charge of some native cavalry. But this time they came in silence. No whooping and yelling. They came on with a purpose and drawn swords.

"I don't like this," said Morganus. "Stand to arms!" Everyone drew, everyone except me. But, in truth, I was little more disadvantaged than the rest, because for all its formidable utility in foot combat. It is hard to imagine a more useless weapon than the gladius, the Roman army sword, for the task of defending a carriage against horsemen.

Thus the riders separated into two wings, and sped around and behind us in a pounding roar of hoof beats. Then they came back and nipped in beside us, and rode alongside, and easily kept pace as our team took fright, and shot forward flat out, rocking the vehicle so hard that we had to hang on just to keep our seats. Nobody had a chance to use a sword, even if the horseman had come within reach; but neither did they strike at us. Instead, two men, one left, one right, leaped from their horses, and threw themselves on our team, in the wild, care-not abandon of savages, and hacked at the harness with sharp knives. Then one slipped as our driver, in his fury, yelled the legion's battle shout, drew a pugio and threw it at the Celt. The heavy dirk struck hard, butt first into the side of his face, half stunning him; so, he lost hold, screamed, and fell beneath four pairs of pounding hooves and two sets of wheels, and we bounced high as we ran him over. The horsemen yelled, and the lightning heaved, and the team ran mad and off the road, and the wheels found one of the pair of drainage ditches that run to either side of a Roman road, and a wheel splintered. The lightning went over and smashed and shattered and broke, and threw all seven of us tumbling and hurtling out.

I came down with a jar on my right side. The ground was soaked with rain and very soft, and it was covered with thick grass, and I rolled and rolled, and sat up. I was dizzy, but unharmed. If I had landed on the road I would have been smashed in all my limbs. But I had not. So I got up. I staggered. I looked around. About a hundred yards off, some of the horsemen were picking up the body of the man who'd been trampled. He was still moving. Others were yelling and struggling with the horses that had pulled the lightning. Then there a furious whinny from the horses and a wild kicking in all directions, then the solid *SMACK* of a hoof striking home, and a man was thrown down. The rest scattered as the front pair of the team broke free, and sped off, still linked in their harness. The Celts would have mounted and given chase, but their leader, a man I had not seen before, yelled at them and brought them back to his side, and the two horses ran off into the distance.

I looked at my companions. The driver and three of the bodyguards were either getting up like me, or were sitting with heads in hands, obviously unharmed. But one of the bodyguards lay unmoving, and Morganus sat, with one leg crooked at an angle below the knee. He blinked at it and I went to him first, but he waved me away.

"It's broken, that's all," he said, and pointed at the silent bodyguard. "See about him. I did, and he was dead. His neck was snapped and he was lost beyond help. He was the youngest bodyguard. The one with the smooth cheeks. The one the Corvidic sisters had played with. If he really was as pure as they thought, he would never lose his innocence now. I raised hands over him, and the others came to do the same, even as the Celtic horseman encircled us, with their horses stamping and tossing their heads.

"Has he gone to his ancestors?" said Morganus.

"Yes," I said, and Morganus looked at the horsemen. They still made no move, so he judged them to be in no immediate threat. He looked back at us. "Then we will give blessing upon the dead in the name of Jupiter Maximus," he said. "We shall give blessing together, over the body of the fallen one, and you men will get me up and help me stand." Which we did. We said it together, and one of the Celts, who proved not to be a Celt at all, dismounted, and removed his helmet and recited the prayer with us. He was Aulus Magrix Drusillius, once drill master of the Twentieth Legion and now captain to the foot guards of King Cogidubnus. He had not taken part in the wild charge. He had ridden up afterwards, jarring awkwardly in the saddle like a Roman.

Morganus saw him, and when the prayer was finished and himself still held up by two of the bodyguards, he turned on Drusillius.

"So whose side are you on now?" he said, and Drusillius looked away, unable to face him.

Chapter 32

Drusillius fiddled with his helmet straps. He was embarrassed. He put on his helmet, and looked round for the leader of the horsemen, and shouted something at him in Britannic. The man shouted back at Drusillius. There was a brief argument between them, then Drusillius gave up and walked to where I was standing. Morganus was supported by two of the bodyguards, with his right shin stuck out and beginning to swell.

Drusillius took off his helmet again. It was a Celtic helmet, elaborate and decorated, and with two bronze horns. He made a gesture of apology, then bowed to Morganus.

"Huh!" said Morganus. So Drusillius turned to me.

"I speak Greek," he said. "Not good, but I speak it." He said it in Greek and he was right. It was not good Greek. The accent and inflections were atrocious. It was Greek he'd learned in some gutter, because not all Greeks are scholars, and we have pot men, thieves and whores like any other people. But, it was Greek and, as he spoke, the horseman leader rode forward, and shouted at Drusillius, and the two had another argument. But Drusillius was the fiercer. Finally the horseman backed off, but pointed to his men, as if to emphasise that they were still there. Which, they were, in a ring all round us. Drusillius looked at me, and jabbed his thumb at the horseman. He forced a smile trying to ingratiate himself.

"He said ..."

"I know," I said. "You told him to take his men away, and he wouldn't.

Then he told you not to use a language he doesn't understand, but you insisted and told him again to go away, and he wouldn't."

Drusillius was impressed. He reverted to Latin. "You really do it, don't you? Read minds. 'Cos I know you don't speak Britannic." He looked at Morganus. "Or does he?"

Morganus sneered. "Don't talk to me, you traitor," he said, and Drusillius sighed.

"I got to speak Greek," he said to Morganus. "Can you follow it, honoured sir?"

"No," said Morganus.

"So talk to me," I said, because he had something to say, and I wanted to know what it was. Drusillius nodded and spoke Greek.

"Tell the big man that I saved your lives," he said. "Tell him Maligoterix wanted you dead. Bodies burned. Carriage burned. Horses burned. Everything. But I said if they killed Morganus and the legion found out, then the legion would march! Nobody could stop them. The men would lead, the centurions would follow, and the legate would have nothing to say. The legion would come here and kill all the people and piss on the bodies." He paused, and looked at me, and I wondered what side he was really on.

"Are you saying that Maligoterix knew we were coming?" I said.

"Yes," he said, "and he knew why."

"How could he have known? We came as fast as man can move. How could a message have got here before us?"

"A pigeon," said Drusillius. "They sent one from Londinium, and it was here before dusk on the day you left." So there it was. Proof positive of how the druids gathered information.

"Who sent the pigeon?" I said, and he shook his head. So I went round the question. "I assume some Celt actually released the bird." His face said *'yes'*. "Drusillius," I said, "I don't need the names of whatever Celts were involved in Londinium. But I must know which Roman, or servant of Rome, passed on this information to the Celts." He shook his head again, and fixed his mouth in a stubborn line. I would get no more from him on this.

So I pointed at the wrecked lightning, and the dead bodyguard. "How will you explain this?" I said. "You've broken the treaty with Rome. You attacked us." He grinned at that. The answer was already cooked and seasoned and needed only bringing to table.

"We thought you were another attempt on the life of His Majesty King Cogidubnus," he said. "They happen all the time, see? And they're getting clever. We'd heard they were coming in disguise this time, and when we saw you, we thought you were them, dressed as Romans." He sneered. "Now wasn't that a nasty mistake? 'Cos everyone's away, see? Maligoterix, Cogidubnus and the rest. Everyone senior is away. Even pretty-boy Lachanig, the ladies' darling. There's nobody here who'd know you. Nobody that counts."

"What about you?"

"Me? I'm not even here! I'm somewhere else, with witnesses to swear to it."

"But Morganus has seen you."

"And Cogidubnus has seen me somewhere else!"

I thought that over. Cogidubnus, the man we wanted on our side, the man who had friends in Rome, the man we wanted to prize apart from Maligoterix. It looked as if Maligoterix had long since won this particular battle. So I looked at the old veteran in his outlandish Celtic gear and asked him a question just for curiosity.

"Why do you stand for this, Drusillius?" I said, and gestured at the riders. "Why are you with them? You're a Roman! Why did you make no attempt to warn us? You knew we were coming down the Great South Road. You could have sent a message to any of the way stations."

"Oh yes!" he said, and came close. "I'm a Roman. But you've seen how I live in there." He looked at the Palace. "I live like an emperor, and that's how they catch you, see? And then one day you find you've been here ten years and you've got a wife and kids. Native wife and kids. And do you know what they do to you, here, if you betray them?"

"No," I said.

"They kill your family, one by one. They do it in front of you, then they kill you."

I was barely listening. My mind was heaving. His words had thrown me back to the dream of the closed door. I was in another world. I was on the point of remembering something.

"Greek!" said Drusillius. "Are you listening?"

"Yes," I said, and forced myself to pay attention. "So what will you do with us now?"

"Nothing!" he said. "It was all a terrible mistake, see? It was all the fault of this lot here." He looked at the horsemen. "It was all their fault and they'll pay for it." He waved at the riders, and called out to them. "You don't know yet, do you, my lovely lads?" Then he turned back to me. "This is why I'm speaking Greek. So. We'll say how very sorry we are, and we'll explain that these idiots *did* get a vague idea they'd attacked the wrong people, so they rode back to the palace, and locked all the doors, and waited for their masters to come back to sort it all out. But nobody came for days. So wasn't that a shame?"

"What will Cogidubnus say about all this?" I said. Drusillius laughed.

"Whatever Maligoterix tells him!" I nodded. It had seemed like a good idea to come here, but I saw that the cause was lost before we set forth.

"And you will just leave us out here?" I said.

"That's right."

"Can you not even give us fresh horses?"

"No. Not until it's done. This what's-it-called? The ..."

"The Silanianum?"

"Yes," he said. "Someone wants you dead Greek. You and all the rest."

"So you will leave us out here, without help or horses, and your old comrade badly injured? You'll do that to Leonius Morganus Fortis Victrix?"

Drusillius said nothing, but his face showed a great shame.

"So what are you doing here?" I said. "If you're going to pretend you weren't here, why did you bother coming?"

"For him," he said, looking at Morganus. "For the big man. I want him to know I risked my life for him. They wanted him chopped, see? But I said if they did, I'd tell the legion, and that meant Maligoterix had to do a little sum, see? He had to work out what my guardsmen would do if he killed me and, by the luck of the gods, he decided my lads might turn nasty, and he'd rather have them on his side, 'cos they really are always trying to chop one another in there." He looked at the palace. "It all depends which one has the most men behind him." He turned to Morganus. "So you just tell Morganus I saved his life," he said. "Because Maligoterix wanted him dead." He looked at me, "You too, Greek, especially you. So you owe me one as well. But I don't care about you, only the big man."

So he bowed to Morganus, yelled at the Celts in Britannic, got back on his horse and rode off. They all did, taking their dead and wounded, and the two remaining horses from the lightning. They left us alone on the idyllic parkland of Cogidubnus' castle, in the bright sunshine, with just one day and one night to go before the Silanianum, and not even all of one day at that.

"What did he say, Greek?" said Morganus. So I told him, and Morganus cursed Drusillius in the name of Mithras. Then, since all else seemed hopeless, I set my mind to the troubles in front of me. I looked at Morganus's leg.

"We'd best set that," I said. "Broken bones heal best if set at once. If they're left they become difficult."

"Do you know how to do it?" he said.

"Yes," I said. "In my city, every schoolboy was taught the early care of injury. We called it *first aid*."

"In your city," he said. "Apollonis?" and seemed about to say something. But he did not.

"So," I said, "I'll need the help of your men."

"Do as the Greek gentleman says," he said to them.

"Yes, honoured sir."

"But wrap up the lad in his cloak first," said Morganus, looking the dead bodyguard. "Lay him out with dignity, and cover him up."

"Yes honoured, sir."

While they gave respect to the dead man, I went to the wreck of the lightning, and took out a big wine flask. Having been caught without wine once before, I had made sure that we had some aboard, and two large flasks were still unbroken. Then Morganus was sat down on his cloak and I told him to drink the flask.

"All of it?"

"As much as you can. It relaxes the muscles and dulls the pain."

"Pain?" said Morganus. "I'm not afraid of him. He's my old friend of forty years' service."

"Drink it anyway." I said. So he did, and I followed the drill taught to me by an Apollonite surgeon in my youth. It is no surprise to report that Morganus was very brave. He made no sound, as two of bodyguards held his shoulders, and I straightened his leg, and set it in splints chopped out of the remains of the lightning body, and secured with bandages cut from its hood. Then we propped him up, as best we could, on cushions taken from the lightning. I got the three remaining bodyguards to take out the rest of the hood from the lightning to improvise a shelter in case the rain came back, which it did not, but the work kept them busy while I spoke to Morganus, who was sleepy from the effects of the wine.

"What do we do now, Greek?" he said.

"I've sent the driver to the fort at Noviomagus Reginorum," I said. "He's younger than me, your boys aren't built for speed, and it's about ten miles by road, to the fort. He'd be the fastest of us. So, if he steps out smartly, they should have a cavalry unit back here before dusk, and we won't have another night in the rain."

"Good," he said. "But what about the Silanianum?"

"I don't know," I said.

"You did all that a man could do," he said. "But the gods were against us." He tried to concentrate, but his head nodded and his eyes closed, where he lay covered in cloaks, with a cushion at his head. Then he opened his eyes and looked at me. "What do we do now, Greek?" he said again. "What can we do?"

I did not know what to say. So I dealt with another matter of practicality, even though it turned my stomach and brought pain to my mind.

"You can't be there tomorrow," I said, "at the house of Fortunus. So who will take charge? Who will … who will … organise it?"

"If I'm absent, then my duties fall to the Second Javelin," he said. "He's my deputy and he knows my ways. He's a good man."

"Does he know about … ?" I would have asked if the Second Javelin knew about the Apollonite merciful stroke between neck and collar bone. But Morganus'ss eyes closed. More than that, my voice failed me, and I could not have put the thought into words anyway. At the same time, my mind was working. It was juggling a burden of facts concerning the murder of Scorteus and the business of the shields, and with something else besides, something from my past. I did not know what it was, but I was reaching back towards something. I had the same, thick, sick, bloated feeling in my head, that a man has in his belly in the moments before he vomits.

But nothing came forth, not until a few hours from sunset when were visited by a miracle. The two carriage horses came cantering back, as runaway horses do, because the horse is not solitary like a cat. He is a herd animal. He is highly social, he detests loneliness, and when he is lost he will try to find the place where last he was together with his herd. So the two lost horses came back to us, although one was being dragged by the other. It was running on three sound limbs and one broken.

I went towards them, and let them smell me. I took care to keep always in their sight and to make no sudden gesture. I hoped that they remembered me, and perhaps they did, but I was bred up to horses. There are a thousand small ways that a man may reassure a horse, and when trained from childhood a man forgets that he even does them. In any case, the horses let me come to them, and speak to them, and pet them. And so we became friends and they stood steady and calm.

"How do you do it, Greek?" said one of the bodyguards. "Is it more magic?"

"If you wish," I said, too tired to argue. Also I was afflicted with sudden hope, which comes painful to a man wallowing in the comfort of despair, because it demands action and brings fear of further disappointment. With the speed of a horse, I might still get back to Londinium before dawn. But if I did, what would I do there?

I think that, even in that moment, there were new thoughts in my mind as to who might be our real enemy and who might be our friend. But I put aside the thought because there was a task to be done first.

The broken leg of a man may be set, but not that of a horse, and the men of my city were taught how to end the pain of horses. So I called the bodyguards to me.

"Take this one's bridle," I said to the eldest, "and stand by him, and stroke his head, while I take off the other."

"Yes, honoured sir."

The wounded horse, a mare, staggered and whimpered as I drew her from her companion. A front leg was ruined. Badly broken, with blood and bone showing. I was full of sorrow, because I love horses dearly. They are the noblest creatures on earth. They are beautiful and strong and splendid. So I stroked the mare's head and led her off, and spoke to her all the while, small words, kind words, soft words. So she hopped and staggered, but came on, and I called another of the bodyguards.

"Help me now. Draw your dirk. But do it slowly and don't let her see it. Keep it behind you and come and stand to my right."

One man cannot do it by himself. It takes two men to send a horse into the shades. One must hold the head and keep the animal free from fear, while the other stabs with a sharp knife into the great vessels of the neck. It is the kindest way, I had done it before, and it is part of life. But this time my hands shook and my mind heaved with the thought, not of the killing of horses but of men, killing them in the kindest way: men, women and youngsters. I sneered at myself for being so clever in knowing how to do such things, but so stupid in being unable to prevent them. And, all the time, some great matter was closed within my mind, because I myself would not let it come into the light. I felt sick. I grasped the mare for comfort. I put my arms around her head, I pressed my brow to hers. I reached into the groove that runs down a horse's neck, and I spoke softly to the bodyguard.

"Do you see where my finger points?" I said.

"Yes, honoured sir."

"Then, when I count to three, you will drive your dirk deeply into this place. But first put your own finger on the spot to feel the pulse of the vessel, so that you are quite sure what you are aiming at. Can you do that?"

"Yes, honoured sir."

He did as I asked, and my heart thundered within me, as a mist began to clear, and a vision came to me sharp and bright from my memory. I stood at the door of my house, in the smoke and flames of the siege, yet still I was in the present, with a duty to perform.

"One," I said, as I opened my own front door. "Two," I said, as I stood before my family, sword in hand. "Three!" I said, and the bodyguard stabbed, and blood spouted such that the horse fell not to my stroke, but to that of another. Which actuality of truth finally opened that part of my mind that had been closed for ten years.

I saw my wife, Iphigenia daughter of Eurypheos, granddaughter of Iphigenios of the Clan of the Eagle, and of the city of Apollonis, a noblewoman of lineage greater than mine. I saw her face in sharp recall, and the faces of my children too: all four sweet faces that had been denied me for so long. I looked again to my-lady-their-mother and saw a proud woman who would not be a slave nor allow her children to be slaves. As I watched, she blindfolded our children, then cut their throats, and then her own, and I sank to my knees in their blood.

Chapter 33

I was sitting with Morganus, and he was talking, but I was not listening. I had gone and sat by him when I realised that the bodyguards were staring at me. They were worried that I was weeping over the death of a cart horse. But they were infantrymen, they did not understand about horses and, in any case, I was not weeping for the death of a horse. But I looked at their faces, and thought of the youngest of them, who was now lying cold on the ground, and I realised that I was not only far older than them, but had become a figure of respect to them, such that it was my duty to set them an example, an example of dignity in grief. So I wiped my eyes and stood up straight, and smiled at them.

They looked at one another, much relieved, and I went to sit by Morganus, who stirred and woke up. But I was so deeply within my own thoughts, that he was talking to me for some time before I realised it.

"Greek?" said Morganus, shaking my arm. "What is it?" He looked up at the bodyguards. "Has he been at the wine?"

"No, honoured sir!" They were shocked at the suggestion.

"Well what's wrong with him?"

"We don't know, honoured sir," said the eldest bodyguard. "He was upset when we killed the horse."

"Greek!" said Morganus, and shook me again, but there was a vast clamouring of ideas within my mind, and all of them calling for my attention, and begging to be organised and told where to stand. I felt sick and dizzy. I was in danger of losing my capacity to reason. So I focused on what seemed the most important of the facts swirling within me

"I am Ikaros," I said. "Son of Cleon, Grandson of Ikaros of the Clan Philhippos, of the City of Apollonis, and I know that I did not kill my children, and I know why I never had the will to take my own life. This was because I was shamed that my wife had done what I could not and thereby I was condemned to live as a slave. I was shamed then, I was shamed since, and I will be shamed for ever."

"What's he talking about?" said Morganus, "Greek! Ikaros! What is it?" So I told him what my mind had kept hidden for ten years. He listened, and the bodyguards listened and when I was done, Morganus took my arm again.

"Why did you never mention this?" he said, "About your wife?"

"I didn't know until now."

"No. Of course you didn't," he said. And he looked at me, and looked at the bodyguards and he pondered and worried, and came to a decision. "You men," he said to the bodyguards. "What is our faith? To whom do we pray?" He made the bull sign. They did likewise.

"Mithras the Bull Slayer," they said.

"Yes," said Morganus. "We keep the secrets and the oaths of our faith, do we not?"

"Yes, honoured sir!"

"But sometimes we must break rules. Even the rules of the gods!"

The bodyguards looked at one another with deep unease.

"So this is what we are going to do. I am going to tell the Greek gentleman one of our rituals, and you men will give witness to the truth of what I say. Is that understood?"

"Yes, honoured sir."

"So!" said Morganus and pointed to the scar on his face where the artillery bolt had gone in. "I got this at the siege of Apollonis. Did you know that?"

"Yes," I said. "I guessed. Our best marksmen were told to shoot your officers."

"And so they did!" he said. "Now listen to me, Ikaros son of Cleon. We have a toast in our Legionary Temple of Mithras. We have a toast for hard times when we must do our duty. We fill our cups and we give a toast that is an act of worship. We toast *The Women of Apollonis.*" He looked at the bodyguards. "Isn't that right, lads?"

"Yes," they said.

"You weren't the only one," he said to me. "You weren't the only man that couldn't kill his children. And what sort of a men would you be if you could? So the men of your city didn't do it, but we still didn't find any families alive in the great houses because the women did it! It wasn't just your wife, it was all of them. All of the nobility. That's how they were bred! The slaves told us afterwards. They told us the women had talked among themselves, and planned it. And when they killed, they did it with a great blood letting, as an insult to those that found them. They didn't use your quick sword that makes no mess. They left a defiance to Rome, a defiance in blood. Do you understand? Didn't you know?"

"No," I said. "I didn't know. Our women were not like those of the other Greeks. They were independent. They had their own temples and mystery cults. Some were philosophers and artists. They had a life beyond the house. A life separate from men."

"Well there you are then," said Morganus. "They'd planned it, they'd made peace with their gods, and they led their children to the next world, and saved them from disgrace. And that is why we toast your women and ask that, if we were in their place, we might have the same courage." He looked at the bodyguards. "That's how we honour a brave enemy, isn't it lads?"

"Yes," they said. Morganus nodded and looked at me.

"And it's the only toast that the legion makes to women. It's unique. Do you understand?"

I did understand. But it was hard to let go the guilt that had shaped my character for so long. It was hard, but with Morganus'ss words to guide me, I looked again at the memory of my wife's face as she took up the knife. She had looked at me and nodded. Just one gesture that I had profoundly forgotten. But now it was in my eyes. It was one small sign, but that is all I need to read deeply, except that I had been blinded by the horror of the moment, such that I did not read it but hid it away. But now, that nod told me that she did not look upon me with contempt, which emotion from her, or rather the dreadful fear of it, was the source of my shame, my nightmares, my insomnia. It was probably the self-destructive remarks I had made to the Lord Chief Justice concerning Roman inferiority, or to Allicanda on every occasion that I ever grew close to her.

But by the grace of the gods, there had been no contempt in my wife's expression, only a grim fixation upon a dreadful task that she believed was hers alone and not mine. So, while I was not yet whole and cured, I was ready to do what I always do when troubles come in such legions, that they cannot be faced together. I took refuge in practicality. I got up.

"We have a good horse," I said. "I'll ride to Londinium. When I get there I'll go to Tertia again. She's our only hope. I'll beg her to do anything she can to stop the Silanianum. Perhaps Africanus will obey her and arrest Petros and Veranius? Perhaps I can get something out of them. Veranius certainly knows who took gold from the treasury to pay Scorteus! If he'll admit it was Petros, we've got proof of corruption in the body politic, and Tertia may be able to persuade Josephus at least to delay the Silanianum until Teutonius returns, if ever he does."

They looked at me. The bodyguards were nodding. They were convinced I could do it. But they really did believe I was magic. They believed it from the helmets on their heads to the hobnails in their boots. Morganus was not so sure.

"Why don't we wait for the cavalry to arrive?" he said. "That driver's been gone for hours. And if I could get on a horse, I could come with you. Maybe they've got another lightning at Noviomagus Reginorum? Then we could all go to Londinium together. You're a clever man Greek, but they might listen to me where they wouldn't listen to you."

"You shouldn't ride," I said, "Not hard and fast, and certainly not on a lightning. Things can go wrong with broken leg. Vessels might be severed and bleed inside the leg. Then you'd lose it."

"Bah!" he said. "What's a leg compared to four hundred people? And you're one of them, Greek!"

"No!" I said. "I beg you in the name of every god of Greece and

Rome. I've got to get on that horse, and it's got to be me, because none of you can ride like me. We haven't even got a saddle! And I've got all the facts of the case in my head, and we can't wait because who knows where the driver is? Perhaps he's lost. Perhaps the Celts went after him. He might never get to Noviomagus"

"Well at least go there yourself," said Morganus. "I'll give you a written message to the officer commanding the garrison. I've got a tablet in my baggage. I'll write to him begging his help." That made me think. There was much to recommend the suggestion. With the army behind me I would move at maximum speed, with fresh horses at every stage. But I was unsure.

"No," I said. "I'd have to turn back off the road to get to the fort, which would add more time to the journey. They don't know me and they might not believe me, and they might think I wrote the message myself, and waste time arguing, or sending messages up the line to Londinium." I shook my head, "No! We can't take the risk, I'll ride straight to Londinium. The posting stations do know me, by now, and if you want to write a message, you could write an order giving me the power to commandeer horses."

"That won't help," he said. "The post-station ostlers can't read. They're peasants. But you can take this." He unbuckled the money pouch from his belt and gave it to me. That'll be more use than written orders." He smiled. "There's gold in there, so don't spend all of it on wine."

I laughed at his joke, but I had something more to say.

"You know where my notes are? In your house?"

"Yes," he said. "In your bedroom."

"Then here is a fresh idea," I said. "If the worst happens ... if they do it ... the Silanianum, and I'm dead," I paused, trying to sort out ideas that were unformed in my mind, "if Tertia can't help us, or won't help us, or if I'm killed, to stop me ..."

"Yes?" he said.

"Then this is what I want you to do. I want you do it for justice and for Rome."

So I told him, and he did not like it, but finally he agreed.

Then I contrived a bridle and reins from the lightning harness, threw my cloak on the horse's back, and I spoke to the animal, explaining what we had to do, and I mounted up. Morganus and the bodyguards waved and I record with pride that at no time did any one of them show even the slightest suspicion that I might ride off and save my own life, rather than go to Londinium and fight for four hundred others. In letting me go free, Morganus risked his honour, and even his life, but he trusted me and I tried to be worthy of him.

Now I had to cover some seventy miles, all of it on good roads, but with only a few hours left of daylight. I would be mostly riding in the dark, which horses do not like, or at least they do not like to go fast. Even if they did, no horse could cover seventy miles at the gallop. If a horse is fresh and strong, and well fed on oats, then he can gallop for a few miles, but no more. For long distance riding, the trot or canter is best, and the horse should be rested frequently, and allowed to walk. That is why Roman roads have posting stations every ten miles, so that tired horses can be changed for fresh ones.

Of course there are wicked men who will drive a horse beyond its natural limits, and thereby cover astonishing distances at great speed. But such despicable cruelty will ruin or even kill the horse, and a Knight of Apollonis would rather lose his soul than ride a horse to death. But, in my haste to reach Londinium in time, I was riding for the lives of four hundred human beings, and I prayed that Apollo in his gracious mercy might forgive me if I was less than kind to the horses I rode that night, because I fear that sometimes I was brutal.

My memory of the journey is confused. I was very tired, even when I set out, and night came down. I was over ten hours on horseback, and the way-station ostlers were reluctant to give me a horse. This was mostly they did *not* remember me, because Romans notice masters not slaves, and they certainly did not trust a wild-eyed Greek, yelling in the moonlight. Morganus's purse was my saviour. The ostlers might not recognise me, but they knew a gold piece when they saw one. Even so, at least one of the way stations did not have any horses at all, because others had taken them. When I reached the half way post mansion, I saw light burning and the busy activity of some Roman unit that was there for the night, with centurions shouting orders and men stamping to attention. I sat in the cold night, swaying on my latest horse, aching in all my limbs, tired and weary, and patting the horse's neck, and wondering if I dared meet Roman troops. Roman troops and Roman officers, who might not believe my story, and might delay me? I could not risk it. Time was so short. So I rode on, pushing my mount beyond his tiredness, because even the shortest delay might cause me to arrive in Londinium after dawn, when the massacre was complete, and nothing left but corpses, and the House of Fortunus empty and silent.

The worst time was at the Thames ferry. The ferry was run by a dozen engineers from the Twentieth. Their pontoon barge was made fast to a small jetty, the troops were asleep in a wooden hut inside a fenced compound that was locked up for the night, and just one man was on sentry duty outside. By then I was almost falling off the back of my latest mount, and I showed nothing like the polite respect that a Roman soldier expects from a slave. So I fell into a stupid argument with the sentry, which was more my fault than his, and he refused to turn out the unit to man the ferry, and soon I was hanging on to my horse yelling abuse at him, while he yelled back.

"Sod off!" he cried. "Or I'll have you off that bleedin' horse, and put my boot so far up your arse it'll come out your mouth!"

"You moron!" I said. "You idiot! I'm here in the name of Leonius Morganus!"

"Don't you get clever with me you bleedin' Greek!"

"Just let me in, or call your officer," I begged.

"Sod off!" he cried. "We're shut down till dawn and that's it!"

I groaned. I looked up at the black sky and the moon and the stars, and looked across the black river to the black mass of the city on the other side and, most tantalising of all, I looked at the huge span of the Thames bridge, that I could have crossed at the gallop if only the centre had not been taken out for the quinquireme! Then I looked at the ferry and wondered if I could move it by myself. It worked on a cable strung across the river. The cable passed through ring bolts on waist-high posts at either end of the pontoon, so that the crew could haul on the cable and move the pontoon. But the pontoon was over thirty feet long and twenty wide. It was designed to take heavy wagons and it was far too big for me to move alone, even if the angry sentry would let me, which he would not.

So I had the mad idea of swimming the river, of forcing the horse to take me across. It was the only thing left to do. So I turned the horse and drove him towards the sinister, wild width of the night-time river. The horse was terrified and fought back hard, but I dug in my heels and urged him on without the least kindness or gentleness, and he cried out in fear, and his legs splashed, and spattered the icy-cold water, so that it drenched my legs and my waist, and finally my whole body. But still he would not commit himself to the waters, and if ever I despaired it was in that moment, because I was denied even the small satisfaction of drowning in my attempt to cross the river, which was the most likely outcome of what I was trying to do.

So I cried aloud to Apollo, the god of my fathers. I was done. I was finished. I had failed.

Chapter 34

"Oi!" cried a loud voice. "You there! Greek boy!" I turned on the horse and saw an optio. He had come out of the compound. The gates were open and there were legionaries behind him, holding lanterns. "You! Boy!" cried the optio. "Lay off that bleedin' noise and come here!" My horse splashed in fright. I wondered what to do. Then the optio shouted again, "Here!" he said. "I know you. You're that clever-dick Greek. You're Morganus's boy." He thought about that and his manner changed. He became almost polite. "Will you come over here?" he said. "Get yourself out of that water and tell me what you want?"

Enormous relief. Wonderful hope. I let the horse take me to shore, got off him, and poured out words to the optio. I was tired and confused and he did not follow all of it. But he understood one thing.

"This is for Morganus?" he said. "For the big man?"

"Yes!" I said.

"*RIGHT!*" yelled the optio, to his men. "Get that bleedin' pontoon manned, and I want it across that bleedin' river, fastest you've ever done it because this is for Leonius Morganus Felix Victrix!"

"Gods bless him!" they cried. They hauled on the cable with all their might and the optio yelling the time.

"Pull together! *Pull!* Pull together! *Pull!*"

As the pontoon moved, I was forced to stand still, holding the horse's head and do nothing for the first time in hours. In the quiet, an odd feeling of satisfaction grew in the deep of my mind, where previously there had been a mad jumbling of facts. It was not much, but it was there.

On the north bank I mounted again, and rode off and the soldiers cheered as I went. I had another argument at the city gates, which were closed. But, again, I was recognised, and the name of Morganus turned the great timbers on their hinges, and let me into the dark of the city, except that it was not really dark. The mansions had lights burning and their slave doors open, while citizens were gathering outside with their torches and lanterns awaiting the salutatio.

I groaned, knowing that dawn was approaching and the army would be ready at the House of Fortunes with side streets closed, mass grave open, wagons for the dead, men separated from women, and a place found for the executions. I wondered if the Apollonite sword would be used, or some other method? The army would do everything else by the book, right down to picking out their psychotics to do the killing, which would begin the moment the sun cleared the horizon, the army's definition of dawn.

So I forced my horse through the crowds of slaves and tradesmen, and ignored the curses of citizens and rode at utmost speed to Government House, where the Governor's Guard was on duty in much-polished, antique gear. An officer challenged me as I rode up, the horse staggering and myself gasping in exhaustion and in dreadful fear that I might yet be too late.

"Halt!" cried the officer, with his gilded cuirass, and republican helmet. Behind, his men charged spears and locked shields. There were fifty of them, in two lines, blocking the great staircase into Government House. "State your business!" cried the officer. I tried to, but I was so tired and my breath coming so harsh and hard, that he did not understand me. So I invoked the name of Morganus.

"I come in the name of the First Javelin of the Twentieth!" I gasped. But the magic did not work. Not with the men of the Governor's Guard. They just sneered.

"Oh do you really?" said the officer. "And what makes you think I take orders from a legionary boot slogger?" His men laughed. "Or a Greek pansy-boy? So you just go round the back with all the other toe rags."

I hesitated, so dull with tiredness that I did not know what he meant, and tiredness took the opportunity to fall upon me such that with my mind empty, the feeling of satisfaction came again, but stronger. It was a sense of order, which I love, coming out of chaos, which I detest. But then the feeling was gone as I realised that, of course, there was neither trades door nor slave door at the front of Government House. Those would be at the back. So I kicked the horse, we galloped round the great building, and there, while soldiers ludicrously guarded the front entrance, there was a huge river of traffic freely going in and out at the back! So I slid off the horse, pushed into the crowd of goods-laden slaves and tradesmen, and nobody even tried to stop me as I went in through the back door. In fact nobody would look at me. They were behaving oddly, and at first I was so stupid with tiredness that I could not guess the reason.

"Where are the Lady Tertia's rooms?" I asked a butcher's porter, with a half side of pork over his shoulder.

"Dunno," he said. "None o' my business!" He hurried off, and I stood dazed, in a crowded corridor, with lamps and life, and all the bustle of a household community, and its daily incomers, except that there was a dark mood upon them. No morning jokes, no teasing and chatter, and suddenly I knew why. They knew, as all the city knew, that another household community, just like this one, was lined up waiting to be taken into the killing room. While, somewhere else, the children screamed for the parents they'd been torn from, because the world was coming to an end.

"Where are the Lady Tertia's rooms?" I asked a slave woman with a basket of loaves. But she ignored me and pushed past with head bowed. I asked others, but nobody would answer. The Silanianum was already doing its work. It was driving terror into the minds of slaves. I asked again and again. Then a senior slave woman recognised me. She was very well dressed, a head of department. She took me aside.

"What are you doing here?" she whispered. "You're that Greek boy, aren't you? Scorteus's boy?" She whispered still more softly, "Have you run away?"

"No!" I said. "I must speak to the Lady Tertia. She can stop it."

"The Silanianum?"

"Yes!"

"You can stop it? Really stop it?"

"I don't know," I said. "But if I don't try then it will surely go ahead."

I would like to believe that the gods rewarded my passion for truth, but perhaps she was simply a kind woman because she pointed to her right.

"Through the pastry kitchen, out into the little garden, then turn right and up a flight of stairs. That's the service stairs up to My Lady's personal quarters. I blessed her and the feeling of satisfaction came back in overpowering strength. A feeling of right and correctness, such that I had the answer even before it was prompted out of me by what I saw next. My mind had been active all that long journey, during all those hours on horseback and the disparate facts, that I could not reconcile, had finally drawn themselves up in ranks, as if on parade.

So I ran through the pastry kitchen, out into the dark garden and then I heard the shrill cries of children, reacting in horrified mirth, and I felt something bump into my legs and run off into the bushes. It felt like a creature gone mad, which indeed it was. Children's faces appeared at a window and the children shrieked and laughed. Then I looked through the light of an open door and saw the tableau that put all else into perspective.

Tertia's beloved slave Merloura was at work in a neat, private kitchen. She was preparing poultry, but she was making a black-humoured show of it. She had a basket of live chickens at her feet, and half a dozen slave children for an audience. She took a cackling bird from the basket, she put the bird on a block, and secured its head in a loop of thong fastened to one end of the block. Then she laughed, and pulled on the chicken's legs so that the bird's neck was extended to maximum. Then she picked up a large cleaver, and waved the blade in the air.

"One," she said.

"One!" cried the children.

"Two," she said.

"Two!" they cried.

"Three," she said.

"Three!" they cried, and then shrieked again, as Merloura brought down the blade with such precision, that only the head of the bird was left in the loop, and the bird's neck, body and legs continued alive. Merloura carefully lowered the bird on to the ground and, to further shrieking from the children, the decapitated bird ran around the kitchen, spouting blood, with blind, mindless vigour.

The sight alone would have done it: her fierce energy, nasty cruelty, merciless efficiency, and the callous desecration of a living thing. But the sound of her voice gave proof. It was deep as a man's and harsh and grating. As I stepped forward for a better look, she saw me. I read her face, she read mine, and she growled and stood up, took a grasp of the cleaver, and came after me with murderous determination. But the door opened outwards, and I seized it and slammed it hard into her face. It was a heavy door, it struck hard and she fell.

I found the service staircase and ran up it and opened another door, straight into Tertia's private dressing room where her slave girls were preparing her for the day. They gasped, then leapt forward in a row to protect their mistress. But Tertia stood slowly and deliberately. She was wearing only a white, under robe, and she was very lovely. She looked at me, and frowned. I am sure she guessed what was in my mind as quickly as Merloura had.

"You!" she said, pointing at one of her girls. "Fetch the guards!"

"No!" I said. "Hear me first, or the guards and everyone else will hear." She considered that. She considered it very carefully indeed. Then she smiled. She looked at me as if completely relaxed, and not caring what I might say.

"Leave us," she said, and the girls were gone in an instant and I was alone with her. The room was fragrant with perfumes, filled with garments and cosmetics, bright lit by elaborate lamps, and there was an ornate water clock on a stand beside the still-dark window. It was in the form of a big bronze urn, with a dial representing the hours. In addition, this one had marks on the dial to indicate dawn and sunset. So I looked at it and saw that there much less than half an hour to dawn.

"If you go to Josephus now," I said, "you could stop the Silanianum.

He is lodged in this house. He has the power to stop it, and he would do it for you. You rank highest in all the province."

"Perhaps," she said. "But why should I?"

"It was you," I said. "Not Petros. You wanted a war for your husband to win, and Scorteus came to you with a plan. So what did he want in return? Citizenship?" She smirked. It was citizenship. I read it in her face, but I read it only because she let me, and then she closed shutters on all unintended emotions. She was a fine actress, one of the very few people who had ever deceived me, which indeed she had, most thoroughly and completely.

"You offered him citizenship," I said, "but he didn't trust you, so he wanted gold as well. Massive quantities of gold, authorised by you out of the treasury. That's why Scapula won't speak. He thinks, if he betrays you, he betrays the Emperor." She affected a puzzled expression.

"How would I speak to Scorteus on so private a matter?" she said. "When my every movement is the gossip of all the world."

"You spoke to nobody! Scorteus approached you. He sent the Syrian to Merloura. They arranged it between them, and it was her in a cloak that he took aboard ship to prove the shields were loaded. Then they signed the cipher book, and Scorteus got the gold. They did that each time a ship went out with a load of shields."

She replaced puzzlement with a cold smile, as if changing masks.

"You will be thrown to the beasts for this," she said.

"And I know why you threatened the tribune Rufinus at Aquae Sulis," I said. "You were taking too much gold from the treasury weren't you? To pay Scorteus. And you needed to get the mines working to cover your theft! That was the main reason for going to Aquae Sulis. Cursing the girl was just a bonus. But I do wonder why you bothered. Were you that jealous?"

"She gave him a son," she said. "That barbarian bitch. She gave him a son, which I could not." Her face was cold, but the words were hot, because even Tertia had her limits and she was finally showing her feelings.

"So you were jealous of the German girl?" I said, and she sneered in infinite contempt. "Then the girl was cured with my drug," I said, "by Scorteus, and you had him killed. You had him killed by Merloura." I studied her face as I made the accusation, but she revealed nothing. The anger was gone, the control was back. So I continued. "We never understood how someone got into the bath chamber that morning and then got out again. But, of course, Merloura *didn't go into the bath chamber on that morning*! She went a few times, on earlier days. She went round the house dressed as a Corvidic sister, so the slaves got used to her, then she entered the house on the day *before* the murder, and hid in the cupboard in Scorteus's bath chamber, which she knew about from slave gossip. She stayed there all day and all night. Then, as on every morning, Scorteus took a hot plunge then dozed off to sleep in a chair to await the barber. She knew that from slave gossip too. So, she waited until he was in the chair, then crept out and cut his throat, so he was dead before the barber came in! Then she waited in the cupboard until she could escape. I think she draped herself in a linen towel and mingled with the rest when the bath chamber was full of people in mourning sheets, and she left the rags behind."

"This is fantasy," said Tertia.

"Then she killed the Syrian," I said, "because he knew her name and yours. She arranged to meet him in his rooms, she drugged him, pulled him into his bath chamber, and scalded him to death."

Tertia stared at me, showing no emotion.

"And the Tribune Severus?" I said. "The one who ordered away the door guard when Merloura killed the Syrian? She killed him because he also knew her name and yours. She poisoned him with mushrooms. I wonder how she did it? And what about Maligoterix the druid? It was you that sent word that I was on my way to Cogidubnus. You or Merloura, you told some Celt who was in touch with the druids."

She smiled and spoke. "Dreams and delusions," she said. "You are facing death, and inventing any story to save you, however unlikely or wrong!" She smiled nastily. "For instance, you say that I killed Scorteus because I was jealous over a slave girl?" She laughed. "The very idea is nonsensical!"

I shook my head. "I didn't say that. I said you were jealous, and I said that you had Scorteus killed, but I didn't say you did it for jealousy. You had him killed because he was useful to you while he *wanted* citizenship, but dangerous if he *got* it. As a citizen he would've shot up the Roman hierarchy and gained power over you because of what he knew, so you would never have made him a citizen. But, then he won citizenship anyway, with my drug, and the entire business of shields became irrelevant, but could not be stopped. All those deaths, and all for nothing!"

She just shrugged at that. What did she care about barbarians? Or soldiers, or slaves? This time she had no need to hide her emotions because none were moving within her. But she did begin to admit guilt.

"So, is there anything at all that you have not calculated for yourself?" she said. "Worked out in your clever Greek mind? Do you not seek my explanation of anything?"

"Yes," I said. "How did you manage to poison the Tribune Severus?"

"Oh that was easy," she said. I made use of his attempted connection with my daughter Velia." She gave a dismissive gesture. "He had the impertinent hope that he might marry her. It was ludicrous, but useful. It enabled Merloura to offer him the girl if he would withdraw the guard on the Syrian's side door." She laughed. "He objected to the threat against the soldier's family, but we insisted upon that. Then he was invited to a betrothal meal, but sadly my daughter never arrived, and he was served a dish of mushrooms while he waited. Merloura is an excellent cook and he enjoyed the meal."

"Then your daughter was sent away." I said.

"Yes," she said. "So now you have a complete story, rounded and polished in all respects. But what you will do with it? I shall most certainly not take it to Josephus, and I don't think that you will either."

I looked at the water clock. Dawn was close, and a huge anxiety fell upon me.

"Why not?" I said.

"Because it's not in your own interest." She looked round the room as if searching for something. "Ah!" she said, "There it is!" She found a large, double writing tablet, such as the mistress of a house would use to give the day's orders to her staff. She placed the tablet under a good light.

"Open it," she said. I snatched it open. I looked down. Two sheets of fine wax.

"It's blank," I said, "and there isn't time for this!"

"Really?" she said. "Look harder. It's your freedom and salvation."

"What?" I said, and even with the clock dial moving, I looked again.

"It's a codicil to the will of Scorteus," she said, and pointed to the bottom of the second page. "See here, where it is signed by him, and dated this day one year ago; and witnessed by signatures including that of his lawyer, Dolbius." She gave the cold smile again "By whose oversight it was mislaid, until today." I groaned in anxiety, but still I asked, "And what does it say?"

She glanced at the blank sheets.

"It's your freedom," she said. "Your reward for faithful service." Her finger tapped the wax. "Your freedom enacts retrospectively upon the date of the signing of the document, which means," she looked me straight in the eye, "you're saved from the Silanianum because that applies only to slaves and you're a freedman. And, see here, an enormous sum of money has been left to you, together with two other things that your late master has given you out of his intimate knowledge of your personality, especially your hatred of Britannia and its foul climate."

I nodded. I was dazed. Time was rushing by. Mass murder was about to begin. But still she pulled me with her words, and I guessed that she had taken precautions against my finding out too much. She had researched me by setting her slaves to ask questions, such that she knew my likes and dislikes, my hopes and my fears. And, she was right. Yes, I hated the foul, damp cold of Britannia. Yes, I dreamed of the clear skies and blessed warmth of my homeland. She was pulling me like a dog on a chain.

"Thus here," she said, pointing at the empty wax, "is your title to Scorteus's villa at the southern tip of Italy, where the sun smiles in his glory, and the sea is indigo-deep in warmth of blue." She moved her finger, as if following words. "See here," she said, "the number of rooms, the view over the sea, the olive groves, the pastures, the works of art, the staff of slaves and the livestock." I nodded again. "And, take note," she said, "that this is a region favoured by men of learning. There are philosophers, historians, artists, and engineers, and there is a vigorous culture among them of inquiry and debate." She paused, because she knew that she was looking into the innermost desires of my heart. But she was not done. "Finally, here at the bottom is another small bequest." She smiled, and spoke as if quoting the words of Scorteus. "Knowing Ikaros so well," she said, "and knowing his love of gossip, I bequeath him possession of my cook slave, Allicanda the Hibernian, and may he take pleasure of her for many years to come." Then she closed the document, stood back and looked at me.

"So." she said. Just that and no more. I stood with head bowed, and finally asked a practical question.

"Why should Dolbius be party to forgery?"

She smiled. "Your silence will free him from fear of a death sentence for trafficking with the druids. And levers will be pulled to provide such other signatures as may be needed."

"Obviously you propose an agreement," I said.

"Obviously," she said.

"Such that this non-existent document will become reality if I keep silent."

I glanced at the water clock. There was little time left.

"Yes," she said. "It will become reality in its every detail, as proclaimed before witnesses in City Hall. You will become a rich, free, landowner in the Mediterranean sunshine, with the red-headed girl beside you in your bed."

The clock gave a distinct *clop*, as some gear or wheel shifted in its mechanism and the dial moved again. I looked at the clock. There was only the quarter of an hour left.

Chapter 35

Tertia was far more dangerous that I had thought, and more ruthless and practical too. Her codicil to the will of Scorteus was a masterwork of invention, aimed at my soul, with a precision greater than that of a first class artillery machine in the hands of a gifted marksman. It was simply beyond imagination to devise any greater temptation of my own specific desires.

But that was not the only reason why she held my attention locked into the pages of a tablet that bore no words, while keeping her calm expression, and never blinking nor wavering, and talking constantly. Indeed she spoke almost as Maligoterix had done to work his hypnotic trance, except that perhaps she succeeded where he failed.

So I heard nothing and saw nothing except what she wanted me to see and hear, and I am alive and writing these words now, only by the chance that I looked up into her face just as her eyes widened and focused on something behind me. Though perhaps I did hear something? Perhaps she gasped? Perhaps a shoe scraped behind me? Or do I flatter myself in memory? Probably it was the will of the gods, as so much is in the real world, for all efforts of philosophers to find rational cause and effect. But in whatever case, I looked over my shoulder.

Merloura's face, contorted and bloody, nose broken, brow smashed, cheek split, one eye closed, arms raised with bright steel, a door open behind her, a trail of blood and slime, a soundless snarl of rage, and my mind frozen. Mind, but not body, and the body once a soldier, and the body darting under the blade and grappling and kicking and wrestling, in heart-thundering, manic frenzy, and the woman biting and kicking and growling and wriggling and exerting every sinew to slice the cleaver blade into my flesh. The heavy blows to my back were from someone else, that I felt without pain, and then I wrenched free the cleaver, struck the flat of it many times to Merloura's head, and shoved free, as her grip failed, and I stood up. Tertia threw aside the remains of the book tablet, battered into fragments, and leapt for the water clock, heavy and bronze, and snatched it up as a club, with water splashing out and gear wheels rattling. But she gasped and stopped as she saw what I did next.

I reached down and grabbed Merloura's hair, as she lay half conscious and exhausted, and I jerked up her head and put the blade to her throat, and looked at Tertia.

"Nooooooo!" she cried, and every atom of her being shrieked in horror, and she fell to her knees and raised hands in prayer, and begged, and begged with her eyes. She who cared nothing for the unknown murdered thousands whom she would never meet, was transported with dread that she might see her adopted mother killed before her eyes. And it was not just fear and dread. It was love. It was real deep love. I saw it. I read it. I record it here. Such is the limitless perversity of mankind and womankind too, that even the worst of us may sometimes love someone else more than themselves.

So I threw the cleaver away. It clanged and rattled into a corner. I gathered my breath. I stood up straight.

"Listen to me, Tertia, wife of Teutonius, and born of the Clan Ulpius. I reject your bribe with contempt. I reject it and demand two things from you." But, she ignored me. She raised up Merloura, she embraced her. She wiped her face. She kissed her. Then she snarled as the door opened and her slaves looked in, wide eyed and frightened by the noises they had heard.

"*Get out!*" cried Tertia, and the door slammed. Then she looked at me with poisonous, silent hatred.

"You will go at once to Josephus," I said. "You will tell him that Merloura killed Scorteus. You will stop the Silanianum." Her eyes blinked fast. The immediate threat to Merloura was gone. The blade was thrown away. Tertia was a formidable woman and fought back, even when cornered. Perhaps especially when cornered.

"No," she said. "I will not go to him ... *boy*." She sneered horribly. "Why don't you go ... *boy*? Try your word against mine ... *boy*! Who will listen to a slave against a daughter of the Imperial House? You've lost the game!" She was gaining strength with every word, and Merloura was nodding and gasping and stroking her face. The two of them twined around each other, like snakes round the staff of Mercury. "You've lost," she said, "because Josephus is on my husband's side in Imperial politics. Perhaps you didn't know that?" She shouted her final words. "*So you can't break my reputation by going to him!*"

I sighed. These very thoughts had been in my mind for hours, or rather they had formed and grown and taken shape. They had done so on the ride to Londinium, and waiting for horses at the way stations, and especially on the pontoon crossing the Thames, and finally, and sharply, when I saw Merloura beheading the chickens.

This is how great ideas form.

They do not come suddenly and out of nothing.

Not to me, anyway.

"You are correct, my lady," I said. "So I won't try to destroy your reputation by going to Josephus. What I shall do, instead, is to destroy the reputation of your *husband* by going to Felemid, Duovir of the Council of the Province!"

She frowned and bit her lip. She had not expected that. She blinked and turned over the thought in her mind, and real fear showed on her face.

"I shall take my evidence to Felemid," I said. "because he likes me, and he doesn't like Romans, and it is his duty to write a report on the Governor at the end of his reign. Believe me, he will be delighted to destroy the reputation of a senatorial nobleman, because it will hugely increase the power of the Council of the Province, and will make Felemid feared throughout the Empire. So he'll report that your husband is an idiot, ruled by his wife, which Rome will believe, because Rome already knows it to be true. He will report that your husband's recent victory was a fraud, which Rome will believe because your husband's rivals, led by Urban's faction, will believe it with delight and they will persuade the rest." I paused to let her think about that. "And of course, my lady, you personally will be revealed as a liar, a murderer, a hypocrite and a traitor."

She nearly fell over. Now Merloura was holding her upright, and whispering urgently into her ear. She nodded and stroked Merloura's hair.

"Yes, yes," she said, to Merloura, then she glared at me. "I'll call the guards and have you cut down on the spot," she said. But she spoke without conviction. If she had believed it she would have called out, not threatened. I think she had guessed my response. She was a very clever woman.

"No," I said. "Killing me won't help you. My comrade Morganus has my notes, he knows the case, and if I die he will go to Felemid." I nodded. "We agreed that he will do that should the Silanianum be inflicted, or should I be killed." She sagged and sank and shed tears, because, just as she loved Merloura, she loved her husband. She really and truly loved him, and everything she had done, she had done for him. I saw it in her face.

Then she struck away the tears, and stood tall, and acted like a noblewoman.

"So what do you want?" she said.

"What I told you," I said. "Go to Josephus and stop the Silanianum. If Merloura is guilty, the slaves are innocent."

"And?" she said, because she could see there was more.

"You know that I have the political power to break your husband?"
"Yes."

"And you know that I couldn't win against you in a court of law, where a far higher standard of evidence would be required?"
"Yes."

"But there must be justice for the innocent people who have died."

She said nothing, but her face said *yes* because she had accepted the inevitable, and knew what she must do.

Teutonius returned to Londinium five days after the Kalends of May, when the shadow of death covered the city like a shroud. He rode south with a cavalry escort, having finally provoked the Caledonian savages into a major battle, and won it massively, and left the Fourteenth and its auxiliaries to the grim task of pacifying the tribal homelands. Now he wanted to be in Londinium to enjoy his victory before the adoring eyes of the province's capital city. Besides that, he was doubtless missing his German girl and their infant son. So he sent fast riders before him, to carry the news, which presented Petros of Athens with a major dilemma.

Obviously the city should be turned out to welcome His Grace, and it would be relatively easy to repeat the overwhelming reception given to Josephus, only twelve days earlier. The same guilds and societies could be ordered on to the streets, with their floats and banners suitably adapted. They would do it with ease, because Romans loved processions and were infinitely ingenious in contriving them. But there was a problem, because the people were in mourning over a great loss of life.

"So what did you say to Tertia?" said Petros, speaking in Greek, standing beside me on the steps of Government House. "It was yourself, was it not, that sent her to Josephus to stop the Silanianum?"

I told him everything, and he nodded. I could not keep these details from him. Not when there was great need to repair any damage that might have been done to his attitude to myself, and him the most powerful man in Britannia.

"So this accounts for the sudden announcement of cancer of the breast," he said, "and why the noble lady, disdaining such a death, went to her bath and opened her veins with her faithful Merloura beside her doing the same."

"Yes," I said. "And Josephus approved. With Tertia's word that Merloura acted on her own initiative, there need be no scandal and no Silanianum. And now the whole city sorrows for the death of their princess, their darling, their leader of fashion, and patron of the arts. She whose every move was the gossip of them all."

He nodded again, and I looked at the great crowds all around us and gave credit to Petros for the elegance of his compromise. He had ordered that the people should line the streets and greet His Grace with cries of *Imperator*, which supreme acclaim was usually reserved for the Emperor, but which strictly meant the commander of a victorious army. It was a bold step because it would be reported in Rome, and the Urban faction might seize upon it as an example of dangerous ambition. But Petros hoped that Rome would be smiling upon Teutonius, because he had shown that, even in Britannia beyond the edge of the world, Rome could crucify rebellion with iron nails.

Then, having dealt with honouring the Governor, Petros had cleverly squared the circle, respecting the sorrow of the people, by ordering that the streets should be hung with funeral white, which should also be the colour of all the floats and costumes.

We did not see Teutonius pass down the Via Principalis, but we heard the noise, the deep and solemn cries of *Imperator* that rolled over the city in waves. I was on the steps of Government House, waiting with those dignitaries that had not gone to welcome Teutonius at the North Gate. Thus Josephus stood in the centre of the highest step, with Horatius the Vice Governor, and the elite of Josephus's own staff. Other lesser men stood in order of rank, and among them I was on the second step, beside Petros and behind Africanus and Morganus, while others stood below us, and below them the Governor's guard held back the common people.

The cavalry from the Noviomagus Fort had come with the lightning driver, to rescue Morganus and the bodyguards some hours after I left, and Morganus now wore a set of army splints secured with straps. He could stand with the aid of a stick, but could not walk. Nor would he do so for a couple of months, according to the surgeons at the army hospital. So Morganus was being carried everywhere, shoulder high on a chair fasted to poles. The men of the Twentieth were dicing for the honour of carrying him, and the latest team of six was hidden out of sight behind Government House. Africanus had not seen me since my expedition to the palace of Cogidubnus, but seemed to have forgiven me for defying his orders. When we arrived, and Morganus got out of his chair, Africanus smiled at him.

"Look at you, First Javelin," he said, "carried like a woman in a litter!"

He gestured at me. "I hear that this Greek set your leg. Greeks know everything, don't they?" He looked at me, "You're going to be useful to the Empire, boy. You should be pleased." I did not know what he meant, but at least he was not angry.

Then there was a blaring from the buglers of the Governor's Guard as Teutonius finally came in sight, riding a white horse, and accompanied on foot by a great entourage. So we too joined in the cries of Imperator, and raised our right arms in salute. Teutonius was beaming as he dismounted, and Josephus and Horatius stepped forward to embrace him. Then Josephus snapped fingers, a slave handed him a laurel wreath, Teutonius passed his helmet to an attendant, and Josephus placed the wreath on Teutonius' head.

"Imperator!" cried Josephus, and thousands of voices took up the chant. I glanced at Petros, just in time to see the relief on his face. If Josephus had used the word, then it would be all right with Rome.

The greeting was followed by hours of ceremony, beginning with a formal reading of Teutonius' field report to the mass of citizens crammed and jammed into the Great Hall. There, with Africanus gone to stand by Teutonius, and Morganus unable to push into the crowd, Petros and I moved through the togas, bowing and smiling and found a place at the back of the hall where we could talk. We could see nothing there, only the backs of eager citizens stretched on tip-toe trying to show their faces to Teutonius. But Petros had questions to ask and things to say.

"I think that I owe you my life, Ikaros of Apollonis," he said.

"Why is that, Petros of Athens?"

"Josephus spoke to me after you went to him with your ideas."

"What ideas?"

"In particular, the idea that I was behind the business of shields." He shook his head as I began to apologise. "Do not worry," he said. "It was the obvious conclusion. I am far more concerned that you disproved it, than that you made it!"

I was relieved that he took the matter so philosophically. I was also surprised by his fear of Josephus, who I had thought to be somewhat on his side. But Josephus was a politician, probably protecting himself by seeking someone to blame if need be. And Josephus was famous for his capacity to inspire fear.

"So what did Josephus say?"

Petros tried to remember the moment, and particularly Josephus's attitude. "It was all very indirect. He was trying to find out what I knew, without telling me what he knew."

"And what did you know? I asked, and he studied me, making his judgement of my ability to judge him. Then he asked a question, which seemed to have no relevance to mine.

"Have you heard that the slaves of the late Scorteus are raising a stone in your honour?"

"Yes," I said. I knew because Agidox had come to me with a delegation of slaves, and very embarrassing it had been too, because to the unsophisticated, which meant most of the slaves, the distinction between a memorial stone and a holy altar is unclear. While I expected to become their hero, I did not expect to become a god. Petros focused on this uncomfortable point.

"In their innocence," he said, "they believe you to have a *numen* as the Romans say, meaning a projection of the self into the spirit world." He explained further. "His Imperial Majesty has a similar divine presence," his lips flickered a brief smile, "as everybody knows," he added.

"Gods bless His Majesty," I said, carefully, and he shrugged his shoulders.

"Indeed," he said. "And these grateful slaves will pay for the stone from their own savings, which will cost them a fortune because it will stand in the Temple of the Capitoline Triad in the centre of the Forum, where all the city can see it." He paused. He was coming to his main point. "Now hear me, Ikaros of Apollonis, because I am no house boy who believes you to be divine. But everyone also knows that you look inside men's heads. So look inside mine and see that I knew nothing of this plot. Yes, I was happy for my master that this unexpected rebellion arose giving him the chance of military glory, and I took care to protect the German girl and her child while he was away. I did that for him, because once he was gone, Tertia would have killed them. She would have found a way."

"I see," I said, and decided to dig no further. Whatever Petros may actually have known or not known, he was very powerful indeed, and he wanted me as a friend. Then a great roar of laughter shook the hall, as Teutonius made some joke, and every sycophant in the hall laughed until he ached, and Teutonius laughed with them.

"He shows little grief for his wife," I said.

"He is excited by the moment," said Petros. "Entranced by it. But he will do everything that is proper. Her body has already been embalmed, and will be sent back to Rome and placed in a tomb, with full honours. Meanwhile, you know the limits of his mind, and that he never loved her. The marriage was a political alliance, and we may seek another in due course, but he will fall at once into the arms of the German girl to conceive another son if he can." Petros paused to applaud, when, for some reason, everyone else did. Then he resumed. "We, that is to say His Grace, has already planned for the firstborn who will take the name Germanicus. He will be educated, he will run the cursus honorum and, if he shows promise, he will be adopted and the moron Horatius set aside. The mother may even be freed and married. If we get the next step, as Governor of Italia, we shall please ourselves who wears the stola in the house!"

Then bugle calls announced the beginning of another ceremony, this time outside, and there was a great parting of the crowd, while Teutonius led the company out through the great doors. Petros and I talked as we went.

"There are two other things I must tell you, Ikaros of Apollonis," he said.

"Yes?"

"We, that is to say His Grace, has decided that among the trophies to be brought back from Caledonia, there is no place for any shields taken from the enemy's dead."

"Ah!" I said.

"All such will be burned and the metal fittings gathered and thrown into the sea."

"Good," I said. "Everyone who was guilty in this matter is either dead or has been punished enough." It was true. It was one reason I never published my evidence at the time. Even Dolbius the lawyer was imprisoned for life. He would never dare return to the Roman world in case it took note of his contact with druids. He was therefore sentenced to live among the small world, and murderous intrigues of the court of Cogidubnus.

"The other thing concerns yourself," said Petros. "Teutonius will be persuaded that he must reward you for your efforts in this case. It will be easy, because he detests the Silanianum. He thinks it a disgrace to Rome, and he is pleased that you prevented it. So he will do something for you."

My emotions stirred. I dared to hope.

"Will I be freed?" I said, and Petros laughed, as if at some absurdity.

"No, no, no!" he said. "You are far too useful to the Empire. The Legate Africanus has asked for you to be compulsorily purchased as an Imperial slave seconded to the Twentieth Legion. So we, that is to say His Grace, will arrange that. You will be interested to know that Josephus and I have discussed you with the Legate Africanus. You should know that Africanus is deeply impressed with you, as is Josephus. As are we all."

"And may I know your conclusions?"

"Yes. We believe that we have found something exceptional in the combination of yourself as an agent of inquiry, and Morganus as the strength of the army. Each is powerful by itself, but in combination you become something entirely new and formidable, and we believe that there will many further uses for this combination." He looked at me. "What do you think of that, Ikaros of Apollonis?"

"I think you are correct," I said, and he continued.

"As you know, an Imperial slave, such as myself," he bowed, "is legally the property of the Emperor. But in practice someone may stand *in loco Imperatoris*, which means *in place of the Emperor*, and we, that is to say His Grace, will appoint Morganus to that duty. It is a formal process of law, with documents signed and the originals kept in Rome." I nodded and Petros continued. "Take note that that this does not make Morganus your owner, but the man responsible to the Emperor for your safe keeping. It is a unique relationship, and you will be obliged to live in his house. I hope that presents no problems."

"It does not," I said.

"Then, finally, know that we ..."

"... that is to say, His Grace," I said, and he smiled.

"Yes. He asks if anything more is needed to bury this matter for good?"

"What about the druids?" I said. "Josephus said that something would be done."

"It will indeed!" he said. "As regards the attack on your lightning, we have already received emissaries from Cogidubnus, bringing profuse apology, and wicker baskets containing the heads of twenty three men. It is politic that we accept this atonement." He waved a hand. "You may view the heads if you like. You might recognise them."

"No thank you," I said, and sorrow fell upon me as I thought of the young horsemen, in their beauty and pride, with their muscles and tattoos and moustaches, and their easy grace in the saddle.

"A wise choice," said Petros. "The heads are no longer fresh. And, as regards to druidic activities beyond the client states, a private warning has been given, and will be followed by a public demonstration. Five cohorts of the Twentieth will go on manoeuvres just outside the borders of Cogidubnus' kingdom, and his majesty and other client kings will be invited to inspect the army's heavy siege equipment. They will be shown how completely the army can demolish stone walls, and they will take the hint because they do so dearly love their palaces." He paused. "And is there anything else?"

"There is," I said. "As part of my investigations I deeply regret that I was obliged to insult a noble Roman lady."

"Oh?" he said. "I would not have thought you capable of it. Who is she?"

"The lady Aggripina, mother of the Tribune Severus. We had to search her house, and it was a shameful act."

"And so?"

"Could an Imperial pension, a generous one, be found for the lady and her family? They are Equestrian Knights, but impoverished." Petros nodded. "And perhaps there could be some word that this comes in apology for my ..." But, I stopped. If forgiveness is not freely given, it cannot be bought with money. "No," I said, "Just give her the pension."

Then we went out together, and for once the Britannic weather was kind, and the sun was shining. Morganus was there, with the bodyguards getting him into his chair, and six legionaries stood ready to man the shafts and hoist him up. He grinned, as if helpless in their hands, and so I smiled.

I was still a slave, but I was liberated from guilt. I was freed from nightmares. I could not be sold down the mines by Badrogid, nor purchased by Felemid for his perversions. As for Allicanda, I did not know my own mind, because I loved my wife again. I loved her without restraint or impediment. She was safe in my heart beside our children, and I remembered all their faces. Meanwhile, I had found another family and a place to call home.

I was at peace for the first time since my city fell.

Epilogue

Morganus got back on his legs in the astonishing time of six weeks. The surgeons said it was impossible at his age, but he walked nonetheless. He was so pleased that he came to the Legionary Headquarters where I had been given an office and a staff of clerks. I was under orders to improve the army's ciphers, and I was explaining some of the methods we had used in Apollonis when Morganus came in.

"Look!" he said, pointing to his leg. "And the bodyguards grinned behind him, including the new one, chosen from hundreds of volunteers. "And look at this," he said, "Straight from the legate! The runner found me coming out of the hospital." He handed me a wax tablet, and I read it and looked back at him.

"That's very odd," I said. "And very serious. What does it mean?"

"Nobody knows," he said, "Which is why we have to go and find out!"

Afterword

Why I wrote this book.

In the hope of fame, and of putting a few bob in the bank, naturally. But also for the following reasons.

The Senatus Consultum Silanianum was real. (Ref: 1, 2) and there really was a notorious case when four hundred household slaves were sentenced to death following the murder of their master Lucius Pedanius Secundus. (Ref: 3) He was a millionaire who was murdered in a fit of jealousy by his *previous* best boy, who found him in the arms of the latest. The case went all the way to the Senate (the Roman parliament) where it was fiercely debated, and the final conclusion reached that the executions must proceed because otherwise no slave-owning master (which meant everybody with political power) could be safe in his house.

The decision sparked outrage from the Roman people and a mob besieged the senate for three days. But, finally, with troops lining the streets, the four hundred were taken out and killed. That was the Romans. They were like us in many ways, but not in others, and you can't beat history for a really good story, so I pinched it for this book.

As a footnote, the words Senatus Consultum Silanianum mean: *the Senate Decree enacted in the year when Dolbella and Silanus were Consuls*. See below for an explanation of this unique Roman method of dating the years.

The other reason for writing this book is my life-long fascination with Roman history, and I cannot read about the Roman Empire without thinking of the British Empire. Both were built by military force, both were greedy and opportunist in their acquisition of territories, but both involved a claimed duty to civilise the barbarians. For their part, the barbarians fought and died to resist being civilised, but once they were, then Monty Python has listed what the Romans did for them, and I will give just one further example to add to the list.

Two years ago I visited Pompeii and, of all the fascinating things I saw there, one comes first to mind. Walking along a street I looked down to see a perfectly-preserved lead pipe just showing where the paving stones had worn away. It was a Roman water main, laid under the pavement by a Roman plumber nearly two thousand years ago. As I said, they were very like us in some ways.

Historical accuracy?

Please remember that I write fiction. This is not a history book. But I have tried very hard indeed to describe Roman life and Roman ways as accurately as I can, and to avoid putting twenty-first century opinions into the minds of my characters. Thus Ikaros accepts slavery, capital punishment and torture as part of normal life. He may despise torturers, but accepts that, like the night-soil men, they do a necessary job, if a dirty one.

So Ikaros is not a liberal democrat, female-suffragist atheist. He honours the gods of Olympus and he is genuinely astonished that the early Christians could not offer up prayers to The Divine Genius of the Emperor. I think these authentic attitudes are far more important than the fact that I have made up a few things. Thus there were no *cennad angau* assassins, but the words are my attempt at translating *messengers of death* into Welsh, which true, native and British language is the direct descendant of first-century Britannic.

Historians are welcome to go through the book with a pencil, marking out truth from falsehood and, as long as they buy it and I get my percentage, I don't mind. And, so to other matters.

In the Presence of Heroes.

I describe, in Chapter 12, the reaction of the Fourth Cohort, Second Augusta to the sudden arrival of one of the Roman Army's great heroes:

Leonius Morganus Fortis Victrix. In doing so I borrow from life an experience I had in the 1980s at an ICI Pharmaceuticals launch conference, I worked the company's TV unit in those days. At the formal dinner in the evening there were about five hundred sales reps present, mainly men, and we had been promised a special guest speaker.

Came the moment when we were all sitting down awaiting the speaker, and the chairman of the evening entered the room with no less than the heavyweight boxer Henry Cooper, one of the best loved sportsmen in Britain, a complete gentleman, and famous for having knocked down Mohammed Ali when Ali got a bit too clever *floating like a butterfly* and discovered that Henry Cooper could sting, not like a bee but like a battering ram. Wallop! Down went Ali. Rule Britannia! Land of Hope and Glory!

My point is that, when Henry Cooper entered the room, there was a sudden and enormous cheer and a vast scraping of chairs and thundering applause as five hundred men leapt to their feet and welcomed a great hero. The looks on their faces and their boundless joy were as I have described in Chapter 12. So this too was real and I didn't make it up.

I record with enormous pride that I had the opportunity to shake Henry Cooper's hand. Given that, and since he was famous for his left hook, I insisted in shaking his left hand, known to us Cockneys as *'enry's 'ammer'*.

In which year did Ikaros solve the murder of Scorteus?

This is a Roman story, so we shall think of years as Romans would. (Ref: 4) Thus Romans identified a year by the names of the two Consuls (leaders of the Senate) who first served in that year. So: Britannia was conquered by Rome in The Year of Claudius and Lucius Vitellius; and Boudicca's rebellion occurred in The Year of Nero and Cossus Cornelius Lentulus. (See below for comment on Roman names and meanwhile note that the names of emperors, who automatically served as consuls, could be reduced to one name, such as Nero and Claudius.)

This consular dating system worked perfectly well for educated persons who could refer to lists showing which consuls served when. (Ref: 5) But, for the simple minded there was also a numerical reckoning, starting from the beginnings of Rome, and years were numbered as *Ab Urbe Condita*, meaning *from the founding of The City*, commonly abbreviated to AUC (which looks like AVC on Roman inscriptions because V served for both v and u). Thus Julius Caesar made his two expeditions into Britannia in the years 699 AUC and 700 AUC, and the Emperor Claudius returned, ninety-six years later for the serious job of conquest, in the year 796 AUC (the year of Claudius and Lucius Vitellius, as above).

But others reckon differently. Thus the Jewish minority sect that worshipped the rabbi Jesus Bar Joseph as a slain and risen god, eventually grew into a more widespread organisation which measures time from the birth of their supposed divinity, which they claim to have occurred in the year of C. Julius Caesar (not the famous one, another one) and Lucius Aemilius Paullus (754 AUC). The story of the murder of Scorteus, which took place in the year of Trajan and Iulius Frontinus (854 AUC), is therefore set in the year 100 AD.

Roman names.

Very, very roughly it went like this, taking the example of Gaius Julius Caesar. Gaius was his given name, or *Praenomen*. Julius was the name of the clan he belonged to, and was his *nomen*. Finally, Caesar was his surname, or *Cognomen*. In his particular case, his descendants became so powerful that the surname *Caesar* became equivalent to *emperor*, and has passed into later languages as words like Czar, Kaiser, and Shah.

Still following? Beyond that, some famous Romans earned a fourth name, or *Agnomen*, as personal nicknames, such as the *Teutonius* I added to the names of my fictional character for his victories over the German tribes. Beyond even that, Emperors had more names, to proclaim their pedigrees and achievements. Thus Trajan, the emperor of this book, was *Caesar Marcus Ulpius Nerva Traianus Augustus*. But then, our own

Queen (God bless her) is Elizabeth Alexandra Maria of the House of Windsor. So Trajan's list wasn't excessive.

But, as I said, this is only a very, very rough guide to Roman names. So anybody who wants to learn more, could go to a library and seek help. But my advice is not to bother, which is why I quote no references here, because the relatively simple explanation above, relates mainly to the Roman Republic, the system changed under the Empire, and experts tie themselves in knots on this subject, some saying that nomen was the clan name and cognomen the surname, and others the other way round. It's very confusing. It's my guess that in using names the Romans followed oddities of fashion and local usage, now long forgotten. So, in choosing which of my characters' names to use in the book, because the full set is too long: for example, which from Fabius Gentillius Scorteus? I have, in general, and arbitrarily, used the last.

The City of Apollonis.

There was no city of Apollonis. I invented it to provide comparison to assist understanding of Roman life. For instance, I had to explain that the Romans had no police force or public prosecutor. But it would be tedious and boring to the reader (you wouldn't thank me for it) to explain the absence of a police force without using the words *police force*, so I said that Apollonis had one.

Roman surgery under anaesthesia.

It is only my invention, in Chapter 2, that an ancient author wrote a formula for the preparation of an anaesthetic based on poppy resin extracted in alcohol, even though these are the two oldest drugs known to mankind. As far as I know, it wasn't until the sixteenth century that European pharmacopoeias recorded such a drug, as *laudanum*, a powerful painkiller. But even then it wasn't routinely used for surgical anaesthesia, perhaps because it is so addictive, though I have personally discussed this non-event with modern anaesthetists who find it as puzzling as I do.

The explanation may be that surgery is entirely painless to surgeons, who therefore remained unconcerned about the sufferings of patients: *Brace up, old chap it won't take long*! On the other hand, perhaps there were other and nastier side effects, and I have guessed that with dosage difficult to control, it might have been dangerous and difficult to prepare, as well as expensive.

As for the capacity of Roman surgeons to treat vaginal fistula, there is in the National Archaeological Museum of Naples, a complex and beautifully-designed surgical instrument, (Ref: 7), dating from the Roman Empire, and designed specifically to dilate the vagina for surgical procedures. This sophisticated device is proof that Roman surgeons carried out gynaecological procedures, while the modern procedure for repair of vaginal fistula (Ref: 8) was developed by the controversial American surgeon J. Marion Sims (he operated on slaves without anaesthesia) (Ref: 9) who worked in the 1840s when contemporary surgical technique was no more advanced than that of Rome. All in all, I think the happy cure of the beautiful German girl was entirely within the reach of my unnamed surgeon and Ikaros the Greek.

Racial Characteristics of British Celtic Tribes.

In Chapter 22 I make play of visible distinction between the features of members of the ancient Britannic Celtic: *their features cried Silure, Belgae, Parisii and the rest,* and: *his sleight, almost child-like stature* typical of *the Brigantes tribe of the north west.* I stress that this is my fiction, but very reasonable fiction, based on such facts as the visible differences between Cheyenne, Apache and Sioux in nineteenth century America. My contention is that, in first century Europe, the members of the native tribes would instantly have guessed each other's ethnic origins just by looking at one another.

Not Pagans, please.

A personal gripe. Please don't call the Greeks and Romans *Pagans.* The word derives from the Latin *paganus*, meaning someone who lives in the wilds. It suggests a midnight jamboree of naked savages, howling the moon, rolling their eyes, and leaping through the flames, to throbbing drums and the scent of singing hair, none of which was the typical behaviour of the gentlemen who built the Parthenon, the Pantheon, and the seven aqueducts of Rome.

I suggest instead the term *Olympian Pantheists*, meaning those who worship the classical gods of Mount Olympus: Jupiter, Athena, Mars and the rest. This dignified term is far more appropriate to the sophisticated religious practices of classical civilization, and the magnificent temples wherein their faith was proclaimed and celebrated.

No man can be a slave who knows how to die.

Seneca didn't say it quite like that, as quoted by Ikaros in Chapter 1. Seneca said: *qui mori didicit servire dedidicit*, meaning: *he who has learned how to die has unlearned to be a slave.* I am grateful to Sam Foster of Harvard University who pointed this out to me.

The quote is elegant in Latin, but clumsy in English, so I have altered it. But having ruined the beauty of the original Latin, I must do duty to Seneca by pointing out that he was no poseur who told others to do what he could not do himself. In 65 AD he was accused (probably unjustly) of being in a plot to kill Nero. He was given the opportunity of committing suicide as an honourable death. Which opportunity he took, by opening his veins. So we should not forget him completely.

The Salutatio

I cannot sufficiently stress the importance of this daily event to Roman life. (Ref: 10, 11) To understand how important it was, first consider some of the things that Romans did not have: social security, state pensions, a health service, a police force (see above!), professional qualifications, legal aid, or newspapers. Nor did they have any belief that contracts should be awarded on merit to the supplier who gave the best quote.

What they did have was something close to the opening scene of *The Godfather*, where men kiss Don Corleone's hand to ask a favour. They ask because he is rich, powerful, well connected and can get things done. And that is exactly what the Roman patron did for his clients. He would pay a pension to a starving artist, fix an army contract for a tent maker, find a lawyer for a man being sued, get a doctor for a family with a sick child, and punish hooligans by sending his slaves to beat them up. All that and more.

In return, the clients gave him social status by marching behind him to the forum during the many civic or religious ceremonies of the Roman calendar (which events were tremendously important to Romans) and, of course, they voted as he told them in elections. Thus a patron's status was directly proportional the number of his clients, and the greater his status the greater his power and the more he could do for his clients: a virtuous circle of mutual self-interest.

There was still more. I repeat that there were no newspapers in ancient Rome (let alone TV and radio). So the Salutatio was the occasion when everyone heard the news. Thus the patron would pass on news of civic and wider events, which he would have because he was a member of the class that made all the decisions and looked beyond the city, and the clients would pass on all the latest street gossip. So the patron told the clients when a new theatre was promised, or a war was threatening, and the clients (one of them) told the patron that His Grace the Governor was in love with a beautiful slave girl who couldn't stand the pain of the surgery needed to cure a vaginal fistula.

I can think of no other Roman civic institution anywhere nearly so important as the Salutatio: not for ordinary Romans going about their daily lives.

The *Cursus Honorum*

But there was another institution that deserves a mention, as compared with the modern British equivalent. This was the *cursus honorum*, the noble pathway of jobs that a young Roman aristocrat had to follow if he sought high rank in public life. (Ref: 12)

When the boy was in his teens, his father's influence would get him one of a series of jobs such as Warden of the Streets, Overseer of Law Suits, Governor of The City Mint, or Officer for Capital Punishment, I paraphrase these titles for clarity. He would do jobs like these for about one year each, climbing a ladder of increasing responsibility and authority. Then, when he was in his early twenties, he would serve in the army as a Military Tribune (roughly equivalent to a modern colonel) and would do so for several years. This was vital because the Roman Empire was built and held by the army, and Romans would not consider a man as seriously fit for government if he had not served as a soldier.

Once in the army, the young man might see action, he would travel the Empire, and he would learn how a huge and efficient organisation (the Roman army) works. Also, he would need to win the respect of the men who ran the army: the centurions. These grim veterans, with their scars and battle honours, would either break him or make a man of him, just as a regimental sergeant major makes or breaks the young officer cadet of today.

But even then he wasn't ready for top political office. When he came out of the army, he would do further and still more senior jobs, and if he wanted to get into the senate, he could not do so until he was at least thirty years old, and preferably older, by which time he really was a man.

Compare this with modern Britain, where children go from school, to university and straight into parliamentary politics, without ever setting foot in the real world. The Romans would have thought we were barmy.

How clever were the Greeks?

I have had much fun contrasting the intellectual achievements of Greece with the military power of Rome. So how clever were the Greeks? I will give two examples. First, in Chapter 4, a slave dealer asks Ikaros if he knows how Eratosthenes of Syrene who (in c.200 BC) calculated the circumference of the Earth, having seen his own reflection down a well. Second, in Chapter 12, Ikaros explains how Eupalinos of Megara (in c.600 BC) drove a tunnel through a mountain, working from each end and meeting in the middle.

I did not make this up. These events were real. Have a look at the details on the internet. (Ref: 13, 14) Have a look and be amazed at the intellect of these Greek gentlemen, and understand why I object to their being called *pagans*. As a final comment I point out that, like all educated Greeks of his time, Eratosthenes knew that the Earth was a sphere. It was not flat. It was not a disc, sitting on a turtle floating in the mists of time on the back of four elephants, or any other monstrosity of ignorance. It was a sphere. In 200 BC, the Greeks had long since worked that out. Yes, they really were clever.

How important was Britannia to the Roman Empire?

Very. It took an enormous army, three legions plus auxiliaries, to keep and hold Britannia, and if it were not worthwhile the Romans would not have done it. So why did they do it? It wasn't like keeping back the wild German tribes beyond the Rhine, who were a threat to the Empire. It wasn't like seizing the fabulously wealthy provinces to the east that were rich in civilisation. I believe that Britannia was taken and held for glory and for propaganda. Britannia showed the world what Rome could do.

So having taken it, and kept it, Britannia was decorated with some spectacular building projects. The Basilica (town hall) in Londinium, and the great palace of Cogidubnus were two of the largest buildings in the Empire. (Ref: 15) What I have called the *Palace of Cogidubnus* is, of course, the palace at Fishbourne in West Sussex, first excavated in the 1960s, and a true whopper by Roman or any other standards. It was bigger than Buckingham Palace and contained every luxury known to the classical world.

Cogidubnus was a real person, and was king of the Regni tribe in the first century AD. But nobody knows who owned the Fishbourne palace, and it is only my invention that the palace was a bribe, built by the Romans to persuade the kings of the Regni to accept Roman rule. It is a very reasonable invention nonetheless, and it makes a good tale. Which is what I try to do.

References

1. Robinson, O.F., *The Criminal Law of Ancient Rome*, The John Hopkins University Press, 1995, page 45.
2. *Lewis, N., and Reinhold, M., Roman Civilisation Volume II: Selected Readings, The Empire, Columbia University Press, Third Edition, 1990, page 177.*
3. Internet http://en.wikipedia.org/wiki/Lucius_Pedanius_Secundus

(The dreadful tale itself: the main reason I wrote this book)

4. Internet http://www.web40571.clarahost.co.uk/roman/calhis.htm

(Summary of roman dating system and calendar)

5. Internet http://en.wikipedia.org/wiki/List_of_Roman_consuls

(List of consuls showing in which years BC or AD they held office)

6. *Stratham, P., A Brief History of Medicine: from Hippocrates to Gene Therapy, Caroll and Graf, 2005. (See index re laudanum)*
7. Internet http://www.hsl.virginia.edu/historical/artifacts/roman_surgical/

(Picture of the instrument itself and other Roman surgical devices)

8. Speert, H., *Obstetrics and Gynecologic Milestones*, The MacMillan Co., New York, 1958, pages 442–54.
9. Internet http://en.wikipedia.org/wiki/J._Marion_Sims

(Discussion of the ethics of Marion Sims's work)

10. Balsdon, J.P.V.D., *Life and Leisure in Ancient Rome*, Phoenix Press, Third Impression, 2004, pages 21 – 24.
11. Smith, W., Wayte, W., Marindin G.E., *A Dictionary of Greek and Roman Antiquities*, John Murray, Albermarle Street, London 1890.
12. Birley, A., *The Roman Government of Britain*, Oxford University Press, 2005, page 3 onwards.
13. Internet http://en.wikipedia.org/wiki/Tunnel_of_Eupalinos
14. Internet http://en.wikipedia.org/wiki/Eratosthenes
15. De L Bédoyère, G., *Roman Britain*, Thames and Hudson, 2006.

(See index re Londinium Basilica and Fishbourne Palace)

Milton Keynes UK
Ingram Content Group UK Ltd.
UKHW041307271223
435059UK00008B/48

9 781839 015144